MON

Clea's Moon

Clea's Moon

Edward Wright

LARGE PRINT

This large print edition published in 2004 by
RB Large Print
A division of Recorded Books
A Haights Cross Communications Company
270 Skipjack Road
Prince Frederick, MD 20678

Published by arrangement with Penguin Putnam, Inc.

Publisher's Cataloging In Publication Data
(Prepared by Donohue Group, Inc.)

Wright, Edward.
   Clea's moon / Edward Wright.

   p. (large print) ; cm.

   ISBN: 1-4025-7919-5

1. Collection agencies—Fiction. 2. Large type books. 3. Los Angeles (Calif.)—
Fiction. 4. Historical fiction. 5. Mystery fiction. I. Title.

PS3623.R535 C43 2004
813/.6

Printed in the United States of America

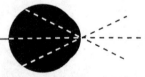

**This Large Print Book carries the
Seal of Approval of N.A.V.H.**

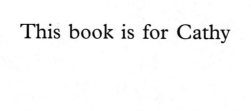

This book is for Cathy

ACKNOWLEDGMENTS

My thanks to Todd Keithley, who offered expertise and encouragement early on; Jane Conway-Gordon and the Crime Writers' Association of Great Britain, who together made the first breakthrough possible; Elizabeth Winick, Neil Nyren, and Gail Fortune, who surprisingly made it happen again; Mimi Cazort and Bob McLarty, the kind of kinfolk everyone should have; Marsha and Ted Baker, for their sharp eyes; the Los Angeles writers of The Group, for helping me get started; and my wife, Cathy, for everything. I'm also grateful to those who, many years ago, created a Los Angeles on film so vivid that I would feel compelled to revisit it on the page. And I remember Al "Lash" La Rue, who gave a little boy his autograph back in a time when movie cowboys were the most memorable heroes of all.

Horn, John Ray—B. 1909, Green Springs, Arkansas. Star of dozens of low-budget westerns for Medallion Pictures, 1937–1945. Described by one reviewer as "a cross between two silent-movie icons, William S. Hart and Harry Carey," Horn was memorable for his laconic manner, penetrating gaze, and lanky frame. Most of his films featured him as Sierra Lane, an ex-cavalryman who seldom used a gun but who, when provoked, revealed a deadly side under his quiet demeanor. (In *No Man's Town*, he methodically tears up a bunkhouse to get at the three men who killed his friend the sheriff.) Many of his films co-starred American Indian actor Joseph Mad Crow.

Horn's career was interrupted by Army service in World War II. Discharged after being wounded, he resumed his place as one of Medallion's reliable money-makers. In 1945, he was imprisoned for two years following a controversial conviction for assault and battery, and his career in films was effectively ended. His current occupation and whereabouts are unknown.

Films: *Bloody Trail, Border Bad Men, Carbine Justice, Empty Holster, Hell's Rockpile, The Lost Mine, No Man's Town, Six Bullets, Smoke on the Mountain, Wyoming Thunder,* many others.

—FROM *White Hats: An Encyclopedia of Western Movie Heroes,* EDITED BY JEFFERS AND BLOCK, 1949

CHAPTER 1

The street smelled of dust and regret. The loser's side of town, Horn said to himself as he approached the rooming house, eyeing the front windows for any sign of movement.

The neighborhood had the look of impermanence. The shingle-sided wood-frame houses had been thrown up more than twenty years ago as people migrated to Los Angeles looking for jobs. When the Depression hit, the houses sat vacant. Then the war came, and the houses filled up again. But now the war was over, the defense jobs were gone, and all the little front yards on the street looked patchy and ill-tended. The people on this street weren't exactly poor, Horn thought, they were just passing through. They kept at least one of their bags packed, waiting for him to knock on the door. Or someone like him.

First he checked out the car. It was one of two in the cracked-concrete driveway, a Chevy sedan maybe ten years old, and the Kansas license number matched the one on the scrap of paper in his pocket. It was the collateral, all right. The windows were rolled down because of the heat, and he stood

1

for a moment by the driver's window looking in, making sure of the ignition. He could manage it without a key if he had to.

Up the steps, the wood almost soft from the tread of countless feet, then through the unlocked screen door and down the hall—smelling of old food—a short distance to the first door on the right, the front room. As he rapped on the door with his left hand, his right curled around the roll of poker chips in the pocket of his cotton jacket. No harm in being prepared. *This one could be bad,* the Indian had told him with one of his hard-to-read grins. *Not like one of your pictures, where you wipe the floor with everybody 'cause that's the way it's supposed to turn out.*

Horn hoped it would be no worse than the two fisherman brothers down in San Pedro, the ones the Indian had been ready to write off if Horn couldn't collect. He had found them playing gin at a card table set up in their kitchen, a loaf of bread and a jar of peanut butter beside them. When he told them why he was there, one of the men went for Horn's eye with a knife. It was only a table knife, dull-edged and slicked with peanut butter, but it was his eye. The affair ended violently but reasonably well, and thereafter the Indian enjoyed referring to it as "the Showdown at Peanut Gulch."

He rapped on the door again. The woman who opened it could have been anywhere from thirty to forty. The lower half of her apron was darkened

2

with the grime of all her hand-wipings. She looked resigned to whatever he had brought with him on this summer afternoon.

Horn hadn't expected a woman, and some of the tension went out of his right hand. He tried to see past her into the room's interior, caught sight of what looked like a young boy sitting on a sofa in the gloom. "Afternoon, ma'am," he said. "I'd like to see Mr. Buddy Taro, if he's in."

"I'm Buddy." The man moved into Horn's line of sight. He was medium height and pudgy, wearing dress slacks with suspenders over an undershirt. His shoes were well-shined, and a single roll of flesh, smooth and pink, cradled his chin.

The man made a slight sideways shooing motion, and the woman moved back from the doorway, hands tucked protectively in her apron. He stepped into the hall. "We can talk out here," he said easily. His face seemed open and friendly. *Buddy puts on a good front*, the Indian had said.

Horn gave the man one more good look up and down, then pulled his right hand out of his jacket. Maybe the Indian had been wrong. "I'm here for Joseph Mad Crow," Horn said quietly after waiting for the door to close. "You're into him for five twenty-five. He's extended you twice. Today's collection day."

"Sure," Buddy Taro said, nodding earnestly. "I knew it was today. Here's the thing." He touched Horn lightly on the elbow, a friendly touch. "I've got two hundred even. You can take it. The rest

3

I'll have real soon." His voice was smart and light and a little amused. A good gambler's voice, Horn thought, for telling stories to the boys around the table, between hands, without giving anything away.

Taro pulled a small roll of bills out of his pants pocket and handed it to Horn. "Here it is," he said. "Just tell him—"

Horn shoved the bills into the jacket pocket with the rolled-up chips. "I'll have to take the car," he said.

"What?"

"The Chevy. You put it up for collateral. Today's the day. I'll be taking it." He started for the front door.

"I can't let you do that," Taro said, the easy tone gone from his voice as he followed Horn heavily through the hall to the door. "I need that car. I need to get places." He sounded out of breath.

Horn pushed through the screen door, took the porch in two strides and the steps in two more, then waited by the car. *Get this over with*, he thought. "Can I have the keys?"

Taro stood a few feet away from him, talking through clenched teeth. "Look, I got a sick kid in there, and the woman doesn't do anything to bring in money. I got to get places. I got to find games."

"That's what got you into trouble," Horn said to him in a tone that was not unkind. "Get your-self a regular job."

"That's right, a regular job. Maybe I could get one like yours." Underneath the smart talk Horn

4

could hear the desperation pushing to the surface. "I worked at Lockheed for a while, making airplanes, but there's no more of that. So I guess I should get a job like yours, taking people's grocery money."

"If that's what you like to do." Horn made a come-on motion. "Keys." Out of the corner of his eye he saw a slight movement. The curtain had parted at the front window to show the boy's thin, pale face, watching.

"Huh-uh." Buddy Taro was now the picture of comic defiance, arms crossed, face flushed, his middle straining at the undershirt over his trouser top.

"Never mind." Horn reached inside the car window, pulled up on the door handle, and seated himself behind the wheel. From his left-hand jacket pocket he extracted a small screwdriver and a pocket knife. "I can manage." He leaned sideways to study the ignition.

The other man was suddenly upon him, dragging at his left arm. Fearing a weapon, Horn came out quickly, the screwdriver held up protectively. But Buddy Taro simply stood there in front of him in an awkward crouch, eyes wide, as he doubled up a round fist and drew it back. Horn placed the flat of his hand on Taro's face, fingers spread, and pushed quickly, hard. The man went over backward and sat down abruptly on the concrete pathway, his back against the lowest step. He stared straight ahead, looking dazed.

"Don't do that again, all right?" Horn debated searching the man's pockets for the car keys. But he caught another glimpse of the face at the window and decided to get back to work on the ignition. For a few minutes he could hear Taro's labored breathing, then heard him heave himself to his feet, mount the steps, and go inside. Horn had the ignition pried out of its housing and was beginning to work on the insulation over the wires when he heard the screen door open.

"Here!" He looked up to see Taro fling a wad of bills into the front yard and driveway. They scattered over a wide area, like green leaves dropping off the trees too soon. "There's the rest. Take it. You better count it." He turned to the door. "Part of that's milk money. I hope you get a big cut."

It took Horn a long time to retrieve all the bills. He was counting them a second time on the hood of the car when he heard the voice. "Are you Sierra Lane?"

The boy was standing with one arm wrapped around the pillar by the front steps. He was maybe thirteen or fourteen, extremely thin, barefoot and wearing corduroy pants and a multicolored T-shirt. Horn could see that one ankle, the one bearing no weight, was shrunken over the bone, like dried meat. Polio, Horn guessed, which meant that the whole leg probably looked that way.

"Who?"

"Sierra Lane. The cowboy."

Horn shook his head.

The boy's gaze never left Horn's face. "Bet you are," he said finally. "I seen enough of his movies. You're dressed different, but . . . What I mean is, I bet you're the guy who plays him. Aren't you?"

"No."

"My favorite was *Border Bad Men*," the boy said in almost a sing-song voice. "I seen it when I was little. You know, at the end, where Sierra talks the other guys into taking off their guns, then he fights all of 'em. My friend Lee likes Sunset Carson, but I told him if we was in a tight spot, we'd want Sierra Lane on our side, 'cause he could whup Sunset Carson any time."

Horn shrugged as he rolled up the bills and put them in his pocket. "Maybe he could."

"You sure you're not him?"

"I'm sure."

The front curtains rustled, and Horn saw the woman. "Come on in, honey," she said.

The boy didn't move. "Why'd you push my dad?"

Horn took a deep breath. "I didn't want to," he said finally. "You better get on inside." Turning to the window, he said: "Ma'am, please tell Mr. Taro his account is square."

Twenty minutes later, Horn slid into a seat aboard the trolley for the trip back. It was stifling in the car, and he shucked off his jacket and put his hat on his lap. His fingers were slick and stained, because some of the bills had landed in a puddle of engine oil in the driveway. He wiped his hands with his handkerchief, then leaned against the window and closed his eyes as the trolley bucked and rattled. The car was crowded and smelled of sweat. He heard the spark of the trolley against the overhead wire, and the air tasted as if he had a copper penny under his tongue. *This is where I ride off and everybody cheers*, he thought. *Nice job, cowboy. You come back and see us.*

"Here's your money." Horn tossed the roll of bills on the desk. The Indian, occupied as usual in financial matters, was toting up figures on his desktop adding machine, eyes scanning a ledger, the fingers of his left hand stabbing at the keys as his right worked the handle, ratcheting up the totals. He stopped, looked up.

"How'd it go?" he grunted.

"I bet you know how it went. Want to count it?"

Joseph Mad Crow was almost as tall as Horn but thicker in the chest and shoulders. He wore a white silk shirt with embroidery across the front. On his left wrist was an expensive Bulova, on his right a hammered silver bracelet with a turquoise the size of his thumb. He picked up the roll, stripped off the rubber band, and quickly flipped through the bills. Halfway through the wad, he stopped and looked up, his face gone sour. "They're greasy."

"It's oil," Horn said. "Some of them landed in the driveway when he threw them at me."

"Threw 'em at you." Mad Crow suddenly broke into a grin. "That's old Buddy." In repose, his face was about as expressive as the face on the buffalo

8

nickel. When animated, though, it was capable of a broad range, from a pixyish glee to the kind of clouded-over threat that would cause large men to duck their heads and quickly cross the street.

This time his expression suggested enjoyment of a secret joke. "I told you it could be bad."

"I thought you meant different," Horn said, taking the chair across the desk. To his left, most of the office wall was glass, allowing the Indian to look down on his domain, the Mad Crow Casino, biggest card parlor in this corner of Los Angeles County. Thirty tables and a bar crammed into a smoky, warehouse-like room. It was now late on a Saturday afternoon, and the place was beginning to fill up. Horn recognized some of the regulars, and he spotted the photographer who, later in the evening, would make the rounds of the tables taking souvenir photos for the high rollers who wanted them.

"What happened?"

"Not much. Buddy got worked up and came at me when I went for his car—"

"So you didn't drive there?"

"Figured I'd better not. I left the Ford here and rode the Red Car, just in case." Horn pulled a pouch of Bull Durham and a packet of cigarette papers out of his shirt pocket.

"Come on," Mad Crow said disgustedly when he saw the tobacco. "Worst habit you picked up in that place. Don't know how you can smoke that stuff. Here," he said, leaning toward Horn and

9

shaking a Lucky out of an open pack. "Be civilized, okay?"

Horn smiled, having heard the gibe several times, and took one. "I don't mind. Anyway, Buddy wasn't hard to handle. Only there was a woman there, and a crippled kid. That's the part I didn't like."

"I knew you wouldn't," Mad Crow said. "But who else was I going to send? Any of the other boys, it could've gotten messy. They might have come back with old Buddy's scalp. You're my diplomat."

"Why didn't you say that at the trial?" Horn asked, his attention on the cigarette as he lit up.

Mad Crow ran both hands over his hair, which was gathered in a short ponytail, and his face turned grim. "I did my best," he said. "We all did. That son of a bitch had you in his sights, and that's all it was. Clarence Darrow himself couldn't have gotten you off that rap, my friend."

The swivel chair creaked as he shifted his solid frame in it. "You hungry? I could send one of the girls out for a pastrami. What say?"

"I wouldn't mind one of your beers."

"Lula!" Mad Crow hollered through the closed door to his assistant in the outer office. "Couple of Blue Ribbons, if you please, honey." He peeled several bills off the roll that Horn had brought in and laid them on the other side of the desk. "Your cut," he said. "Hope you don't mind some of the dirty ones. I threw in a little extra. Now you can get your phone turned back on."

"It's back on. I paid them the other day." Noticing

10

Mad Crow's look, he went on: "I wasn't broke or anything. I just let things slide, that's all."

"Good," the Indian said patiently. "Well, now you can talk to people again, make contact with the world. I got awful tired of leaving messages for you at that rinky-dink garage. It's like sending out smoke signals—you know, like in the cowboy movies." He looked hard at Horn. "Something bothering you?"

Horn shrugged. "Just the kid," he said finally. "He recognized me."

"Ah." Mad Crow leaned back in his chair. "I get it. One of your old posse. I don't imagine you signed any autographs, did you? Sorry you didn't run into him under better circumstances." His face brightened. "Lookie-here." He pointed to the corner of the room over Horn's right shoulder. On the wall was a large, framed movie poster, what theater owners called a one-sheet. The movie was *Carbine Justice*, and the artist's illustration, done in broad strokes, showed the profiles of two men on horseback—Horn, in western garb, in the foreground, and Mad Crow wearing buckskins, with a feather in his hair.

"Ain't it a beauty?" Mad Crow said. "I found it in the prop room over at the studio, and I got 'em to give it to me. Of all the ones we did together, this is the only time they ran a decent picture of me."

"It's a good one," Horn said. "You look very noble."

"Noble red man, that's me. White man speak truth."

A young woman entered, wearing a gaudy satin shirt, boots, and a fringed skirt, and placed two bottles of beer, still flecked with ice from the cooler, on the desk. "Thanks, sugar," Mad Crow said as she left. He popped the two caps on the scarred edge of his desk, passed one to Horn, and raised his bottle. "Here's to Sierra Lane, the gol-dangedest cowpoke who ever busted up a saloon." He took a long pull on the bottle and belched noisily. "You got any of your old posters?"

"No," Horn said. He was picking absent-mindedly at the label on the bottle with his thumbnail.

"The kid got to you, didn't he?"

When Horn didn't answer, Mad Crow went on: "Tell you what, I won't give you anything to do with widows or orphans, okay? Just hardcore gamblers, tough guys, bad apples. Then you can keep your conscience clear."

The Indian finished his beer and dropped the bottle into a waste-basket with a loud clatter. "Two guys who never finished high school," he said, his voice softening a little. "We sure fooled 'em, didn't we? We had it pretty good for a while. Nobody ever seemed to notice neither one of us could act worth a hoot." He shook his head, remembering, and laughed. "We just went around dispensing justice in the old west, by God. The cowboy and his faithful Indian—"

"It was all crap, and you know it."

12

"Who says? Cecil B. De-fucking-Mille? Okay, we turned out a lot of forgettable movies, for anybody who had a quarter in his pocket. But the kids liked us. And along the way, we had a few laughs, we made a few bucks."

"Guess I should have saved some of them," Horn said. "Wouldn't be working for you, picking up greasy money off the pavement."

"Please, a little less gratitude. You're embarrassing me. I didn't see anybody else standing in line to offer you a job. Not after Bernie Rome put out the word and you couldn't get a job at any studio in town, even mucking out their stables. Look," he went on when Horn didn't respond. "Who cares? We're saddle pals again, and I say to hell with all of 'em."

"Saddle pals. Right." Horn got up. "I appreciate the work, Indian. I do. Every now and then, I just get a little tired of it, you know?"

"Wait a minute." Mad Crow reached in a drawer. "I almost forgot. You got a call today." He handed him a slip of paper.

"MUtual 3224," Horn read aloud. "Scotty?"

"Yep. I didn't tell him I knew where you were, just said I'd pass it on if I ever ran into you."

Horn crumpled up the paper and dropped it into the wastebasket alongside the empty bottle.

"Not going to call him?" When Horn didn't answer, he said: "I thought you all were good friends. Whatever happened to Horn and Bullard, the terrors of the Sunset Strip?"

13

"I don't know," Horn said, making sure he sounded as if he didn't care. "I've lost touch with the guy."

"He was at the trial, wasn't he?"

"That's right. Bought me a drink just before I went upstate, wrote me a couple of letters, and that was it. Last I heard from him was almost three years ago. I suppose when Iris dumped me, he had to pick sides, and he'd known her longer. Or maybe it was just that Scotty's old man wouldn't have approved of him hanging out with a jailbird. Bad for business. Bad for the family image."

"Well, he doesn't have to worry about Daddy's opinion anymore," Mad Crow said with a snort. "You heard, right?"

"I saw it in the paper. Big funeral. They said it took an hour to clear all the cars out of Forest Lawn afterward."

"So your old buddy's a rich guy now."

Horn shrugged. "Good for him." He turned to leave.

"Why not give him a call? You can use every friend you've got."

"Go to hell," Horn said pleasantly as he closed the door behind him.

"Happy trails, amigo," Mad Crow called loudly after him. "Keep in touch."

CHAPTER 2

Normally, Horn would have headed home to fix some dinner, but he was newly flush and felt like eating out. He drove downtown to Cole's Buffet, in the basement of the Pacific Electric Building on Sixth. Down the stairs off the sidewalk, the place was cool and dimly lit. The counterman made him a roast beef sandwich with a side of potato salad and drew him a draft beer. Horn settled into a table near the back.

Cole's was one of the places where he still felt at home. Those places seemed to be vanishing, the way things dissolve in one of those long, slow fadeouts on the screen, when you know the movie is over. Horn had spent little time in the city during the past few years. First had been the war, and not long after that came prison. Now he was back, but from time to time he was troubled by small, unsettling surprises—the sight of a new building where there had been grass and trees, or a vacant lot where a hotel had once stood. Los Angeles, the city that had welcomed him in his youth with sunshine and promise, was beginning to present a different face to him, a little like an ex-girlfriend who had changed, who now preferred other men.

As he ate, he felt a mixture of shame and anger. Shame over the work he did, anger at everyone— Buddy Taro for being a fool, the boy for recognizing him. Anger even at the Indian, one of the few friends he had left, for putting him in the position of accepting charity, for handing him a job that made him feel low and mean. He went for another beer, to soften the edges of the anger. He had to be careful about the feeling. Sometimes, anger could fester and erupt in rage. It was rage that had put him in Cold Creek for two years.

The beer made him feel better, and he felt something soften in him. After a while he went over to the pay phone in the corner, paged through the phone book to find Scott Bullard's number at work, and dialed it.

"Scotty, it's John Ray."

"Hey, my friend. Thanks for calling me. Been a while, hasn't it?"

"I suppose it has. Sorry about your father."

"I appreciate that. At least it was quick—his heart. The old man wouldn't have wanted to stick around with some long illness. He told me that, back when we were still talking." Although Scotty spoke quickly, as always, with the words tumbling over one another, he sounded tired and distracted. "It's almost as if he picked the way he wanted to go. Just like he arranged everything else."

"I guess so," Horn said. "You needed something?"

"Look, I, uh . . ." Scotty stopped, uncharacteristically at a loss for words. "Yeah, I need to talk to you. Where are you right now?"

"Cole's. On my second beer."

"Mind if I come by and try to catch up?"

Horn nursed the second draft while he waited. The place was getting busier as the nearby office buildings emptied for the day, and he idly watched the countermen as they sliced rare roast beef off the bone, dipped the bread into the juice, and slid the sandwiches across to the customers. *Nice to have a useful trade*, he thought. *Man comes in off the job hungry, his starched collar wilting in the heat, and this guy in a white apron hands him a juicy French dip with a glistening kosher dill on the side and a mug of cold beer to wash it all down. Now there's a service that's appreciated. Me? I take people's grocery money.*

He thought about Scotty, trying to focus on the good times. Years earlier, the two had eased into a solid friendship. Each had something to offer the other. Horn had introduced his friend to the slower rhythms of a ranch and had invited him onto movie sets while some of his "oaters" were being shot. He showed him how to use a rifle and took him coyote hunting a few times up in the San Gabriels. For his part, Scotty, as the son of one of Los Angeles's biggest land developers, had showed Horn the joy of irresponsibility—and how

17

intensely two young men could carouse when financed by Bullard Senior's money.

Even after Horn and Iris were married, she never seemed to mind when he and Scotty went off somewhere. She had worked for the Bullard company as a secretary and knew the family— Scotty had introduced her to Horn, in fact—and, like most people, seemed to genuinely enjoy Scotty's company. She and Horn would sometimes go on double dates with Scotty and his current girlfriend, who might be a file clerk with the family firm, a department-store model, or a debutante from back East. Scotty was undiscriminating when it came to women. He liked them all, and they returned the affection.

When Horn began his two-year stretch upstate and Scotty let things lapse after a couple of letters, Horn reluctantly wrote the other man off as the kind of friend he didn't need. Then came the letter from Iris, giving him someone else to write off. . . .

The street door opened, and Scotty stepped inside with his usual quick, fluid movement. He waved to an acquaintance standing at the counter, patted another on the back, then looked around, spotted Horn, and came over.

"John Ray Horn," he said with mock seriousness, sticking out his hand as he sat down.

"Scott Bullard, Esquire," Horn replied, taking it.

Scotty looked much the same. Lithe build, sharp features, sandy hair with a pronounced widow's

18

peak. The ever-present slight grin was in place, except now it looked strained. He was wearing a well-cut tropical-weight gray suit, apparently having come over directly from the family offices. The only difference Horn noticed was the circles under the other man's eyes. *Guess that's what losing a father does to some people*, Horn thought. *Wonder if it'll do that to me.*

"You doing all right?" Scotty asked, looking at Horn searchingly, taking in his clothes, the slightly tousled hair, the one-day stubble, the overall look of a man for whom good grooming had ceased to be a priority. "Someone said you're working with Joseph now."

"*For* him," Horn grunted. "It's not much, but I didn't find many topdrawer jobs waiting for me when I got back. You want a beer?"

"Maybe later. What about the studio?"

Horn laughed. "What do you think?"

"What about another studio?"

Horn shifted impatiently in his chair. "I've got a felony on my record. I'm what they call black-listed. Might as well be a goddamn Red or something."

"I'm sorry," Scotty said. "Look—"

"Hey, Bullard, if you're about to offer me a job, save it. You're a little late, anyway, know what I mean?"

The other man nodded, looking down at the table. Horn said, "So I guess you're the big dog at Bullard Development now."

Scotty shook his head. "The old man was too smart for that. He knew I wasn't the one to carry the company banner. Just to make sure I didn't tear down everything he worked to build—" His voice rose dramatically in mimicry of Arthur Bullard's oratory. "Anyway, he set up a trust fund for me. My dear old mom and the board of directors are going to be running the company, which is fine with me." He leaned back in his chair and unbuttoned his suit jacket. "I think I disappointed him from the day I first poked my head out into the world. Even though I wanted him to be proud of me, I never wanted to go into his business. He thinks all I ever wanted to do was spend his money."

"Well," Horn said, "you had a real talent in that department."

"I did indeed," Scotty chuckled. "I think he had this secret hope that I'd mature, buckle down at the office, get married, and sire a lot of Bullard grandchildren to carry on the line. But none of that ever happened. Then, when the war came and I wound up 4-F, I think that finished me for him. Not only was I a disappointment in every other department, now I wasn't even good enough to die for my country."

"Not your fault you were 4-F," Horn said.

"You couldn't tell him that," Scotty replied, shaking his head. "I saw you and a bunch of others come back from the war, and I was jealous of you. When you wouldn't even talk about what you'd done, that somehow made me feel even worse."

Horn regarded him uneasily. Once Scotty had sat down, what energy he had left since his father's funeral seemed to drain out of him, and his voice and gestures were growing slower. Scotty had always been able to throw himself into everything—a new car, a new girl, even a conversation. It was one of the things that made him likable. But his heart wasn't in this conversation. He took long breaths, and his eyes flitted around the room, rarely meeting Horn's.

"We didn't have much to say to each other in the last few years," Scotty went on. "Oh, I made a good show of it, so he could tell his friends at his club how he was grooming me to take over things some day. I'd show up for work, shuffle papers for a few hours, and go home without ever seeing him . . ." Scotty stared at Horn for a few seconds. "What the hell. Enough of this. Have you seen Iris?"

"No."

"Or Clea?"

"Nope. Not since I went up."

"That was almost three years ago."

"I know it was three years ago," Horn said, more loudly than he intended. "I went in married, came out divorced. Why do I need to see either one of them?"

"Well, I know Clea was special to you . . ." Scotty trailed off, looking uncomfortable.

"Just let it go, all right?" Horn leaned forward impatiently. "Come on, Bullard. If you're not going to get a beer, at least you can tell me what you wanted to see me about."

Scotty nodded slowly, as if he'd been waiting for those words. "Can we get out of here? I want to show you something."

Horn stood at the window looking down at the street twelve stories below. Beneath a cloudless, ink-dark sky, Spring Street danced with the lights of cars and the quick movements of the last workers exiting the office buildings on their way home. The heavy, wide-paned windows were thrown up, and the evening air was beginning to cool the room. He and Scotty were in Arthur Bullard's office on the top floor of the Braly Building, where Bullard Development occupied the top two floors. Except for the occasional cleaning woman, most of the other offices were dark and unoccupied. The room where they stood was lit only by a study lamp atop the desk in one corner.

"Some view, huh?" he heard Scotty say behind him. "My office is on the other side, looking east out toward the rail yards." Scotty nudged him and handed him a glass. Horn guessed it contained Bullard Senior's favorite scotch, and a sniff confirmed it. He sipped appreciatively.

"But I like my view too," Scotty went on. "Did you know this was the first skyscraper around here? It's still pretty goddamn impressive."

Although Horn had visited Iris at work in the building a few times before they were married, he

22

had never been in this office. The place was a statement of power, with richly paneled walls and plush leather furniture. He walked around the large oak desk to study a row of framed photos on the wall, squinting to make out the figures in the dim light. He saw Scotty's father standing with the mayor, the archbishop, the governor, the occasional movie-studio chief, and groups of friends on hunting and skiing trips. Although Horn had little interest in business or government, he nevertheless recognized some of the men known to be the oligarchs of Los Angeles. They were the big businessmen who, earlier in the century, had sensed the city's coming greatness and, by methods both legal and questionable, had accumulated enough of the vital pieces on the board—oil, rails, water, real estate—to ensure their fortunes. Arthur Bullard had been one of the last surviving oligarchs, and now he too was gone.

Scotty sat down in his father's old chair and gestured for Horn to sit across from him.

"How's the view from behind the big desk?" Horn asked.

"Pretty grand. But I don't plan on getting used to it. Where are you living these days?"

Horn told him, explaining how to find his place, and wrote down the phone number on Arthur Bullard's monogrammed notepad.

"So . . ." Scotty cleared his throat, looking vaguely ill at ease. "I guess I should have written you more. Maybe driven up there a few times."

"You probably had more important things."

"I don't know about that. Did you get along all right?"

"Sure. I made a few friends, tried not to make too many enemies—although that's not easy in a place like that. Kept my head down, my nose clean, you know. I even learned a little bit of a trade, tooling leather and working metal. I made this belt I'm wearing. Started on a saddle, but then my time ran out."

Scotty's mind appeared to be elsewhere. "Maybe this isn't much of a reason," he said. "But I heard people say you really tried to kill that guy."

"Maybe I did."

Scotty grinned ruefully. "And then I heard a few others say maybe he deserved it."

"Maybe he did."

"All right, here it is: My father had some things to say about you. You can imagine what they were. I tried to avoid being Daddy's good little boy most of the time, but this was one time I guess I listened to him. He said you had gone crazy and were dangerous. I admit, I was a little scared of you, scared of what my old friend had turned into. Make sense?"

"No."

"I know it doesn't, but that's the reason you didn't hear from me after that first couple of letters. I feel bad about it. If you've got any hard feelings, take a poke at me, and we'll call it even." He glanced down at Horn's oversized right hand

24

cupped around his glass, the knuckles whitened with old calluses. "Maybe that's not a good idea. Why don't you just call me some names?"

Horn suppressed the desire to laugh. Although he wasn't rid of his resentment, it was hard to dislike Scotty for long. Still, there remained one thing, buried deep, that he needed to unearth. "For a while there, I was wondering," he said. "When I didn't hear from you, and then when Iris said she was divorcing me . . ."

"You thought I was romancing your wife?" Scotty looked astonished.

Horn shrugged. "Sounded reasonable to me at the time."

"Well, it's crazy. She's a great gal, and I always liked her. But hell, John Ray, I fixed you up with her. She'd never get serious about me. I was only good for laughs. Besides, she's married again."

"You know anything about the guy?" Horn asked casually.

"A little. You know how I never turn down an invitation? Well, I just might have been at the party where they met each other. At least that's the way I recall it through the haze of alcohol. Also, I think they both showed up at the old man's funeral the other day, although there was such a crowd . . . I haven't talked to her for a long time. He's some kind of business type. A few months ago there was a picture of the two of them in the society page, some event. He's a decent-looking guy." He glanced quickly at Horn. "Apparently she's well fixed."

25

"Well, good for her," Horn said, trying to mean it. "Like they say, third time's the charm." The subject was making him uncomfortable, and he wondered what he was doing sitting in a dead man's office. "Is this what you wanted to show me?" he asked, gesturing around the room.

Something passed over Scotty's face. "No," he said. "There's more. When the old man died, my mother and I went through everything of his, all his papers. He was organized, like you'd expect. We opened his lock boxes, found a lot of things related to the business. Even a pile of her old letters to him, which made her happy that he'd bothered to keep them. Some people said he didn't have a conscience. When it came to business, he could be ruthless. But my mother said they just didn't know the real Arthur, the man who'd keep old letters from his wife."

Scotty paused, and Horn simply nodded, waiting. "We knew he'd written a will," Scotty went on, "but it didn't turn up in the lock boxes, so we came here to look in his desk. He kept the drawers locked, but we had all the keys from his key ring. Sure enough, we turned up the will down in the bottom drawer."

Scotty finished off his scotch in one gulp. "There was one other thing in the drawer—this," he said, reaching downward. He turned a key in a lock, opened the drawer, and extracted an ordinary manila envelope, which he laid on the desk. "I looked inside and told my mother it was just business details, not anything she needed to worry about." His eyes evading Horn's, he said quietly, "Now I want you to look at it."

The envelope was about nine inches by twelve, bearing the logotype of Bullard Development and no other markings. Horn picked it up, opened the clasp, and let the contents slide onto the desk. It was a packet of photos secured by a rubber band. He slid the band off and spread them around the desktop. Fifteen pictures, warped and dog-eared by Arthur Bullard's handling. Horn instantly knew the photos. Not because he had seen them before, but because he had seen many like them. The first had been at a county fair, when a cousin had taken him behind a stall and showed him a sepia-toned snapshot he had bought on the street in St. Louis, a picture of a woman lounging on a couch, naked, with her thighs apart.

Horn picked up his glass. "I've seen dirty pictures," he said. "A guy in my platoon over in Italy had a bunch of them. Said they were all of his girlfriend, and if he didn't make it back to New Jersey, he wanted us to bury 'em with him."

"I don't think they were like these," Scotty said.

"Hmm?" Horn looked over them again. The photos, like all those he'd seen, gave off a whiff of sinister energy: They were furtive, blatant, and forbidden all at once. Men and women, doing things few cameras ever recorded. The women were all naked, the men were covered in some way, wearing bulky robes, open in front. Their faces were hooded. Horn's eyes swept over the inescapable details—the erect male organs, grasping hands, awkwardly sprawled legs, open mouths, joined bodies. Then he leaned forward, blinking. He'd had too much to drink, and something wasn't right. He fanned the remaining photos out on the desk and stared.

There were no women in the pictures. Only girls. Children. The oldest, he guessed, were in their mid-teens. They appeared in the tableaus featuring men and sex. The youngest were usually posed alone, naked and in a semblance of seductiveness, their small fingers sometimes touching themselves in ways they couldn't yet understand. These girls were young, so young he didn't want to guess their ages.

Horn pushed his chair back and got up. "Don't know why you went to all this trouble just to show me your old man's photo album. You want my opinion, he had a sick hobby. Maybe he should have asked the family to bury these with him in Forest Lawn."

"Wait," Scotty said. "Give me another minute. Just keep looking."

Horn stared at him, sighed, then leaned over the desk, bracing himself with his hands. "I see a few guys who belong in jail, who don't want their faces to show," he said, sounding bored. "I see a bunch of little girls who are going to be messed up for a long . . ."

He reached for one photo, held it up close to

28

the desk light. Then he sat down slowly. A small girl, no more than four or five years old, stood in a doorway, smiling at the camera. Her weight was on one leg, her hip cocked and the other leg slightly bent. Her right hand cupped a nonexistent breast, her thumb toying with her tiny nipple. The girl's face was rouged and lipsticked, but underneath the grotesque mask, her smile was full and eager, as if she wanted to please whoever operated the camera.

It was the face that had stopped him. Even in this childish form, it bore features he recognized. He knew the full upper lip, the well-defined jaw, the pale, wide-set eyes. *I didn't know her then*, he thought distractedly, *I knew her later.*

He looked up to find Scotty staring at him. "I was right," Scotty said. "It's her, isn't it?"

Horn nodded slowly, not wanting to say the name. "It's Clea."

CHAPTER 3

They sat there for a while, listening to the distant sounds of traffic. Horn's face was set in an expression that was hard and yet unfocused, as if he wanted to lash out at someone but couldn't yet make out his adversary.

A cleaning woman opened the door and started in, her water pail trailing behind her. She saw the two men and stopped. "This is Mr. Bullard's office," she said hesitantly in a thick accent.

"I'm the other Mr. Bullard, the junior one," Scotty said to her, not unkindly. "Come back later, would you?"

She closed the door behind her. "Fifteen years at this fucking company," Scotty said quietly, "and some of the help still don't know me. Guess that's what I get for only working half-days, huh?"

Horn just stared at the photo of the little girl who had once been his stepdaughter. Finally he said, "You know where he got this stuff?"

Scotty shook his head. "There must be dozens of photographers in L.A., and it wouldn't surprise me if a lot of them sell this sort of thing. My father had a lot of money, and I'm sure he had people

30

who could get this for him. This town's got something for everybody." He looked around, as if searching for something. "But I did find this." Reaching in the top center drawer of the desk, he brought out a small card and slid it across to Horn.

It was a business card. It read GEIGER'S RARE BOOKS, with a phone number and an address in Hollywood.

"This place is one of several bookstores along that stretch of Hollywood Boulevard," Scotty said. "I've been in most of them. Geiger's is a little different. They sell first editions, but they've also got dirty books under the counter—expensive ones, leather bindings and all that—if you've got the money to spend and know what to ask for."

"You know about this sort of thing, do you?"

"I know about a lot of things, John Ray. Don't go getting holy on me. You asked me, and I told you what I know."

"All right," Horn said. "But your father probably had a lot of business cards."

"Hundreds of them," Scott said. "All arranged very neatly and alphabetically in that box." He pointed to a long and narrow teakwood box resting by Arthur Bullard's telephone.

"So why—"

"But this card wasn't in the box," Scotty interrupted. "It was underneath the desk blotter. The only thing I found there."

Horn thought about that for a moment, then put the card in his pocket.

"Here's a laugh," Scotty went on. "I've finally got the goods on the old man. But if he were sitting here right now, I wouldn't have the nerve to ask him what he was doing with these pictures."

"I know one thing," Horn said, looking again at the photo. "He held this one in his hands and looked at it. He was a sick son of a bitch." He sat back, his face drawn, and rubbed his eyes. "How the hell could Clea—"

"Get her picture taken like this? That's what's been bothering me. Who took it? Where was she? Where was her mother when this happened? Tell me how old she looks here."

"Maybe four or five. She was five when I married Iris, and she looks a little younger here. She—" He stopped for a second, swallowing hard. "She was growing real fast right about then. This was either while Iris was still married to Clea's dad or after she divorced him."

"Any chance Iris could have known about this?"

Horn had had the same thought, and his face twisted with something close to pain. "How am I supposed to answer that? Look, she's not one of my favorite people right now, and I'm sure it's mutual. But one thing I know—she loves this girl."

Scotty nodded. "I would have said the same thing."

Horn raised his gaze to him, and the look was not friendly. "Why did you show me all this?"

Scotty shoved his chair back until it rested against a bookshelf behind him. Horn had never seen him look so tired. "Maybe I want to get even with my old man," he said, his words a little slurred. "For not letting a day go by without dropping a hint about what a disappointment I was to him. Maybe I just want somebody to know he wasn't the high-and-mighty Arthur, the guy in those pictures up there on the wall. I don't want his name in the papers or anything like that. My mother is pretty strong, but I'm not sure she could handle this. I don't want to tell the police. These pictures are old, and who are they going to arrest after all this time? I just want somebody to know, and I guess you're the one I want to know." He stopped, breathing deeply, and Horn heard the clatter of the cleaning woman's mop against her pail far down the hall.

"All right, now I know," Horn said. "But what do you want me to do?"

"Somebody needs to tell Iris about this."

"You tell her."

"Come on. I'm just a friend, and I haven't talked to her in years. Clea was your daughter for a while."

"Right. Stepdaughter, anyway. And Iris was my wife, until she resigned. I'm not exactly part of the family anymore." Horn was beginning to feel that Scotty was pushing him somewhere he didn't want to be. "What good would it do to tell her, anyway? It would just make her sick. I'll say what you just said: This picture's more than ten years old. We don't know where your old man got it, and we'll probably never know. Clea's a big girl by now. Let's leave it alone." Horn got up. "I'm tired."

33

"What do you think I should do with these?" Scotty asked, sweeping his hand over the photos.

Horn glanced once again at the painted little face, younger than he had ever seen it, then tossed it back onto the pile. "Burn 'em," he said, turning to leave.

As he closed the door, he heard Scotty say quietly, "I hope she's doing all right."

An insistent knocking at the cabin's front door awoke him when the morning light was still gray. He opened the door to find a little man with a thinning head of hair and an improbably bushy mustache.

"I want to show the property this afternoon," Harry Flye said without preamble, the volume of his voice turned louder than necessary, as always. "I talked to you about the weeds. The place looks awful. You said you'd take care of it. Get up there today, all right? This morning."

"All right," Horn said.

"The place looks awful," Flye said again, as if it had just occurred to him. "I can't sell it the way it looks. You're supposed to keep it up."

"I will, Mr. Flye," Horn said with what he hoped sounded like proper respect. *You used to be an actor,* he told himself. *So pretend he's not a weasel, and act friendly.* "Today."

"This morning," the other man said as he stomped down the stairs to his car. "The swimming pool can wait a while, but the weeds can't.

You don't take care of the place, lots of others be glad to get the job, I bet."

"Nice to see you again," Horn said as he closed the door.

After breakfast, he put on dungarees and an undershirt, fetched the long-handled scythe, and started up the path that led around his cabin and up the steep hillside through the trees.

The cabin sat on a densely wooded hillside near the head of Culebra Canyon, which wound like the snake after which it was named for a few miles until it dead-ended in the Santa Monica Mountains. The little building was made of rough, old-wood siding, but it had a solid foundation and a fireplace, both made of stone, and a brick chimney that leaned only a few degrees. Inside was one medium-sized room with a couch where he slept. Behind a door was the bathroom, and behind a curtain was a tiny kitchen.

Harry Flye, the only other person who held a key to the gate, was his landlord. Flye had used the war to build an impressive little empire of new money—buying low and selling high, turning over property at precisely the right moment to make a buck, reading the market like a Gypsy fortune-teller reads a mark's palm. At present, he was the owner of the old Ricardo Aguilar place here in Culebra Canyon, a relic of the silent-movie days when Hollywood royalty built estates to match their screen images. The property was mostly in ruins, but the caretaker's cabin still stood, and

Horn was allowed to live there rent-free in exchange for keeping up the grounds. Flye knew about his prison record and didn't seem to care. What he cared about was cheap labor.

Within five minutes, Horn stood on a large plateau rimmed with eucalyptus trees, from which he could see the Pacific, far off to the southwest. Twenty-five years earlier, Aguilar had built his estate here, a Greek-revival palace where Valentino and Swanson, Fairbanks and Pickford, the gods of the silent screen, had gathered for their revels. When the movies found their voice in the late 1920s, Aguilar's reedy tenor drew only laughter from audiences. He retired to his hilltop, and years later a fire swept the property and took his life. Horn had heard the stories that the fire was set by Aguilar himself in an attempt at one final dramatic moment. Now the Villa Aguilar was a scorched ruin, with the fire-blackened remnants of the mansion and outbuildings standing here and there like decayed and broken teeth.

Waist-deep weeds were everywhere. Horn picked a spot near the old swimming pool and went to work, swinging the scythe in long arcs. It felt awkward at first, but then he settled into a rhythm, taking pleasure in the easy motion, the snick of blade against weeds, the pause at the top of the arc before letting the weight of the scythe decide the timing of its return. After an hour, he had worked his way around the tennis court and the foundations of some of the outbuildings and could look back and see more clearly the shape of the estate. *Not a bad life you lived up here, Ricardo.*

Before tackling the grounds around the site of the main house, he pulled some tobacco and papers from his pocket, sat on a chunk of concrete that once had been part of the foundation of the house, and rolled a smoke. His mind wandered, and for a second he saw Clea's face in last night's photo. But he forced the image away, and its place was taken by the thin, pinched face of the boy from the rooming house. Horn remembered the way one lock of hair had fallen over the kid's eyebrow, again heard him ask: *Are you Sierra Lane?*

He had met a lot of kids like that, at rodeos and horse shows and public appearances on small-town streets in front of the only theater in town. He signed autographs for them, shook their fathers' hands. He liked the way they looked at Sierra Lane, the goldangedest cowpoke who ever pretended to bust up a saloon. No one had looked at him like that in quite a while. Even that kid yesterday—Horn thought he had seen something different in that look, something full of disappointment, even contempt.

Why'd you push my dad?

He attacked the weeds with new energy, sweat flying off his face. "I could whup Sunset Carson any day of the week," he panted aloud, "and twice on Sundays."

He worked until mid-afternoon, then had a cool bath in the rusty, claw-footed tub and took a nap.

For dinner, he grilled two pork chops, sliced up a tomato, opened a High Life, and carried it all out to the rocker on his front porch, where he sat and ate and listened to the early-evening noises of the canyon. Since the nearest house was a half-mile away and there was almost no traffic down on the road at this end of the canyon, most of the sounds were natural ones—a slow breeze in the eucalyptus and oak trees, an occasional bird call. At night, he could often hear the call of a coyote way up the slope behind him.

The ringing of the phone inside startled him. Until settling up his overdue bill with the phone company a few days earlier, he'd been without a telephone for weeks, and he wasn't used to its sound. He went in and picked it up.

"Cowboy." Mad Crow's voice was a relaxed rumble from deep in the chest, and Horn imagined him sunken in the hefty chair in his living room with something tall and cold in his fist.

"Yeah."

"How you doing?"

"Not bad." The Indian was not given to idle conversation, so Horn waited to see what he wanted.

"Got to thinking. Guess I shouldn't have sent you after Buddy—"

"You said that already."

"I know what I said, dammit. How come I can't say something twice if I want to?" The Indian's voice lowered a notch. "Look, I don't want you to get sour on the work. I need you around. We're good for each other."

Horn said nothing. He could hear the clink of ice cubes as Mad Crow sipped at whatever was in his glass.

"What you need, you need to stay busy," the Indian went on. "Got a job for you. It's over by MacArthur Park. A dentist. Thinks he's God's gift to poker. Into me for a couple of hundred. He's a pillar of society, so he'll pay up quick and—"

"No," Horn cut in. "I can't do it right now."

"Come on."

"Something's come up. I'll tell you about it later, okay? But get somebody else." That was a lie. Nothing else was competing for his time. But yesterday's job *had* soured him on the work, just as the Indian had guessed. And his talk with Scotty the night before had left him with a sense of unease that he didn't know how to deal with.

Mad Crow sighed. "Okay, amigo. But remember, I got a business to run, and this is work you can do. You scratch mine, I scratch yours. Not a lot of jobs waiting for you out there."

The Indian sounded impatient, and Horn felt a rising anger. Their friendship stretched back years, but it had been uneven. In the beginning, Horn had been the successful one, the name on the marquee, and Mad Crow had been his companion, both in their movies and away from the camera. Now the earth had shifted, and Horn found himself the hanger-on, the one who had to earn his pay.

Would we still be friends, he wondered now, *if I didn't work for him?*

He was tempted to tell Mad Crow to go to hell, as he had back at the casino. But that had been in jest, and he doubted he could keep the edge out of his voice this time. So he simply said, "Talk to you later," and hung up.

As the sun dropped behind the cabin and the light turned pale green in the trees, he rolled a smoke, lit it, and looked through a day-old copy of the *Mirror*. He was restless—had been restless, in fact, since seeing Scotty—and turned to the movie ads.

There was a double bill at the Hitching Post on Hollywood Boulevard, a new Gene Autry paired with a revival of *The Lost Mine*, one of Horn's movies from a few years ago. Although he never admitted it, he had once enjoyed seeing himself on the screen. But possibly as a joke on the part of the guard who selected the weekly entertainment, one of Horn's films had made its way up to the California State Prison at Cold Creek. Sitting there in the dark, watching himself ride Raincloud in pursuit of justice while listening to the catcalls of his fellow inmates, he knew that the heroic image would never fit him again.

The phone rang again. *Damn, I'm popular tonight.*

"Hi. Not bothering you, I hope." It was Scotty.

"Not at all. I was just having my town car brought around. Thought I'd pick up Linda Darnell and hit the Trocadero."

40

"Capital idea. She got a friend?"

"I'll ask."

"You're a prince. A prince among cowpokes." Once again, Scotty sounded tired. Horn wondered when he'd hear the real Scott Bullard again, the playboy hell-raiser who could lift anyone out of a bad mood. "I've had a long day. Been driving all over the place. Thought I'd see if you'd like to go up to the lodge with me tomorrow."

"Maybe," Horn said. "What have you got in mind?"

"Oh, I just thought it might be fun. Get out of the heat, breathe some good air. Maybe go for a long walk, bag a few squirrels, I don't know. I'll pack some beer in the ice chest. We can leave early and be back by night. Sound okay?"

"Sure. Want me to bring some food?"

"I'll take care of it." Scotty was quiet for a moment.

"Anything else?" Horn asked.

"I've been thinking about those goddamned pictures."

Horn made an impatient sound. "You didn't get rid of them, did you?"

"Not yet. Plenty of time for that. I, uh . . . I think there's more to them than we thought. Want to see if you agree."

"I don't understand a word you're saying, but I disagree anyway."

"Not so fast, cowboy. Give me by the end of the day. You tell me you want to burn the whole pile

41

of them, we'll build a little campfire up in the wilderness and do just that."

"Fair enough."

"We might even have time for those war stories you never got around to telling me."

"I already told you, Scotty—"

"At least how you got the Purple Heart."

"No war stories from me. Not ever."

"All right, don't get mad." Horn heard what sounded like a yawn. "Look, I'm really worn out," Scotty said. "Just meet me at my place by eight tomorrow. I'm still at the Moose. We'll have a good time."

"Bet you could use one."

"I could definitely use one. Funerals do that to you. Want to hear something strange? I stopped in at the office for a couple of hours this morning, and Dad's secretary told me someone went through all his desk drawers sometime last night after we left. Even the locked ones, apparently. Might have been one of the cleaning people, looking for souvenirs now that the old man's gone." He didn't sound convinced.

"Did they find the pictures?"

"No. I took them with me after you left. Didn't want to haul them around with me all day, though, so I stashed them away, where the cleaning brigade'll never find 'em." Scotty yawned again. "You probably could, though. So could she."

"So could who? You're not making much sense, Bullard."

"Too tired to make any sense," Scotty said. "Don't be late." He mumbled a goodbye and hung up.

Horn sat up for a long time. It was that time of evening when, if he wasn't careful, his mind went for a walk, sometimes opening old doors and entering rooms where it didn't belong. He wondered how Iris was with her new husband, and Clea with her new father. When he'd been her father, he'd found that nothing came naturally. His own father had given him little to go on. So he made mistakes. Most obvious was the drinking, and the way it affected his relationship with both mother and daughter. Iris drank too, and once in a while the two of them would wind up in a shouting match that sent the girl into some far corner of the house. Afterward, they would coax her out and try to soothe her, but her eyes darted between them like those of a small animal cornered by two predators.

Neither one of them ever struck Clea. He wished he could say they had never struck each other, but some of their worst fights had ended in blows. The memory still sickened him.

His last memory of Clea was of the night before he was to surrender himself for the trip upstate, when she had locked herself in her room and screamed over and over that he was leaving her. He could still hear the screams, the absolute despair in her thirteen-year-old voice.

CHAPTER 4

Horn left early, to make sure he had time to get to Scotty's apartment. The drive along Pacific Coast Highway went smoothly, and he was able to enjoy the way the growing sunlight picked out the humped back of Santa Catalina Island, far off to the south. He had always liked driving in the early morning, windows open and the fresh ocean air rushing noisily past his ears. As he took Sunset up from the coast road, the light was pearly gray, no sun in sight yet, but the cool air felt thin, as if the coming heat could break through it like tissue paper whenever it wanted.

It was only about half-past seven when he pulled into the parking lot behind the apartment building. Scotty lived in the Blue Moor, an eight-story, U-shaped building with a landscaped courtyard in front and decorated in ornate plaster Spanish-Moorish trim. The higher-up apartments, which included Scotty's, had a grand view of the Hollywood Hills, including the old sign reading HOLLYWOODLAND, a tattered relic of a 1920s real estate development, the *H* sagging and near collapse. True to its name, the Moor was painted an almost garish shade of blue that made first-time visitors gape. Scotty liked to refer to the place as the Blue Moose. The apartments were peopled by an assortment of dowagers, well-heeled bachelors, and sometimes a name or two from the movies.

Horn spotted Scotty's car in the lot, a new Lincoln Continental convertible he had first seen the night before last, when they had left Cole's. The top was down, ready to travel, and sitting on the backseat were a jacket, some heavy-duty pants, a pair of hunting boots, and an ice chest. On the dashboard was a grease-stained paper bag bearing the name of a bakery Horn recognized. When the two had gone on excursions in the old days, Scotty's main responsibility was procuring doughnuts.

Horn entered the building through the back door and walked down a corridor that gave onto the lobby, a high-ceilinged room of tile and potted ferns. The doorman, he noticed as he rang for the elevator, was not at his usual place behind the desk. Through the glass panes of the big front doors, traffic moved along the street almost at a crawl. Too slowly for this time of day. Across the street, a small group of neighbors, some in bathrobes, stood motionless, apparently staring at the front of the building.

Maybe a traffic accident. Horn hesitated for a second in front of the elevator, then turned and strode across the lobby, pushing through the doors. On the street directly in front of the building stood a police car and an ambulance. Behind the ambulance a mix of police and white-uniformed men stood not far from a stretcher covered with a sheet. He cut across the lawn toward the ambulance, passing a brick walkway that fronted the building. The walkway was stained with a large pool of crimson, still glistening as it seeped into the crevices.

Horn approached the stretcher. "Who is it?" he asked an ambulance attendant standing nearby.

The man was young and black-haired, with bad skin and eyes that had seen a lot. "Some guy who lived up there," he said, indicating the blue building. "Looks like he fell."

"I want to see him."

"That's not a good idea," the young man said. "The cops just got an ID on him, and they don't like . . . *Hey.*" He reached out to stop him, but Horn had a hand on the corner of the bloodied sheet, and something in his face made the other man drop his hand.

Horn pulled back a corner of the sheet far enough to reveal Scotty's face. The left temple was crushed, and his hair was matted with drying blood. His eyes were open but just barely, the eyelids slitted, as if the world had suddenly grown too bright to look at. The twisted mouth, half open with blood pooled inside, was not Scotty's anymore.

"You know him?" A cop was speaking to him, in a voice that said keep your hands off.

"No," Horn said.

"Then why don't you turn loose of the sheet and step back?" The cop was taking in Horn's appearance, his scuffed shoes. "You live here?"

"No." Horn replaced the sheet. "Just waiting for somebody."

The cop's face didn't change expression, but Horn could see the man had him tagged as someone he could push. The cop moved toward him until they stood almost chest to chest. "Back on the sidewalk."

"Sure." Horn faked a smile, as easily as if the camera had been rolling. "Sorry." He stepped away, looking at the ground, knowing he didn't want to risk an arrest, even a frivolous one.

He went over to the front steps of the building and sat down, then pulled out a toothpick and began chewing on it. He was there for a long time, slowly spitting out the pieces, his eyes focused on the bricks at his feet, as the morning warmed and the ambulance left with Scotty's body and most of the gawkers dispersed. Finally most of the police were gone too, including the man who had spoken to him, and only one squad car was left.

Without knowing exactly why, Horn wanted to see Scotty's apartment. He avoided the elevator and took the stairs. When he reached the seventh floor, he took off his cotton jacket and sport shirt, folded them, and left them on the landing. Then, dressed in khaki pants, an undershirt, and the same heavy, high-topped work shoes he had worn while weeding the day before, he walked down the

47

corridor to Scotty's apartment. The door was open, and he went in. A different policeman sat on the sofa in the living room, filling out some kind of report.

"They need a broken window fixed in here?" Horn asked him.

"I don't think so," the man said, going back to his report.

"Mind if I look? I don't want to get in trouble with the manager. They don't call him *Il Duce* for nothing."

The cop laughed without looking up. "Sure."

Horn went into the bedroom. One of the two windows was wide open. Far up in the hills, the HOLLYWOODLAND sign was hard to pick out in the morning haze. He leaned out and saw, seven stories down and precisely below the window, the stained bricks on the walkway. Nothing else on the street seemed abnormal. A woman walked a small dog, and not far away, two kids played catch in a driveway.

He looked around the bedroom, saw nothing unusual. The bed was casually made. He went back to the window, leaning in close to the sill, and saw three faint parallel scratches on the painted surface near the corner. They were not very noticeable and could have been made by almost anything. Fingernails could have made them, Horn thought, if a man was trying to save himself from falling out the window. Or being thrown out.

He noticed that the cop had gone, leaving the apartment door open. Horn decided not to close

48

it, reasoning that he would look less suspicious that way. But he was running out of time, especially if the manager or a neighbor should walk in on him. His mind darted back to Scotty's comment about someone going through his father's desk. The same impulse, barely thought out, that had sent him up to this apartment now told him to hunt for the envelope and the photos. He began looking quickly around the apartment, starting in the bedroom, where he searched under the bed and the mattress and opened all the bedroom drawers, then checked the closet. Then on to the bathroom and kitchen. Breakfast dishes were in the kitchen sink, but nothing seemed out of place.

He went out to the living room and glanced around, recalling the last time he'd been there. It was years ago, after he had come back from the war. He and Iris had gone out to dinner with Scotty and his current flame, a young woman who worked behind the cosmetics counter at one of the big department stores on Wilshire Boulevard. Afterward, they came here. Scotty had entertained them for a while with jokes about the stuffed shirts at his father's club, and Horn told a story about the owner of Medallion Studios trying to turn his girlfriend into a movie star, with disastrous results. Then Scotty put on some Glenn Miller records and mixed a pitcher of martinis, and they all seemed content to sit there, eyes closed, and hum along. Horn sat on the sofa with his arm around Iris. It had been a nice evening.

He looked under cushions and furniture and between the records, then moved to the big, glass-fronted bookcase. The thin film of dust that lay on the edge of the shelves and in the occasional gaps between books had been disturbed. In a couple of places, gaps were totally free of dust, as if books had sat there until recently. The shelves looked as if someone had removed handfuls of books, looked behind them, and then replaced them—but not always precisely where they had been.

He heard voices in the hall, gave one last look around, and left, almost bumping into two women, obviously neighbors, who looked at him curiously. Retrieving his shirt and jacket, he left by the back door. In the lot, he stopped again by his friend's convertible. The trunk lock, he discovered, had been forced. Inside he found only the spare and the jack. *Did they find what they were looking for?*

He looked in the glove compartment and behind the sun visors, felt under the seats. Nothing. The clothing, the ice chest—containing only beer and ice, barely melting—and even the bag of dough-nuts were as before, telling him that the trunk had been forced open before he'd arrived. He berated himself for not noticing.

He sat in his car. The sun was higher now, and in the glare on the windshield he saw Scotty's dead face. He had seen too many others like it in Italy. On the way up from Salerno he had marched past Germans stacked in a ditch, waiting for someone to cart them off. Most of them had that same look—the slitted eyelids framing an awful stare, one that focused on something farther away than living men could see.

It had not occurred to him to tell the cop that he knew Scotty. To Horn's thinking, a policeman was not someone you trusted with a confidence. Or the truth. Two years at Cold Creek had taught him the value of not giving anything away.

He was not as reflective as some people. He either met problems head-on or ignored them in the hope that they would go away. Sometimes they did. During one of the bad times toward the end, Iris had told him that he was oblivious to others, that he didn't give enough thought to consequences. By the time he got around to asking himself whether she was right, it was too late.

He shook his head, trying to decide what to do next. Scotty had wanted Horn to go with him up to the lodge, a place the two of them hadn't visited together in years. What was it Scotty had said to him on the phone? *Been driving all over the place.* Could Scotty have been up there earlier in the day? If so, why? And why go back?

Horn visited the Lincoln once more, then returned and placed the grease-stained bag and the ice chest on his front seat. He got in and started the engine. An hour later he was passing through Glendale, heading for the foothills of the San Gabriels. He turned in at a gas station and told the pump jockey to fill 'er up. Even though the war was long over, Horn still reveled in the absence of the hated gas-rationing stamps and the luxury of a guilt-free full tank. After all, he reminded himself, he had spent two of those years in a cell where everything was rationed—time most of all.

While the kid gassed up the Ford and checked it over, Horn pulled on his shirt and went to a diner next-door for a cup of coffee. No one was behind the counter. He spotted the waitress and a couple of customers over in a corner, huddled around one of the new television sets. It was almost as big as a jukebox, done mostly in wood, with a small glass window high up, like the porthole of a boat. The manager fiddled with the controls, and soon a black-and-white image took shape, a man on a galloping horse, firing his six-shooter at someone. Man and horse looked tiny and mis-shapen, as if they were made of modeling clay left out in the sun, and the gunshots sounded like crumpled tinfoil.

"Look at that," one of the customers said excitedly. "It's a movie."

"Hoot Gibson," another said knowledgeably.

Tex Ritter, you idiot. Horn finally got the waitress's attention. She brought him a coffee, then gave him a look when he took one of the dough-nuts out of the bag and began to eat it. He left her no tip.

The attendant was finishing up the windshield. "Lot of miles on that right rear," he said as Horn paid him for the gas. "It's almost bald. You'll want to keep an eye on it."

"Thanks."

"Or," the kid said, grinning, "you could just leave me the keys and get yourself one of those." He pointed to a billboard that loomed over the gas station, showing one of the new Cadillacs.

"If I had five thousand burning a hole in my pocket, I might," Horn said. "But what the hell are those bumps on the rear?"

"They call 'em tail fins," the kid said. "Neat, huh?"

"If you say so."

Another half-hour and he was into the mountains, climbing the narrow two-lane road that snaked along the crest of the San Gabriels east of Los Angeles. He was almost a mile up, and the air, although no cooler, was sweeter up here. The road wound on and on, through brown and rugged mountains dotted by boulders and patches of evergreens. To his right; the road skirted a chasm hundreds of feet deep.

The government was acquiring much of the San Gabriels, but pockets of the mountain land were held by a small number of companies and rich individuals who used their property as retreats for hunting or camping. Arthur Bullard had been one of those.

A few miles past the road that led to the observatory atop Mount Wilson, Horn turned off to the left onto an unmarked, poorly maintained dirt road. It quickly became a rutted lane shaded by big pines. A few hundred yards took him to a sturdy iron gate. The chain that usually secured it was wrapped loosely around the uprights, and Horn was somehow not surprised to see that the lock was broken. He opened the gate and drove through, slowing to a crawl as he fought the ruts with the steering wheel. Not a good place for a flat tire.

But good enough for an ambush. Someone could still be around. He scanned the trees and underbrush on both sides of the narrow road, but saw nothing. Fifty yards down the road, he came to a familiar clearing and a large one-story building made of roughly hewn logs under a sharply pitched shingle roof. There were no cars in the clearing, which allowed him to relax somewhat. But to make sure, he got out and walked carefully around the perimeter of the lodge. Nothing. Whoever had broken through the gate had finished their business and gone.

Three stone-and-concrete steps led to a porch that held chunky wooden furniture. The lock on the heavy front door had been forced. Inside, the pine-paneled rooms smelled of dust and mildew, but otherwise little had changed. The fire-blackened stone fireplace was clean and ready for use, the firewood piled on the hearth. The big sofas and chairs and tables in the main room were rough and functional. The three small bedrooms held bedframes and mattresses and crude dressers, with a dog-eared copy of *Collier's* atop one of them. In the kitchen, he found that clean-tasting well water still flowed from the faucet.

He took ten minutes to go through the place—every closet, every drawer, every cabinet. It was impossible to tell if anything had been moved, but the broken locks told him that someone had been here before him.

He sat back on the couch, eating the last doughnut and pulling at one of the beers he had extracted from Scotty's cooler. *The pictures.* It was only a guess, of course, but this is where the guess took him: Someone wanted them, and someone had searched Bullard Senior's office for them. Somehow, they found out that Scotty had them, and they killed Scotty for them. Horn, who hated and feared the police, was beginning to think he had no choice but to talk to them about this. He doubted that they would accept his flimsy theory based on what little he could tell them. But it didn't matter who believed or doubted him. As he sat there, the guess grew into something more certain.

He wiped the sugar off his hands on the sofa cushion and looked idly around the room. Like Scotty's apartment, this place held memories for him. One winter, during one of the times when Arthur Bullard was not using the lodge, Scotty had impulsively invited Horn, Iris, and Clea up for a long weekend in the mountains. They had gone for walks in the snow, done some target shooting, and played three-handed poker in the evenings by the light of the fire. It was to be their only visit. Hearing about it later, Arthur had

55

exploded at his son, telling him that no one outside the family was welcome at the lodge.

The fireplace, six feet from where he sat, smelled strongly of soot. Clea had been about nine when they'd been here, he remembered, and she'd been unusually quiet. After dinner, when the three grown-ups sat around with drinks, she would play by the hearth, talking softly to herself, arranging an assortment of pebbles she'd collected on their walks. At bedtime, the pebbles went into a Mason jar that she'd hide away until the next morning. Hide somewhere in the fireplace, he recalled.

What had Scotty said on the phone? He'd put the pictures where the cleaning women would never find them. *You probably could, though,* he had said. *So could she.*

Horn went over to the hearth. The hiding place was to the right, high up, where a little girl could barely reach. He soon found the loose stone. Inserting his penknife between stone and mortar, he wiggled it until the stone edged out a fraction of an inch, then pulled it out with his fingertips. Inside was a ledge about ten inches deep, and there, folded into a V-shape in order to fit, was the manila envelope.

He spread out the pictures on the small table in front of the sofa. They lay there like a deck of obscene playing cards, and the dark energy came at him again, a whiff of brimstone from some hidden place. The young faces and bodies, the male organs, the whole carnival tableau of

56

children being dragged into the kind of knowledge usually forbidden to them, made his stomach clench. He was no stranger to his own animal side, indeed had reveled in it when he was younger, and he had to admit that there was a power in the photos that called to that side of him. But then he looked at the girls' faces again, and he felt not desire but only sickness.

His father, of course, would feel no such ambivalence, because he saw none in life. John Jacob Horn would look at these pictures, catch the scent of brimstone, and know it for what it was. Sin, he would call it.

Horn himself never used that word. Although Sierra Lane would disagree, Horn had long since decided that not much in the world was easily reducible to labels of good and evil. In this case, though . . . He focused on the photo of Clea. In this case, the word just might fit.

There appeared to be at least a dozen girls in the pictures. Some, like Clea, were white. Two were colored, several looked Mexican. One, he thought, might be Oriental.

He couldn't look at their faces any more, so he began looking elsewhere in the photos, to see if he noticed anything unusual. The youngest girls were sometimes posed alone, sometimes with a single male figure. The sexual tableaus involving the older girls featured either one or two men. The robed and hooded figures were impossible to identify, but there were differences in body types and skin tones. It appeared that one was uncircumcised. Another was on the beefy side and wore a ring on each hand. Horn thought at least three men were in the pictures. And possibly another behind the camera.

The photos were all of excellent quality, he noted, printed on heavy paper. The details were sharp, the framing was expert, even the lighting was precise. The backgrounds told him almost nothing. Furniture was barely visible, except for the ubiquitous mattresses. Since he could see no windows, he couldn't tell if it had been day or night. About the only distinctive thing was in the single photo of Clea. Just beyond the frame of the door the little girl leaned against was a strip of paneling—pine, apparently, because not far from her shoulder he could see an odd-shaped knot about two inches across. Stranger yet, it looked almost familiar.

He got up abruptly and began pacing through the rooms of the lodge. When he came to the bedroom at the end of the hall, he turned and immediately saw it. He held up the photo to make sure. The pine knot was shaped like a slightly irregular horseshoe, a shoe for a tiny pony, perhaps, one that might have figured in a little girl's bedtime story.

He sat heavily on the dusty mattress. It had happened here. The pictures were taken here. *I think there's more to them than we thought*, Scotty had said to him the night before he died. His father hadn't bought the pictures from someone; he had been present when they were taken. He, and a few of his friends. They had brought children up here, Clea among them. And when she had come back with her family, years later, she had been quiet and withdrawn, playing alone, talking only to her collection of pebbles.

Now he knew why.

CHAPTER 5

I guess I can tell you my war story now. It won't be what you expected, since most war stories have heroes in them, and mine doesn't. But you asked for it. And since you're dead, you have to just sit there and listen. All right?

Horn sat in the back of the chapel. The place was nearly full, since Scotty had had a lot of friends. Nearby, a large floor fan drew in warm air, mixed it with the heavy scent of the floral arrangements, and pushed it noisily out the stained-glass Sermon on the Mount window, whose lower panel had been cranked open a few degrees. Because of the hum, Horn could barely hear the drone of the minister's voice, but that didn't matter, since Horn was sure the man hadn't known Scotty anyway.

It was in the mountains outside Cassino. We had been trying to take the old abbey for months. I can't really tell you how bad it was, my 4-F friend, but I will say I'm glad you didn't have to be there. The mud stuck to your boots like molasses in the daytime and froze rock-hard around you in the foxholes at night. We were hungry and tired all the time. Just dug in there, in the ice and snow, shooting and being shot at. Every now

60

and then I would think about being a cowboy hero, riding a big horse, chasing bad men, saving good people. Then I would look around me, think about how scared I was, and laugh and be ashamed.

His gaze absent-mindedly swept the crowd, looking for Iris, but he didn't see her there. The gray-haired woman with the dignified bearing, sitting up front, was Scotty's mother, the widow Bullard. The minister was commenting, a bit melo-dramatically, on how Scotty had been prepared to carry on his father's tradition as a "pillar in the business community." *Make that the golfing and nightclubbing communities*, Horn thought.

One morning I woke up and found that three of my friends had been hit by a mortar round and blown up. Just gone, barely enough left to bury. I must have been behaving a little crazy and careless after that, because a German sniper put one through my shoulder, just above the collarbone. They took me to a field hospital, where I hurt for two days. On the third day I was having a conversation with the guy on the next cot who was about to be shipped out. He had just finished wondering if his girlfriend would still love him with most of his jaw missing. Then he stopped, coughed, and died. Medics said it was a blood clot that had been swimming around inside him until it finally reached his brain.

I cried all that day, and the next day I couldn't talk. Couldn't focus my eyes, couldn't eat, couldn't get up to pee, couldn't do anything. They shipped me out, and I spent some time in a hospital and was discharged long before the war was over. For a while, I'd go places in my uniform, and people would buy me drinks, treat me like a hero. You were there some of those times, remember? But in my head I was still the guy in the hospital. Afraid people would find out who I really was. Maybe that's one reason I went after Bernie Junior.

So you see, Scotty, I'm not the guy you thought I was. I'm someone who'll always remember that time I was so full of fear that I would almost rather die than be that way.

He heard scattered coughing and shuffling and realized that the service was over.

I'm sorry you're dead. I don't know yet if there's anything I can do about it.

The crowd filtered out, carrying him slowly with it. Helen Bullard, Scotty's mother, stood outside the door accepting condolences. Horn barely knew her, and his few meetings with her had been strained by her sour relations with her son. Standing straight-backed and wearing a long black dress with hat and veil, she looked small and lonely. But he knew the appearance was deceptive. "My mother's a good match for my father," Scotty had told him once. "Both of them can smell weakness in another person."

He started to edge out but was surprised to see Helen Bullard acknowledge him with a little wave. To his further surprise, she beckoned him over.

"Thank you, John Ray," she said quietly, squeezing his hand. "You were his best friend. I know he'd be glad you were here."

Horn squeezed back, smiled, and muttered something appropriate, then started to move on. But she held his hand. "Would you stop by sometime? I have something for you. Maybe day after tomorrow, in the afternoon, if that's convenient? It would be nice to see you."

Seeing no way out, he said, "I'd be glad to, Mrs. Bullard," and started down the stairs as a woman enveloped in a heavy floral scent moved up to take the widow's hand. He stood under the shade of a tree, waiting. In the noonday sun, Horn was uncomfortable in his blue serge suit. It was the only good one he owned, but heavy for this time of year. Finally Iris came out. The man holding her arm must be her new husband, he thought. From what Horn could tell at this distance, the man wore his suit in a way some men have, the ones who don't have to try very hard. Horn was disappointed not to see Clea with them.

Iris wore an expensive-looking black suit with big shoulders and a nipped-in waist that emphasized her figure. For jewelry she wore only pearls. She looked almost elegant, he thought. The word had never before seemed appropriate for a woman who was married first to a hotel clerk and then to a B-movie actor, but it fit her now. He felt a stab of jealousy directed at this new man, angry that she should look this good for him.

They paused at the top of the chapel steps, about fifty feet from him, and as Iris glanced around, she saw him. He lifted his chin in greeting, but she looked quickly away.

Horn took off his hat and wiped his handkerchief around the inside. *No easy way to do this*, he thought, and began walking toward them. Seeing him approach, Iris touched her husband on the arm and spoke to him. They descended the steps and began crossing the lawn toward the parking lot, walking diagonally away from him. He quickened his pace, almost to a run. Iris glanced at him over her shoulder, and Horn could see the tension in the look. In another moment, she pulled her husband to a halt and spoke urgently to him. The man hesitated and seemed about to object but then, after giving Horn a dark look, he went on toward the parking lot.

As Horn walked up to her, Iris smoothed her dress and set her face in a polite smile. "Hello, John Ray." She pulled a pair of dark glasses out of her purse and put them on. He wasn't sure it was entirely because of the glare.

"Iris."

"It's awful about Scotty. So soon after his father."

He nodded.

Her look of discomfort surprised him a little, because Iris was anything but frail. Years of working as a secretary and rearing a daughter through a bad marriage—*make that two*, he corrected himself—had made her tough when she needed to be. The surprise gave way to satisfaction. *I'm making her nervous*, he thought. *Good.*

He studied her. It was his first good look at her in almost three years. She looked fine. No, better than that. Iris had never been a great beauty, but that had never hindered her. Men had always responded to a sense of urgency about her, a kind of hunger that translated into sexuality. It also drove her to fiercely protect and nurture her daughter. And those who knew her well could discern another hunger in Iris, the need for comfort and security—even wealth. Horn had seen hints of it during their marriage and knew he could never satisfy that side of her. Now, apparently, she had a man who could.

Her pale brown hair under her tiny hat was a little longer now, gathered in two large waves at the side, then allowed to fall down the back, where it pillowed out softly on her shoulders. The same two nervous tendons stood out on her neck. He couldn't quite make out the wide-set brown eyes behind her glasses, but the sharp cheekbones were the same, along with that full upper lip she shared with Clea. And she still wore Evening in Paris, a scent he'd always liked. He still hated her, of course.

"I hope you're doing all right." She was getting her nerves under control. And her voice, one of the things he'd liked best about her, was the same— soft and yet direct.

"Me? I'm fine. Was that your new husband?"

She nodded. "That's Paul. He's getting the car. My name is Fairbrass now." She spelled it for him.

"Fairbrass." He didn't care for the name, nor

had he expected to. "Didn't you want him to meet me?"

"Not particularly." She said it without emphasis, then allowed herself to laugh, as if admitting the awkwardness of it all.

"Fair enough. What does he do?"

"He owns Fairbrass Pipe Fittings in Long Beach."

"He's a plumber."

"No, he's a . . ." She stopped. "You're making a joke. No, he's not a plumber. His company installs pipe fitting for steam plants and oil-pumping systems and I don't know what else. Paul took over the firm when his father died. Then the war came, and government contracts. They did a lot of work for the Navy. Anyway, Paul's done well."

"I'm glad for you," he said, wondering if she could tell he didn't mean it. "So where are you living now?"

"Hancock Park."

"Nice neighborhood, huh?"

"I suppose."

"I hear the mayor lives around there somewhere."

She only shrugged, and he was almost disappointed that she wouldn't take the bait, to meet his veiled sarcasm with something pointed of her own. Iris had never been one to shrink from a fight.

She extracted one of the new filter-tip cigarettes from a case and, when he didn't offer to light it, fished a delicate lighter out of her black leather purse and clicked a flame alive. She studied the tip of the cigarette for so long he thought she was

66

about to mention the divorce, but she was silent.

"How's Clea?" he asked. "I expected to see her here, since I know she liked Scotty."

"She couldn't be here," Iris said vaguely. She looked over her shoulder, watching for the car.

He wanted to talk more, to ease into the horrible subject that was coming, but there wasn't time. Scotty's funeral might be the only occasion when she'd let her guard down enough to listen to him. It had to be now.

"I need to talk to you," he said. "Not long before he died, Scotty showed me something he'd found in his father's office. It was a bunch of photos, what you'd call dirty pictures." Iris, who was about to brush the hair away from her face, stopped. Her expression—what he could see of it—did not change. *Jesus, does she know?* "They weren't the usual kind. They had little girls in them. Very little." He knew he was talking too fast, but there was no going back now. He plowed ahead, feeling the sweat break out on the back of his neck. "There was one picture he wanted me to see. He . . . It was a little girl who looked like Clea."

She drew in her breath. There. It was done. Only one thing left. He pulled the picture from his inside suit pocket and held it out to her.

She studied it without removing the glasses. He saw her wince, set her lips in a thin line, shake her head. "Oh, Lord," she said. "The poor girl."

"I know," he said awkwardly. "I didn't want to show you this, but—"

She handed it back to him. "It's not her," she said flatly.

"What?"

"It's not her. Oh, it looks a little bit like her back then, before you knew her. But it's not Clea. At that age, she had longer legs, and the shape of her head was very different. I'd know better than anybody." She shook her head. "But it makes me sick to look at that picture. I feel so sorry for her. How could anyone—"

"Come on, Iris." He felt himself getting angry. "Scotty recognized her. So did I."

She backed away from him slightly. "What do you want me to do? You got this idea, and it turns out to be wrong. It was good of you to worry about us, but you didn't need to." She looked over her shoulder. "There's Paul."

He felt desperate. "I think Scotty was killed because of this," he blurted out.

That stopped her. She seemed to be studying him. "The paper said it was probably an accident," she said carefully.

"Just listen to me. The pictures were taken at the Bullards' hunting lodge, the place we went to once, and Arthur Bullard was one of the men who took them." He thought she reacted to that, with a flicker of her eyelids, but he couldn't be sure. "Scotty was killed by someone who wanted the pictures back."

She hesitated, taking it in, then reached over and touched his arm. "Oh, John Ray," she said, and

68

he could hear the sadness in her voice. "You've had a bad time, and I'm part of the reason. I'm sorry for everything. I just hope you get things back in order. I really want you to be happy."

"Thanks," he said, laying on the sarcasm. "Would you do me one favor?"

She waited, fidgeting with the purse strap around her shoulder.

"I'd like to see Clea once. Just to talk. All right?"

Her face turned hard as she shook her head. "No, you can't," she said.

"She was my daughter," he said. "For a while."

"You could have adopted her, but you didn't. Paul did."

"I wanted to," he said, hearing the tightness in his voice. "We talked about it."

"Once," she said. "You were drunk. You made a lot of promises whenever you were drunk."

"If I was drunk, there's a good chance you were too. Remember?"

She turned away. "I have to go now, John Ray. I don't think we should talk any more."

"Believe me, I don't want to bother you," he called after her. "But why can't I see her, just once?"

"Because she's run away," Iris said without looking back.

The Glendale diner where he'd stopped for coffee on the way to the lodge was only a few blocks away, so he drove there for lunch. The day's special was hot turkey sandwich, mashed potatoes on the side, and choice of apple or cherry pie. He ate slowly, trying to keep his thoughts away from Iris lest he feel the anger build again. So he focused on his food, thinking how much better the sliced turkey and gravy would taste if the white bread was replaced with his mother's cornbread. But Horn was generally an unfussy eater, and he cleaned his plate.

He rolled a cigarette and smoked over his cherry pie and coffee. In the corner, the television set sat unattended, the small screen glowing with a geometric test pattern accompanied by a steady, irritating hum. He noticed that the waitress was the same woman he'd had before, the one he'd imagined was looking down on him for bringing in doughnuts for his coffee. But today she looked tired, not disdainful, and she kept shifting her position against the far counter as if her feet hurt. He left her a tip this time.

Back at the cabin, he found a note on the door. DON'T FORGET POOL, it said, and was signed H.F. A week earlier, Harry Flye had told him to clean out the old swimming pool up at the estate. It had not been touched by the fire, but over the years it had accumulated a layer of sediment that hid a mass of junk left there by a generation of bums and hoboes who stayed there for a while and then moved on. With the brush cleared, this was Horn's next project.

He changed into his work clothes. Then he hoisted

an old folded tarpaulin over his shoulder, picked up a shovel, and hiked up to the estate. The deep end of the pool was two feet deep in dried mud. He began digging it out, tossing the shovelfuls over his shoulder and stopping every now and then to pluck out a piece of trash, which he deposited on the tarp. The trash heap grew steadily: empty cigarette packs, beer and whisky bottles, tin cans that once held beans, or tomatoes, or soup, or sliced peaches. Tattered clothing. A deflated football. The charred remnants of campfires.

After three hours, most of the sediment was shoveled out, and he could barely drag the tarp back down to the cabin. Later, he decided, he'd carry it in the car down the canyon to one of the big public trash barrels near the highway.

He took a bath, then opened a bottle of beer and a can of beef stew for dinner. After his meal, he put his plate in the sink and wiped his hands on a dish towel, then sat on the sofa by the phone for a while.

Scotty was dead. Clea had run away, and Iris wanted nothing to do with him. Horn felt powerless about all of it. Almost absent-mindedly, he thumbed through the bills in his wallet. Twelve dollars, and a few more dollars in change in his pocket. If he was frugal, he could live on that for a week or more, but after that . . .

He picked up the phone and dialed the casino. At least, he thought, he could earn some money. There was that dentist Mad Crow had mentioned,

God's gift to poker but slow to honor his debts. Horn could tell the Indian he had changed his mind.

Lula, Mad Crow's secretary, answered the phone and went to look for him. Minutes later, she came back. "Finally found him out in the loading area. They're bringing in some cases of beer," she said. She paused.

"So is he coming to the phone or not?"

"No," she said carefully. "He's in what you might call a bad mood."

"What did he say?"

"Well, he cussed a little, and then he said he'd try to call you back if he gets a chance."

"Tell him never mind. Maybe you can help me, Lula." They spoke for another minute, and he hung up. He stacked some records on the spindle of his boxy phonograph. They were all by Jimmy Rodgers, "the singing brakeman," who had recorded for six years in the 1920s and then died. Out on the porch, Horn rocked and smoked, listening to *Blue Yodel No. 9*, and pulled slowly at what remained of his beer.

Mad Crow's moods could shift like the weather in the mountains, and all Horn could do was ride them out. But it was Iris who was on his mind now. How could their marriage have started so well and ended so badly? He knew he'd loved her, she'd loved him. What happened? Was it just the drinking? There were a handful of memories in Horn's life that were almost too shameful, too painful, to summon up. His time up in the mountains in Italy was one of them. And then there were the times with Iris when things turned bad. Or sorrowful. Or violent. When he saw her today, he'd stolen a glance at her left arm, which was bare between her glove and elbow, to see if it looked different from the other. It didn't, of course, but he knew that if he rubbed his thumb along the tendon below her elbow, he could feel the knot of a broken bone that had healed improperly. And remember how it was broken.

One of the worst memories was of the last time he saw Clea. He'd been given a day to settle his affairs before surrendering himself for the trip up to Cold Creek Prison. She locked herself in her room, screaming at him through the door. *You're not my real father anyway*, she told him. *No wonder I can't count on you.* He understood that it was just a young girl's hysteria, but the words hurt nonetheless. He'd thought he would have a chance to prove her wrong once prison was behind him. But one day at mail call, the letter from Iris arrived, forever closing the book on that part of his life.

Once out of prison, he had held back from contacting Clea. He told himself he was still too full of hatred for Iris, and there was truth in that. But by keeping his distance, wasn't he validating Clea's own words—that she couldn't count on him?

Clea was not the girl in the picture, Iris said. She seemed sure. Was she lying, or just wrong?

This wasn't the first time Clea had run away. About a year before Horn had gone to prison, Clea frightened them by disappearing. She and a girlfriend, whose name he'd forgotten, took a bus out to Santa Monica and then hitchhiked several miles up the coast to a spot where he and Iris had once taken Clea on a holiday. Guessing where she'd gone, he spent two days showing her picture up and down the coast before he finally found the two girls in a motel, smoking cigarettes and reading movie magazines. At the sight of him, the look on Clea's face said, *I knew you'd come.*

All the way back in the car, the two girls giggled in the backseat, reliving their adventure. Although he lectured Clea on the dangers of hitchhiking, secretly he admired her courage in heading off on her own. It was something he might have done at her age. Iris too.

Now she was gone again. Her mother wanted nothing to do with him, and even Clea had screamed at him that last day he had seen her. He retained his strong suspicions about Scotty's death, but how could he know there was any connection to Clea? Maybe she was off with a friend some-where, having some forbidden fun. Eventually she might call home, or even come back on her own. Horn had been raised to stay out of other people's business. Why should he get involved in this? Why not let her new father find her this time?

After a while, he went to bed. Sometime before dawn, when the first birdcalls began to break the quiet of the canyon, he drifted into a half-dream, half-memory of a little girl, not much more than six, her face frozen in a mixture of fear and fascination as she reached out a hand to touch a horse's muzzle for the first time in her young life. Later in the dream-memory, he lifted her astride Raincloud, his big hands encircling her waist, and she tossed her corn-silk ponytail and shrieked with delight as he took the reins and walked horse and girl around the corral.

Then the little girl's face changed, and she seemed to be asking him for something, and he wanted to protect her against a threat neither of them could see. He felt his chest tighten with sadness, knowing that she'd never be six again and that no one would ever ride Raincloud again. He tried to will himself out of the dream, but just before he was able, he saw the thin-faced boy with the bad leg standing some distance away, leaning on a fence post and watching them, his face full of sadness and contempt.

Horn woke up sweating and went out to the porch, where he sat and watched the half-light begin to define the trees. He felt his thoughts take shape the same way. He remembered Scotty's words that night in his father's office: *I hope she's doing all right.*

He knew he had to find her.

CHAPTER 6

In Horn's old movies, hunting down badmen had presented only nominal problems, usually hinging on the search for a particular brand on a horse's flank, or a distinctively hand-tooled holster, or a pony's shoe that left a peculiar mark on the trail. It never took Sierra Lane more than a few reels to get his man. Horn, on the other hand, had no formal training as a policeman or an investigator. But a year of collecting debts for the Indian had taught him a few things about finding people.

He started early, right after breakfast. He drove methodically up the coast as far as Santa Barbara, stopping at every motel and gas station and cafe and gift shop to ask about Clea. He portrayed himself as a distraught father looking for his little girl. That was partly true, of course. But he had to lie about being her father, and even though he desperately wanted to find her, the lie came too easily, and he felt uncomfortably like an actor reading lines, making up a story to gain people's sympathy.

He had forgotten to bring a picture of her, he

told people apologetically, but she was sixteen, fair-haired, and a little tall for her age, and she might be traveling with a friend. Having not seen her for three years, he was reluctant to be too specific about her appearance, the kind of clothes she liked or how she wore her hair. Most of the waitresses and motel keepers seemed sympathetic and not inclined to question him too closely.

The drive turned up nothing. The next day he drove down the coast as far as Laguna Beach, repeating his inquiries. Again, nothing. As he drove, he racked his brain to come up with new searches, new avenues to explore. *A girl runs away from home. Where does she go?* It would help if he knew why she was gone, but presumably only Iris could tell him that. If Clea stayed missing, maybe her mother would eventually welcome his help.

She was likely to be traveling or staying with someone, and he was handicapped by not knowing who her current friends were. In fact, he knew little about Clea at sixteen. When he last saw her, she was partial to horses, hair ribbons, Edgar Bergen, and Charlie McCarthy. Now, she was probably using lipstick and going out with boys, he reflected with some discomfort.

After he returned, he spent some time with the information operator and was able to get a number for Mr. and Mrs. Paul Fairbrass, with an address in the Hancock Park neighborhood. When Iris answered, he said, "It's John Ray. Any news about Clea?"

She sighed. "Please . . ."

"I'm not going to make trouble for you. I just want to know."

He heard a man's voice in the background, and Iris put her hand over the mouthpiece for a moment, then came back on. "Well, there's some good news," she said, a little too brightly. "Clea called us. She said not to worry. She'll be home soon."

"Where is she?"

"She didn't say, but . . ." She stopped. Something in her voice, something he'd always been able to hear, gave her away.

"I don't think you're telling me the truth."

She said nothing. He tried again: "Did she really run away?"

"Yes," she said quietly.

"Do you want to tell me why?"

"It's not any of your business."

"Tell me who her friends are."

"Please, I have to go."

"Have you called the police?"

"Of course we have," she said bitterly. "Why don't you just stay out of this?"

"I can't," he said, and hung up.

Like most of those who had worked in and around Hollywood, Horn knew Hollywood Boulevard well, from the Hollywood Palms Hotel near Vine to Grauman's Chinese Theatre several blocks west, but he had never been in Geiger's bookstore. For one thing, he wasn't much for serious reading.

For another, the interior visible through the awninged and curtained window always reminded him of a gentleman's club—deep carpet, leather chairs, and shelves of rare and expensive-looking volumes resting behind glass-front bookcases. Not the place to pick up a copy of *Wanderer of the Wasteland* or *The Last Trail*.

But Scotty had told him that Geiger's did business in more forbidden material, and he hoped to find out if old man Bullard and his friends had frequented the place. It was the only fresh idea he had at the moment.

A small bell sounded as he opened the door, as if he'd entered an old-world tea shop. The place was cool after the heat of the pavement, and it smelled of leather, mildewed pages, and pipe tobacco. No customers, only a man behind the counter who looked up as Horn entered.

"May I help you find something?" The man was somewhere in his early forties, with regular features and thinning hair combed forward Roman-style. He wore a starched white shirt with bow tie and sober black suspenders. Thick, wire-rimmed glasses gave him a studious look, but he appeared more athletic than the average bookstore worker.

"Mr. Geiger?"

"No, Mr. Geiger is deceased," the man said, blinking at him through the glasses. "I'm his nephew."

"My name is Horn." He held out his hand.

"Calvin St. George," the man responded, taking

the hand in a firm grip. "Are you interested in fiction or nonfiction?"

"Ah . . . To tell you the truth, I don't know much about rare books. I guess you'd say I'm interested in the kind of things you don't normally find in a bookstore."

Calvin St. George nodded encouragingly, a trace of a smile on his face. "Anything in particular?"

"Well," Horn said, lowering his voice and leaning forward even though no one else was around, "a friend of mine mentioned that I could find some unusual things here."

The faint smile never left St. George's face, but he was clearly waiting for more.

"If he were here, I'm sure he wouldn't mind if I mentioned his name. Arthur Bullard. Sad to hear of his death the other day. I'd known him for years. His family too."

It was hard to read St. George's expression behind the lenses. "I've had gentlemen coming in here for ages without ever telling me their names."

"I understand perfectly," Horn said. "Did you take those?" he asked, pointing over the other man's shoulder to a couple of framed photos on the wall. One was a portrait of a young woman in a bathing suit, reclining on a piece of gnarled driftwood in the sand. The other, also taken on the beach, showed a little girl, age four or five, posing behind a straw hat with an enormous brim. Both were in black and white and showed dramatic composition of light and shadow.

"Yes, I did, actually," St. George said, apparently pleased. "I'm a bit of an amateur photographer."

"They're very well done." Horn glanced at his watch. "So, do you think can you help me?"

The eyes blinked once behind the lenses. Then he tapped the fingers of both hands lightly on the counter and said, "Would you have a seat? I'll just be a minute."

Horn had barely settled into one of the oxblood-hued tufted leather chairs when St. George returned bearing in both hands a leather-bound volume which he carefully placed on the side table by the chair. "This is a French translation of the first four volumes of Casanova's memoirs, published in 1890. Do you read French?"

"I barely read English."

"I'm sure you're being modest. This would be a valuable addition to your library even if you're not fluent in the language, because of the beautiful hand-tooled binding and also because of the twenty full-page engraved illustrations." He indicated that Horn should have a look. "Please."

The illustrations, each one protected by a page of onionskin, depicted diverse and athletic sexual activity. The details were graphic.

"Very nice," Horn said, turning the pages.

"I also just received a *Justine* that you should look at—it's French as well. I think you'd be interested in the—"

"Do you have any pictures?"

St. George looked blank.

81

"Photos, I mean."

"I'm afraid not."

Horn drew from his pocket one of the more explicit hunting lodge photos. "This sort of thing."

St. George stared at it for a brief moment. "Where . . . ah, where did you—?"

"Oh, I got this from Arthur. And a bunch of others like them. I think he took these himself, or maybe a friend did. So, since he mentioned your store, I naturally thought you might be familiar with them."

St. George shook his head. The faint smile had departed.

"Have you ever sold any like these?"

"Ah, not exactly. You see, these are . . . what you might call very unusual."

"You mean because of the girl's age?"

"Exactly."

"But someone took them, didn't they?"

"Well, yes," St. George said patiently, "but we don't know if these were commercially done, do we?"

"I don't understand."

"They might have been made strictly for private use. In fact, I'd bet on it. I can assure you, the market for something like this is so small and so . . . ah, problematic, you're not likely to find anything like it anywhere in the city." St. George handed back the photo. He hadn't looked at it again.

"Well, I'm sure I can trust you," Horn said,

getting up. "I'd like to leave you my phone number. I know it's unlikely, but if you ever come across any more like these, would you give me a call? I wouldn't haggle over the price, if you know what I mean."

Outside, the late-afternoon heat struck him like the opening of an oven door, but he barely noticed it. He was thinking about the way St. George had barely glanced at the picture, almost as if he'd seen it before.

Did you lie to me about that, Calvin? And what other kinds of pictures do you take?

The Bullard home was in Pasadena, on a street where Horn imagined the homes spoke quietly among themselves of large amounts of money, old and new. The house was big, mostly stone, and in a style that Horn had once heard called Tudor. People hereabouts who had money would borrow from any architecture that suited them. Sometimes the house looked like it belonged on the land, other times it looked more like a visitor from another country. In the center of the graveled circular drive was a pond full of koi that, he recalled, were ministered to tenderly by the Japanese yard man. Under big shade trees, the backyard sloped gently down to a low stone wall beyond which the ground dropped away into the Arroyo Seco, a deep, dry gorge that cut through the west end of Pasadena like an unhealed wound.

He parked the dusty Ford next to a stone lion

bearing a shield, went up the front steps, and lifted the brass knocker. After only a moment, Helen Bullard opened the door. "John Ray," she said, smiling a welcome. "I'm really happy you could come."

"Mrs. Bullard," he responded, taking off his hat and stepping inside. It was, by his count, only his third visit to the house. Arthur and Helen Bullard had not liked many of Scotty's friends, and Horn had suspected that, as a second-rate actor in forgettable movies, he was especially undesirable.

"You know, if you had gotten to know me a little better, you'd probably be calling me Helen by now," she said, leading him down two steps into a large parlor, its curtains pulled back to let in the afternoon sun. She waved him to a comfortable chair by the window, and before long a Mexican girl brought a tray with a pitcher of lemonade and two glasses. He looked around at the room, the old books on the shelves, fresh-cut flowers on the central table, pictures of her and her husband on the piano. Somewhere upstairs, Scotty had told him once, in a room not seen by visitors, was a portrait of his mother as a Broadway showgirl. *Dad snatched her out of the arms of Flo Ziegfeld*, Scotty put it, *and she never looked back. He told her California was where people could reinvent themselves, and damned if she didn't reinvent herself into the most perfect hostess this town ever saw. Got to hand it to her.*

Helen Bullard was still in mourning, but the black dress was smart, nipped in at the waist and edged with black velvet at the collar and cuffs. Her gray hair was wound tightly in a bun. "I hope you like your lemonade," she said. "I told you I had something for you." She reached for an object on the table and handed it to him. At first he thought it was a book, but when he opened it he saw it was a leather frame for a photo. He recognized the picture. Scotty had taken it years before, on a riding trip up the back side of the San Gabriels. In the photo sat three people on horseback—Horn, Iris, and one of Scotty's girlfriends, her name long forgotten. He hefted the frame, noting the quality of the leather. Even though the photo reflected Scotty's usual expertise with a camera, it was still just a snapshot, and the mounting was ridiculously overdone. "Well, it's very nice," he said finally.

"He'd want you to have it," she said simply. "You were his best friend."

"I suppose I was."

"Sometimes I think we—Arthur and I—should have gone to more trouble to know Scotty's friends, but . . ." She trailed off, as if to say, You know how it is, don't you?

Not much point getting to know people you think are trash, he thought idly. But he knew what kind of face to put on for her. "I'm sorry about what happened," he said. "Couldn't have been easy for you, losing first a husband and then a son."

She nodded. "At least with Arthur we had some warning," she said. "He'd had several minor heart attacks. We both knew it would come someday.

We even had a chance to talk about it, to . . . prepare. I'm grateful for that. With Scotty, though . . . I'd always heard that there's no grief like that of a parent losing a child, and it's true. And when they die suddenly, unexpectedly, violently . . . You wonder how God, when he makes plans for us, can have room for something like that."

She sat stiffly, perched on the edge of the comfortable chair, as if fearing that by letting herself droop she would give in too obviously to her grief. *She's the tough one*, Scotty had told him. *Tougher than the old man, even. If she has a single weakness, I've never seen it. Except for this one: She's afraid to let anything show.*

She gazed at him for a while as if hoping he'd say something, but he only sipped at his lemonade, waiting. She wanted something, he knew, and the snapshot was just an excuse to get him there.

He drained his glass, and she refilled it. "Would you like to walk a little?" she asked. "I've felt so cooped up here ever since Arthur died. Let's go outside. Bring your lemonade."

She led him into the backyard. About fifty yards down the green and landscaped slope, the bluff dropped off into the gigantic arroyo. Horn pointed to a sprawling oak. "Isn't that where Scotty had his tree house when he was a kid?" he asked her. "Last time I was here you could still see parts of it. He told me he used to imagine he was Robin Hood, and Maid Marian would climb up to be with him." He didn't add the rest: *That was the one place I couldn't hear them yelling at each other,* Scotty had said. *Or at me.*

"Oh, he had his little imaginary world up there," she said with a laugh. "We used to try to get him to come down during parties, meet the guests, and he wouldn't budge. Anyway, the thing was an absolute ruin, an eyesore, really. We had it torn down a couple of years ago."

She took his arm as they descended a flagstone path toward a gazebo. "Scotty was a little wild growing up," she said. "Even as a young man, he seemed . . . unfocused. But in recent years he seemed to mature, he settled down at the firm. I'm convinced he would have made a fine businessman, he would have taken the reins from Arthur, if he'd just had . . ."

"More time," Horn finished for her.

"Yes. More time." They arrived at the gazebo and sat on a bench, looking out over the arroyo. In the heat, the shimmering air over the dry gulch looked like dirty water, and the homes on the far side were indistinct, their edges blurred.

"I want to be honest with you, John Ray," she said carefully, looking into the distance. "My husband had a lot of interests that didn't concern me. One in particular. I knew about it, I didn't approve, but I knew it was important to him. Does this make any sense to you?"

"Yes, ma'am," he replied. *Scotty tried to protect her,* he said to himself with surprise, *but she knew all along.*

87

"Thank God for that," she said grimly. "I don't know if I'd be up to explaining. I had a feeling you might know. Did Scotty tell you?"

"Yes, ma'am."

"Just a week ago, I would have said this knowledge you have is a terrible thing. I would have preferred that no one in the world have it. You can imagine why. I want my husband remembered for the good things he did, the things he built, and not for . . . *that*." Her voice went sour at the last word. "Now, I don't know. . . . Something tells me if Scotty knew, it's all right for you to know too. I just have to be sure that you won't do anything to harm Arthur's memory. Can I trust you?"

All his distaste for the memory of Arthur Bullard rose in his throat, but he needed this woman's trust. "I think you can count on me to do the right thing," he said carefully.

She stared at him. "Maybe I'll have to be satisfied with that. Just remember one thing about me. You don't want to have me for an enemy. You know that, don't you?"

He put on a look of exaggerated concern. "I know your reputation, Mrs. Bullard."

"Good." She patted his arm, but there was little affection in the gesture. "Do you have the feeling that there was something not right about the way Scotty died?"

Smart lady. "Yes, I do."

"So do I. In fact, I'm convinced it was not an accident. Further, I believe what happened to him was a result of what he knew about Arthur. I can't be more explicit than that, and I certainly don't know who might have been involved, who might have had anything to gain in Scotty's death. But I know my son didn't fall out that window, and he certainly didn't jump."

"I agree with you, Mrs. Bullard."

"I don't dare go to the police with this. Too many questions would be asked. But I'm talking to you about it in the hope that you can help. Is there anything you can tell me?"

"I'm afraid not," he said. "I'm at just about the same place you are. We're stuck with a lot of suspicions and not much information."

"If you find out anything about Scotty's death, will you tell me?" When he hesitated, she went on hurriedly: "I never ask anything for free, John Ray. If you help me, I can help you."

"If you mean money—"

"I mean anything. If you ask people about me, they may tell you they admire me or they dislike me or they're afraid of me. But all of them will tell you I'm in a position to help people if I want to help them. I raised two hundred thousand dollars for war orphans last year, and I don't know if there are many other women in this town who could have done that. I'm a good friend. Scotty told me you might be having trouble getting steady work. I could do something about that."

"Let's not get ahead of ourselves," he said. "Just see what happens, all right?"

He waited for her response, but none came. Instead, she looked off toward the big oak where the tree house had once been. "Do you believe in second chances, John Ray?" she asked.

"I want to."

"Maybe I wasn't the best mother. Arthur and I both wanted Scotty to be as strong as we were. I suppose we were harsh with him from time to time, and every time we tried to instill strength in him, he would just turn away—never confront us, just turn away. He'd make a joke or get quiet. We wanted him to stand tall and fight, and he'd bend like a reed."

"That sounds like him," Horn said. "Nobody could avoid a battle like Scotty. He was a born diplomat."

"I know," she said. "Isn't it sad that I couldn't see it? I thought he was a failure, and he was just developing into his own kind of man. A gentle man, a good man."

She gripped his arm, and this time he felt her urgency. "This is my second chance. I'll do whatever's necessary to find out what happened to him. I'll do anything. Do you believe me?"

"Yes, ma'am."

"Good." She got up, signaling that the visit was over. "Thank you for coming."

CHAPTER 7

Horn and Mad Crow sat in a thickly varnished booth at the South Seas on Western Avenue. It was a typical nightclub, with a bar, about twenty tables, a bandstand, and a tiny dance floor. The decor was ersatz Polynesian—bamboo partitions, grass skirts on the waitresses, Hawaiian shirts on the bartenders. It was still late afternoon, and the place was mostly quiet. Beers arrived, and the two men began working on them.

Horn slid a wad of bills across the table. "The dentist," he said. "I took my cut."

Mad Crow grunted an acknowledgment and pocketed the money. "Any trouble?"

"No. He invited me in, introduced me to his wife, offered me a Dr. Pepper. We went into another room, where he apologized for putting it off so long and paid up, just like that."

"See," Mad Crow said with a grin. "You're made for this work." He took a long pull at the bottle. "I'm real sorry about Scotty Bullard. Didn't know him well, but I know you used to be friends."

"Thanks."

"Did you ever call him?"

"Yep." Horn hesitated for a few seconds and then began talking, describing everything that had happened in the last few days. By the time he had finished, a second round had arrived, and the Indian's brow was knotted, his face frozen in a look of near-disbelief.

"I'll be goddamned," he said finally. "Do you think there's any connection—"

"Between Scotty being killed and Clea being missing? Uh-huh. There's just too much coincidence, him finding her picture and then dying like that. I can't prove the connection. But I believe it. That's why I've got to find her."

"They say she ran away."

"Maybe she did. That's bad enough by itself. But I think Scotty was killed by somebody who's involved with those photos. Maybe by the same sick piece of crap who took dirty pictures of Clea when she was a little girl. That means it could be a lot more serious than some girl running away from home. Maybe somebody's taken her, maybe they've . . ."

"I get you. You want the police in this?"

"They're already in. Iris called them. Let them work, and I'll work too."

"Bet you have her home quick."

"Be nice, wouldn't it? You know, I don't fool myself thinking she's really my daughter. But I'm still worried about her. I got a right to be."

"Then good luck, amigo," Mad Crow said.

"Haven't seen her in years, but she was always a nice little thing. I got a feeling that it's not as serious as you think, that she's just off having some fun, like that other time. That's what youngsters do, right? She wants a taste of that sweet grass on the other side of the fence. Bet you a stack of chips she comes home on her own. Three more days."

"Maybe," Horn said with a sigh. "A lot of things could happen to a sixteen-year-old girl out there. Before I came over here tonight, I spent some time on the Santa Monica Pier, just walking up and down. She used to love going there—"

"I remember. She used to bust broncs on the carousel, right?"

"I took her there on her birthday a couple of times. She'd try to ride the same white horse every time, 'cause she said the color was a little like Raincloud. You should have seen her riding that thing, the way her face lit up. Anyway, there I was, walking around, kind of looking for her, hearing the music, watching all the couples enjoying themselves. But every girl I saw, I thought: Is this one happy, or is she in some kind of trouble? Are her folks worried about her?" He ground out his cigarette hard.

"Come on," Mad Crow said uneasily. "Ease up. I bet she's off having a good time somewhere. She and some boy drove down to Tijuana—"

"That's not what I want to hear."

"Okay. Maybe that's not what she's doing. Tell

you one thing: If I was her father, I'd think about keeping a tighter rein on her."

"Lock her up in her room, you mean?" Horn made a face. "She's just a kid. Far as I know, this is only the second time she's done this. She's had three fathers in the last ten years. Let's let her finish growing up."

Mad Crow held up his palms, I-surrender style. "Fine. So how's the lovely Iris?"

"I just saw her for a few minutes at the funeral. That guy she married is a rich pipefitter from Long Beach. They've got a place in Hancock Park, where the real estate's not cheap. After bad luck with husbands One and Two, maybe she's finally found herself a solid citizen."

"You were solid enough, at least until things went to hell. From what I hear, her real disaster was Number One, Wesley What's-His-Name. You started to tell me about him once, but we ran out of beer, as I recall."

"Wendell. Wendell Brand. I don't know much about him," Horn said. "She showed me a couple of pictures. Nice-enough-looking little guy. From what she told me, though, he didn't have much personality or ambition. He was happy working behind the reception desk at the Hollywood Palms Hotel back when Scotty's dad owned the place. Just a clerk. Sometime after Clea was born, she must've realized she'd made a mistake marrying him."

"So she dumped him," Mad Crow said.

"The year before I met her. He was sickly—TB, I think she said. He moved up to San Francisco to be with some relatives, and a few years later he died. I remember she went up for the funeral, because she'd always gotten along with his sisters. I thought it was pretty nice of her, considering."

Mad Crow was staring at him. "You know what I'm wondering?"

"You're wondering," Horn drawled, "if Wendell had anything to do with the picture of Clea. Me too. Somebody took her up to the lodge." His jaw set hard. "If it was him, it's a good thing he's dead now, 'cause . . ."

"If Iris went to his funeral, that doesn't sound like she thought of him as a child molester," the Indian put in. "Anyway, not much chance of finding out now, I guess."

A woman walked unsteadily from the bar over to the jukebox and put in a nickel. Soon the lounge was full of the sounds of a whining Hawaiian electric guitar. Horn winced.

"I keep going back to Scotty and how he died," he said. "Let's say Wendell and Scotty's father were playing with little girls, taking their pictures and all those other things. If you look at the photos, you can tell there were at least three men there. Let's say three. That means there's somebody else out there. And since I think Scotty was killed for the pictures, that means whoever is out there isn't just hiding, he's killing people, to keep their little games secret." *Don't think of Clea,* he said to himself.

95

"I think I see where this is going, and I'm going to tell you something you should already know," Mad Crow said evenly. "Those movies we made were just pretend. We never really lassoed bad hombres and brought 'em in to be tried by the territorial judge. We never shot it out with a bunch of rustlers up in some box canyon. Those were just stories—"

"Come on," Horn tried to break in.

"I mean it. We probably thought we were hard guys, because we rode horses fast and the other guys always fell down when we threw a punch. But we were just *actors*." He stressed the word, as if Horn was hard of hearing. "I'm a businessman now, and I'm getting a belly from all the good meals I can afford. You're a guy who needs to keep his nose clean, *comprende*? If you know anything about somebody killing people, take it to the police."

"I don't get along with the police. And why would they listen to some half-assed hunch of mine?"

Mad Crow leaned toward him. "If you stick your fool neck out and get in trouble, they might just put you away again. If that happens, who's going to collect for me?"

When Horn didn't answer, the Indian looked around for their waitress. "I thought we came here to have a good time," he said. He lifted his glass and drained it. "Here's to all the husbands of the lovely Iris," he said dramatically. He spotted the waitress, waved her over, and ordered two more.

"And one for Annie," he said, gesturing toward the front door.

"Annie can't drink on the job," the waitress said.

"Then make it a lemonade." Mad Crow's silver bracelet glinted as he placed some money on her tray. "Keep it."

Portuguese Annie was the South Seas' legendary greeter/hostess/bouncer. Weighing in somewhere north of two-fifty, she sat planted on a stool just inside the front door. Often the first sight to greet patrons was the blue and crimson anchor tattooed on Annie's enormous bicep. To hear Mad Crow tell it, she had once drop-kicked an unruly drunk all the way across the sidewalk, where he bounced off a taxi.

Somewhere along the way, Horn had learned that she had been born Mary Ann Rourke, and she seemed to enjoy it when he addressed her as Mary Ann. He hadn't been in the South Seas since before he was sent up, and when he and the Indian had come in this afternoon, she'd grinned and said, "Hey, gunslinger."

The beers arrived. "So, the Mick still own this joint?" Horn asked.

Mad Crow nodded.

"I heard you two weren't getting along. Think I should have picked a different place for us to meet?"

"No, it's all right. We got it straightened out. He wanted a piece of the casino, and I didn't want him in. It was just business. All settled now. Besides, he hardly ever comes in this early." Mad Crow's eyes idly followed a grass skirt as it went by. "When you called, you said you needed something."

"Right. Can I use Douglas? For addresses and stuff. It should take only a few days." Douglas Greenleaf was one of the people Mad Crow called his "Dog Soldiers," Oglala Sioux cousins, nephews, and more distant relatives who did various jobs for him. Greenleaf was married to the sister of an L.A. cop, and one of his gambling buddies worked in the Department of Motor Vehicles. When chasing skips, Horn often asked him to run a name, a license plate, or a phone number.

Mad Crow hesitated a moment. "Sure, why not?" he said finally. "Just don't overload him, okay? He still works for me."

"I know. Appreciate it." Horn looked up. "I think the Mick needs to get his watch fixed."

"Hmm?" Mad Crow followed Horn's eyes across the room, where he caught sight of Mickey Cohen approaching.

"Now don't bust up the place," the mobster said when he reached their table. "You two go in a saloon, you always bust up the place. I seen some of those movies. Neither one of you guys could act worth a crap."

"Hello, Mick," said Mad Crow.

"My girls treating you all right?" Mickey Cohen was short and squat, with a round, chipmunk-cheeked face and a cupid's-bow mouth that clashed with his eyes, which were blank and heavy-browed.

He wore an expensive linen jacket over a silk sport shirt buttoned to the neck, along with razor-creased slacks and two-tone shoes.

"Just fine," Mad Crow said. He seemed ill at ease.

"I hear you got set up with a new partner," Cohen said, leaning slightly over Mad Crow's side of the table. His right hand was buried in his pants pocket, and Horn could hear the rhythmic jingling of keys.

"That's right," the Indian said with a smile. "You know, just a business decision."

"Just business," Cohen echoed, nodding, his face still expressionless. "Maybe we'll do business sometime."

"Sure." Mad Crow studied the tabletop as he wiped at a damp spot with his napkin.

Cohen turned to Horn. "How about you? Big Chief doesn't like me. Maybe you and I, we can do business. I hear you're a hotshot collector. You want to come collect for me?"

"Thanks, anyway."

Cohen's face registered no change. "They show any of your movies up in the joint, or they got better taste than that?"

"No, the place was too highbrow," Horn said. "Mostly old Shirley Temple movies, so the boys wouldn't get all stirred up."

"She stirs me up," Cohen said. "She's legal now, but even when she was jailbait, she stirred me up." The jingling in his pocket grew more vigorous. "She ever walks in here, I'll tell her I got something for her."

Horn got up. "Guess I should go," he said to Mad Crow. "Coming?"

Outside, they stood for a moment by the Indian's white Cadillac convertible, which gleamed in the multicolored light from the neon sign over the South Seas' entrance. The seats were covered in pinto hide.

"You're a man of understatement, aren't you?" Horn said, nodding toward the car.

"Hell, people expect me to act like this. It's good for business."

"So who's your new partner?"

"Nobody you know," Mad Crow shrugged. "He's from Reno. And he's only got a minority interest, so the place is still mine. The Reno crowd's been sniffing around for a while now, and it seemed better to let them get their nose under the tent than to partner up with somebody like the Mick."

"Don't know why you'd say that," Horn said. "He's such a sweetheart."

"Wouldn't hurt you to be polite to him, though. You could use a few more friends."

"Maybe. I'm just not in the mood to hear anybody talk about jailbait right now, you know?"

"Sure." Mad Crow punched him lightly on the shoulder. "I been wondering, though. Even though I always admired the lovely Iris, she cleaned you out good and proper. I'm surprised you're helping her out. After a divorce like yours, some guys would be real bitter."

"Who says I'm helping her out?"

"All right, you're not. You okay for money?"

"For now."

"Come back to work when you're ready," Mad Crow said. "And don't worry about the little girl. You'll find her."

"Sure. See you."

"Hey, did I ever tell you I saw Maggie? It was at a horse show a couple of months ago, and she was looking good. Said to say hi. I bet she wouldn't mind if you gave her a call sometime, get caught up on . . ."

But Horn was already walking away.

He wanted to resume his search the next morning, but he felt under pressure to finish the job up on the hill. He couldn't afford to antagonize Harry Flye and risk losing the cabin. So he spent several hours working on Ricardo Aguilar's old swimming pool. By early afternoon he had cleaned it out down to the concrete, and he loaded the accumulated trash in his car and drove it down the canyon to one of the big public trash barrels. He fixed himself a late lunch, and as he ate, the name of one of Clea's friends suddenly surfaced in his memory. A boy her age named Peter Binyon had lived with his parents not far away from the Horns' place in the Valley. From age ten on, they had played together, visited each other. Turning twelve, they had started at the same junior high school. At some point Horn lost track of the boy, but he needed to find him now.

After a half-hour, Douglas Greenleaf called him back with the address and phone number. The family had moved east of downtown, several miles away from their old address. He called the number and got Peter's mother, a woman he had never known well. Unsure how she would feel about hearing from him, he told her he was doing a survey for the Board of Education and needed to check some information with her son.

"He's working this summer," she said proudly. She told him where.

He cleaned up quickly, put on a fresh shirt, and left. It was mid-afternoon. The traffic began building on Sunset as he approached downtown, the smell of auto exhaust grew more intense, and Horn was reminded of how much the city had changed in just a few years.

Before the war, he and Iris had had a little ranch out in the San Fernando Valley, a few acres of lawn and pasture and horse corrals almost surrounded by citrus groves. Back then, it seemed that wherever you went in Los Angeles, you were never more than a twenty-minute drive from open land or the ocean. When he came back from the war, though, that sprawling adolescent of a city he'd known had matured into something bigger and rougher and less forgiving, where the scent of orange blossoms now had to fight it out with the smells of the automobile. A few years ago they had finished a wide new road connecting L.A. with Pasadena to the northeast, something called a parkway. They were working on others, because now this city was in a hurry.

Wouldn't mind one of those parkways right now, he thought as he caught sight of City Hall up ahead, white and sharp-topped, the colossus of downtown. Twenty minutes later, he parked by a loading dock in the warehouse district near the railroad tracks in downtown L.A., a few miles southeast of the white tower. The warehouse was owned by a toy company. Inside, a foreman told him where to find Peter Binyon. Horn spotted him down a row of high shelves, wrestling crates onto a handcart. "Hey, Peter," he said.

The boy was wearing dungarees and an undershirt and was sweating in the still air of the building. He was much bigger than Horn remembered, three inches taller and shoulders turning to muscle. The young face had matured into something lumpier, with the remnants of old acne scars.

"It's Pete," the boy spat out in a tone that said, *I use a tough gay's name now.*

"Okay, Pete. Do you remember me?"

Pete squinted. "Yeah," he said slowly. "You're Clea's dad."

"That's right. Can you take a break for just a minute? I'd like to ask you something."

The boy looked around. "I guess." They stepped out onto the shade of the loading dock, where a carton had burst and spilled out small cast-metal soldiers. They lay in a jumble, frozen in various fighting postures—throwing grenades, aiming rifles, loading mortars. One planted a flag, the red and white stripes glinting on the metallic surface. Horn stooped and picked up an officer's figure, its right arm pointing out some imaginary enemy position.

"You can take that," Pete said. "We pick up stuff around here. I take things home for my little brother."

"Thanks," Horn said as he put the figure back. "I guess you know I'm not Clea's dad any more."

The boy nodded, looking wary. *You probably know some other things about me too*, Horn thought, then went on.

"I had to tell your mother a little story, since I wasn't sure she'd want me talking to you. But the reason I'm here, I'm worried about Clea. Her mother tells me she's run away, and I want to help them find her. I'm hoping you might have some ideas about where she went, who she might be with."

The boy laughed. "She and me, we aren't exactly friends anymore."

"Why's that?"

"Oh, I got the idea her mother didn't like me after a while. Maybe thought I wasn't good enough to go out with her little girl." It sounded like Iris, Horn thought. She wasn't a snob, but when it came to Clea, only the best would do.

"Did you go out with her?"

"Once, I did." Pete pulled out a pack of Old Golds and lit one. He handled the cigarette carefully between thumb and forefinger, like a new smoker. "She told me her mother wouldn't let her do it again."

"What about Clea? Did she like you?"

"Yeah, I think so. She was all right. I liked her. But people go different ways, you know? I got a new girlfriend now."

"Good for you. So who was she close to? Who were her best friends, the last year or so?"

Pete thought, scuffing his shoe on the rough flooring of the dock. "Well, there was Addie Webb."

Addie. The name was familiar. Adele Webb. She was the girl Clea had run off with that time they went up the coast. A dark-haired little thing, pretty. He asked where she lived, and Pete told him.

"Anybody else?"

"Yeah." Pete's face twisted into a kind of sneer. "This guy. Tommy something-or-other. He was older. Maybe a lot older. He looked like some kind of college guy."

"What was he doing with her?"

"I don't know. Somebody said he had a brother or sister at school, and that's how he met her. Anyway, he used to pick her up at school. He had a convertible."

"What kind?"

"Chrysler. Light blue. He was hot stuff. Or thought he was."

"You know where he lived? Or any places they went?"

Pete shook his head.

"Did she like him?"

"Sure, I guess." The boy looked bored. "Maybe they were just right for each other."

"What do you mean?"

"Oh, you know. Maybe she thought she was too good for the rest of us, she wanted to hang around with somebody older. Somebody who had a snazzy car, who kept a pint under the dashboard."

"So she was drinking?"

Pete nodded. "She wasn't wild, exactly, but she was trying to be, you know what I mean?"

"You don't sound as if you like her much."

The boy shrugged. "I used to. Before she got high and mighty, started ignoring everybody her age."

"You know Tommy's last name?"

"Huh-uh. You think she's in trouble?"

"Maybe."

"How bad?"

"I don't want to worry anybody, but . . ."

The boy picked up one of the toy soldiers and studied it for a moment. "Well," he said finally. "I used to like her."

"Thanks, Pete." Horn pulled out a couple of silver dollars and handed them to the boy. "Next time you take your girlfriend out, it's my treat."

CHAPTER 8

He drove back through downtown and stopped at Olvera Street for a Mexican dinner, walked around the old buildings, and sat in the plaza until the heat had slipped away. It was almost fully dark by the time he reached his turnoff near the head of Culebra Canyon. The heavily forested canyon floor was deep black around the tunnel carved out by his headlights, and he drove slowly, alert for wildlife.

As he swung left onto the gravel road leading to the cabin, his lights swept past a car. Cars were unusual in the canyon at night. Sometimes couples went to the trouble to drive all the way up there just to find a private spot. But Horn was feeling jumpy. He stopped, then backed the Ford up into the road until his headlights shone dead on the other car, about thirty feet away.

It was a new Packard, parked halfway off the road just beyond his turnoff and facing him, lights off. Two men sat in the front seat.

Horn leaned out his window and called out. "Hey, boys, it's not smart to sit on a public road in the dark. If you're looking for a place to bed down, try the campground a couple of miles back thataway. Boy Scouts use it sometimes. Look for the pup tents."

The driver got out and walked over, squinting in the headlights, a solidly built man in a creased lightweight suit and a hat that needed blocking. The lights shone on a stark white bandage that ran diagonally from his left ear down toward his jaw. When he reached Horn's car, he rested his fingertips lightly on the door and said, "Fellow over there wants to see you."

His intonation was polite. But the man reeked of cop, Horn thought. Or ex-military. Or both. It wasn't exactly a threat he exuded, more like the kind of authority that didn't need to threaten.

"You wouldn't be police, would you?"

"Not at all."

"What's he want to see me about?"

"I'll let him tell you."

"You'll let him step out of the car so I can see him."

The man grinned lightly and went back over to the other car, where he spoke briefly through the driver's-side window. The other man emerged and walked around the front of the car to stand in the glare of the Ford's headlights.

"Mr. Horn? I tried to call you. I'm—"

"Iris's husband. I saw you at the funeral."

"Paul Fairbrass. I hope you don't mind my coming by like this."

Horn got out and walked over to him. "Only

thing I mind is being called over like an errand boy," he said. "Something I can do for you?"

When the other man hesitated, looking around, Horn said: "We can talk right here. I'd ask you in, but it's late, and I'm not feeling very neighborly."

Paul Fairbrass wore a well-cut suit, lighter in color than the one he'd worn at the funeral. He had slightly boyish features and a conventionally handsome face that didn't say much, except for the eyes, which Horn could barely make out under the man's snap brim. They were heavy-lidded and almost sad.

"Who's your friend?" Horn asked, indicating the other man, who had resumed his seat behind the wheel.

"He works for me," Fairbrass said simply. "He won't bother us." There was an edge of impatience in his voice. *He likes to ask the questions*, Horn thought.

"All right." Horn leaned against the Packard's fender, his vision angled so as to keep both men in view.

Fairbrass cleared his throat. "Iris doesn't know I'm here. I don't like going behind her back, but I think I have to. She told me what you said to her at the funeral. About Scott Bullard's death. About the picture of the little girl, the one you think might be Clea—"

"It is Clea."

"All right. The point is, after you called yesterday,

109

she told me you're determined to go looking for our daughter."

"That's right," Horn said. "I'm going to find her. For some reason, I seem to be the only one who's really worried about what might have happened to her—"

"You're wrong."

"You and your sidekick came here with the idea of changing my mind."

"No. I came here to help."

"What does that mean? Do you believe what I told her?"

"I don't know. Iris doesn't believe you. But what matters to me is that you might find our daughter. If you did, I'd be grateful to you."

"And just how can you help?"

Out of the corner of his eye Horn saw the man inside the car make a sudden movement, reaching outside the window to flick on the car's search-light. Looking ahead intently, he trained it down the road. Following the beam, Horn saw a coyote standing silently in the middle of the pavement, staring at them, its eyes luminous with reflection like tiny lanterns. For ten seconds the animal was frozen in the light; then it shifted and was gone into the brush like a shadow.

Fairbrass laughed nervously. "A neighbor?" It was the first time his composure had slipped.

"It can be wild out here," Horn said. "That's why I like it. I was saying, how can you help?"

"By telling you some things, things Iris doesn't

110

know. Such as, for a couple of months Clea has been going out with a young man."

"Is his name Tommy?"

Fairbrass looked at him appraisingly. "Right, Tommy Dell. She was very secretive about seeing him. I only found out about him after she ran away and I asked some questions around her school . . ."

"What did you learn about him?"

"Well, that he was too old for her, somewhere in his twenties. Very good-looking, very well dressed, very polite. I gave the police his name and description, the kind of car he drove, thinking she might be with him. A few days later, they told me they couldn't find anyone by that name."

"He was using a phony name?"

Fairbrass nodded, looking embarrassed. "Apparently so. It was bad enough having her run away, but hearing that really got me worried. I put one of my men on it full-time—Sykes, the man in the car there—"

"What do you mean, put him on it? Just who is he?"

"He's someone who does jobs for me. Look, I own a business, and sometimes businesses have to deal with things. Before the war, we had serious labor trouble. Communists, Wobblies. First pickets, then little acts of sabotage. It was the Depression, the police had their hands full. So I hired a few men like Sykes, who knew how to deal with things."

111

"Strikebreakers. I know the type."

"Maybe, maybe not. Some of them, like Sykes, were ex-policemen, family men. They know how to investigate, find out things."

"Get tough. Crack heads."

"When they had to."

"Are you a tough guy, Mr. Fairbrass? I'm just curious."

"When it comes to my wife or daughter . . . yes, I am."

Horn laughed softly. "Fair enough." He didn't particularly like Iris's new husband, but he was beginning to dislike him a little less.

"Anyway," Fairbrass continued, "I gave Sykes a few ideas. Clea told one of her friends that Tommy had taken her shopping on Wilshire once, so Sykes showed her picture around the stores. Coming out of one store, pure luck, he spotted what looked like Tommy's car parked across the street. He started over to get the license number, but just then Tommy walked up and got in. Sykes was able to follow him, up into the Hollywood Hills. Sykes is good at following people, and he was pretty sure the other man wasn't aware of him. But . . .

"He turned a corner, and there was the car, blocking the road, Tommy standing there, looking relaxed. He came over. Sykes got out. They talked. Sykes said the guy acted friendly but clearly gave him the message that he didn't want to be followed any more. Tommy was cleaning his fingernails with a little penknife while he talked. Smiling, you know?

And right in the middle of something he was saying, he used the knife, very fast. Reached up and cut him below the ear. Then he was gone."

"I can't believe this," Horn said, his voice tight with anger. "This guy who was spending hours with her, who may be with her now . . . he was able to fool you, to sneak around with her, use a phony name. And now you tell me he cuts people with a knife for fun."

"I know," Fairbrass said curtly. "I know. He's dangerous. This is my fault. You can see why I have to find her, especially if there's any chance she might be with him. And why I don't want Iris to know any of this."

"Damn right this is your fault," Horn said. "You should have taken better care of her."

"You can't say anything to me that will make me feel any worse than I already do."

Horn paced in front of the car for a moment, casting long shadows on the road. He breathed deeply. Finally he said, "So how bad did he cut him?"

"Twelve stitches," Fairbrass said. "Plus, the seat cover in his car was ruined. He's very embarrassed. Says he won't make that mistake again."

"I'm sure he won't. But even slipping up like he did, old Sykes sounds better at this sort of thing than I would be. Why—"

"Look, Mr. Horn, Iris told me two things about you. You're stubborn, and you love Clea. I'm hoping you can help us find her."

"Did she tell you where I was until about a year ago?"

"Yes. I don't care. Besides, she told me what happened. I think you got a raw deal."

Horn didn't want to take it any further, but the words came out before he could stop them. "Did she tell you how she broke her arm?"

"This isn't what I came here to talk about," Fairbrass said, his face grim. "If you really want to know, I don't think you're a particularly nice person—"

"We were both drunk. Arguing. She fell. That's just for the record. I didn't hit her."

Fairbrass made no response. The asphalt had given off the last of the day's heat, and the night air was beginning to feel cool. Horn stepped over to his car to get his jacket and put it on. Fairbrass followed him, reached in a pocket, and brought out a medium-sized photo, which he handed to him.

"Here's a picture of Clea. She's probably a couple of inches taller than she was last time you saw her. She dresses like most kids her age—big skirts, sweaters, blouses, bobby socks, usually saddle shoes or loafers. Her hair's long, and she pins it back a lot." He paused, as if thinking. "She likes to clip pictures of horses out of magazines. She said she wants a dog, and we promised to get one. She likes strawberry ice cream and strawberry malts." Another pause. "Her favorite places are the ocean and, I'd say, the Santa Monica Pier, especially the carousel."

I already knew that. "Have you looked there?"

"Yes, more than once. She said some of her friends have kidded her about the carousel being for little girls. They go for the roller coaster. But Clea's got her own mind. In some ways, she's growing up very fast, but in others she seems content to take her time. Her mother says it's hard to tell which girl she is from one day to the next."

"You think you know her pretty well?"

"I haven't been her father for long, but I try."

"Have you talked to Addie Webb?"

"Adele? I tried. I spoke to her mother on the phone, but the woman wasn't very cooperative, and she didn't seem willing to let me talk to her daughter. However, she did say Adele's at home, so she couldn't be off somewhere with Clea."

"What about her father?"

"I'm not sure there is one."

"Well, there was a few years ago," Horn told him. "The two girls went off together once. I fetched them back, and when I took Addie home, he didn't even say thanks."

"I see," Fairbrass said in a flat tone. "Anyway, we haven't been able to talk to her. Maybe you can."

"I'll try. One thing we need to talk about. There's a chance that something might have happened to Clea."

"You mean . . . ? I know. We've been making inquiries along those lines too. Sykes has called the emergency rooms at all the hospitals and checked with the county coroner's office about unidentified white girls. Nothing."

"How do you know this Tommy—or somebody else—didn't just take her?"

"You mean kidnap her?" Fairbrass's expression suggested that the thought had occurred to him. "I suppose we don't know anything for sure. But I'd say it's not likely. For one thing, she's run off before. For another, I'd noticed a lot of tension between Clea and her mother. Couldn't put my finger on it, but it was there."

"How bad?"

"Pretty bad." Fairbrass stuck his hands in his pockets and studied the ground for a few seconds. "Almost from the time I became her father, Clea's been angry. At first I thought it was me and that she would learn to like me. But it went on, and in all honesty I couldn't say it was directed at me. It was something between the two of them. She's been almost impossible to control—"

"What about the horses and the strawberry malts? All that sounds pretty normal to me."

"She was normal, I suppose, except in the way she treated us," Fairbrass said. "There was a tug-of-war whenever we tried to put any limits on her. I didn't want to be the one to discipline her, at least not at first. But after a while I realized that neither one of us could. She would leave the house without telling us, that sort of thing. We suspected she might have been drinking with some of her friends . . ." He gestured vaguely. "Anyway, one morning she was just . . . gone."

"All right," Horn said. "Is that it?"

116

"Just about," Fairbrass said. "Except for how much this is worth to me."

"We're not going to talk about money. This isn't a job."

"How about expenses?"

"If I run into any, I'll let you know. Your man Sykes still on this?"

"He is if you need him to be." Fairbrass got into the car, and Sykes started the engine. "I won't keep you any longer."

"You may not hear from me for a while." Horn walked around to the driver's side to get another look at Sykes. "You got a first name?" he asked the man.

"Dewey." The bandage almost glowed in the dashboard light.

"I guess I'm not very friendly when I find strangers waiting for me in the dark."

"I guess I get paid enough so I don't mind," Sykes said. "One thing to remember, though."

"Uh-huh?"

"If you find Tommy, watch his right hand."

At mid-morning the next day, Horn pulled up in front of Addie Webb's place, a one-story duplex in Echo Park that sat in one of those apartment courts that began to spring up all over L.A. about twenty years earlier. The duplex was a wood-frame cottage with a green shingle roof and two entrances about ten feet apart on the front porch. The court-yard, which held a dozen of the cottages, was

117

mostly concrete pathways with ill-tended little patches of grass here and there. A half-inflated beach ball sagged on the grass beneath the lone shade tree.

Pete Binyon's directions had been fairly accurate, but two phone conversations with Douglas Greenleaf the night before had yielded both the precise address and the name of Addie's mother, Thelda.

The apartment he wanted was the left-hand entrance in the second building. He knocked on the door and heard a woman's raised voice inside, then the door opened. Thelda Webb wore a loose-fitting housecoat and an air of distraction. She held the door open with one hand as the other, holding a cigarette poised between two fingers, brushed her hair from her face. She looked at him wordlessly.

"Good morning, ma'am," he said, hat in hand. "I'm John Ray Horn, a friend of Clea Fairbrass's parents. She's left home, and I'm helping them look for her."

Thelda Webb studied him up and down, a little boldly. She appeared a few years younger than Horn, attractive in a way that suggested she worked hard at it. Her auburn hair—from a bottle, he suspected—was freshly brushed and fell lavishly over her shoulders. But she gave off the mixed scent of cigarette smoke and what he guessed was last night's perfume.

"Somebody called—" she began.

118

"Her father."

She shrugged. "I told him we don't know where she is."

Somewhere inside, Horn heard a shower start up. "Is Addie here? I'd just like to talk to her for a minute."

She shook her head. "She's off someplace with friends," she said with little interest. "Playing tennis or something. All summer, it's like this."

"Well, I'd really like to talk to her." He handed her a slip of paper on which he had written his name and phone number. "Would you mind asking her to call me?"

She made no move to take it. Her expression hardened by a fraction. "You sure that's what this is all about?"

"I don't know what you mean."

She leaned into the door and brought the cigarette up to her lips. "Look, I'm getting very tired of swatting guys off of her like flies. I've told her she better stick with boys her own age or she's going to have trouble with me. But she's at that age. All of a sudden, she likes *men*." Her voice went sour on the word. "College boys. Older, even. She doesn't understand all the trouble she can get into."

Horn fought to hold down his anger. "Mrs. Webb, I'm not a college boy. I'm looking for a sixteen-year-old girl who may be in trouble herself, and I just want to talk to your daughter."

"Maybe. If that's so, it's like I told you. Addie

can't help you." She eyed him through a haze of exhaled smoke. "You look familiar."

"A few years ago," he said, "when you were living someplace else. Clea and Addie went off together. I brought them back, spoke to your husband. You probably saw me then." He heard the shower being turned off, and he looked past her into the small sitting room. "Is he here? Maybe I could—"

"Mr. Webb is long gone," she said with no expression. She delicately picked a strand of tobacco off her tongue and studied him with renewed interest. "I remember. You're the cowboy, aren't you?"

"I used to do that."

"Addie showed me a picture of you in a magazine." She eyed his scuffed shoes and unpressed pants. "You sure look different. Anyway, she thought you were really something. You know, one of those crushes. Sorry to say, she's way past crushes these days."

"Yes, ma'am."

"I work at the Cocoanut Grove," she said brightly. "A hostess. You wouldn't believe all the movie people we see there. Errol Flynn was in the other night. And Red Skelton. You should come in sometime." Once again, she took in his appearance. "But people dress up there. You know, elegant." She spoke that word as if it were one of her favorites.

"I know," he said. The year they were married, he and Iris had gone dancing at the Cocoanut Grove on New Year's Eve. He remembered the lush sounds of the orchestra, the tinsel and confetti, and the feel of Iris next to him. But the memory, once vivid, was now so faint it could have belonged to another lifetime.

He said goodbye to Thelda Webb. As she closed the door, he heard her call out to someone inside: "Isn't it time for you to get to work? I need to use the bathroom."

Walking down the steps, still angry over her attitude, he noticed a little girl on the porch of the adjacent duplex. He hesitated. She appeared to be about five or six, wore a pale blue pinafore, and stood with her arms resting on the top porch railing, rocking back and forth, looking at him.

"Hi," he said.

"Hi."

"You live here?"

She nodded.

"You know Addie?"

Another nod. "She gave me her *com*-pact," the girl said, still rocking, reciting the words like a nursery rhyme. "With a *mir*-ror. 'Cause somebody gave her a *new* one. You want to *see* it?"

"Maybe some other time, honey." He walked over to her. "Would you do something really important for me?" He laid the slip of paper on the top railing next to her and weighted it down with a twenty-five-cent piece from his pocket. "It's kind of secret. If you give this note to Addie when nobody's looking, and don't tell anybody about it, you can have this quarter."

She regarded him solemnly. "Secret?"

121

"That's right. Secret. And the quarter's yours, for candy or anything you want to buy for yourself."

Her eyes drifted to the quarter. "For Gold Bricks?"

"Sure. You can buy five Gold Bricks with this. Just be sure you don't eat them all at once, all right?"

CHAPTER 9

On the way home, Horn stopped at a fruit stand on Pacific Coast Highway and bought a watermelon and a bag of lemons. In the kitchen, he sliced up several lemons and squeezed the juice into a jug, then added water and a fistful of sugar. He poured a glassful and sat in the rocker out on the porch, swirling the ice cubes around in the glass and taking an occasional sip. The porch was hot but shady in the late morning, and the cold lemonade bit gently at the back of his throat with each swallow.

Fresh watermelon and lemonade were two of the things that could instantly take him back in memory to the hill country of northwestern Arkansas, where he grew up. Sometimes he and his little brother, Lamar, would steal watermelons, because the stolen ones tasted better. If his father caught them at it, he would take them out to the tool shed and whip them both with his belt. John Ray, as the elder, merited twice the number of licks because he had led his brother astray. Their father's mastery of Scripture was so complete that he was able to quote the relevant passage in time with his blows, each syllable distinct, ending with a thunderous "Amen!" on the final stroke.

The memories should have been painful. But the passage of time had softened them, Horn realized. The blows of the belt fell in slow motion, and his father's shouts and his own cries now sounded far away. They had resurfaced briefly only the other night, when he heard Scotty talk about getting even with his old man and Horn had realized that he knew the feeling only too well. *Amen to that, brother.*

In his last letter, Lamar had said their father still preached every Sunday, even though his congregation had been shrunken by the war and other changes to the little town. Horn took a long, cool swig. *When you're a man of God*, he reflected, *it must be hard to have a son like the one I turned out to be*. Running away from home, winding up in a Sodom called Los Angeles, working in a godless enterprise called the movies, and finally going to prison. For a while, during his acting days, Horn had thought his father might have cause to be proud of him, but no word came. The Reverend Horn had always considered motion pictures frivolous and almost certainly dismissed cowboy movies as unworthy of any attention. Horn wondered if the preacher's voice was still strong and sure and if the old man ever thought about him.

He picked up a day-old newspaper and paged through it. There was a new Bette Davis playing at the Egyptian, and Horn considered going. Somewhat to his surprise, he'd developed a liking for Bette Davis while up at Cold Creek, where the inmates had no choice about the movies they saw. One week the film was *Jezebel*, and Horn, desperate for some diversion, went to see it. He came out impressed with her character's guts and determination and her willingness to admit foolish, destructive behavior and try to change. The woman seemed more real to him than most male characters he was seeing on the screen, certainly more real than anyone he had portrayed. Since then, he had tried to see more of her movies, but he was careful not to mention it to anyone, especially Mad Crow. *What's next for you, amigo?* he could hear his friend drawl. *Joan Crawford? Ethel Barrymore? Tallulah Bankhead?*

He put aside the paper, picked up the phone, dialed the long-distance operator, and asked her for a number. She said she'd call back. While he waited, he sat on the porch and smoked as Rose Maddox, on the record player, sang *I Want to Be a Cowboy's Sweetheart* with her brothers accompanying her. Horn liked the song and let it repeat twice.

The operator rang, and in a few seconds he heard a familiar voice.

"Hey, little brother," he said.

"Hey, John Ray! Son of a gun. Knew this had to be you, 'cause I don't know anybody else out in California. How you doin'?"

"Just fine. I thought I'd give you a call and see how Sally was doing."

Horn heard him cover up the receiver and yell to his wife that it was John Ray calling to ask about her. "She says that's real nice of you." There was a little static on the line, and Lamar's voice, although clear, sounded as if it was coming from the next room. He and Horn always seemed to end up shouting on long-distance calls, as if they simply didn't trust the equipment to do its job. "She got out of the hospital three days ago, and she's getting around. Doctors said having your appendix out ain't nearly as big a thing as it used to be."

"Glad to hear it. You tell her thank you for sending those strawberry preserves. Kids all right?"

"Everybody's fine. We saw one of your movies a couple of weeks ago, over in Rogers."

"Which one?"

"*The Lost Mine.*"

"That's been around for a while. Guess they're getting a little extra mileage out of it."

"It was playing with a Charlie Chan. We'd seen 'em both, but you know, we don't get many new movies around here. The kids hadn't seen it, though, and they had a good time. They talk about you a lot."

"So, uh . . ." *Why is this so hard?* "You seen the old man lately?"

"Sure, just the other day."

"How's he doing?"

"Well, I don't know . . . I guess he's just getting old. He's using a cane now. Don't know if I told you that. He wouldn't want me to. And I think he's having some trouble with his hearing. But he still preaches every Sunday. Some of the congregation, they make jokes about how his sermons are twice as loud now that his hearing is bad."

"I don't suppose he went to that movie." Horn hadn't meant to ask. The words just came out.

"The one with you in it? No, he didn't." Lamar's response was quiet, and Horn had to strain to hear it. "But you know, he doesn't go to the movies much at all, unless they've got something about God or Jesus. So . . ."

"I know. That's all right."

"You want me to tell him anything?"

"No," Horn said. "Just that you talked to me, and I asked about him."

"Well, he'd appreciate that," Lamar said, but he didn't sound convinced.

After hanging up, Horn went to a table by the couch where he had left the photo that Paul Fairbrass had given him. It was about five by seven inches and on heavy paper, printed with a matte finish, and it looked like the work of a professional studio. He stared at it. Clea wore a sweater over a blouse with a Peter Pan collar. She looked up and to the left, smiling, her pale hair backlit and almost aglow. She had become what you would call a very pretty girl. Her looks hinted at the woman to come, not yet there but visible not far off. It was her smile that seemed most familiar to him—open and trusting, speaking of little-girl delights in horses and pebbles in jars, of carousels and skinny crescent moons. *Look at this face too long*, he thought, *and it could break your heart.*

Fairbrass had said they'd looked for her at the Santa Monica Pier. Horn remembered her riding one of the garishly painted carousel horses at the pier one Fourth of July weekend, her jaw set grimly, leaning way over to grab the brass ring but missing it by several inches each time. "Wait 'til you're bigger!" he had yelled to her over the calliope music, but she just shook her head and leaned out farther.

The phone rang.

"Mr. Horn? It's Addie Webb."

"Addie! I'm glad I found you."

"I was surprised you wanted to talk to me. I haven't seen you for a long time." She sounded much older, more self-assured. But she spoke softly and guardedly, as if worried someone might overhear her.

"It has been a long time." They exchanged small-talk for a while, and then Horn said, "Listen, Addie, did you know Clea was gone?"

"No," she said, sounding puzzled.

"Her parents say she's run away, like the other time. I'm hoping you can help us—"

"I think my mom's waking up from her nap," she said in a low voice. "She wouldn't want me—"

"Addie, I really need to talk to you."

For a moment, he could hear only her breathing. Then she spoke urgently: "Listen, I need to go out to Malibu this afternoon. If you'll take me, we can talk."

"Sure. Your house?"

"No, better not. I'm getting a ride as far as Pacific Coast Highway. You can take me the rest of the way. Do you know the gas station at Entrada and PCH?"

"Uh-huh?"

"I'll meet you there in an hour."

She was waiting by one of the pumps at the Flying A station, wearing sunglasses, a short beach robe, and espadrilles. He pulled up next to her. "Hi, Mr. Horn," she said excitedly, coming over to the car.

"Hello, Addie." He wouldn't have recognized her. She was taller and had filled out, but there was more. Dark eyes, outrageous lashes only partly hidden by brunette hair that swept lazily over part of her face, Veronica Lake—style. If Clea's picture spoke of the young woman to come, in Addie she had arrived.

Without meaning to, he studied her. Boldly, the broad smile still on her face, she studied him right back, just as her mother had done. Finally, he reached over to his right and opened the door. She came around and got in.

"It's really nice to see you again," she said. "I'm meeting some friends at the beach. It's not far."

He pulled back onto the highway and headed up the coast. Almost directly overhead, the sun burned through the coastal haze, but a breeze off the ocean tempered the heat a few degrees. A few cottages hung precariously off the cliffs that loomed to the right. The houses had a temporary look, as if they had been placed there by the children of a race of giants who would soon return and capriciously move them elsewhere.

Addie undid the sash on her robe and rolled down her window, letting the warm air wash over her. Underneath she was wearing a tight-fitting white two-piece bathing suit. Her hair was held in place by a band that matched the color of the suit, and her legs were tanned. "This is fun," she said.

"I talked to your mother today," he said. "She didn't want me to see you."

"She doesn't want me to see anybody," she said lightly. "Especially lately. She wants me to stay little Adele, and I'm not that girl anymore. She tries to chase away every boy—"

"It's not just boys she's worried about."

"She's jealous," Addie said, and Horn heard satisfaction in the words. "She thinks I'm trying to steal her boyfriends."

"Are you?"

She made a sound of disgust. "I can do better. This one's an auto-parts salesman." She giggled. "Who smacks when he chews."

"Did she meet him at the Cocoanut Grove?"

"I don't know. I suppose she told you she's a hostess there?"

"Uh-huh."

"She's a waitress," Addie said. "Except on Saturday nights, when she's the cigarette girl." She leaned back in her seat and looked sideways at him. There was something devilish about her smile. "A bunch of us at school went with Clea to see one of your movies. We thought you were *very* cute."

"I don't do that anymore," he said. "It was just a job, and nobody takes that sort of thing seriously anyway." *Except for the ones who do*, he said to himself, thinking of the boy on the porch with the withered leg.

"Clea did."

"For a while, maybe. Then, when she was older, she was embarrassed to have a cowboy actor for a father. She would rather have had Tony Martin. Or maybe John Payne. Those were the pictures she had on her wall."

"You said she hasn't come home?"

"That's right. Addie, I need to know anything you can think of that would help me find her. Friends she might be with. Places where she might go. Anything." When she didn't respond, he went on: "This Tommy Dell. She might be with him. Do you know him?"

"I know him." She spoke quietly. "He's a creep."

"Do you know where he lives?"

"No, why would I?"

"Can you think of any way we could locate him?"

She thought for a moment, then suddenly clapped her hands together and leaned forward. "I know exactly how. Do you know Central Avenue?"

"Sure." Central Avenue was L.A.'s Harlem, the place to go for music and dancing and excitement off the beaten path. He and Iris had had some good times there.

"Well, I just remembered," she said, sounding breathless. "Tommy told Clea once that he had business at some of the nightclubs. I don't know what he meant exactly, but he said he goes down there a lot. From the way he talked about it, he made it sound . . . I don't know, I've always wanted to go. We could do it tonight."

"We?"

"Sure. White people go there all the time, don't they? They say it's the best music around. You like jazz, don't you?"

"There are a whole lot of clubs on Central."

"We can look for him, one place at a time."

"I don't know about you going, Addie."

"Don't be stuffy, Mr. Horn. You need somebody to point out Tommy, don't you? And besides, you'd fit in better if you had a date. I'll be your date." She giggled. "Your pretend date. Oh!" She gestured to the left. "Here. This is where I get off."

He pulled onto the shoulder and stopped. She hopped out and ran around to the driver's side. Off to the left the Pacific lay, broad, blue, and passive under the sun. The beach, rippled like another ocean, sloped down from the road to end fifty yards away where a few delicate whitecaps nibbled at the sand. A few houses, shacks really, dotted the ocean side of the road. Through the wide gap between two of them, Horn saw a group of young people lounging on blankets. Spotting Addie, one of them waved.

"Well?" she asked, resting her hand lightly on his arm.

"Just one thing," he said. "If we spot him, I'll probably try to follow him. I'll have to put you in a cab."

"No! I'd miss out on the fun."

"It's too dangerous, Addie."

"Tommy? There's nothing dangerous—"

"I know something about him you don't. We have to do it my way, or I'm afraid you can't come."

Her face turned sour. "All right, then. But I think it's silly."

From far off, he heard someone call her name. "Your friends are waiting," he said. "Seven o'clock tonight. Do I call at your door, like a date?"

"You must be kidding," she said. "I'll be waiting outside."

Horn drove home, where he fetched a beer from the fridge. It was too hot to sit outside, so he took off his shoes and lay down on the couch/bed, sipping and reflecting on what he'd learned. Fairbrass's story of his man Sykes's encounter on the road had made Horn's stomach churn.

He was drowsy from the heat and allowed himself to drift off to sleep. When he awoke, the front porch was in shadow, and the heat had eased a little. Around six-thirty, he washed up and laid out his good suit. It was time to go nightclubbing.

Addie was waiting for him on the sidewalk outside the apartments. When she got in, he took a good look at her, marveling at her appearance. She was wearing an emerald-green silk dress, tightly belted, with black, ankle-strapped high heels and a small hat perched at a precarious angle.

"You look very nice, Mr. Horn," she said animatedly, arranging herself in the seat. She tilted the rearview mirror in her direction and checked her lipstick and makeup. He had to admit to himself that the transformation was impressive.

"So do you," he said as they pulled away. "But I hope you're not thinking about ordering any drinks tonight."

"Oh, don't be that way," she said happily. "I'm eighteen. I know you don't believe it, but it's true. I had some problems in grade school, and they held me back a year. I'm a year older than just about everyone I know. As soon as I graduate, I'm getting my own place."

"That's wonderful, but you're still not old enough to drink." Thinking of Addie as a young woman was a stretch for him, but the way she was dressed was helping him adjust. He caught a whiff of a sweet scent and noticed that she was wearing a fresh gardenia at her waist.

134

"If we spot Tommy, will he recognize you?" he asked.

"I don't think so. He's never seen me like this. Besides, I'll let this down," she said, indicating the light veil rolled up over her hat. "I'll be the sophisticated lady, the one in the Duke Ellington song." She turned on the car radio and began dialing through the stations.

"What's wrong with your radio?"

"Hmm? Oh, you mean the static? It's not much of a radio. This is an old stunt car."

"A what?"

"A stunt car. From the studio where I worked. It's restored now, but it was used for rolling over and crashing and things like that. You know, for serials and gangster movies. Also for driving very fast. It has a Mercury engine and a heavy-duty suspension. The head of the motor pool at Medallion thought it had enough mileage on it, and he sold it to me cheap when I . . . when I needed a car."

She found a good station, one that pulled in a dance band from somewhere, and the sound of a ballad from the war years filled the car, a story about a love gone away, and the tenor saxophones told it in a voice ripe with longing. As he turned onto Sunset Boulevard, the air was beginning to cool. "I heard about your troubles," Addie said. "All of us at school did. The divorce and all the rest. I'm very sorry."

"I appreciate that."

135

They talked about random subjects, mostly things that interested Addie. She joked about the day he had "rescued" the two girls from the motel up the coast, "just like in one of your movies."

"Except I wasn't exactly on horseback."

"Didn't matter," she said. "We were both glad to see you. I was getting sick from all those cigarettes."

She told him about some of the singers the girls liked, some of the new dances. She said she hoped they could dance tonight, and he said he'd see about it. He steered the car along Sunset into downtown, where he picked up Broadway and headed south. They passed the Million Dollar Theater, one of the movie palaces built before the Depression. "My mom was an usher there once," Addie told him. "She says movies were more exciting back then. Her favorite was Clara Bow. You didn't know her, did you?"

"I'm not quite that old, Addie."

"I know," she said quickly. "I just thought that since you—"

"I was never a real movie star, either. Not like the kind your mother remembers."

"You don't mean that."

"I'm not sure you'd understand."

An old memory surfaced. Years before, just after he and Iris were married, Horn had stopped by the bar at the Hollywood Palms Hotel, which was then owned by Scotty's father. The bar was a famous watering hole and often attracted tourists who waited in line to get inside in hopes of a celebrity sighting. Horn was with a wrangler friend who worked on some of his movies, both of them still in their western gear. Before long, Horn found himself entertaining some of the tourists with stories of movie stunts, location shoots, and rodeo rides.

Standing there in his dusty chaps, signing an occasional autograph, he felt himself very much the center of that particular universe. That is, until William Powell entered the room. Nick Charles himself, of the *Thin Man* movies. A little past his prime, perhaps, but there was no question that a movie star was among them. Little by little, those in Horn's audience drifted away and soon had assembled around the latest arrival. Horn drank too much that evening, and when he got home, he quarreled with Iris over nothing.

He considered telling the story to Addie, then thought better of it. If she wanted to think of him the way she did, why not?

At 40th Street, he turned left. The sky was almost fully dark when, a few blocks later, he turned south on Central.

The street was ablaze with lights. As far as they could see, Central Avenue teemed with people and nightclubs, bars, theaters, lunch counters, barbershops, drugstores. Many of the night spots' doors were open to the street, and they could hear snatches of jazz. As they passed a cafe with its windows open, he caught the smell of grilled meat.

"Isn't this something?" Addie said excitedly. "It's like Hollywood, only more so. Let's stop."

He pulled into a lot around the corner on 42nd Place, across from the Hotel Dunbar. On the sidewalk, the faces were every hue of the colored spectrum, and almost everyone was well-dressed, the men in sharp suits, the women in fancy dresses and showy hats. He spotted a few zoot suits, holdovers from the war years, tucked and pleated into an outrageous style. Now that the war was over and more material was available, women's skirts were longer, a development Horn had often noted with some disappointment. Yet the way the women of Central Avenue wore their clothes had nothing to do with skirt length and everything to do with flair. Free of their day jobs as housemaids or dishwashers, they promenaded on the arms of their men, wearing an attitude that said *Look at me*.

Horn guided Addie toward the Club Alabam, on the corner next to the Dunbar. As the biggest and best-known of all the nightclubs on Central, it was a good place to start.

Inside, they were shown to a table. Across the dance floor—where he and Iris had danced once—a band was playing *How High the Moon*. Even on this weeknight the crowd was large and enthusiastic. Everyone was drinking, and the place had a familiar, heady smell that combined alcohol, pomade, perfume, and cigarette smoke—and the occasional reefer. When the waiter arrived, Addie started to order, but Horn interrupted her. "Planter's punch for the lady," he said. "Heavy on the fruit, easy on the rum. For me, bourbon and water."

She made a face at him but appeared too excited to hold a grudge. "Look over there," she said, nudging him. "That's a movie star. Isn't she?"

"I don't know," he said without turning. "Listen, Addie, remember why we're here."

"All right." She sighed, adjusted her veil, and looked intently around the room for a few seconds. Her hat resembled a miniature version of the cap Errol Flynn had worn in *The Adventures of Robin Hood*, complete with jaunty feather, but on her it looked cute and feminine. "I'm afraid I don't see him. Does that mean we have to leave?"

"Not right now. You can have some of your drink if you want to. But we have a lot of territory to cover."

Twenty minutes later, they were out on the street again. They looked in on one spot after another— either going in and sitting down or, if the place was small, looking around from the door. The places came and went—the Down Beat, the Last Word, the Memo, the Oasis, even the lounge in the Dunbar. All pulsed with music and the electricity of the crowd, but none of them contained Tommy Dell.

Coming out of a luncheonette, where they had stopped for sandwiches and milkshakes, Addie pointed across the street. "How about that one?"

It was a joint called the Dixie Belle, and it looked small and shabby next to its brightly lit neighbors, but Horn was running out of ideas and beginning to regret the excursion. "Why not?"

Inside, the Dixie Belle had a long bar on the right, a small bandstand against the far wall, and no dance floor. The band was a combo fronted by a round-faced man the color of mahogany who stood, head back and eyes closed, working an alto sax. The tune was *My Funny Valentine*, but Horn took a while to recognize it through the horn man's playing—complex, introspective, almost tortured. The crowd seemed rapt, but Horn's ear was used to melody, and he found the music grating.

It was too gloomy to see much of the interior from the door, so they asked for a table. When they were seated, Addie turned to the waiter and said quickly, "I'd like a whisky sour, please. And bourbon and water for the gentleman."

He gave her a look but decided not to press it. "That's strange music," Addie said.

"That's called bebop, ma'am," the waiter said. "You like it?"

"Not particularly," Horn said before she could answer. Satisfied with her small victory over the drink, Addie lit a Pall Mall and grinned at him. Then, suddenly aware of how her veil would interfere with the cigarette, she rolled it back onto her hat. "I almost set fire to this thing," she said. "Be glad you're not a woman."

"Look around," he told her.

She did so, scanning the room from left to right,

then back again. Suddenly she stopped, grabbing his arm. "Over there."

"Don't point. Just tell me."

"Against the wall, in the booth next to the bandstand."

He turned casually. Four men sat in the booth, two white and two colored, all wearing dark suits. The mustached white man on the far left appeared to be in his mid-thirties, with high cheekbones, a muscular neck, and an expressionless face. The man next to him was slim and almost aristocratic, with slicked-back hair and features that just missed Valentino's. He was talking animatedly to the colored man next to him.

Horn turned his back to the booth. "Hello, Tommy," he said under his breath.

CHAPTER 10

"I need to get a closer look," he said to Addie. "Will you be all right for a while?"

"Sure." Her eyes shone with excitement. "Let me know if I can help."

He picked up his drink and headed toward the bar, which was somewhat closer to the booth. On the way, he intercepted their waiter, laid a hand on the man's shoulder, and said, "Keep an eye on the lady, will you? Get her whatever she needs."

He found a place at the bar that was about twenty feet from the booth, leaned his back against the scarred wood and pretended to idly gaze around the room. He worked over his rough-hewn plan. His car was a block away. If Tommy left, Horn would pick up Addie and exit with her—just another couple having a good time. If Tommy went to another club, they'd follow. There were enough white couples in the Central Avenue clubs tonight to ensure that the two of them wouldn't stand out too much. If their quarry got in a car—Horn prayed it was the oh-so-visible Chrysler convertible—he'd slip her taxi money, make it to his car as quickly as he could, and try to pick up the target on the street. The plan was ragged at best, but it was all he could devise. The alternative was to confront the other man, and Horn quickly rejected that notion. With his prison record, even a minor incident could put him in jail.

"Hey there."

A young waiter holding an empty tray stood next to Horn, looking at him quizzically. He had a wiry build and an amused expression. "I know you," the man said. "I used to wait tables over at the Alabam. You and your lady—"

"Sure," Horn said. "I remember you. It's Gene, isn't it?"

"That's me. Eugene. You Mr. Horn. You give me an autograph once."

"I don't give autographs anymore, Eugene."

"I know that. It was in all the papers. I don't mind. You give me some good tips too."

"I'm afraid I don't do that any more either."

"Well, goodbye to you, then," the man said, swiveling on his heel into a kind of pirouette, tray held aloft, turning gracefully all the way around to finish facing front again, a huge grin on his face. "Just kiddin'. I do a dance routine now, with my brothers. We over at the Lincoln Theater every weekend. I do this job in between. Uh oh—" He peered across the room. "Somebody wavin' at one of my tables."

Eugene sped off to take the order. In a moment he was back, waiting as the bartender mixed the drinks. He took them to the table and returned. "So how you been?"

"Not too bad. Could I ask you something? Do you know that white man in the booth over there? Second from the left?"

Eugene looked briefly. "Him? Sure. Don't know his name, but he's here a lot, maybe once a week. Sometime for fun, sometime for business, like now. He talk to the Creole—that's my boss, next to him. He buys, he sells, I don't know. You don't ask, know what I mean?"

"Sure."

"When he on business, he with his friend there, the one look like you don't want him mad at you. They have one drink, they leave. Other times, he come with a lady, he stay longer."

Something chilled him. "A lady?" He pulled the class photo of Clea from his coat pocket. "Does she look anything like this?"

Eugene studied it. He whistled. "Pretty. Well, I don't know. One time, he come here with a blond lady, but she didn't look as young as this one. It's hard to tell. Other times, different ladies. That one you with tonight—" He gestured toward the table where Addie sat. Through the smoky haze, Horn could see her in conversation with a good-looking young colored man, part of a group at the next table. She was laughing.

"What about her?"

"One of his ladies look a little like her."

"Really?"

"Well, you know. Hard to tell in a place like this, with this light. And she got that veil. Besides, a

144

lot of white ladies look alike to me." He made a tentative grin. "That's a joke." He looked across the room. "Table wants me."

Horn nodded, only half hearing. "Thanks, Eugene," he said, laying four bits on the tray as the man walked away.

He was turning that last bit of information over in his mind when he saw the mustached man get up and move aside to let his companion out. Tommy Dell headed for a curtained doorway just to the left of the bar and went through it. Squinting, Horn could make out a sign on the wall that read LADIES AND GENTS. He waited. After five minutes, he began to get nervous. He glanced over at Addie, saw she was still happily involved in conversation with the young blade at the next table. She also had a fresh drink. He wasn't sure whether to be relieved or concerned.

Making an abrupt decision, Horn crossed the room and pushed through the curtain. Inside was a dimly lit corridor about twenty feet long. To his immediate left was a door marked PRIVATE. At the far end were three doors. Two faced each other; the third, at the end, stood open, apparently to let in some fresh air. He entered the men's room, the one on the left, and saw quickly that it was empty. Stepping through the end door, he saw a row of trash cans and found himself in an alley illuminated only by a lamp some fifty feet away, where alley met street.

Tommy Dell stood not far away, leaning against

the near wall, hands in his pockets, staring at his shoes. He seemed lost in some kind of reverie, listening to the muted wail of the sax inside the club. The song was different now. It might have been *Stella by Starlight,* but Horn wouldn't have put money on it.

He had a second to decide what to do. *I'll be a drunk who wandered out the wrong door.* He looked around aimlessly and muttered a few words, as if to himself.

Tommy noticed him. "Hot in there, huh?" he said. "I swear those spades water their drinks. I don't care, though. It's fun to come down here, don't you think?"

"You bet," Horn said, slurring his words just a little. "Fun place."

"You like that alto sax?" Tommy wore a snappy-looking pin collar, and the small knot in his tie stuck out above the pin like a flag on the prow of a yacht. On the toes of his well-shined black shoes, the lone streetlight showed as twin pinpoints of light.

"Not much."

"Guy your age, I bet you're more of a swing man. Let's see. Miller, Goodman, James, the Dorseys. All the big bands. Am I right?" Tommy had a playful voice, but Horn thought he could detect something underneath the play.

"I suppose."

"You got a light?" Tommy reached into an inside jacket pocket, extracted a cigarette case, and flipped open the lid. "Want a smoke?"

"Sure." Horn went over to him, fumbling for his matches. His senses were on full alert. *Watch the right hand.* But the right hand held only the cigarette case, and the left was reassuringly empty. He reached for a cigarette, careful not to stand too close.

A small sound behind him. Horn twisted to one side, throwing up an arm, and he was almost too late. The blow, although glancing, struck his right temple with a terrible weight behind it. Horn staggered to one side, stumbled and fell to one knee on the cracked pavement. In the brief moment he was allowed, he cursed his failure to remember the other man, who had quietly approached as Tommy distracted him.

The man was quickly upon him. With something in his fist, he drew back his right arm and swung it as he would swing a hammer. Horn tried to block the blow with his left arm. It landed at the point where the deltoid muscle met the upper arm, with an explosive pain, and he felt the arm go limp. It dropped uselessly, and he knelt there, waiting.

Seeing the results, the other man paused, a fleeting look of satisfaction on his face. Tommy stepped forward. "Let me use that," he said casually. "You just do what you do."

The man grunted and tossed Tommy the object he'd been holding. In the dim light, Horn could make out the outline of a sap. He guessed that the stitched leather covered a couple of pounds

147

of lead, and he knew he was in for a bad time. You could break bones with a sap. If it was your intention and you knew what you were doing, you could kill a man.

Left arm hanging limp, he struggled to his feet, fishing in his jacket pocket for the roll of chips he'd brought along. As he wrapped his fist around the cylinder, it seemed pitiably light. It was all he had.

The mustached man removed his suit coat and tossed it over the lid of a trash can. Then, clenching gloved fists, he assumed a practiced stance and moved in on Horn. He didn't bother to bob and feint but began throwing serious jabs and hooks. Crouching, Horn took most of them on his numb shoulder, waiting for a chance to use his right. He also tried to keep his opponent between himself and Tommy. Whenever he failed, Tommy swung the sap, sometimes landing painful blows on Horn's back or shoulder. But Tommy was apparently not an experienced street fighter. He seemed largely content to watch the one-sided fight unfolding in front of him.

Out of the corner of his eye, Horn saw that some people had gathered at the mouth of the alley. Once he heard an indignant voice cry out, "You leave that man alone." But no one moved to stop it.

Horn felt a warm, sticky trickle course down his right temple, wetting his neck and shirt collar. His left arm ached, and the man's punches were finding his ribs and face. Once he saw an opening and, throwing all his weight behind it, launched a right cross that landed with a satisfying thud on the man's neck and jaw, sending him to the concrete. But the man seemed to have barely touched the ground when, with a graceful backward roll, he was up and advancing once again, fists high.

Horn was tiring. He thought he had one more good punch in him. Evading an awkward swing by Tommy, he waited a split second and then caught the boxer squarely in the sternum. It was a roundhouse punch. But, amazingly, the man once again hit the ground with a roll and was up again. *What the hell?*

The distraction had lasted an instant too long. The sap caught him in the back, at the junction of neck and shoulder, and he went to his knees again. This time, he could not get up. He stayed down, breathing raggedly, bloody spit running from his mouth to pool between his hands.

"I've had enough fun, haven't you?" he heard Tommy say. "Hold him."

The other man caught him in a headlock from behind, then got a grip in his hair and forced his head back.

Horn saw Tommy approach, the streetlight now glinting off the mother-of-pearl finish on the small knife in his hand. "Somebody ought to get the police," said a voice from the street without too much concern.

Delicately, Tommy unfolded the blade, then leaned forward. "Looking for somebody?" he whispered. "Maybe they don't want to be found."

The blade rested lightly on Horn's cheekbone, just below the left eye. Involuntarily, Horn shut his eyes tight. But he had already focused on his target. Jerking his imprisoned head slightly to the right to evade the blade, he collapsed his weight onto his deadened left arm, freeing up the other arm. At the same instant, he grabbed for Tommy's testicles with his right hand, finding them and twisting with whatever strength he had left. The scream told him it was enough.

The mustached man flung him to the ground. Horn pulled himself into a ball as the man began aiming kicks at him.

Then, over Tommy's hoarse screams, he heard a squeal of brakes as someone shouted from the street. "*Po*-lice comin'," the voice said. "*Po*-lice comin'." A car door slammed.

"Fuck," the man looming over him said quietly. "It's the cops." His only answer was a moan. "Come on," Horn heard him say, followed by scuffling sounds.

Horn lay there, breathing raggedly. He didn't know how much time passed until he heard the next voice. "Sir?" it said. "Can you get up?"

A moment later he was leaning against an unmarked patrol car, head still ringing, amid a crowd of onlookers. The policeman who had helped him up—a plainclothes cop whose partner stood nearby—swiveled the car's searchlight around and flicked it on, bathing Horn and the sidewalk in glaring light. As Horn leaned against the car, head down, the cop casually patted him down, then asked him for ID.

"You know you take a chance coming down here," the detective said, holding out a hand for Horn's wallet. He was somewhere in his mid-forties, and his necktie stopped short of covering his expansive middle. His expression and manner said he'd seen everything. "You get rolled?"

"Not exactly."

"Two white men," said one in the crowd. "They going to cut him, then you showed up."

"White men? Is that right?"

"Yeah," Horn said. "They were crazy."

"Well, you ought to be careful," the cop said. "You're going to need a doctor to look at you." He flipped open the wallet, studied the inside, and his polite demeanor dissolved. "Well, son of a gun. Hey, Chick, you know who we got? John Ray Horn. Remember this guy? Used to be in the movies. He beat up some guy half his size, did time for it. I knew the arresting officer, he told me all about it. Yes sir, this fellow is mean and bad. Aren't you, cowboy?"

"Not particularly."

"Well, you sure weren't tonight."

The other cop came around the car. He was maybe ten years younger. He studied Horn's face. "These guys rob you or anything?"

151

Horn's breath was coming back, and he straightened up. "No, they just jumped me," he said. "Something about music. I told them I liked swing, and I said bebop sounded like a couple of cats fighting. They went crazy. I guess they really take their jazz seriously."

The young cop's face showed nothing. "I guess so."

Horn pulled out his handkerchief and blotted at the blood on his temple. His head had stopped ringing and was beginning to ache.

"Sounds like bullshit to me," the older cop said. But he didn't seem sure.

"Well, that's what happened," Horn said.

The older cop plucked a flashlight out of the car and walked into the alley, playing the light around.

"Your partner want to run me in?" Horn said to the younger cop.

"Titus? Oh, he might," the detective said. "But I think I can talk him out of it. The thing is, when we bump into a felon all covered with blood, we get suspicious. Me, I don't care about your record. If you didn't do a crime tonight, you got nothing to worry about."

"I appreciate that," Horn said. "What's your name?"

"Loder. Why you ask?"

"I haven't run into many cops who played straight with me, that's all."

The stocky detective came out of the alley carrying Horn's roll of poker chips. "These yours?"

"I might have dropped them in there."

"Must've been a high-stakes game, huh?" He broke the seal on the end with his thumbnail and extracted a chip, held it up to the light. "Mad Crow Casino," he read. "You work there?"

"Sometimes."

"I'll keep a couple of these for a souvenir," he said, handing Horn the rest. "Maybe they'll be good for a drink."

"Here he is, ma'am," someone said urgently. Horn turned to find Addie and Eugene, the waiter.

"Oh, no." Addie grabbed at his arm. "Oh, no. What happened?"

"I'll tell you all about it," he said, shooting her a look intended to mean, *Not here.*

Eugene handed him his hat, which he'd left inside. "I saw what was going on," Eugene said. "Went looking for you and saw it. Ran out to Central. They's a po-lice car out there this time of night, usually. I yelled to 'em."

"Thanks."

The beefy cop stared at Addie. "We don't like to see white women down here, miss. It's not safe."

"I'm not worried," she said. "I have an escort."

"He wasn't much good at protecting himself tonight."

She turned to Horn. "Why don't we just go?"

"That's a good idea," he said. Then, to the policemen: "You arresting anybody?"

The older cop was about to answer when a colored man in a white jacket stepped up and

153

spoke to him in a low voice. Horn recognized the bartender from the Dixie Belle. The cop listened, then turned to Horn. "You need to come with me," he said.

A minute later they were inside the club, standing in the corridor beyond the bar, and the detective was knocking on the door marked PRIVATE. Hearing a response, he opened it and went in. A minute later he came out and gestured Horn inside.

"Thank you, Titus," said the man behind the desk as the detective stepped back into the corridor and closed the door. To Horn he said, "You like to sit down?"

The office was small, windowless, and ill-furnished, with a scarred desk and a few chairs. Since the bandstand was only about thirty feet away beyond the wall to Horn's left, the floor throbbed with the vibrations of bass and drum. Smells of liquor seeped in from the bar, and someone had smoked a lot of cigars in the tiny space. Horn felt nauseated.

"I'm in a little bit of a hurry," he said, studying the individual Eugene had called the Creole. The man's face was an ethnic map of the bayou country, with sharp cheekbones and skin that looked almost golden in the overhead light. His wavy hair was slick with pomade. The original shape of his nose was hard to read, since its topography had been changed over the years by contact with fists or something harder.

"Well, I won't take much of your time," the man

said, his right hand fiddling with a half-dollar. "Just want to apologize for what happen outside. They told me you got jumped in the alley. I don't like that. Make people think they can't come down here. Bad for Central, you know? Bad for business. Can I offer you a drink?" In contrast to the face, his voice was soft, almost silken. He was one of those men who didn't have to raise their voices, Horn thought. Sometimes it was just a trick, speaking softly to get people to listen harder. But sometimes it was for real.

Horn shook his head. "Where's Addie?"

"The young lady? She fine. One of my boys sitting with her close to the bandstand. She be just fine."

"I need to—" He suddenly felt dizzy and reached out for the edge of the desk.

"Whoa, man." The Creole got up and helped him into a chair. "You wait right here." In a few minutes he was back with a steaming cup, which he placed on the desk. "You drink this."

"What is it?"

"It's tea, with orange peel and chicory and lots of other stuff." He smiled briefly, showing a glint of what might be gold in one of his front teeth. "My mama used to give me that when I was sick. I make it behind the bar for me and a few friends. I don't drink hard stuff anymore." He patted his stomach. "Ulcer."

Horn took a sip, then another. "Thanks."

"So, you get a look at the boys who jump you?"

"Sure," Horn said, wrapping both hands around the cup. "They're friends of yours. Or maybe I should say business associates."

"Hmm?"

"Saw you talking to them earlier tonight, over at your table."

The Creole's face went blank. *He didn't know*, Horn thought. "Didn't the cop tell you?"

"He say couple of white men. That's all he say."

"He wasn't there. They were the same two you were having a drink with, just a few minutes ago. I guess they left in a hurry, huh?" Horn wondered if he'd just made an enemy of this man, and he knew he didn't want him for an enemy. In the next few seconds, he knew he had to decide whether to be cagey with the Creole or to be honest with him.

What the hell, he thought, *I'm too tired and sore to be cagey. And besides, the tea tastes good.*

"Here's the way it is," he said, leaning forward in his chair. "I came down here looking for my daughter. I've got nothing to do with the police, and I'm not interested in whatever business you have going with anybody. If I was police, that fat cop you're on such good terms with, he'd have shown me a little more respect."

The Creole smiled at that, and this time Horn was sure he saw gold.

"She's missing. This guy Tommy Dell, or whatever the hell his name is—I think she's with him. She's just sixteen, and he's got no right to be with

156

her." He pulled Clea's picture from his pocket and slid it across the desk. The Creole glanced down at it. If he recognized her, he gave no sign.

"Tommy and his friend, they knew I was looking for them, and they set me up in the alley. Now they're gone. I could use some help finding them."

"And if you ask the police, they wouldn't help," the Creole said lazily, yawning and stretching his arms over his head. "Because you got a record."

"He told you that too, huh? What else did he tell you?"

"Oh, that you used to act in the movies, before you get in trouble. I think I seen one or two of them. Me, I like Bob Steele. He's a scrappy little man, ain't he? Nobody punch like him. Anyway, now you fetch and carry for Joe Mad Crow over at his gambling place." He fiddled some more with the coin, then tossed it onto the desktop. It wasn't a half-dollar, it was one of the casino chips the cop had taken.

"Joseph," Horn said. "He likes Joseph."

"Man like to use his formal name, that's fine with me." The Creole slid the photo back across the desk. "Nice looking young lady," he said. "Well, I ain't the one to help you. Ain't none of my business."

"What is your business? Tommy got anything to do with it?"

The other man leaned back in his chair and half-closed his eyes, as if to show Horn he had no concerns. "My business legal, mostly, just like your

157

friend Mad Crow's place, what I hear. And this Tommy, you call him, he's legal too, mostly. If you think you got something on us, you wrong."

"I'll come back," Horn said. "Until I find him."

"Not in my club you won't." There was no threat in the voice, just fact. "You not walking inside. My boys escort you right back out. And if they don't—"

"Your friend Titus will."

"Maybe. Don't want to make it sound like he work for me, though. He just a police detective stationed down here, and he got friends all up and down this street. Sometimes he help out a friend, you know how it is."

"What about his partner? Is he your friend too?"

The Creole shrugged. "Him I don't know about."

Horn pocketed the photo and rose unsteadily. "Thanks for the tea."

"You better wash that shirt fast," the Creole said without much interest. "Blood's bad for clothes. But be sure you use cold water. My mama teach me that too."

At the door, Horn turned. "This is more than just a missing girl," he said wearily. "Friend of mine is dead too. And there's something else going on. I've learned about a bunch of men who take advantage of little girls. Have sex with them. Girls so little, you don't want to know. All this is connected, but I just don't know how."

"What are you talking about?" The Creole was staring at him, his head cocked to one side.

"I don't know how to prove—"

"About the little girls." Something flickered in the Creole's eyes. Was it interest?

"I've got pictures they took," Horn said, leaning against the door. "The girls are all different ages."

"What this got to do with your friend?"

"He had the pictures. I think he was killed because of them."

The Creole said nothing. For a moment he had seemed interested, but now Horn felt him slipping away.

"My daughter was in one of the pictures."

The Creole stared at his desktop for a moment, as if making up his mind. But when he looked up, there was nothing in his eyes. "Sorry you had a bad time here," he said. "You drive careful going home."

"You said I could help." Addie was sulking as she drove, but it was a halfhearted sulk, and she was clearly still high from the drinks and the excitement. Horn had been happy to learn she could drive. As they headed back, he leaned against the doorpost on the passenger's side, head throbbing, the bloody handkerchief crumpled in his hand. The bleeding had stopped as he talked to the Creole.

"You helped a lot," he said. "You pointed him out."

"I'm so sorry, Mr. Horn," she said. "I feel responsible, asking you to—"

159

"Don't feel bad," he said thickly through his bruised lips. "Wasn't your fault."

"You need to see a doctor. Your shirt's all bloody."

"No, I don't. This looks worse than it is. When I was bull-riding a long time ago, I broke a few bones. Nothing that bad happened to me tonight. I'm going to be real sore tomorrow, that's all."

"At least we found Tommy."

"Turn right on Broadway." He sighed. "Yeah. Lot of good it did. I need to know where the man lives. And I still don't." He closed his eyes. "I'm no closer to Clea. But at least I feel like I know this Tommy now. Maybe I'll be more ready for him next time."

They rode in silence for many blocks. Finally she stopped in front of her house.

"Thanks, Addie. I can take it the rest of the way." She got out and he slid over. "I'm not going to be in touch with you for a while. This was a little too dangerous tonight." He pointed to his shirt. "For both of us. But I appreciate your help."

"All right," she said. With the streetlight behind her, she seemed suddenly older, as if she'd grown into her glamorous outfit in the course of the night. He remembered the sight of her from across the room, laughing as she raised her whisky sour amid the smoke and the jazz.

"Good night," he said to her.

Yawning, she plucked the gardenia from her waist. "Look at this," she said with a frown. "It's already turning brown." She dropped it on the street. "Good night, Mr. Horn."

"Addie," he said, pulling away from the curb, "after all the fun we've had tonight, I think you can call me John Ray."

CHAPTER 11

The next morning, Horn filled the tub with hot water and lay there for a long time, trying to soak the soreness out of his muscles. He found ugly varicolored bruises on his ribs, shoulders, and kidneys—the last no doubt left by his adversary's departing kicks. While shaving, he inspected his swollen face. "You ought to be in pictures," he said to his reflection through swollen lips. The worst was the cut left by the sap near his right eyebrow. Now finished bleeding, it presented a dark, crusty scab. A stitch or two might help, but he didn't want to take the time to find a doctor. Instead, he placed a tightly folded rectangle of gauze over the cut and sealed it with layers of adhesive tape. Then he took a look at his shirt. The stain on the collar, and the smaller spots farther down, had darkened and stiffened. He briefly considered following the Creole's advice, then decided it was too late and tossed the shirt into the fireplace.

He had found and lost Tommy Dell and gotten a beating. Not a good scorecard for a night's work. And there was something else. Facing those two men in the alley, he had felt something stirring in him, and he knew it was the fear he had encountered in the mountains below the old monastery, the kind of bone-chilling dread that disables the mind and paralyzes the limbs. There had not been enough time in the alley for the fear to take him over, just enough for him to recognize it. This old enemy, whose face he'd last seen years before, had returned. Wherever he went now, down streets and alleys, around corners, through doorways, he knew he might find it waiting for him.

He was surprised to find his stomach rumbling, then remembered that he'd had little to eat the day before. He fried up some bacon and scrambled three eggs, and later, still hungry, he used a slice of nearly stale bread to sop up a little of the bacon grease. Then he carried his coffee cup out to the rocker. The morning was still cool, and only an occasional birdcall broke the canyon's silence.

A couple of thoughts fought for space in his mind. First, Clea was with Tommy Dell, or whatever his name was. Tommy knew Horn was looking for her, and he was ready to go to great lengths to make sure she wasn't found. The second thing had to do with the man who worked him over last night, the man with the unusual fighting skills. It wasn't the way he worked with his fists, which was merely competent. It was the graceful way he absorbed punches and rolled to his feet. Some kind of athlete, Horn thought. Like a tumbler, a gymnast, an acrobat.

A stunt man.

That was it. Over the years, Horn had watched dozens of stunt men work, some of them the best in Hollywood. Risking death or dismemberment in staging their "gags," or stunts, they needed the balance of a gymnast, the recovery skills of a tumbler, the fist work of a street fighter. They were in peak physical condition. They knew how to fight effectively and convincingly for the camera, but more important, how to fight without themselves getting hurt. How to hit the ground rolling.

The man he'd fought last night had worked in the movies, he was willing to bet—possibly still did. Knowing that he was no closer to running the elusive Tommy Dell to ground, Horn thought he just might know how to find his companion.

The telephone interrupted his thoughts. "Paul Fairbrass," the voice said without preamble. "I forgot to give you a phone number. Do you have a pencil?"

Horn wrote the number down. "This is my work number at the plant in Long Beach," Fairbrass went on. "You can reach Sykes here too. It's best if you don't call me at home. As I mentioned, I don't want to disturb Iris."

"I don't either. I found Tommy."

"What?"

"And lost him. It's a long story, but he's got somebody working with him."

"Did anything happen?"

"I got a little careless. I'll spare you the details.

But you and Sykes were right about him. He's dangerous. And something else: He knows I'm looking for Clea."

"How could he know that?"

"I don't know. Maybe someone told him."

Fairbrass was silent for a moment. "Well, it couldn't have been me."

"I'm not blaming anybody. I'm just getting more worried about her. Are the police still looking for her?"

"Yes."

"Stay on them. Tell them you heard Tommy sometimes hangs out at a place on Central Avenue called the Dixie Belle and maybe some other places down there too. I hope they find him, because I'm not sure I feel qualified to go up against this guy and his friend."

"I didn't think you'd be afraid."

Horn felt his original dislike of Paul Fairbrass returning.

"Then you were wrong."

He parked the Ford on Gower just south of Sunset, walked back to the intersection, and looked around. Up and down the street, standing in knots of two and three, leaning or sitting on cars, were men in western clothing—hats, boots, dungarees, bandannas.

This was "Gower Gulch." During the silent era, a studio had stood at the northwest corner of Sunset and Gower. Later, other small studios sprang up in the neighborhood, some that would last only a few years. Somehow, the interesection became a hangout for cowboy actors between jobs. They were not stars. Some were not really cowboys but could wear the clothes and stay in the saddle well enough to work as extras. Others were the real thing, who could ride and rope expertly and work either in front of the camera or behind the scenes as wranglers.

On Gower Gulch they socialized, drank coffee or something stronger, and swapped tales. Some even found work, when a harried low-budget producer would drive up, point to a few of the most authentic-looking, and say, "You with the hat, you with the fancy vest, you with the big belt, you with the lariat . . ."

Of the two dozen or so on the sidewalk, Horn saw only one familiar face. He started over, then stopped and decided to watch Tuck Brown for a while. The man was medium height, lean and leathery, somewhere in his mid-forties. He wore a big hat low on his face, a plain shirt, and dunga-rees rolled high up over worn boots. With his gloved right hand poised over the sidewalk, he made the free end of a lariat do a little dance, first jumping into a wide slipknot, then back out to hang loose, then back into the knot, then out again. Through it all he stood quite still, gazing off down the street, working the rope as gracefully as if he were an orchestra conductor leading his musicians through a measured, elegant waltz.

Horn laughed out loud, then walked over. Tuck Brown looked up. "Well, I'll be damned to perdition," he said. "John Ray Horn."

"Hey there, Tuck."

"It's been a while, hasn't it? You doing all right?"

"Just fine." Horn was sure Brown knew all about his troubles, but he also knew the man wasn't the sort to bring up the subject—or even mention his bruised face. He pointed at the lariat, now hanging loose. "You haven't lost your touch."

"Thank you, sir. Did I ever tell you I learned this by watching Will Rogers? He came to Kansas City once, did a stage show. I swear, that man could rope . . ."

"He was the best."

A man wearing a shirt with horses embroidered on it walked over. "I don't think there's any work for you here," he said to Horn.

"I'm not looking for work," Horn said.

"Good thing, too," the man said. He seemed ready to add something when Brown broke in.

"Don't mind him," he said to Horn, staring into the other man's face. "We two, we worked on a Hopalong Cassidy movie once. Never even learned this old boy's name, but he got his boot caught in the stirrup during his dismount once, almost broke his fool neck. After that, everybody in the chow line called him Little Hoppy."

The other man stared at Horn for a second more and walked away.

"Like I said—"

"Don't worry about it," Horn said. "Could I ask you something?"

"Sure." Brown began making the lariat dance again.

"I need to find a stunt man. I know what he looks like, but I don't know his name."

"Cowboy type?"

"No. I mean, he could be. But my guess is, he works all kinds of stunts."

"Studio?"

"I don't know which one."

"Well, that's a tall order," Brown said. "Stunt men, if they're any good, they don't hang out here much, 'cause they can get work easier than cowboys. Fact of it is, almost anybody can get work easier these days. Cowboy movies are dying. You know that, don't you? Oh, they're still making 'em, especially over at Republic and Medallion, your old outfit. But there's less and less every year. It was the war, I think. Nobody's interested in cowboys anymore, just musicals. Or these gangster movies, where it's so danged dark you can't see who's who."

"I know. So what are you going to do?"

"The missus wants me to invest in this dry cleaner's out in Van Nuys."

Horn smiled. "I can't see you doing that, Tuck. You'd miss the smell of horseshit."

"You bet I would." He speeded up the rhythm of the lariat. "Do you miss it?"

"Sometimes. Listen . . ."

168

"Oh, the guy you're looking for. Sorry, I get to rambling. Well, here's an idea. The stunt men have their own association now, kind of a union, but it's strictly local and pretty informal. There's, oh, dozens of 'em working. I got a couple of friends belong. The one who tries to keep track of the membership list is Maggie O'Dare." He looked away from Horn for a moment. "You remember Maggie, don't you?" he asked casually.

"Yes, sure I do."

"I know you been out of touch. Well, she's not in the business anymore. Got a little horse ranch out in the north Valley, where it's unincorporated. She gives riding lessons, rents out to the studios, that kind of stuff. It's called the O Bar D. Haven't seen her for a while, but we did *Bandit Girl* together, and it was fun. Say hi for me."

"Thanks, Tuck."

In the year or so since he'd gotten out, Horn had found few reasons to drive over the hill into the San Fernando Valley, the place where he'd once lived and worked. He made the drive now, taking the broad new Cahuenga Pass Parkway, gunning the car's engine northward up the grade toward the top of the pass. When the road leveled off, he saw the Valley spread out before him, and he made an involuntary noise. He was still not used to the sight.

The Valley was taking on the look of a city. Flatter, perhaps, with no skyscrapers and more space

169

between the buildings, but nonetheless a city in the making. A network of neat streets laid out in a grid, filled with well-ordered little lots each containing a one-story house. Only when he looked off into the distance did Horn see the land open up to resemble the Valley he once knew, an expanse of open land, of farms and ranches and groves of trees. He could imagine that the sea of houses was washing slowly and steadily to the north, lapping up the open land.

It was the way Mad Crow had described it, soon after Horn had gotten out of prison. The Valley, the Indian said sadly, was turning into a giant bedroom, just a place where people go when they finish working over the hill in the big city.

As he guided his car along the downslope of the pass, he saw just another California city in the making—houses, stores, schools, churches. It all looked unbearably settled, tamed . . . *civilized*. He cursed softly.

Medallion Pictures, his old workplace, was only a few miles away, but he wasn't headed there. He turned left on Ventura Boulevard and drove for half an hour, paralleling the low range of the Santa Monica Mountains that hid Hollywood and the rest of L.A. Then he swung north, and little by little the houses thinned out. After twenty minutes, orchards and ranches began to appear on either side of the road, and soon the rising bulk of two mountain ranges stood out clearly, the Santa Susanas to the left, the San Gabriels up ahead. He was almost in the foothills now, and the ranch land began to roll, dotted with big rock outcrops.

Up to the left was the Santa Susana Pass, cutting its way through the mountains. He had ridden there, sometimes spending an entire day on Raincloud, climbing higher and higher until there were no houses and all he could see was green and brown and sky. Miles to the northeast, up in the high desert, was the Devil's Punchbowl, where he and Mad Crow would go hunting deer and coyote in the winter, the ground lightly dusted with snow. And somewhere up ahead was Vasquez Rocks, where a Mexican bandit had hid out from the law a hundred years ago. It was up there in the rocks that he and the Indian had ridden against Three-Finger Teale and his outfit. A bad day, that one. He remembered the heat and the smell of gunsmoke. . . .

Horn shook his head, feeling foolish. That was a movie. *Carbine Justice*. No, wait. *Hell's Rockpile*. That was it. Not him, but Sierra Lane. Not a real memory, just a movie.

He stopped once to ask directions at an isolated gas station emblazoned with garish signs advertising everything from engine oil to cigarettes to baby powder. Before long, he spotted the sign for the O Bar D Ranch. He turned up a dirt road toward a group of buildings and parked in front of the one that most resembled a residence. It had the rough look of a bunkhouse to which someone had added a coat of paint and a row of flowering plants all along the front of the house.

No one answered his knock on the door, so he walked around to the rear. Beyond a fence he saw a man exercising a horse on a long lead. Farther out in the pasture, two riders, going at a walk, followed a trail along a fence. The big door to the stables stood open. He entered, struck at once by the cool air and by the smell, at once loamy and ammoniac, a rich mixture of manure and urine and hay and fodder and oiled leather and big animals. It was a smell he had missed.

He walked along, making out the shapes of horses in the darkened stalls and hearing their whuffling and snorting sounds. As his vision adjusted, a woman came out of one of the far stalls and headed his way, a bridle slung over her shoulder.

She saw him. "Something I can—?" she began, then broke off as she drew close enough to recognize him.

"Hello, Maggie."

She took her time looking him up and down, then finally answered. "Hello, John Ray."

"Long time."

"I'll say. You been all right?"

"Pretty much. I heard about your ranch." They walked out of the stables, and he gestured toward the pasture. "Is this all yours?"

"Yep. Or will be when I finish paying for it."

"I'm impressed." In the bright sunlight, he took a good look at her. If Iris seemed almost the same after three years, time had worked more changes on Maggie. Folks who had followed the career of Margaret O'Dare, queen of the Medallion serials, might not have recognized her right away. She wore a shapeless plaid work shirt and baggy jeans. Her dark auburn hair, which always flowed free in her movies, was pulled back tightly into a pony-tail to keep it out of the way. Without makeup over her fair skin, the freckles showed plainly on her nose and cheeks. Her features seemed softer, less angular, and fine lines now framed her eyes. She was no longer the young woman he'd first met more than ten years earlier at Medallion, when she was doing stunt work and he was on his way to becoming Sierra Lane.

Yet she still had the same long-legged horse-woman's build, hips a little on the narrow side. Her lips were still full, her eyes still clear, and the lines around them looked natural and earned. He had no trouble liking this face as much as he'd liked the other.

"Tuck Brown says hi. I found him on Gower Gulch, and he put me on to you. He's still doing rope tricks."

She smiled. "You want a cup of coffee?"

"Sure."

He sat on a sofa covered with Indian blankets in the small front room of the main house while she made coffee in the tiny kitchen. "What happened to you?" she asked over the clatter of pots. "Your face."

"It's not important."

"All right."

"Tell me about yourself."

"Well, you probably heard I got married."

"I think somebody mentioned it. Who's the lucky guy?"

"Name's David Peake," she said over the clatter in the sink. "Davey, everybody calls him. You might have heard of him. He rides the rodeo, got a couple of championship belts riding broncs last year."

"Is he around?"

"Huh-uh. He's out on the circuit. Should be in Tucson this week. He's only thirty-one, says he wants to get everything he can out of the next few years."

"You married a young stud."

"Ain't I entitled?" she said as she entered the room, using the drawl he had last heard in *Bandit Girl*.

"Sure you are. What else you been up to?"

She laid a steaming mug on a rough wood table in front of him. "Well, like I told you in the letters, I quit the movies."

"You just never said why."

"Oh, it was a bunch of things. I did love it, you know. I had almost ten wonderful years. I worked with good people and made good money, and I sure liked all the attention. Every time somebody asked me for an autograph, I swear that for just a second I couldn't believe they meant me. Did I tell you I met the Duke of Windsor?"

174

"No."

"He was visiting over here after the war, and he came out to the set with the mayor one day. *Mask of Monterrey*, it was. That's him and me in that picture on the wall."

"You look like you're having a good time. What did you two talk about?"

"Oh . . . how to fall out of the saddle without getting hurt. Who's best at jumping, us or the English. You know, your usual elegant tea-party conversation." She smiled. "The Duke of Windsor. For a little girl from Arizona, that's about the ultimate."

"So why'd you quit?"

"For one thing, the injuries were piling up. Especially that time I chipped my spine when I did that fall from the car. We were shooting *The Secret Code* down in Long Beach. That one stayed with me for a while." She blew into her coffee cup. "There were younger actresses coming along at Medallion, and Bernie Rome was using them in the kind of pictures I was good at. Bernie Junior told me once I could work more if I would just put out." She laughed softly. "I left and slammed his door, broke one of the panes in it. You know, I try never to think ill of man nor beast. But for a few seconds there, I was glad you'd broken the little shit's jaw."

"Me too."

"I suppose I was finally getting tired of it. So one day, it was a week or so before we were supposed to start shooting another fifteen-chapter epic—with me in some kind of leopard-skin thing—

I realized that my contract was up for renewal. I told Junior to get one of his starlets. I was done."

"Good for you."

"I bought this place, and God, do I love it," she said. "Got a couple dozen quarter horses and three or four hands, depending on how busy we are. People rent horses from me, take them out on the back roads. Some of them bring their kids here for riding lessons. When a studio's shooting something with a lot of horses, they can lease some from me. Business is all right."

"I'm glad for you, Maggie," he said. He studied her as she leaned back in her blanket-covered chair, her boots up on the table. The hands that framed her coffee mug were graceful and strong, their backs freckled like her face. *There was a time*, he thought, *when I knew just where all those freckles ended.*

"So, are you married?" she asked.

"Nope. Once was enough."

"Not for Iris, what I hear." She caught his look. "I shouldn't have said that. Now you tell me about you. What have you been up to?"

"Since I got out? Working for Mad Crow."

"Gambling?"

"More like bookkeeping."

"Oh." She didn't sound convinced.

"I haven't had a chance to thank you for the letters," he said. "They meant a lot. I'm sorry I only answered a few, but—"

"Well, if you'd have answered more, I would've

written more," she said. "And I'm still holding your things for you. Pick 'em up any time you want." Noting his confused look, she laughed and said, "You forgot? It's a trunk full of odds and ends you'd left with Joseph, but when he was building his new place he ran out of storage space and asked me to take it."

"I clean forgot, Maggie," he said. "I guess it's all old stuff I don't need anymore. But thanks for hanging on to it. Anyway, the reason I'm here, I need a favor." He took a few minutes to describe his search for Clea and what he had found out so far. To keep it simple, he omitted any mention of Scotty or old man Bullard, or the photos.

"So I think this guy does stunt work, or used to," he summarized. "Tuck told me you've got the list of all the stunt men in town. Can I look through it?"

She gazed at him evenly, as if trying to read his intent. He thought he knew what was on her mind: Was he there only because she could help him? He didn't want her to think that.

But if she felt hurt, it didn't show. "You bet," she said with a smile, getting up and reaching for something high on a shelf. She handed it across the table to him, a clipboard thick with pages. "I think they elected me to this job because I'm the only one who has the patience for it," she said. "Each one has several pages, with vital statistics and work history. Most have a photo too. They're alphabetical. More coffee?"

He began leafing through the pages while she refilled his cup. Then she sat quietly as he looked. Some of the faces were familiar to him, men he'd worked with while making dozens of westerns at Medallion. A few of the faces were female.

He was about three-quarters of the way through when he spotted the man. The face that stared up at him was clean-shaven, but there was no mistaking it. Expressionless as it had been in the alley the night before, the face looked vaguely menacing, the cords in the neck visible. Horn felt an ache in his kidneys and silently cursed the man.

"Something?" Maggie asked him.

"Something," he said.

CHAPTER 12

Horn eased the Ford down the dirt slope, stopped under the shade of a big valley oak, and set the brake. A few dozen yards downhill stood a row of equipment trucks and trailers, and beyond them the shooting location, a valley of high grass and big trees and abrupt, knobby hills, all crisscrossed by a network of dirt trails.

This was the southeastern corner of the Medallion Ranch, where the studio shot most of its rural scenes. Horn had ridden after many a villain in this valley, cut off many a runaway buckboard bearing a gingham-dressed leading lady, defended many a stagecoach against marauding Indians or masked desperadoes. "If they saved up the gunpowder in all those caps we popped," Mad Crow had said to him once, "we could have invaded Mexico."

Although the ranch had hosted hundreds of westerns, it had also played as backdrop for Nazi spies, French musketeers, and invading Mongols. Today, Horn knew, it was the location for a sequence in one of the studio's many serials, *Air Ace and the*

Ray of Death. By making a few inquiries, Maggie had determined that the stunt man Horn sought was working here today.

His name was Gabriel Falco. Maggie's file on him was not much help. He was thirty-three and from New York City and had done stunt work for several studios around town, notably Republic and Medallion. The last association newsletter she had mailed out to him had come back with no forwarding address.

The sun had been up for an hour or so. Horn noted some activity clustered around a canvas-sided truck out on the valley's main dirt road. But it didn't look as if anything important was going to happen in the next few minutes.

Coming here involved risk, he knew. His muscles and face still ached, and the prospect of encountering Falco again made his stomach flutter unpleasantly. But finding the man could bring him one step closer to Clea. He decided to go ahead, be careful, and not waste time worrying about the consequences.

He walked down the slope and along the row of vehicles. He wore his hat pulled low, hoping he'd spot his man before the other got a look at him. He noticed a few familiar faces among the crew, and one or two of the men appeared to recognize him, but there were no greetings. After a minute, he found the director sitting at a work table under an awning stretched out from the side of a trailer. "Hello, Dex," he said quietly.

The other man looked up. "Hello, John Ray," he said after only a second's hesitation.

"How you been?"

Dexter Diggs had a square face and a stocky build and wore khakis and a hunting vest over a canvas work shirt. Years before, he had written and directed big-budget features during the silent era and had been a man with a future. But he liked the bottle too much and lost a series of jobs before landing at Medallion, where he became known as an all-purpose director of B-pictures. Diggs obviously knew he was doing hack work, but he always tried to turn out a respectable product, on time and under budget. He never yelled at his actors. Horn liked him.

"Oh, you know," Diggs said, pushing to one side the script he had been reading. "Still managing to fool 'em." He looked Horn up and down, as if to measure the man he saw against his memories.

"You mind if I watch you shoot today?"

"Ah, well, that might be a problem."

"Nobody has to know," Horn said with what he hoped was an ingratiating grin.

"Father and Son are coming over this morning to watch," Diggs said. "You know what that means. You're not supposed to be around here."

"Look, Dex, I don't want to get you in trouble. I won't hang around for the shoot, all right? Just help me out a little for a minute. I need to find out something about one of your boys, Gabriel Falco. I hear he's working today."

181

Diggs looked toward the truck out on the main road as he drummed his fingers on the script. Finally he indicated a folding camp chair next to the table, and Horn sat down. "I don't want to be rude," the director said. "But I don't want to lose my job either."

"I know."

"I'm glad to see you back. You working?"

"Uh-huh. I'm doing a little work for Mad Crow."

"That's good," Diggs said without much enthusiasm. "Joseph's come a long way since he was working around here, wearing buckskins and talking bad English. He's going to wind up richer than all of us."

"Wouldn't surprise me."

"You, uh, got any other irons in the fire?"

"You mean is anybody offering me honest work? Come on, Dex, you know nobody's hiring me, not after Mr. Rome put out the word to all the studios. I take what I can get, and I can't afford to be picky."

"I'm sorry about what happened. We all are."

Horn shrugged, wanting the subject to go away. "About this Falco?"

"Yeah. He's my lead stunt man on this thing."

"Is he around right now?"

"He was earlier, but now he's over at the air strip, getting ready for this shot. This is his only scene today. You know Air Ace?"

Horn shook his head.

"We got him from the comics. The kids are crazy

about this character. He flies planes, chases spies, that sort of thing. Rod Blakeley's the hero. You remember him. This morning we're shooting the big scene in Chapter Five. Master shot; I'll do the inserts back on the lot tomorrow. It's a transfer, and this guy Falco's doubling for Rod."

"Hell, I used to do those myself, without stunt man's pay," Horn said with a laugh. "You remember? Horse to train, horse to buckboard, horse to stagecoach . . ."

"This transfer's a little different," Diggs said. "Plane to truck."

"Really?"

"No kidding. Hero climbs down a rope ladder from the plane, jumps into a speeding truck. They're gonna love it."

Horn whistled through his teeth. "Wish I could see that." Then, seeing the look on the director's face: "Like I said, I won't stick around. But what do you know about this Falco?"

Diggs looked at his watch. "Enough to know I wouldn't want him mad at me. He's the best stunt man I've ever worked with. Absolutely no fear. But off camera . . . I don't know. He's cold as ice. You know how scuttlebutt spreads around a studio. Word about this guy is he did time for armed robbery back east. One story says he beat a man to death in prison, but they never proved it. I wouldn't find that hard to believe. Whatever reason you have for asking questions about him, I hope you're careful."

"I will be," Horn said. "How's the work going?"

"Oh, it's not like when I was directing Gloria Swanson and that gang. But it's regular. You wouldn't recognize things, though."

"How so?"

"No more westerns, at least not the kind you'd recognize. I haven't shot one in almost a year. Funny thing happened: The big studios discovered 'em. Over at Fox, John Ford lined up Henry Fonda for one of his. And Howard Hawks is shooting one with Montgomery Clift. You imagine Monty Clift on a horse? Anyway, everybody takes westerns very seriously now. They're not fun anymore, and nobody's interested in the cheap kind we do. They don't want a hero who carries a guitar or wears fringe on his shirt."

Horn looked disgusted. "I never did any of that."

Diggs laughed. "Couldn't see your shirt for all the dust. Sierra Lane always looked like he just finished a hundred-mile cattle drive."

"Horn!"

They looked down the row of trailers to see the diminutive figure of Bernie Rome Jr. advancing on them, his face twisted into something ugly. Close behind him was his father.

As the two men reached the tent, Horn came quickly out of his chair, sending it to the ground behind him. Reaching across the table, he grabbed the script and flung it into Diggs's chest. "Go to hell," he said loudly. "I don't need a job around this place."

"You!" Rome yelled, stopping about ten feet away. "Somebody get the police."

"Never mind, I'm leaving," Horn said, brushing past the smaller man. "Your puppy dog there doesn't feel like helping an old friend, so to hell with both of you."

For one second he locked eyes with Bernie Rome Jr., who stood there with clenched fists and reddened face. Horn hadn't seen him since the trial. Junior was a little fleshier but otherwise unchanged. He still affected the dress of a rich sportsman, down to the ascot at his throat. In a quick image, like a single frame of film, Horn glimpsed the man's bloodied face under him, felt the impact of his knuckles on bone. He expected the old hatred to wash over him, blind him, as it had on that day three years earlier. But he felt nothing.

Ignoring him, Horn turned to go, stopping briefly in front of Bernard Rome—*Mister Rome* to his employees—who, as always, was dressed in an immaculate dark suit. The older man's eyes were expressionless behind thick glasses, the fringe of hair around his bald head whiter than Horn remembered. As Horn walked away, he heard the studio chief's son shouting again for the police and Diggs reply, "He's leaving, Bernie."

Horn walked to his car, backed out of the trees, and took the dirt access road farther into the valley until he came to a smaller road that wound up a mountainside. He drove slowly for about ten minutes, the Ford laboring up the steep, rutted road, until he came to a smooth, rounded-off clearing encircled by trees and underbrush. This was Dome Rock, a popular location for the studio because of its panoramic view.

Horn pulled a pair of Army-surplus binoculars from under the car seat, rested them on a rock, and trained them down toward where Diggs's crew was visible. He could see most of the valley, and he wanted to watch Gabriel Falco at work.

The sun was higher now, the day growing hotter. The dry, sage-scented air parched his throat, and he wished he had brought some water. He swept the valley with the binoculars every few minutes, and soon Diggs's boys appeared busier. People climbed into the cab of the canvas-sided truck, and a few seconds later a smaller film truck—outfitted with a rear platform for the 35-millimeter camera along with the director and his assistants—pulled out into the road ahead of it. The film truck was swarming with people. Then he saw a figure he recognized as Diggs climb aboard, and soon thereafter both trucks began moving slowly in Horn's direction. He moved the binoculars up and could make out the speck of an airplane. It grew larger, and then he heard the sound of it. The plane was a twin-engine with a silver fuselage, and it came in just above stall speed, descending gradually until it was about fifty feet off the ground.

A door in the side of the plane opened, and a rope ladder was flung out, whipping wildly in the wind. Then a man came out the door and began descending the ladder. He wore boots and jodhpurs and some kind of jacket along with a flight helmet with goggles and a white scarf around his neck. An outlandish outfit for a flyer today, Horn thought, but just right for the hero of a fifteen-chapter serial aimed at any twelve-year-old boy who had a quarter for the ticket. The man descended lower and lower on the ladder until he was just above the truck, which was moving fast now, but the road was uneven and the truck bounced and pitched. The man on the ladder abruptly rose and dipped as the pilot fought to maintain a steady altitude. At one point the ladder swung inward, slamming the stunt man against the side of the truck, but he recovered. Then it all came together and the man saw his chance. Just as the plane began to pull ahead, dragging the man out of range, the ladder dipped one more time, and he found himself level with the driver's-side door of the truck. He reached out, caught the door, swung himself over onto the running board, then wrenched the door open, grabbed the driver, and extracted him neatly, tossing him onto the road. In an instant he was inside the cab of the truck.

Horn whistled to himself. It was a daring stunt. Not crazy, but almost. He felt a grudging respect for the man who'd battered him the other night.

He watched both trucks come to a halt. The scene was finished, and since this had been Falco's only job of the day, he was probably getting ready to leave. There was always the possibility of a retake, Horn knew, but Dexter Diggs was known as a director who seldom needed retakes.

Horn drove carefully down the hillside and then out the main gate of the ranch and onto the rural road that led back to L.A. About a half-mile down the road was a gas station. Just beyond the pumps, he pulled over. He walked back to the station, fished a grape soda out of the ice chest and paid for it, then took it to the car, where he adjusted his rearview mirror and waited.

It took his man about twenty minutes. Horn saw him coming and, averting his face, had the engine started up as the other car passed, but he waited a while before pulling out onto the road. There was little traffic, so at first he trailed behind by a hundred yards or so. Then, as traffic picked up, Horn moved up closer. Falco was driving a dusty, cream-colored De Soto coupe. He drove it fast and expertly, and Horn had to be careful to keep the proper distance. They went south through the Valley and took Laurel Canyon up into the hills, where Horn could look back the way he had come and see much of the San Fernando Valley laid out like a giant game board, with a few prominent pieces jutting up in the foreground and great stretches of the board unoccupied in the distance. They crossed Mulholland Drive at the summit and headed down the twisting road toward the city.

A couple of miles past the crest, Horn saw his quarry turn off onto a narrow street to the right past a sign marked *Dead End.* He slowed, then eased forward just in time to see the car disappearing up a driveway. He drove slowly up the side road until he could see the De Soto parked in front of a large stone house with a dark shingled roof. Two other cars were parked there. A well-tended, medium-sized lawn sloped down to an iron fence that encircled the property. Horn made note of the address.

He drove back to the main road and parked on the dirt shoulder just above the intersection, facing downhill. He was fairly sure this wasn't the home of a low-paid studio employee. Did it belong to the young man who called himself Tommy Dell? He decided to wait and see what Falco did next.

Horn rolled down all the windows to coax some fresh air into the car. To make himself less visible, he slid over to the passenger side, pulled his hat low, and leaned against the door. He was hungry. In his glove compartment he found a half-finished bag of peanuts. They tasted good but made him thirsty, and he quickly finished the rest of the grape soda.

The afternoon wore on, and the car smelled of hot upholstery. As the sun dipped behind the side of the canyon to his right, the air in the car cooled somewhat.

Patience had never been one of Horn's strengths, but two years at Cold Creek had taught him the value of waiting, of knowing the difference between trying to shape events and letting events take shape on their own. It was a kind of grudging, acquired patience that now was helping him deal with his current condition, a time of little money and no pride.

But sitting in his car, thinking of Scotty murdered and Clea in the company of a dangerous man, frustration began to take over. He felt powerless, miles away from Clea, and he denounced himself for knowing no better way to find her. *Sierra Lane would have done this job days ago,* he thought drowsily. *Would have kicked some asses, brought the girl back to her folks, waved goodbye, and giddyupped right on over the hill. Real life's just a little more complicated, ain't it, cowboy?*

Hours later the canyon darkened, and the headlights of passing cars played up and down the road. Horn's mind was beginning to drift, on the verge of dozing, when through half-open eyes he saw a car pull out from the side road in front of him. It was Falco. Instead of heading down toward the city, the car spun left, throwing gravel, and accelerated up toward Mulholland. Traffic was busy, and as Horn started the engine, three more cars passed him behind the De Soto. He turned around and followed.

He had already lost sight of the De Soto's taillights, and because of oncoming cars and the narrow, twisting road, there was no way he could pass. Over the crest and back down toward the

Valley he went, squinting into the road ahead. He saw an opening and passed one car, then a second, ignoring their outraged horn-blowing. Far down the hill was a pair of disappearing taillights, and he knew it must be the De Soto. Leaning into a hard left turn, he accelerated—but felt the wheel jerk in his hands as a loud noise rocked the car, and he fought to keep the wheel from pulling him off the road and down a dark ravine. He jammed on the brakes, and the car limped onto the shoulder as other cars raced by.

He got out and walked around, teeth clenched, knowing what he'd find. *It's almost bald*, the pump jockey had told him about the right rear tire the other day. Now it was a mess, tire and inner tube blown out. He yelled out a curse and kicked the tire. He heard a derisive honk of the horn and loud laughter from a passing jalopy loaded with youngsters.

Once again, as on Central Avenue, he had found his man and lost him. But this time he had an address. Someone's address.

CHAPTER 13

"You could have told me over the phone," Horn said to Douglas Greenleaf as they sat at a lunch counter in a cafe on Highland Avenue, not far from Hollywood High School. The waitresses wore pink aprons and pink caps, and they expertly balanced burgers and hot dogs and french fries on trays as they threaded their way among the tables. The place resounded with the cries of high schoolers on their lunch hour.

"This is too important for the phone." The young man bit into his ham sandwich and gestured for the ketchup, which he poured liberally over his potato salad. "You should never pass sensitive information over the phone."

"Is that what they tell you in that correspondence course?"

Douglas nodded, wiping his mouth with the paper napkin. "I'm on the last round."

"And then you'll be a private detective."

"No, but I'll have the book work out of the way. Then I'll get a job with a real investigator, and work my way up from there."

"Sure. Samuel Greenleaf Spade." Probably the

smartest of Mad Crow's nephews, Douglas was in his mid-twenties. Asthma had kept him out of the war, but Horn noted that he was wearing his favorite Eisenhower jacket with the Fifth Army patch on the shoulder. When Horn had first known him before the war, he was a kid just off the reservation, come to join his relatives in the big city. Now he was older but still a kid, thin and hungry, full of questions, wanting to make his mark. He was already a whiz at gathering information. Horn enjoyed his company.

"So give me the sensitive dope."

"Okay," Douglas said, lowering his voice. "That guy you chased the other night, the address where he wound up? The house belongs to Vincent Bonsigniore."

"Yeah?"

"You know the name?"

"I think so," Horn said slowly. "Just don't know from where."

"You've seen it in the paper. They usually call him 'the mobster.' He runs rackets in L.A. for the New York syndicate."

"That's right, now I remember. He has some kind of nickname."

"Vinnie B," Douglas said dramatically, talking out of the side of his mouth as he motioned the waitress over to refill his lemonade glass. He loved the movies, and it sometimes spilled over into his behavior. *You've seen too many Jimmy Cagney movies,* Horn once said to him, and Douglas took it as a compliment.

"What do you know about him?"

"He came out here about twenty years ago," Douglas said before taking a long swig of the lemonade. "My contact with the police—"

"Your brother-in-law Charlie," Horn prompted.

"Well, yeah. He says Vinnie makes money off of whorehouses and protection, but his real thing is gambling. He was one of the owners of the Rex, the old gambling ship that used to float off Long Beach, outside the three-mile limit. He runs off-track betting on the races at Santa Anita. And he's starting up small gambling houses here and there around the county, in the unincorporated areas or in towns where he can buy his way in. And a lot of the money gets sent back east. Charlie says the L.A. cops—the honest ones, anyway—have had their eye on him for a long time, but he keeps a low profile, and a lot of his business is legitimate. He owns one of the two or three biggest liquor distributorships in town.

"They raid his places now and then, but they arrest the little guys, and they've never been able to stick him with anything. He likes to sit back and let flashy types like Mickey Cohen get all the attention. You know that bomb that went off in Mickey's apartment awhile back? Charlie says it was probably Vinnie's boys that did it, but nobody can prove it."

"What about Falco?"

"His name has come up a few times. He's got a record, mostly strongarm stuff, but not in

California. Only been in town four or five years. They think he works for Vinnie occasionally. Since they both came out here from New York, it would make sense."

"What about the guy who runs the Dixie Belle?"

"The Creole," Douglas said dramatically. "I like that. Real name Alphonse Doucette. He has a record too. Why doesn't that surprise me? All these characters you hang out with nowadays—"

"My new friends," Horn said. "Ever since I did time, this is the kind of company I like best. They're a lot more real than all you law-abiding folks."

"Yeah. Anyway, this Doucette . . . he had a couple of convictions back in Louisiana, both of them involving a straight razor he carried in his shoe and the rivals for the affections of one young lady or another. Funny when you think about it, 'cause he shouldn't have gotten a liquor license in L.A. County. But it seems he has a friend or two in the police department."

"I think I met one of them the other night. Did you ask Charlie about Tommy Dell?"

"Yeah. Nothing. But if it's not his real name anyway—"

"I know," Horn said. "But I had to try. He's the one I really want. I don't know if any of this gets me any closer to him."

Seeing Douglas's disappointed look, Horn squeezed his arm. "Thanks, though. This is a big help." He put some money on the table. "My treat."

"I could tell you a little more about Vinnie in

New York," Douglas said. "The life of a young thug."

"Not unless it helps me find Tommy," Horn sighed as he rose to leave. "And I doubt if it will."

"Probably right." Douglas followed him out onto the street. "He's had a kind of charmed life, though. Even when he was busting heads for the big guys, he only got arrested a few times, and never for killing anybody. Public drunkenness, sex with a minor, stuff like that."

Horn was beginning to pull his car keys out of his pocket, but he stopped. "Say that again. Sex with a minor?"

"Yeah. Sex with a young girl, they called it. Really young, actually. Something like twelve. They eventually dropped the charges, Charlie says, when the girl's mother decided she wasn't going to testify. They think she might have been bought off or threatened or something like that. What's the matter?"

"Nothing." He grabbed the young man's hand and shook it. "Thanks, Douglas. I owe you."

Horn turned the radio up as he drove toward home, humming along to Charlie Barnett's *Cherokee*. He was excited. He still felt as far away from Clea as ever, and he still didn't know how Tommy Dell figured in this, or in fact if she was even with him. But something had slid into place today. He now wondered if Vincent Bonsigniore— Vinnie B, the gangster who had once molested a child in New York—might be one of the older men in the stack of photos Scotty had given him. If so, it took no great leap of the imagination to conclude that Bonsigniore could have ordered Scotty's murder when it began to appear that the events that had occurred in the hunting lodge might be made public. Even with their faces shrouded in hoods, the men who had assembled at the lodge must have feared what would happen if the photos found their way outside that small circle.

Now Horn had the photos. Could they know it, and could they even now be making plans for him? For that matter, how had they known that Scotty had the photos?

His free hand beat lightly on the roof of the car in time with the music, but his thoughts were elsewhere. How could anyone have known Scotty had them? They almost would have had to see him search his father's office. Or at least have known that he was there. And how could they have known? Maybe by speaking to someone who saw him there.

He pulled over to the curb and turned off the radio. The cleaning woman. The one who tried to enter the office while Horn and Scotty sat at the desk with the photos spread over the desktop.

He turned the car around and headed for downtown. It was midafternoon when he parked near the Braly Building and walked into the lobby. The guard at the desk looked up.

"Sir?"

"Hello," Horn said, putting on an earnest and frazzled look. "I was in here the other day to pick

197

up a delivery for the mayor's office. I had to go up to the tenth floor, and when I left, I didn't take along part of the delivery, some architect's drawings. My boss—he's in the city attorney's office—called over here, but they told him the drawings weren't around. Said because they just looked like rolled-up paper, they might have gone out in the trash last night. I was told to talk to the cleaning woman who worked up there. Do you know her?"

The guard looked at him without much interest. "I didn't see you," he said.

"I walked right past you," Horn said with a grin. "Bunch of people in the lobby, but I knew where I was supposed to go, so I went right up. Look," he went on, "this is really important. I'm not going to say I could lose my job over this, but . . ." He finished with a helpless gesture. "Can you help me out?"

"That's probably Greta," the guard said. "I can't pronounce her last name, and you're lucky if you can understand half of what she says."

"Greta. That's a big help. Know where I can find her?"

The guard looked over at the lobby clock. "In about two hours, you'll find her waltzing right through that door."

Horn walked over to Pershing Square and sat on one of the benches facing the Biltmore Hotel, trying to decide what to do when he saw the cleaning woman, how to approach her, what to say. The square carried its usual complement of office workers, panhandlers, preachers, lecturers,

198

and loonies. Under a palm tree stood two white-robed disciples of Sister Aimee's Church of the Foursquare Gospel handing out leaflets in front of a wide banner that read: *You Can Smell the Roses; Can You Smell the Brimstone?*

The ornate facade of the Biltmore loomed over the west side of the square. It was there, they said, that an aspiring actress named Elizabeth Short had been glimpsed alive for the last time before she walked off into the night. The next time she appeared, it was as a sad, mutilated thing, some butcher having dealt her the ultimate indignity by carefully severing her body, leaving the bled-dry halves on display in a vacant lot.

His mind strayed to Clea, and he shook his head fiercely, not wanting to go down that trail. *She's not dead,* he thought, *just lost. I will find her and put things right. Not for another man's money, but for her sake. And mine.*

At the end of an hour, he walked over to a cafe that fronted the north side of the square, ordered coffee and a cinnamon bun, and nursed both until it was time to head back to the office building. He moved the Ford, parking it between the main entrance and the nearest bus stop, and waited.

Just before five o'clock, he saw her coming. He hadn't been sure he'd recognize her after the brief glimpse he'd had that night, but he knew her—the gray hair under a kerchief, shapeless dress, and sturdy shoes. She carried a large bundle wrapped in brown paper.

He got out and approached her. "Greta?" he said, lightly taking her by the elbow. "Hi. May I talk to you? The guard in the lobby told me you were working tonight."

She looked fearful, pulled back from him a little. He plunged ahead. "You don't know me. I made a pickup here yesterday, and I think I may have left part of it behind. They tell me it may have gone out in the trash." He laughed at the idiocy of it all. "I'd sure appreciate it if I could just explain—" He was guiding her toward the car, opening the door. She seemed genuinely alarmed now and tried to shake him off. "It won't take a minute," he said, increasing the pressure on her arm until she was forced to sit down. "It's all right," he said loudly as he closed the door, his eyes scanning the passers-by to see if they had noticed anything. "Just take a minute."

He walked around quickly and got in. She sat quietly, staring ahead, her bundle huge in her lap. He read her quickly as a woman of little education and not much English. He decided to lean on her.

"Do you recognize me, Greta?" he asked.

She looked at him briefly and uneasily and shook her head. He couldn't tell if she was lying or not, and it didn't really matter.

"I was in Mr. Bullard's office the other night. With his son, Scott. You walked in on us, wanted to clean the place. He asked you to come back later. Remember?"

She said nothing.

"Don't lie to me, Greta. I'll know if you lie. So will the police."

"Police?" It was her first word, heavily accented. *She might be German*, he thought. *If so, she hasn't had an easy time the last few years, no matter where she was.*

"Police," he repeated. "I need to ask you a few questions. When I'm finished, I'll let you go to work and never bother you again. But if you lie to me, I'm going straight to the police, and you can deal with them." *What bullshit*, he thought. *But with her it might work.*

"I do nothing wrong." The skin around her jaws was slack and colorless. There was no telling her age. It would be easy to feel sorry for her. But not now.

"Greta, do you know what happened to Mr. Bullard just two days after you saw him?"

Something like terror flickered over her face, and he knew he was on the right track. "So here's my question," he said. "And I can find out even if you lie to me." *You're sounding like a broken record.* "Did you tell anybody that you saw Scotty—Mr. Bullard—in his father's office?"

She hesitated so long he was about to threaten her again. Then, in a soft voice, she said, "Smitty."

"Who's Smitty?"

"My supervisor."

"When did you tell him?"

"The next day."

"What did he say?"

"Nothing."

"Who else did you tell?"

She exhaled loudly, clutching her bundle, and he could smell the tobacco on her breath. "A man."

"Do you know who he was?"

She shook her head. "He come around the next day, asking if anyone been in the office, if anything been taken out."

"And you told him you saw us?"

She nodded.

"Why?"

She made no answer. "Don't make me wait, Greta," he said, his voice rising. Her breath caught in her throat, and she began to sob quietly. He fought the urge to feel pity for her. "Why?" he demanded again.

"He give me five dollars."

"So you told him who was in the office. Did you know who I was?"

She shook her head, sniffling.

"Did you describe me?"

She shook her head vigorously. "I didn't see you good."

"What else did you tell him?"

"Nothing."

"Someone went through the desk drawers not long after I was in that office. Do you know about that?"

She nodded. "I tell Smitty about that too." Her breathing sounded labored.

Scotty had told him that someone had broken into old man Bullard's desk within a few hours after he and Scotty had sat there. Whoever it was, he found nothing, and so he came back the following day to question Greta.

"Is that all?"

She nodded.

"Now tell me: What did he look like?"

She seemed to be thinking, possibly trying to find the words. "Dark hair. Same size as most other men. On his face—" She held a finger under her nose, the way people used to satirize Hitler.

"A mustache?"

"Mustache."

Sounds like Falco, he thought with a kind of grim satisfaction. *And Greta, do you know you've got some responsibility for what happened to my friend?* He wanted to say that to her, but his anger felt dried up now. Whoever deserved it, it certainly wasn't this defeated and pitiable woman who scrubbed floors for wages.

He walked around, opened her door, and helped her out. "Thank you, Greta," he said, the hardness gone out of his voice. He handed her a couple of dollars—not much on the bribery scale, he thought. "You get on to work now, and I'll try not to bother you any more." He watched her walk slowly away. *Nice work, Horn.*

On his way home, he stopped for dinner just east of Santa Monica. Before placing his order, he went over to the restaurant's pay phone. It was time to check in with Paul Fairbrass. He tried dialing the number, but the operator came on the line and told him a call to Long Beach had to go through her, so he asked her to ring it. Since it was after hours, he wasn't surprised when no one answered the phone at Fairbrass Pipe Fittings. He hesitated to call him at home, knowing Fairbrass wanted to keep Iris out of this. But much had happened since they had met, and even though Clea was still among the missing, her father was entitled to some current information. Horn had no idea if Falco or his employer was any threat to Iris or her husband— most likely, they were not. But if Fairbrass chose to take any precautions, he should probably do so sooner rather than later. And so, there were things he needed to know.

Horn dialed the home number, and Iris answered.

"It's John Ray," he said. "Sorry if I'm bothering you. Just wonder if I could have a word with your husband."

"Hello," she said, sounding almost glad to hear from him. "Paul's not here. He had to go to Chicago for a few days."

"I guess it can wait. Hope I didn't—"

"If it's about Clea, you could tell me."

"I don't know if that's a good idea."

"Please, John Ray. I know Paul's been talking to you. He wants to protect me, but this isn't the way to do it. If you've found out anything, don't you think I should hear it?"

"I haven't found her. I'm sorry. Are the police still looking?"

"I suppose," she said, and he could hear the nervous exhalation of cigarette smoke into the mouthpiece. "But they're not being very encouraging. One of them told me that children run away every day, and if they haven't committed any crime, the police can't devote a lot of energy to finding them."

"Well, I wish I could say something encouraging. But—"

"Have you found out anything at all?" She drew out the vowel sounds the way she sometimes did when she was drinking. *If she is, she has good reason,* he thought.

"A few things." *She doesn't know about Tommy and his fondness for knives, and I'm not going to be the one to tell her.* "Just little pieces, you know? I'm hoping I'll get lucky."

"If you called Paul, you must have something to report."

"Come on, Iris." He was beginning to get angry. "You left me, you took her away from me, and you've tried to keep me out of this from the beginning, even though you know there's no one who wants to get Clea back more than I do. When your husband recruited me, he said it was a deal between the two of us. If you want to know what's going on, ask him."

Over the line, he heard the breath catch in her throat. The sound surprised him, because Iris wasn't a woman who cried often. It was one of the things he'd admired about her.

"Oh, God," she said softly. "I just want her home."

"I know," he said. "I'll do what I can. Promise."

"You know, for days now, I've been thinking: Wouldn't it be nice if she were home for her birthday? I have a present sitting on her bed, all wrapped—"

"Her birthday. It's today, isn't it? I'd forgotten." He turned around, looked out the window, and saw that the sky was almost dark. It was Clea's birthday. "Iris? I have to go."

CHAPTER 14

In ten minutes he was at Ocean Avenue. Far below the Palisades and stretching out to the horizon, the great bulk of the Pacific was gray-black in the fading light. Streetlights were on, and signs lit up one by one along the avenue, advertising the small hotels, the bars and seafood joints.

Below him was the Santa Monica Pier, an avenue of dancing lights suspended over the water, the illuminated outline of its Ferris wheel bright against the sky. He drove down to the pier, parked, and followed other summer-evening strollers out onto the boardwalk. Clea had always liked this place, and he had last been here just days before, on one of his trips in search of her. But this time felt different. Each birthday, she had wanted to celebrate at the carousel.

She was older now, of course, possibly too old for brightly painted make-believe horses. Horn wondered if he was only being wishful—imagining Clea coming to a place like this just as she had as a little girl, in search of a little girl's pleasures. It helped him avoid thinking of her being with men. One man in particular.

As he approached the circular building housing the carousel, he saw that it was dark and shuttered. On the entrance hung a sign: CLOSED FOR REPAIRS.

"Well, hell and damnation," he muttered. He looked around, unwilling to give up so easily. Not far away stood a young couple sipping on iced drinks. The girl looked about Clea's age.

"Hey," he said.

"Hi, there," said the boy.

"Got a question. I'm from out of town, and my date's supposed to meet me here. Said she wanted to go for a ride on the merry-go-round, and the darn thing's closed. So I've got to take her someplace else. Any ideas?"

The boy stared at him. *I know what you're thinking,* Horn said to him silently. *I'm too old to have a girlfriend who rides the merry-go-round. So go ahead and say it.*

"Well," the boy said finally, "just about every pier around here's got one."

"Right. So which one's the best?"

"You mean after this one? I don't know. . . . The one at Lick's Pier is good, because they play swing, not a lot of old organ music. But I think the one at the Pike down in Long Beach is my favorite, because it's the biggest and the fastest. Friend of mine fell off once." He snorted. "Most of the guys like that one."

"Thanks." Horn glanced over at the girl. "You agree?"

"No," she said. "I like the one at Ocean Park Pier."

"How come?"

"The horses," she said. "They're just . . . *beautiful.*"

Ocean Park Pier was a short drive away, on the boundary between Santa Monica and Venice. By the time he got there, the pier was a circus midway, throbbing with light and music and the sounds of a crowd of people out for a good time on a breezy summer night. Halfway down the pier stood the sea-serpent shape of the roller coaster, and the screams of the riders rose to a crescendo, faded, then rose again.

The carousel was lively and crowded, the recorded organ music belting out *Hindustan*. He stood and watched for a few minutes. The horses were fine examples of the woodcarver's art—eyes staring, nostrils flaring, legs rearing, tendons straining. They bucked and pranced in their circular dance, and the kids, along with some grown-ups, clung to them, managing to look both silly and proud.

He scanned the crowd and the riders, trying hard not to expect to see Clea. After a while, the smell of grilled meat spilling in from the boardwalk reminded him that he'd had to postpone dinner. He went outside and bought a hot dog and an orange soda, then walked down to the end of the pier, where he stood and ate and watched the crowd for about twenty minutes. Then he started back past the fortune teller's booth, the cotton candy stand, the guess-your-weight man, the target-shooting booth.

Nearly overhead, the screams of the roller-coaster riders reached a shriek, and he looked up at the cars streaking earthward, the people wailing like lost souls headed straight for perdition. When he lowered his eyes, he saw Clea coming toward him.

She was with a man. Horn ducked his head and strode quickly over to a souvenir booth, where he dropped to one knee and pretended to tie a shoelace. He watched as she passed. She was holding onto Tommy's arm, but Horn barely saw him. They slowly passed, and he lost sight of them in the crowd, but he waited there by the booth, knowing they had to come back this way.

Ten minutes later they appeared again, and he stood in the shadow of the booth, watching, his hat brim pulled low. His throat tightened as he regarded her, not because of his relief at finding her but because of the pure sight of her. Paul Fairbrass's description had not prepared him for how much she had changed. She wore a light summer dress and high heels, and she walked with a long-legged, limber stride. Her fair hair was brushed back from her face; the breeze off the ocean played with it. Her features were more defined, about to cross that hazy boundary between girl and woman.

Tommy was talking, gesturing expansively, obviously having a good time. She said little and wore a half-smile, her eyes looking left and right, seemingly focused on other things. They passed abreast of him. He waited a minute, then fell in behind them, keeping a few dozen people in front of him.

They passed the carousel without stopping. *Must have already had her birthday ride*, he thought. He followed them into the parking lot until he confirmed that they were getting into the sky-blue Chrysler convertible, then sprinted for his own car and was able to pull in behind them as they exited onto the main street.

Off the pier, Tommy turned left and crossed into Santa Monica, where he picked up Santa Monica Boulevard and turned right, headed northeast. As in his pursuit of Falco, Horn tried to keep a couple of cars between himself and the Chrysler. Whenever he got stopped by a traffic signal and had to watch the other car's taillights recede, he drummed his fingers on the wheel and muttered, then darted ahead when the signal changed, closing the distance once again. Working in his favor was the fact that the Ford was the most nondescript of cars, but too much had gone wrong for him to be optimistic. He knew this might be his one chance.

You lost Sykes, and Falco lost me, but I'm with you tonight, Tommy my boy. Or whatever your name is. You won't shake me. And if you know I'm behind you, and you stop and try anything, I swear I'll run you over in the street.

But the pursuit went uneventfully. Up Santa Monica through Beverly Hills they went, and on into Hollywood. Santa Monica doglegged to the right, and a few blocks later Tommy picked up Crescent Heights and turned left up Laurel Canyon. At first, Horn thought they might be headed for Bonsigniore's house high in the hills. But after about a mile, the Chrysler turned off onto a side street. Horn waited ten seconds, cut his headlights, and followed. The street was narrow and twisting, with a blind corner every few dozen yards. He gripped the steering wheel as he squinted for a sight of the Chrysler's taillights, spotting them, losing them, catching them again. A few times he hung his head out the window, the better to see up ahead.

Then he saw brake lights, and the Chrysler was turning up a short, steep drive. Horn stopped, crept forward, finally cut his engine about twenty yards short of the house. He got out and walked up to it. It was an ordinary-looking bungalow near the spot where the street crested and started down-hill again, the small lawn sloping steeply down from the front porch to a five-foot-high stone retaining wall that bordered the narrow street. He could make out the Chrysler parked at the rear of the dark driveway that ran alongside the house.

As he stood there, undecided, lights came on in the front room. Foolishly, he realized that he didn't know exactly what to do. *If I knock on the door, I could get my head blown off*, he thought. *Or at least arrested. The ex-con who's causing trouble for the girl who's not even his daughter anymore. That would do nobody any good.*

The best thing to do, he concluded, would be to tell Paul Fairbrass where he could find his daughter and let him take it from there. Clea might or might not want to go home, but she was certainly underage, and Fairbrass could cause Tommy much grief over that. Once Clea was safe, Horn could find out why she had run away, could determine if there was indeed a connection between her disappearance and Scotty's death.

He went back to the car and wrote down the address of the house. He moved to start the engine, but something held him back. Now that he had found her, he wanted to stay near her for a while. So he made himself as comfortable as the Ford's cramped front seat would allow and watched the lights in the house.

What do you want with her? he asked the man in the house. *Why did she run to you? Is she happy? Have you done anything to hurt her? If you have, Paul Fairbrass isn't the one you need to worry about.*

When the lights in the house went out, he checked his watch and was surprised to see he'd been there more than an hour. It was almost midnight, and the street—barely lit by its widely spaced lights—was so quiet that he could identify the radio music drifting out someone's open window.

He yawned and shifted position, thinking it was time to go, when he heard a sound, like a slamming door. It came from up ahead, in the vicinity of Tommy's house. He leaned out the window, ears straining. After a few seconds, another sound, this one more of a pop. Silence after that, for thirty seconds or so, then another pop, the same pitch and volume as the second sound. All three had been slightly muffled, but Horn knew them—small-caliber gunshots, probably from two different weapons.

As the third shot sounded, he was out of the car and running toward the house. When he reached the stone wall, he ducked below it, listening. Nothing except the furious barking of two dogs apparently reacting to the unusual noises. Peering over the wall, he saw the same darkened house.

He went up the uneven stone steps to a pathway that led to more steps and the front porch. Holding his breath, he quietly tried the front door. Locked. *She's got to be inside. Is she all right?* He made a quick decision, rattled the door handle again, force-fully enough this time to be heard inside the house. "You hear those noises too?" he said loudly, feeling like a fool. "I think it was inside. Tell you what, I'll go around the back, and you all wait here for the cops, okay?"

A few seconds later he heard a noise somewhere in the back—a door closing, footsteps running on gravel, then silence for almost a full minute, then the sound of a car starting up far behind the house, possibly a street away.

He went back to the car and pulled a flashlight out of his glove compartment. Then, feeling his way along the side wall, his breathing shallow and quick, he made it to the rear of the house, where

214

he found the intruder's way in—a door with a jimmied lock.

For an instant, he allowed himself to dwell on the insanity of walking into a house where anything might be waiting for him. *Don't stop to think about it*, the inner voice said. *If you think, you won't do it*. He cleared his throat and said loudly, "Hey, there. It's your neighbor. I'm coming in." He held the screen door ajar, pushed the broken inner door open, and stepped quickly inside. The house was dark. He flicked on the flashlight and saw that he was standing in a small kitchen. Nothing seemed out of order. A hallway led toward the front of the house, and he took it.

"Anybody home? I heard something, and I just—"

Playing the light up ahead, he saw the form on the hall floor almost immediately. *Oh, no.* But it was the size and shape of a man, not a girl. The man lay on his side, head resting on his right arm, almost as if napping. Horn shined the light on the face. The features were slack and the hair was not lacquered in place as usual, but it was Tommy. He wore boldly striped silk pajamas, and he gave off a sweet and pungent scent. The left side of his midsection glistened with blood. Inches beyond the fingers of his right hand lay a large pistol. He didn't move, and a moment later Horn saw why. Tommy's left eye was missing, replaced by a clot of blood that bulged and shone like the ruby eye of a pagan statue.

"Clea!" Oblivious to the danger, Horn rose to his feet and called out. "Clea! Where are you?"

He began going through the one-story house—living room first, followed by both bedrooms. The front bedroom was obviously Tommy's, its closet containing an array of loud but well-tailored and expensive clothes. Atop the dresser he found a wallet and keys and a bottle of Number Six cologne, the source of the scent on the body. The second bedroom had also been used, and the closet held an odd collection of both girls' and women's wear. He checked kitchen, bathrooms, pantry, closets, everywhere. She was not there. Working to stay calm, he went back into the front room and sat in a chair by the fireplace, trying to reconstruct what had happened.

After the two had gone to their separate beds, he theorized, someone began to break in. Tommy had time to grab his gun and make it out to the hallway, where he exchanged fire with the intruder. The gun on the floor was a .45-caliber semiautomatic, the kind of service pistol hundreds of GIs had smuggled home after the war. It was a big, loud, brutish weapon, with formidable stopping power but little accuracy—not a bad choice for the night table if you're mostly interested in scaring someone away. Unless your adversary is not easily scared.

The first shot had come from the .45, Horn was sure, and was answered by something lighter and more accurate, which wounded Tommy and gave the other man time to administer the *coup de grace.* After that, he had taken Clea. Must have taken her, since there was no other possibility.

Horn considered turning on some of the lights, decided against it. He played the flashlight fitfully around the living room, as if asking the answer to jump out at him. The light glinted off something on the fireplace screen. He went over to see. It was a lightweight chain, about three feet long, with a steel ring on one end big enough for an index finger. It was draped carelessly over the screen, almost as if someone had hurriedly flung it toward the fireplace. The final link at the other end was broken.

He carefully unlocked the front door and stepped off the porch onto the front lawn, where he turned and looked back at the house. Like a lot of bungalows, the place had a gabled roof, and the roof peaked about six feet over the ground-floor ceiling. About three feet below the peak in the front wall was an air vent. The house had some kind of attic.

"Hello." Horn turned to see a stocky man in a bathrobe and slippers standing in the adjacent yard. "Any trouble?"

"Well, hey," Horn said. "You heard some noises too, huh, and some yelling? I came outside to look around, but I don't see anything." He swept the front of the house with the flashlight. "Looks like a false alarm. Or somebody fooling around."

The other man stood there fiddling with the sash of his robe, looking from Horn to the house

217

and back again. Horn doubted that Tommy had been the kind of man to stand around and jaw with the neighbors over the back fence, but he wondered if this man realized he wasn't talking to the resident.

"Guess we can sound the all-clear," Horn said with a laugh, then covered a yawn with a hand. "Don't know about you, but I'm going back to bed. Good night."

"Sure. Good night." Horn felt the other man's eyes on his as he went back up the steps and into the house. *Is he wondering what I'm doing out here after midnight fully dressed? Is he headed for his phone to call the cops? I need to get a move on.*

Back inside, he paced the hallway, playing the light along the ceiling. Almost directly over Tommy's body he found it—the outline of a hatch-way with a white-painted steel eye almost invisible in its center. Tommy had just enough time to close the hatch, tear off the chain, and fling it toward the fireplace. To hide something—or someone—in those few seconds he had left to live.

Horn fetched a chair from the kitchen table, stood on it, hooked his forefinger in the eye and pulled. Neatly counterbalanced, the hatch opened and a jointed wooden staircase unfolded and descended slowly to the floor. He went up it.

The place smelled of dust, unfinished wood, and the accumulated heat of the day. With his head above the attic's floor level, he sent the light around the forms of cardboard boxes and unwanted furniture.

In one of the far front corners, the beam found her.

She half-lay, half-sat, huddled on a rumpled blanket, barefoot and in pajamas, eyes wide, face frozen. "Clea." He started up and was halfway over to her when he saw the gun in her hand. It pointed directly at him, the hand shaking wildly, and she pursed her lips with the effort of squeezing the trigger. But the trigger pull was too stiff, and she brought the other hand over to steady the revolver and was squeezing it as he lunged toward her, wrapping one hand around the cylinder as she pulled the trigger, feeling the sudden pinch as the webbed skin near his thumb was caught between the striking hammer and the block.

He wrenched the gun out of her hand, hurting her, and she yelped. "No!" he said. "It's me. Honey, it's me." Even in the near-panic of the moment, he knew enough to realize, *I can't call myself Daddy anymore.* He turned the light on his own face, but she only shrank back against the wall, and he knew he must look like a death mask.

He turned it off, and they both sat in the dark, breathing heavily. "It's John Ray," he said finally, quietly. "I've come to get you. Nobody's going to hurt you."

It took him minutes to coax her to stand up and make her way toward the stairs. He held her hand as they decended, and pointed the way with the light. Just as he remembered the body on the floor, she saw it, and let out a moan. Reaching the floor, she knelt by Tommy, plucking at his sleeve, running her hand over his hair. It was too dark to see the extent of his wounds, but she clearly understood he was dead.

She turned her face up to Horn, and he heard the beginnings of a scream building in her throat. "No, Clea." He covered her mouth roughly with his hand. "I didn't kill him. I swear I didn't. I found him here." She fought against his hand, making little noises. "Someone else killed him. We have to go. It's dangerous to stay here."

Both her hands gripped his wrist. After a few moments, the noises subsided, and he took his hand away and led her to the back door. "Stay here just a minute," he said. He went into Tommy's bedroom and found the man's wallet again. He extracted the driver's license, stared at the name: Anthony Del Vitti. He flipped quickly through the assortment of cards and photos, finally plucking out one picture, which he pocketed with the license. Back in the hallway, he considered taking one of the guns but quickly decided against it. *An ex-con with a gun*, he thought. *Just asking for it.* Then he and Clea were out the back door and moving along the side of the house to the front, where he looked agitatedly around. No one stirred. For the moment, even the dogs were quiet.

Seconds later they were in the car. He started it up, did a tight U-turn over the shoulder and back onto the pavement, and sped down the hill toward Laurel Canyon Boulevard.

He took a breath, glancing over toward Clea, who leaned against the door, feet tucked under her, staring ahead. "You're going to be all right," he said. "I've been looking for you for a long time. You've been a hard girl to find, you know that? It was a lot easier tracking you down out at the beach, that time with Addie, remember?"

"Where are we going?" The first words she'd spoken were just a mutter, so indistinct he barely heard.

"I'm taking you home," he said. "Your mother and father are going to be real—"

"No."

"Clea, you have to go home."

"*No.*" She wrenched at the door handle with both hands, and it flew open. Wildly, she flung her legs out the door just as he leaned over, grabbed a bunch of pajama top in his hand, and dragged her back inside. The car veered, and he fought the wheel as she struggled.

"*No!*" It came out as a scream, and he slammed on the brakes, wrestling her with both hands now as she pummeled him with her fists. Her screams rose, and he sat there, still gripping her pajama top and wondering what to do next. A light came on in a nearby house.

No time for anything else. Holding her steady with his right hand, he cuffed her once with his open left, then again, harder. The second blow took the breath out of her, and she sank back against the seat, sobbing.

"Little girl, I'm sorry to do that," he said, using the name he'd called her a long time ago, when things were at their best. "Why don't you want to go home?"

No answer, just sobs. There was something in her face. He couldn't read it, but it frightened him. Somewhere in the house with the lights on he heard a voice, and he made several quick calculations—and a decision.

"All right," he said. "All right." He gunned the engine, and they descended to the main canyon road. Instead of turning left, he turned right, headed up toward the crest, the route that led to the Valley.

His watch read almost 2 A.M. as he knocked on the door. Maggie opened it, her face blurred with sleep.

"I need some help," he said.

CHAPTER 15

He sat up abruptly on the couch. A rectangle of sunlight on the floor hurt his eyes. Something had awakened him, and then he heard it again: kitchen noises. The smell of coffee hit him, and he looked over the back of the couch to see Maggie beyond the counter, making breakfast.

"Where is she?" His voice came out a croak.

"Good morning," she said without turning around. "In the bedroom. Thought I'd let both of you sleep."

"She's asleep?"

"Yep. Finally. Almost sunup, though, before she dropped off. I made her some warm milk and bourbon, and that did it. I know she's a little young for that, but I didn't think you'd mind."

"Something tells me she's not that young anymore. Where'd you sleep?"

"On the bed next to her. She wouldn't talk to me much, so I just tried to make her comfortable."

He heard crackling sounds and smelled sausage frying. "She's barely said two words to me either."

"She cried some before she went to sleep," Maggie continued, "and once she woke up making noises. Some kind of nightmare, I guess. Don't know what's wrong with her, but she's been through something."

"Do you want me to tell you any of it?"

He saw her shrug, her back still turned. "Not unless you want to. I can still help out without knowing every little thing, right?"

"I don't want to get you in trouble."

"Don't worry about me."

He kicked off the cotton blanket with the Navajo design and stood up, then realized he was wearing only his shorts. He put on pants, shoes, and under-shirt and went back to the bedroom to look in on Clea. She lay with her head turned away, the sheet covering all but her head. Her breathing looked regular.

Heading back to the front room, he paused by the tiny kitchen and cleared his throat. "Thanks, Maggie," he said.

She acknowledged with a little wave of her spatula, and a minute later she was bringing out plates loaded with scrambled eggs, grilled sausage patties, and corn bread. She laid them on the table in front of the couch, added mugs of coffee, then sat down beside him. "I've got a lot to do today," she said. "One of my mares is about to foal. If you can't be around, I'll look in on Clea every now and then, okay?"

"Sounds fine." They ate, and halfway through

the meal, he began to tell her. This time, he included the discovery of the photos, Scotty's death, Sykes's bloody encounter, the murder of the man now known as Anthony Del Vitti.

"Godalmighty, John Ray," Maggie said, wiping her mouth with a paper towel. "This is very scary, you know that?" Without waiting for an answer, she rushed on: "But who's doing this?"

He made a face, as if to acknowledge how little he knew for sure. Nevertheless, he laid out all his guesswork for her: the link between Scotty's death and the forbidden photos, the likely involvement of Vincent Bonsigniore and, through him, the ex-con/stuntman Gabriel Falco.

"The thing is," he went on, "I don't know why Tommy—Del Vitti, I mean—wound up dead last night. Anybody who goes around with a phony name has got something to hide. And since he hung out with Falco, he was likely connected with Bonsigniore too. But who would want to kill him?"

"Maybe there's no connection," Maggie said. "Maybe he just made the wrong enemy, and it's got nothing to do with all of this. But here's something I just thought of: He was keeping Clea at his place, right? Maybe someone who belonged to the group from the lodge didn't like that. So maybe there is a connection."

Horn looked distracted. "But that picture of Clea is years old," he said. "I don't see how she's mixed up in this at all. I think about it 'til my head hurts, and the pieces don't fit."

"You've got too many missing," she said with a smile. "But this all started with the little girls."

"Right. The trips up to the lodge. Arthur Bullard was there for sure. And let's say our friend Vinnie. Another one on my list was Wendell Brand, Clea's father. He used to work for old man Bullard. Besides Iris, he's the only one who could have gotten Clea involved in this, and Iris just isn't capable of it. I think he took his four-year-old daughter up there, turned her over to those . . ."

He stopped, saw he was gripping his fork so tightly the food had shaken off onto the floor. "Sorry." He reached down with his paper towel and cleaned it up.

"You've named three," Maggie said.

"Right. I thought about Falco and Del Vitti. But Falco came out here from New York a few years ago, and the trips to the lodge have been going on for at least ten, if you go by that picture of Clea. Del Vitti seems—*seemed*—too young for that too, and I don't know if he has any connection to any of these other men. But those three I named needed somebody to take the pictures and develop them, since they aren't the kind of thing you could just take down to your local camera shop. I think I've got a good candidate for that—man named Calvin St. George. He runs a rare-book store in Hollywood, sells dirty books under the counter, and he's also a good photographer—pictures of little girls, among other things. He acted a little shifty when I talked to him."

"What's his connection to the others?"

Horn chewed his lower lip. "I'm not sure."

"Well . . ."

"It's just an idea."

She pushed her plate away, looked at him. "What are you thinking?"

"Del Vitti. Just before he died, he made sure Clea was safe. Most of what I know about him is bad, but he did that one good thing."

"I suppose." She finished her coffee. "What do you do next?"

"I'll take her home, soon as she's ready."

"From what you said, she doesn't sound ready."

"I know. At least nobody could say we kidnaped her. But I'll need to tell her folks where she is pretty soon. I've got to find out what's wrong at home. Iris's husband told me Clea and her mother were fighting about something. Maybe that's all it is. We can clear it up, and once Clea sees how glad they are to have her back . . ."

"Do you want to know what happened to her? To those other girls?"

"You mean the details? Not if it means asking her about it. I know what I need to know."

"Are you going to the police about any of this?"

He went out to the kitchen to refill his cup before he answered. "No," he said. "They can all go to hell."

"What about Scotty? He used to be your best friend. Don't you want to—"

"Now that Clea's found, the thing I want most

227

is to find whoever killed Scotty. When I do, I mean to fix him. But every time I see a cop, and he finds out who I am, he treats me like I'm horse-shit. I never met one I'd give the time of day to."

"Well, then, what can you do?"

"I've been thinking," he said slowly. "Scotty's mother. Do you know who she is? She wants real bad to know what happened to him, who's behind it. She's a very elegant lady who helps war orphans and serves great lemonade, but she's got a hard side to her. I wouldn't want her after me. She says she doesn't want to go to the police about any of this because of what might come out about her husband's hobby. But she has a lot of connections. And I have a feeling that if I get some stuff together and turn it over to her, she could find the right way to get it into the hands of the police without mussing up old Arthur's reputation. I think that's what I'll do. Then I won't have to get in the same room with any cops, breathe the same air, see that expression on their faces when they find out who I am."

"You're pretty mad about what happened, aren't you? Prison, I mean. And Iris."

"Damn right," he said, smiling humorlessly. "Wouldn't you be?"

"I suppose. But don't you think it's time you moved on?"

He regarded her curiously.

"I mean, look at you. You used to have a good life, people looked up to you—"

"Kids looked up to me."

"That's right, they did. You meant something to them. Now you go around looking like an out-of-work cowhand. You need a shave most of the time, and those shoes haven't been shined in . . . You know, it's one thing not to have a lot of money; we've all been in that fix one time or another. But John Ray, you act like a man who's got no pride in himself."

He sat with his feet up on the table, head down, cradling his cup in both hands.

"Listen to me, preaching to you," she said. "Forget it. I've got no right. It's just that I used to like you a lot, and I don't like seeing you act like this."

When he looked up at her, it was with an easy grin. "Good breakfast," he said. "That's the first time you ever cooked for me, you know that?"

She didn't return the smile. "That's because you didn't wait around," she said. "You missed out on a lot of things, John Ray. You were in too much of a hurry."

He nodded. "I guess if Iris hadn't come along . . ."

"But she did, didn't she? And you had your heart set on somebody who wore skirts instead of pants and who knew about things like makeup and dancing instead of horses and stables. So don't give me might-have-been, that's just bullshit. We're talking about the way things are. We both moved on, and now I'm married to a good man." She got up and began to clear the table. "I don't blame you. Iris was quite a gal. Still is, I guess. I'm sorry it didn't work out for you."

He couldn't think of anything to say to that, so he went back to the bedroom. Clea had turned in her sleep and was facing him, her mouth slightly open. He sat on the bed and put a hand lightly on her shoulder. Her pajamas, the same ones she'd been wearing when he found her, had a pattern of little lambs jumping over a fence, something a girl would wear. Her hair was matted, and the room retained the sour smell of last night's anxiety.

She stirred, and her eyes opened suddenly. When they focused on him, her shoulder tightened as if a spring had suddenly coiled within it. Her breath came in and out quickly, and he heard the beginning of a whimper in her throat.

"It's all right," he whispered urgently. "It's me, Clea. Do you remember? I brought you here last night. Everything's all right."

The tension slowly left her shoulder. Her mouth was slack, and she brought a small fist up to her mouth, as if she wanted to hide behind it.

"Do you remember?"

She nodded.

"We're here at Maggie's, and she's going to let you stay here as long as you want. She has horses. You'll like it here. Can I get you anything? Are you hungry?"

"Drink of water," she mumbled.

He went to the kitchen and fetched a glass of

water, which he put beside the bed. "Anything else?"

"I want to go back to sleep."

"All right." He patted her shoulder and left. Up front, Maggie was doing the dishes. He finished dressing and sat by the window, looking out at the dirt road and the fenced-in pasture lying beyond, under the warm sun. Some of the horses had been turned out and were grazing. One of Maggie's workers was exercising two of them, riding a gray and leading a chestnut by the reins. Through the open window he could hear the man make a clicking sound, encouraging the horses as he upped their gait to a trot.

"I like this place," he said, as much to himself as to Maggie. "It's peaceful."

He reached into his shirt pocket and pulled out the photo he'd taken from Del Vitti's wallet. It had caught Horn's interest because it showed Del Vitti with Clea. Now he studied it. They were at some kind of nightclub, sitting at a table with drinks in front of them. Del Vitti smiled expansively for the camera, while Clea, wearing a grown-up party dress and holding a cigarette, looked subdued, almost grave. The photo was on heavy paper and apparently had been trimmed down from a larger size in order to fit in a wallet.

Because of the trimming he saw little detail that might tell him where the picture was taken. Besides the table at which they sat, all he could see was a glimpse of a waitress behind them carrying a tray. She wore a fringed skirt. He looked more closely. There was something familiar about the skirt.

"This is one of Davey's," Maggie said, laying a shirt on the varnished pine table next to him. "Might be a little short in the sleeve, but it should fit you otherwise, and it's in a whole lot better shape than that one you've got on. And here's his razor, just in case you—"

He stood up slowly, not hearing her, still staring at the photo. "I'm going to be gone for a while," he said.

When he came through the front door of the casino, the place was not yet open for business. He spotted Mad Crow across the room, talking to someone by the bar. He crossed the room quickly, weaving his way through the poker tables. Mad Crow saw him when he was about ten feet away. The Indian's eyebrows went up, and he started to speak. But Horn was on him in a few more long strides, his fist cocked, and he unleashed a right from the shoulder with all his weight behind it. Mad Crow tried to throw himself to the side, but the right caught him flush on the right cheekbone. His head snapped back and he fell against the bar.

Horn set himself for another punch, this one a left, but he heard cries behind him, and in a second, two of Mad Crow's boys had grabbed him by the arms. They dragged him away from the bar.

"Jesus H. Fucking . . ." Mad Crow crouched

over, eyes bulging, holding his face, staring at Horn. "You crazy? What the hell you trying to do? You a crazy man?"

Horn strained against his captors, but the two were strong. "Easy, John Ray," he heard a quiet voice say. He glanced to his left and recognized one of Mad Crow's nephews, Billy Looks Ahead, a young man with a face like a hatchet blade who, Horn vaguely remembered, had been with the Marines during the war.

"What was that for?" Mad Crow went on. "You want to explain that?"

"Sure, I'll explain it," Horn said, feeling suddenly out of breath. "Something in my pocket I'll show you, if these guys'll turn me loose."

"You going to swing at me again?"

Horn exhaled loudly. "Not right now."

"I'll be ready for you next time, boy, promise you that." He gestured to the others. "Let him go."

Horn pulled out the cut-down picture and tossed it on the bar. Without picking it up, Mad Crow gave it a look. When he raised his eyes, Horn saw recognition in them.

"You know who that is."

Mad Crow nodded.

"And where it was taken."

The Indian sighed. "Why don't you guys find something to do?" he said to Looks Ahead and the other man. Then, to Horn: "You mind if I put some ice on this?"

"You go right ahead, as long as you talk to me."

Mad Crow went around the bar, wrapped some ice in a towel, and applied it to his cheek. "You want a drink?"

"It's early."

"So what? It's my bar." He opened a Blue Ribbon and indicated one of the round tables. They sat.

"Before you say anything," the Indian began.

"No, me first," Horn said. "This guy in the picture is dead."

"*What?*"

"That's right. Somebody shot him through the left eye. Very neat. Professional, almost. And Clea was there, in his house. He managed to hide her before the guy with the gun got inside, and that's why—"

"Is she all right?"

Horn nodded. He briefly recounted the events of the night before. "But you don't get any more answers until I get mine. First, how many times did he bring her here?"

"Once." He saw Horn's look. "Once, John Ray. That time the picture was taken. That's all."

"When?"

"About a month ago. I'm not sure."

"You knew I was looking for her. Why didn't you tell me?"

Mad Crow lowered the towel-wrapped ice long enough to take a long pull on the bottle. "Okay, here it is," he said, not looking at Horn. "You remember how the Mick wanted to buy in with me, and I told you I was taking a partner, some-body from Reno, to keep him off my neck? Well, that was about half true. He's not from Reno, he's more local. His name's Vincent Bonsigniore."

"All right, I know who he is," Horn said. "Why didn't you want me to know?"

"Because by then I knew you were looking for Clea, and I knew she was with this guy Del Vitti."

"So what?"

"Well, Del Vitti worked for Vinnie."

Horn nodded slowly as he rubbed his eyes. Finally, a connection was made, one he had only suspected until now. Clea's disappearance and Scotty's death were not separate and distinct. They were linked by the menacing figure of Vincent Bonsigniore. But how? Clea could tell him, if only she would.

"What did he do for him?"

"I don't know, odd jobs, everything. He came around with Vinnie when we talked about his terms for buying in. Young guy on his way up, you know the type."

"Why didn't you tell me?" Horn asked again.

"Look, it's complicated. I didn't want to tattle on one of Vinnie's guys, get on the wrong side of my new partner. And I swear to God, I thought it was harmless. She showed up with him one evening. She saw me, ran over and gave me a big hug—I hadn't seen her in years, and I was amazed at how grown-up she looked. I didn't like Del Vitti, but I kept an eye on him while they were here, and I saw he was treating her with respect, almost like she was some kind of precious thing he didn't want to see get broken.

"When you said she'd run away from home, I thought she would just spend some time with this character and then go back to her folks, no trouble. I honestly didn't see how there could be any connection with Scotty—looks like I was wrong, and I blame myself for that. But basically, I thought if I kept quiet, it would all sort itself out, you know? I didn't know she'd be in any danger, John Ray, I really didn't."

"She could have been killed. You son of a bitch. You should have said something."

"Maybe." Mad Crow put the towel on the table and looked at Horn under lowered brows. "But try seeing it my way for just a minute. She's got a mother and a father to look after her. You're not her dad anymore, her mother doesn't want you mixed up in this, but you go charging ahead anyway. You spend half your time acting like the world has crapped on you and the rest of your time poking your nose in where it isn't wanted—"

"You going to tell me I need my shoes shined? I just heard that from somebody."

"Well, yeah. You could use a haircut too. Look, I'm glad you were there last night, and I'm glad she's safe now. But my crystal ball's broke, and I didn't know how this was going to turn out. I handled it the best way I knew how."

"You handled it wrong," Horn muttered. He was about to go on, but he glanced at the other man and saw pain on his face, an expression Horn read as guilt and remorse. Mad Crow had always doted on Clea, and he would be slow to forgive himself for this.

Horn decided to let it go. "Did you know Del Vitti called himself Tommy Dell?"

Mad Crow shook his head. "But it doesn't surprise me. Lots of guys like him pick up other names and use 'em for a while. First time I heard the name Dell was when you told me about him over at the South Seas. I had to think about it awhile before I figured it out was the same character."

"You know any reason anybody would want to kill him?"

Mad Crow shrugged. "He was a gangster. Good riddance. I'm just sorry I have to do business with 'em every now and then."

"Why do you have to?"

The Indian gave him a pitying look. "Boy, for a hardened ex-con you sure are innocent, aren't you? Maybe you just don't want to know anything. When you get out and I offer you some work, you don't ask about any of the details, you just say, 'How much does it pay?'"

He waggled his empty bottle in the air, and a moment later one of his workers brought him a fresh one. Elsewhere around the big room, others were sweeping between the tables and cleaning up for the late-afternoon opening.

"Look around you, boy," Mad Crow said. "How much of this you think is legal?"

Horn shrugged. "I don't know. All of it, I thought."

"Well, you're wrong. The poker games are fine. But the blackjack table's unkosher, and so's that wheel I had put in last month."

"So?"

"So this: The poker doesn't bring in enough, so I got to expand. I can't do that without the help of the local *policia* out here in the sticks. That worked for a while, but they started squeezing me, and they know they can get away with it because I'm on my own. I let Vinnie in because he's good at handling that side of things, they won't mess with him, and he leaves me free to just run the place."

"For how much?"

"Fifteen percent of my monthly gross."

"That sounds like a lot."

"Well, he brought in some capital. And anyway, that fifteen percent is worth it in peace of mind."

"Good for you. So how does it feel to be in bed with a piece of garbage?"

"Still mad at me, aren't you?"

"There's some things I could tell you about your friend Vinnie."

"I'm not in bed, I'm in business. And I notice you're not too particular about where your next payday comes from, my rootin'-tootin' friend. Look, maybe you don't care whether you wind up sleeping on satin sheets or out at that shack you call an address. But I care where I wind up. I put in a lot of years playing the silent Indian while you went buggy-riding with the local schoolmarm, all that stuff. I knew there was only so far I could go in that business. And you know something? I didn't resent you being the movie star, because I knew those were the cards I got dealt. And I knew you were a good guy who didn't let that kind of thing go to his head.

"But I didn't plan to wind up sitting on the side-walk outside the Brown Derby, wrapped in my colorful Indian blanket, telling everybody about the time I was in the movies. I took my money and I invested it, and I built this place. And now a lot of relatives are eating better because of me. I'm proud of myself. You want to turn up your nose at the kind of business I'm in, take a good look in your mirror the next time you're ready for your weekly shave. Okay, cowboy?"

They regarded each other evenly. Horn slowly pushed an ashtray back and forth between his cupped hands. Finally he said, "Okay, Indian."

Mad Crow exhaled loudly. "That's fine."

"How's your face?"

"Pretty seriously wounded, I think."

Horn tilted his head slightly, studying him. "I'd call it an improvement."

"My great-grandfathers would call that counting coup. They thought it was the bravest thing they could do—riding up to a strong enemy and striking him with their coup stick." He shook his head. "Fighting was just a game to them. If one side thinks war is playing games, and the other side takes it dead serious, who do you think is going to win?"

"I know."

"That boy who grabbed ahold of you—Billy. You know he was in the war?"

"I've seen that thing on his shirt. Like the one you wear."

"The Ruptured Duck?" Mad Crow glanced down at the gold-colored insignia on his lapel showing an eagle within a ring, its wings spread. "Yeah, most people have gotten out of the habit nowadays; the war's something they just want to forget. But I think it's good for business, so I tell my bartenders and the other boys to keep wearing it. Hell, even I wear the damn thing, and I spent most of my hitch in Special Services, rubbing elbows with the likes of Bob Hope and Dorothy Lamour." His eyes fixed on Horn. "You never wore the duck, even when you first got back. How come?"

"I never needed any piece of metal to remind me where I'd been," Horn said. He didn't like where this was going. Just like Scotty, the Indian had sometimes alluded to Horn's Purple Heart and tried to pump him for war stories. Horn once tried to joke his way out, saying that a Purple Heart only meant a wound, and the medal didn't specify whether you got wounded while facing the enemy or trying to run from him.

"You were going to tell me about Billy," Horn prompted him.

"Yeah," Mad Crow said, clearly unsatisfied with Horn's answer. "Billy, he'd never be satisfied with tapping somebody on the shoulder with a coup stick; he plays for keeps. Brought back a Bronze Star from Iwo Jima. Doesn't talk about what he did, but I met a guy from his unit not long ago. He told me they were pinned down for hours by a handful of Japs in a bunker up on some ridge. Billy volunteered to go up there after dark. They heard shooting and yelling, and the next morning they found Billy sitting there with a bunch of dead Japs. Some shot, some knifed. You want to hear the strange part?"

"Okay."

"Once, over a couple of beers, Billy told me he misses it. Says the war brought out something he didn't even know was there. I worry about him. He's one of those guys they turned loose against the Japs and the Germans, and now, in our quiet little postwar world, these guys are going to be a problem."

"Maybe so," Horn said. "But I'm not going to be a problem. I like things quiet."

"For an hombre who likes quiet, you sure make a racket every now and then. So how's Clea doing?"

"Not good. She saw her boyfriend dead on the floor before I could get her out of the house. And now she acts like she's afraid to go home. Maggie's helping me look after her until she's ready to leave. I don't want anybody to know where she is, all right?"

"Even her folks?"

"Even them. For now."

"Fine with me," the Indian said. "While we're on the subject, your new friend Mr. Fairbrass called here a couple of hours ago, trying to get you."

"He wants to know what's going on," Horn said. "I'll call him later. Don't like keeping him in the dark, but I got too many questions to answer before I tell him where his girl is."

"Now, I don't want to get you started worrying about something brand new," Mad Crow said. "But . . . you've got Scotty dead and this guy Del Vitti dead. Both of them with a connection to Clea. Have you been thinking that somebody out there might—"

"Come after me?"

The Indian nodded.

"I've thought about it," Horn said. "And I don't think so. If they wanted to get at me, they've had plenty of time. It wouldn't take much trouble to find out where I live. If they knew that I was in old man Bullard's office with Scotty that night and saw the pictures, then I know I'd be on their list. But I don't think they've made that jump. As far as anybody knows, I'm just the guy who used to be Clea's daddy and who's been trying to find her as a favor to the man who's her daddy now."

"All right," Mad Crow said. "Hope you're right. One more thing: I don't feel good about . . . you know, what I did. Is there anything I can do to help you out?"

"Sure is," Horn said. "I've been thinking about that while we sat here. Two things: You can have one of your boys bring me a Blue Ribbon."

"And . . . ?"

"I want to meet Vinnie."

"That's not going to happen, John Ray."

"Yes, it is, when you know why. Remember I said I could tell you some things about him? Well, I'm going to tell you now."

CHAPTER 16

When Horn was finished talking, they sat quietly for a while. Behind the bar, the bartender had turned on a radio as he wiped down his collection of glasses. Horn could make out a melancholy song he had once heard in a movie. He couldn't remember the title, but it was one of those New York movies about old friends moving in separate worlds, one straight, one criminal, and he seemed to recall Richard Conte, the bad friend, dying in a church, finally repentant at the end.

The Indian coughed into one of his big hands and said quietly, "So he's the one?"

"I think so," Horn said. "If his police record tells us anything, he's one of the boys who played games up at the lodge. And I'd bet a month's take from your tables, if I had it, that he had Scotty killed."

Mad Crow looked as if he'd swallowed something vile. "Son of a bitch," he said. "I would pick him to throw in with, wouldn't I?"

"Come on. You already knew he wasn't any choirboy."

"This is different, and you know it. What are you going to do?"

"Get Clea home soon as I can. After that, I'll think of something. First off, I'd like to meet your friend, just get a look at him."

"That's all?"

He nodded.

"What if he knows who you are? I mean, knows you're the one who was looking for her?"

"Still looking for her," Horn corrected him. "Story is, she hasn't been found yet, remember? And chances are, he does know who I am, since Del Vitti was working for him all the time he was holding on to Clea. But your friend Vincent doesn't know how much I know about him. Anyway, I still want a look at him. Can you set it up?"

"I don't know." Mad Crow's face was creased with doubt. Horn wasn't used to seeing the big man so unsure. *If I didn't know him better*, Horn thought, *it might even look like fear.*

"He always travels with somebody," Mad Crow continued. "Now that Del Vitti's dead, it might be this guy Falco."

"I don't care. If they see me, they're not going to learn anything about me they don't already know. I'm still your friend, I'm still looking for the girl. Nobody needs to know that I saw the pictures or that I suspect Vinnie of anything."

"What's my excuse for having you sit in?"

"Hmm. I guess you can tell 'em you're working

me more into your business—training me to be your faithful assistant, that kind of thing."

Mad Crow shot him one of his twisted smiles. "I get it. Just like the movies, only I get to be the leading man this time."

"Just don't push it."

In Mad Crow's office, Horn asked the operator to ring Paul Fairbrass's office in Long Beach.

"I tried to reach you all day yesterday," Fairbrass said after answering. "I called your number until late last night. Where were you?"

"Why do you care?"

"I was concerned, that's all. Especially after you told me you had that encounter with Tommy Dell."

"Where did you get Mad Crow's number?"

"Iris told me you were friends," Fairbrass said. "I thought he might know—"

"Don't go tracking me down, okay?"

"All right. But I'd like for you to stay in touch occasionally."

"Mr. Fairbrass, I told you I'd let you know whenever I learned anything."

"And you haven't?"

"No. I'm sorry."

"It wouldn't hurt you to let me know once a day or so." The man sounded reasonable, but something troubled Horn. In the back of his mind was the suspicion that Clea was resisting the idea of going home because her new father had mistreated her in some way. He admitted that it was farfetched and probably due to his knowledge of the poison in Clea's past—that she had once been abused by a group of men. But until he knew Fairbrass was a good father to her, he wasn't inclined to cut the man any slack.

"Look, I'm not your employee," he told him. "I'm not someone you can send off to get his face sliced up, and then stick a few extra dollars in his pay envelope. You came to me, and I'm going to do this my way. You can't fire somebody who's working for free."

On the other end of the long-distance line, he could hear the low background hum of Fairbrass's plant. He wondered idly how many people worked there and just how rich the man was.

"All right," the voice muttered. "I don't like you, nor do I like the way you're handling this. I find it very easy to understand why Iris divorced you. But nevertheless, I appreciate what you're doing, and if you find Clea, it'll all be worthwhile. So . . . ."

"I'll call you when I know something," Horn said, and hung up.

As he parked the Ford in front of Maggie's place, he saw Maggie and Clea standing at the pasture fence, eye to eye with a bay mare. The scent of warm grass tickled his nose and the sun baked the back of his neck as he walked over to them. Clea was wearing a pair of dungarees, loafers, and a brightly colored shirt with the sleeves rolled up. Maggie held a paper bag, and they were feeding the mare wedges of apple from it. "Careful, honey," he heard Maggie say. "Just hold still and let her take it."

Spotting him over her shoulder, Maggie walked over to meet him. "My clothes fit her pretty good," she said in a low voice, taking him by the arm and leading him away from the fence.

"How's she doing?"

"Not good. I let her take a bath and gave her something to wear. She even ate a little breakfast. But she doesn't seem right."

"What do you mean?" He regarded Clea, who still stood with her back to them.

"Hard to describe. She talks about things, but she's not really there. It's like last night, only then it made sense—she was tired and scared. Now she's rested and all, but when you talk to her, she doesn't look at you. She says thank you, and she asks if there's any salt, that sort of thing. But there are things on her mind. She asked me what I would do if anybody ever tried to hurt my horses. She wanted to know if I thought Bonnie—the mare who's about to foal—was going to die. I try to answer her, but I'm not sure she even hears me."

"Do you think it's because—"

"Her friend was killed? I wouldn't be surprised. Remember, she must have heard those gunshots real clear where she was hiding. It would mess up anybody." She brushed the hair out of her face. "I've got to get back to the stable," she said. "The mare—"

"How close is she?"

248

"Pretty close. Next day or so, I think."

"You go ahead. Any chance I could take one of your horses out today?"

"Sure. Try Miss Molly, the hungry one Clea's been feeding. Take her through the pasture and out the north gate, you'll find lots of trails. You need anything, ask one of the boys."

He touched her arm. "Thanks."

He walked over to Clea at the fence. "Hey, little girl."

"Hey," she said without looking at him. Her hair was pulled back in a ponytail and looked freshly washed. Miss Molly, having disposed of the apple, stood a few paces away, regarding the two of them with a calm sideways look.

"How you doing?"

"All right." It was a child's voice, high-pitched and with minimal inflection. She turned her head and looked at him, studying him as if for the first time. Her expression said nothing. He couldn't tell if she was happy in his company.

"Do you remember last night?"

"Uh-huh," she said, turning her gaze back over the pasture. "Somebody shot Tommy, didn't they?"

"Uh-huh."

"Was it you?"

"Oh, god. No, honey. It wasn't me. Don't think that."

"I saw him there in the hall. He was dead, wasn't he?"

"Yes, he was. I know he was your friend, and

I'm sorry. I want you to know you're going to be all right now."

She nodded.

"Do you think you might be ready to go home?"

"No."

"Want to tell me why?"

"No. Can I stay here?"

"Sure, for a while. Do you like Maggie?"

Clea nodded. "She's nice. She showed me the mare that's having a baby."

"She knew you when you were almost a baby," he said. "You probably don't remember, though. Listen, she said we could take out one of the horses. You want to go for a ride?"

"I suppose," she said.

He led Miss Molly to the stable, where he saddled and bridled her, then swung himself up. It was his first time on a horse in years, and it felt both strange and comforting to be sitting there, wearing his ordinary clothes, feeling the large animal tensing and shifting under him, trying to read the horse as the horse tried to read him.

He kicked his left foot back out of the stirrup and reached down for Clea. She put her left foot in the stirrup and took his left hand in both of hers, and he swung her up behind him.

"Let's go," he said, touching the horse lightly with his heels and guiding her out into the pasture. They walked the circuit twice, following the fence. Then he leaned down and opened a gate at the far end and they rode the mare out onto a dirt road that took them north along a scattered collection of other ranches and open land. After a while they were in the foothills and could look back on the enormous reach of the San Fernando Valley.

The sun was hot but soothing, and the mare had an easy gait. Horn adjusted his fedora to keep the sun off his neck. Clea rode quietly behind him, her arms around his waist, as she had ridden many years earlier when he had introduced her to horses. He reminded her of this as they rode, and he talked of other things too, things she had done as a child. He was trying to pierce the wall, find the key that would unlock her defenses, that would allow him to connect with the Clea who had whooped and hollered her way through a hundred childish games they played when she was seven, eight, nine. At the same time, he had the vague hope that she might remember and disclose something that would help him prove who killed Scotty. But she had been a tiny child when she stood before that sinister, all-seeing camera, and Horn's hope was small and forlorn.

After more than an hour, they reached a crest that gave them views both north and south.

"That's the old studio ranch, a few miles off thataway," he said, pointing northwest. "Your mother brought you out once to watch us shoot a movie. See that little mountain? That's Dome Rock. We had a picnic there, remember?"

"Uh-huh," she said, shifting behind him. "I'm getting hot. Can we go back?"

★   ★   ★

251

He found Maggie in the stable, peering over the railing into the pregnant mare's stall. The mare was lying on her side, hugely swollen, her breathing heavy. "John Ray, meet Bonnie," she said quietly. "Her last one was stillborn, couple of years ago. This time it's going to work. Me and her, we talked it over and decided this one's going to be healthy."

"Nice to have it worked out ahead of time." He went down on his haunches, reached through the lower slats and rubbed the mare's great, bony head. "She looks serious about this."

"She is. When you put eleven months into something, you don't want to fail. Oh, I just remembered," she said, patting her shirt pocket. "You got a call awhile ago." She handed him a slip of paper.

"Alphonse Doucette." He read the name out loud and studied the number. The name sounded familiar, but he didn't know the telephone exchange. "What the hell? I'm supposed to be hiding out here, and everybody with a phone knows how to—"

"It was Joseph," she interrupted. "He said this person called for you at the club, and he was passing it on. Said he's getting tired of being your switchboard girl."

He went into Maggie's place and dialed the number. After several rings a voice answered, "Dixie Belle."

"Alphonse Doucette there?"

"Hang on."

A moment later another voice came on the line, and he recognized the Creole.

"It's John Ray Horn."

"Howdy-do," Doucette said. "You recovered from the other night?"

"I'm just fine," Horn said.

"You look like a man can take a punch," Doucette said, his voice soft and musical, as before.

"Maybe not as good as Bob Steele, though."

"No, not as good as him. Tough little nut, that man."

"What's on your mind? Besides asking about my health, I mean."

"I thought you and me, we might talk."

"What about?"

"Just things."

"Want to give me an idea?"

Doucette was silent for a moment. Horn heard voices and the clink of glasses and guessed that the other man was standing near the bar in the club's main room.

"It about that man wound up dead last night," he said finally. "Up in the hills. And about what you said you looking for."

It was a few minutes after five when Horn parked the Ford just off Central, and the Dixie Belle wouldn't be open for an hour or so. As instructed, he went up the alley and in by way of the back door. Passing the scene of his one-sided encounter with Del Vitti and Falco, he remembered the feel of his knees on the bricks and the blood in his mouth.

Inside, the club was fully lit, and he saw some of the staff cleaning the carpet and wiping down tables. The place felt cool, but the smell of liquor and stale cigarette smoke hung in the air like the last, sour note from a horn player who had stopped caring about his music.

Doucette, who was standing at the cash register behind the bar talking to the bartender, motioned him toward a barstool and then came around to sit next to him.

"How you doin'?"

Horn nodded. "Now I remember why I never liked walking into a nightclub in the daytime."

"I know what you mean. Place never look as good in the daylight. Or smell as good. Aftershave and ladies' perfume add a lot, once the people start comin' in. You don't want to see a nightspot 'til the lights are low and the music is going, and it got that . . . *mystery*. Am I right?"

The bartender brought over a cup, filled it from a coffee pot, and pushed it toward his boss, then looked questioningly at Horn, who nodded. The man brought him a cup and filled it.

"So what kind of a name is Doucette?" Horn asked him.

"That's French. 'Cause my daddy was part French, and his daddy too. Louisiana, where I come from, most people are a mixture of one thing or another. We're like gumbo, all different flavors mixed up."

Horn sipped at his coffee. It was strong and, like the tea he was served the other night, it carried a hint of chicory. "I appreciate the hospitality, but I'm a little confused. The last time I saw you, you told me if I came back here I was going to get tossed out on my rear."

"I did say that, sure enough," the Creole said in a mock-serious tone. "Thing is, I learned a few things in the last day or so."

"I'm listening."

"First off, I heard that man you call Tommy, he been found dead in his house last night."

"So?"

"So I figured you caught up with him, that's all."

"Now, wait a minute—"

The Creole held up both hands. "Ain't none of my business. Whatever happen to that man, I don't care."

"Just wait a minute," Horn repeated. "Let's say he is dead. How do you even know about it?"

"That's easy. Somethin' in the paper." Doucette reached in his back pocket, pulled out a folded newspaper, and slid it along the slick bar top. "Page three."

Horn unfolded the paper, the afternoon tabloid *Mirror*, and turned to the third page. GUN VICTIM FOUND IN HILLSIDE HOME, the headline read, followed by a few inches of text on the discovery of Anthony Del Vitti's body by police following a call from a neighbor. The police said Del Vitti had a record of violent crime and was known to hang out with gangsters. The neighbor had reported a conversation with a tall white man in the front yard. But the lighting was bad, he said, and he was not sure if he would recognize the man again.

"I told you I was looking for a man named Tommy Dell," Horn said. "So how did you know—"

Doucette waved that away. "Plenty of time for that."

"Anyway, I didn't kill him. What else do you know?"

"That's more complicated." The Creole turned slightly on his stool and pointed across the room. "See her?"

In a booth against the far wall Horn saw a woman sitting alone. She didn't look familiar. "I see her."

"My sister Lurlene," the other man said. "She the only relative I got left. I brought her out here a few years ago, when this place start to make some money for me. I take care of her. She not real good at taking care of herself, know what I mean?"

"I suppose so."

"She been married twice, had a lot of boyfriends. She got three kids. Her oldest one is Tara, pretty thing. She fourteen now. Lurlene name her after that big place where Scarlett O'Hara live. But everybody call her Tootie." He pulled out his wallet and extracted a small photo. Apparently a class picture, it showed a pretty, light-skinned girl, her hair severely marcelled. Her unforced smile was directed over the photographer's shoulder, as if she'd just spotted her best friend. Horn didn't know what was coming next, but his mind flashed back to the picture of Clea with which he'd begun his search. Pictures are meant to be keepsakes, to capture the image of a loved one for all time. But in the last few days, he reflected, photos had somehow come to represent loss. *I don't want to look at any more pictures of little girls*, he thought fiercely.

"Nice-looking kid," he said.

"You want to come on over here with me?" The Creole slid off his stool and led Horn across the room to the booth where the woman sat. He eased in beside her and motioned for Horn to sit on the far side.

"This here is Mr. John Ray Horn," Doucette said to the woman. His tone was flat, as if he had used up whatever affection he might have felt toward her. "I want you to tell him what you told me."

The woman looked sullen and tired. She was the color of coffee with a splash of milk and very pretty. Her dress was trimmed in lace at the throat and cuffs and looked expensive, but she also looked as if she had dressed carelessly. She had missed fastening one button in the front, and her soft maroon hat perched precariously on the side of her head like an afterthought.

"Can I get another rum and Coke?" Her fingers were curled like claws around a highball glass that was empty save for the melting ice cubes.

Doucette shook his head. "Maybe later. You tell him."

She pursed her lips together in a way that gave her face almost a comic look, but Horn saw something else in her eyes, something that made him almost look away.

"She don't want to tell you," Doucette said quietly, in a tone he might use for a child that wouldn't eat her spinach. "She don't want to tell you how she met him here one night he came around to do business with me. How he start takin' her out, how she introduce Tootie to this nice man. Ain't that right?" he asked her, but she just stared at her glass.

"It was Tootie he wanted," Doucette went on. "He already knew about her, 'cause I'd told him about this niece of mine, I was so proud. Makes me dumb, don't it? He had a thing for little girls. This Del Vitti, he like to call himself Tommy when he scoutin' around for children, for himself and some friends of his. Even had two names for his two jobs, Lurlene tells me. Tony was his real name and his business name, but Tommy was his pimpin' name. Keep things separate. Ain't that slick?

"Anyways . . . he find out what Lurlene, she need the most. She like attention from a good-looking man, she like dinner and dancing. Mostly she like money to feed the habit. So one day this Del Vitti, he tell her he give her three hundred, and all she got to do is let him and his friends spend some time with Tootie. She won't get hurt, he tell her. Did she know what was goin' to happen? Maybe, maybe not. Anyway, she say fine. And he take Tootie off with him, and he bring her back late that night. And she cryin'. And she got ice cream on her dress, 'cause they stop off for a banana split on the way home. But the ice cream don't make her feel any better." He reached over and squeezed his sister's arm, and a single teardrop moved down her cheek, as if formed by the pressure of his hand. "Ain't that right?"

Doucette sat back heavily, and the rest of his words came out in a sigh. "Little bit at a time, Tootie tell her what happen. And Lurlene, some friend tell her about the story in the paper today, and she decide to tell me all about it. I'm not as dumb as she think. That first time I talk to you, I already know something goin' on with the girl, somebody been messin' with her. I just didn't know how bad."

He got up and beckoned her out of the booth. Still silent, she moved quickly past him as if fearing a blow. But his hands were at his sides. "You go on home and take care of your children," he said quietly.

After she had gone, Doucette summoned the bartender over, and soon they had fresh steaming cups in front of them. Horn shifted uneasily in his seat. Doucette looked at him. "I know," he said. "You and me, we not exactly best buddies. So why I telling you all this?"

"I wondered."

"Well, here's the thing. Other night, you just a guy come walking in here looking for trouble. You find some trouble, you expect me to help you out. Nothin' in it for me. Now things change. I done told you what happen to Tootie 'cause I think this tied in with your little girl, and maybe you can use it. And . . ."

"And?"

"And maybe I want something from you now."

"You want to know if I've found out anything."

"That's right. I want to know 'bout Del Vitti's friends."

"So you can go after them?"

Doucette shrugged. "You don't have to worry about that. You found your child?"

"No," Horn lied.

"Well, you got your hands full looking for her. Me, I'm curious about these old boys who like to stick it to little girls, send 'em home cryin'."

"What did Tootie remember about them?"

"Nothin'. Faces was covered, she tell her mama."

Horn sipped at his coffee, trying to think fast. He owed Doucette and wanted to repay him, but not at the cost of letting him interfere. He decided to tell him just enough and no more.

"All right," he said. "Here's what I know. It was probably four men, all of them white. They had a lot of girls, starting years ago. Two of the men are dead now, and you don't need to know their names. The third one I'm not sure about yet. The last one was Vincent Bonsigniore."

He'd never seen any emotion in Doucette's face, but now something like alarm took it over. "Vincent?" he muttered. "Vinnie B? Sweet mother . . ."

"You're surprised?"

Doucette nodded slowly. "Man been selling me liquor for years. So Del Vitti was just—"

"Just doing a job for his boss. When you called him a pimp, you nailed it. He was collecting girls for Vinnie."

"How you know?"

"Bonsigniore was arrested back in New York years ago for the same kind of behavior."

"That don't exactly prove it."

"It's good enough for me."

"You think he get your friend killed?"

"I do. And now that you know about him, what are you going to do about it?"

"How the hell do I know?" Doucette looked angry. "Like to kill him dead, that's what. But Vinnie, he a big man in this town, a lot bigger than this ol' boy. He got soldiers to protect him. So for now, I just keep on doin' business with him. Wait and see. Maybe some day I get my chance."

He drained his cup and set it down with a clatter. "Tootie say they take her 'way back in the woods. You know where?"

Horn nodded. "It was a place up in the mountains belonging to one of the men who's dead now."

"You think any of that still going on?"

"No," Horn said. "Too many of them are dead.

I think it's over. Except for the girls. It won't be over for them. It was worse for the older ones. The little ones, like my daughter—I think they just used them for pictures."

"They the lucky ones," the Creole said, his voice almost a whisper. "If you want to call any of 'em lucky."

Horn picked up his hat from the seat and maneuvered to the edge of the booth. "Before I go," he said, sliding the photo of Clea across the table, "I'd like you to look at this one more time. The other night—"

"I told you I never seen her. That was a big fat lie." The Creole flashed a golden grin. "Sorry 'bout that now. Sure I seen her. That pretty-boy piece of shit, he bring her here once or twice. She get some attention all around the room, I remember. I thought she just some good-looking young thing he picked up somewhere. She sure look eighteen to me. But now I know what been going on, I just feel bad."

"I'm glad to hear that," Horn said.

CHAPTER 17

After leaving the Dixie Belle, he stopped at a place on Central for some chicken and dumplings. It was almost dark when he pulled up in front of the converted bunkhouse. Inside, Maggie and Clea were washing the dinner dishes.

"Hi, you two," he said.

"We couldn't wait for you," Maggie sang out. "Couple of hungry gals here."

"That's fine." He took a seat and turned on Maggie's radio, a big Philco floor model with a molded wood facade that vaguely resembled the Chrysler Building, to see if there was further comment on the shooting in the Hollywood Hills. In a practiced baritone, the announcer was reciting news about Congress looking into Communist infiltration of the movie studios, a suicide attempt by Judy Garland, and a fatal car accident in Santa Monica. Nothing about Anthony Del Vitti.

Maggie and Clea came out to join him. "You want me to find some music?" she asked.

"No, thanks." He turned off the radio. "You mind if Clea and I have a talk?"

"Not at all," she said, and headed for the back door. "You know where to find me."

"She's been in the stable most of the day," Clea said. "The mare looks very sick."

"She's not really sick," he said. "That's just the way they get when they're about to have a baby."

"She's not going to die?"

"Well, I don't think so. Animals are pretty good at that sort of thing."

"I'm glad."

He paused, weighing his next question. "Have you been thinking about Tommy?"

She nodded vaguely. She was still wearing Maggie's shirt and jeans, and she sat with her legs tucked under her, a position she'd favored as long as he'd known her. She had always carried some of her mother's features, but now he could truly see some of Iris the woman in her—the slant of a cheekbone, the tilt of her head, the wary grace of her posture. And although Iris's appeal was as much about sexuality as surface appearance, Clea's features, seen in the soft light from the table lamp, threatened to blossom one day into classic beauty.

Looking at her, Horn felt something like despair. *She's just leaving childhood behind and getting ready to step into grown-up territory*, he thought. *It should be the happiest time of her life. Instead, she's carrying around memories of murder and abuse. And there's not much I can do right now to make it any better.*

"You liked Tommy, didn't you?"

"Uh-huh. He was nice to me." She plucked at a loose thread on her pants leg.

"Did you know his real name wasn't Tommy Dell? It was Anthony Del Vitti."

She looked up at him briefly, then down again.

"I'm sorry somebody killed him, but you need to know he didn't tell you the truth about himself. He worked for a man who . . . well, who liked to spend time with young girls. Very young, even younger than you. And Tommy would find girls for this man. Some of the girls were hurt—"

"Tommy was nice to me," she interrupted.

"Why did you go with him?"

"He said he'd take care of me. He did take care of me."

"Did he—" *Damn. How do you find the words?* "Honey, I'm sorry, but I need to ask you this: Did he do anything sexual with you?"

Clea shook her head.

"You sure? Even touch you or anything?"

"No," she said, her voice rising, looking squarely at him. "He was good."

It's hard to believe. But she doesn't seem to be lying. He tried to imagine another side to Del Vitti, the man who went trolling through Los Angeles for children. He tried to imagine the man keeping Clea in his house and not touching her. The image was out of focus, and he put it away.

"Did he introduce you to any other men he wanted you to spend time with?"

"No." She looked disgusted.

"Okay, I believe you. Why did you run away from home?"

Having abandoned the loose thread, her attention was now on a fingernail, which she picked at carefully. "I just wanted to."

"Were you afraid of anything?"

She said nothing.

"Or anybody?"

No answer.

"Clea, how did your new daddy treat you? Was he all right to you?"

She shrugged. "I guess."

Her long pauses were maddening. "Then why did you run away? Was it your mother?"

No answer.

"Your mother and father are very worried about you, and they asked me to find you. Why don't you want to go home?"

Nothing.

He shifted in his chair, trying not to grow irritated with her. *She's been through a lot,* he told himself. *Don't bully her. But don't let up on her either.*

"All right. Let's talk about something a little different. Do you remember your first father? Your real father?"

"Just a little." She looked apprehensive.

"Do you remember the lodge up in the mountains where your mother and I took you once? And Scotty was there?"

"Uh-huh," she said slowly, as if retrieving the memory from someplace deep.

"We went for walks in the snow, and later you played by the fire while we sat at the table with our cards. You remember?"

"I think so."

"Well, that wasn't the first time you were there. A long time before that, you were at the lodge. But your mother and I weren't there that time. Do you remember anything about—"

She picked more furiously at her fingernail. He couldn't see her downcast eyes, but he was suddenly aware of the blood sprouting around the cuticle. He got up and went to her. "Honey, don't do that." She looked up guiltily and put the finger in her mouth. "Let me have it." He pulled out his handkerchief and wrapped it around the finger. "Hold that there," he said.

He sat next to her, knowing he should push ahead with questions about the lodge, but he didn't have the heart. "You know how many people have been worried about you? People all over this town. I talked to Peter Binyon, one of your old boyfriends— I'm kind of glad you didn't stick with him, by the way. And Addie Webb and I went looking—"

"Addie?"

"Uh-huh."

"Is she all right?"

"She's all right."

"You're sure?"

"I'm sure. Addie can take care of herself. Look, Clea . . ." He turned to face her on the couch. "This is real hard. But if you don't talk to me about why you ran away, don't tell me everything that's going on . . . well, your folks want you back, and I don't feel right about keeping you here anymore." He touched her knee. "You'll have to—"

"Don't take me home," she said in a low, broken voice.

"I won't take you. But I'll have to let them know where you are, and I know they'll come get you. You belong at home."

He got up and stood there for a moment, trying to think of something else to say. Finally he left her there. Was he bluffing? He desperately wanted to keep her where he knew she was safe. But he knew that if Iris and Paul Fairbrass found out what he'd done, he could be in trouble with the police again; he might even go back to prison. His threat to send Clea home was his last chance. He hoped it would work.

He went out to the stable and stood maternity watch with Maggie for a while. When he returned, Clea had gone to bed. He sat by the phone as a thought took shape. Thelda Webb was probably at the Cocoanut Grove tonight. He pulled out a scrap of paper on which he'd written a number, picked up the phone, and dialed it. "Addie, this is John Ray Horn," he said when she answered. He spoke in a low voice so Clea wouldn't overhear. "I need to tell you something."

The dining room at the Hotel Alexandria was high-ceilinged and well lit, and waiters moved around placing silver and napkins and smoothing the white tablecloths. Lunchtime was still a half-hour away, and the big room was almost empty of diners, except for those occupying three tables against the far wall.

"Vinnie likes to eat before the crowd," Mad Crow said to Horn as they stood in the doorway. "The hotel must appreciate his business, 'cause they give him the room early."

"Either that, or they don't like hurting his feelings."

"You still want to do this?"

"You bet."

"Just be careful what you say, okay?"

Mad Crow led the way across the room. At the far-left table against the wall sat an old woman. She wore a long-sleeved black dress and a close-fitting black hat that sat squarely atop her head with a veil wrapped around it. She sat hunched over a bowl of soup and seemed oblivious to everything around her, including the waiter who stood stiffly behind her. As she lifted the spoon to her mouth, she made small slurping sounds that carried faintly across the large room.

Four men watched them approach. Two sat at a table off somewhat to the right, smoking and looking bored. They were in their twenties or early thirties. Neither one was Falco, but Horn had known their type up at Cold Creek. Of the two men at the table directly ahead, one was very young, barely out of his teens, with an unfinished face. He looked not entirely comfortable in his suit. The other man, who sat squarely facing them, was in his sixties, Horn guessed, and heavy. Although he wore a well-cut summer-weight suit in a light gray, everything else about him was dark— black hair only slightly tinged with gray, olive skin, heavy brows over hooded brown eyes. Under a coat of talcum powder, his freshly shaved face showed a hint of heavy beard waiting to sprout again.

Horn tried not to stare. Ever since he had first heard his father thunder in the pulpit, he had been fascinated with evil and wondered where he would encounter it in this world. He had expected to meet it in the war, in the faces of the enemy framed in his gunsights. But he saw only young Germans a little like him, men who got hungry and cold and who carried snapshots of wives and sweethearts. The only evil he'd ever met thus far, he reflected, was in the villains of his movies, those cardboard characters who existed only to confront goodness, in the form of Sierra Lane, and be defeated by it. *So, how about this one?* he wondered as he stood before Vincent Bonsigniore. *What's he made of?*

"Mr. Bonsigniore, this is my friend John Ray Horn," the Indian said. "I told you about him."

"Have a seat." Bonsigniore waved the two of them to chairs. "Excuse me if I get back to this." He dipped a spoon in the bowl of consommé in front of him. *He won't invite us to lunch*, Mad Crow had said earlier. *Vinnie likes to be the emperor in his court.*

"My nephew Dominic," Bonsigniore said, gesturing toward the young man. "My sister's boy. She wanted him to go into dry goods, follow her two-bit husband. He wants to work for me a while. Smart kid." His voice was surprisingly light for such a man, thin and reedy, the kind of voice a small-town businessman might use to interest you in his wares. Horn decided not to be misled by it.

"Been coming here for years," Bonsigniore went on to no one in particular, his attention on his soup. "This used to be the class hotel downtown. Charlie Chaplin's favorite, you know that? Then the Biltmore opened up, and it took away some of the fancy business. But I'm not a particularly fancy guy. This place feels comfortable to me. Mama likes it too," he added, inclining his head toward the table where the old woman sat. He smelled of Old Spice too liberally applied.

The man turned to Horn. "When Joe and me start to talk business, we'll need some privacy," he said. "You can take a seat over there, get some coffee."

"I don't mind," Horn said lightly. "You mind if I have one of these?" He pulled out his Bull Durham and rolling papers.

"Go right ahead," Bonsigniore said, pushing his soup bowl aside and signaling to a waiter. "Saving your pennies, huh? I never had the patience to do that. Plus, I got the habit of smoking these." He pulled out a Dutch Masters and lit it. His fingers were short and thick, and each of his two little

271

fingers bore a sturdy ring. On the left one, Horn could make out the letter B in what looked like garnets and rhinestones—or rubies and diamonds. The ring on the right hand was solid gold. "I hear you were a real cowboy once, before you got into the movies."

"Something like that," Horn said. "I did some rodeo riding after I left home. But the last bull I rode messed me up so bad, I decided to find an easier way to earn a living."

"Riding bulls," the other man said almost dreamily. "Crazy fucking job, if you ask me."

So why don't we talk about your work? Horn thought. *Your hobbies, maybe?*

"I'm ready," Bonsigniore called out to the waiter, and a minute later the man brought over a sandwich on a plate. It was a gigantic pastrami on rye, with a small pot of mustard next to it.

"Want to hear something funny? I have this brought over from Langer's every time I eat here. Food here ain't bad, you understand, but it's hotel food. You know Langer's? Out by MacArthur Park?"

"I been there," Horn said.

"Best deli in town. Good as New York. Guy asked me once how come you grow up in Little Italy and eat at a Jewish place? I told him because most Italian places in this town are crap, you know what I mean? The Jews are good cooks. They just need a little help with the spices sometimes." He slathered mustard on the bread. "So, you know Betty Grable?"

"Afraid not. She's over at Fox. I worked for a small studio out in the Valley."

"She's too good for that guy Harry James," Bonsigniore's nephew piped up in a wise-guy voice. "Too much for him."

"Shut up, Dominic," the older man said without malice. "Go sit with Mama."

The younger man got up and went to the old woman's table, walking in an exaggerated, loose-limbed gait that suggested he was not quite used to his adult frame. When he sat, she did not acknowledge him, her attention now focused on a sandwich the waiter had just placed before her, as massive as the one now being devoured by her son.

"I know where you worked," Bonsigniore went on, his mouth full of pastrami. "Horse operas. They're crap, mostly. No offense. I like George Raft. There's an actor."

"Everybody's got a favorite," Horn said. "I met a guy the other day said he liked Bob Steele."

"Who the hell is that?"

"Just a cowboy actor."

Bonsigniore shook his head. "Never heard of him. But I heard how you beat up that little prick you worked for—"

"He was the son of the man who ran the studio. I didn't really work for him."

"You must have worked him over good. You did some time for it."

Horn nodded.

"Hard time?"

"Not really."

"Make any friends?"

"A few."

The other man stared at him for a moment. Horn didn't like the look. *How much does he really know?* he wondered.

"You ever need a job," Bonsigniore said casually, "maybe you'll look me up sometime."

"Hey," Mad Crow broke in.

"I know, I know," Bonsigniore said. "Don't worry about it. I'm not stealing your guy. Just want him to know." He took a giant bite of the sandwich and chewed without taking his eyes off Horn.

"Everybody's offering me jobs," Horn said.

"Mickey Cohen, he offered you one," Bonsigniore said, still chewing. "The other night. Joe here told me." Horn glanced at the Indian. "You'd be a sap to throw in with him. Crazy little Hebe. He thinks he's independent. It's the independent guys like him who don't last. You watch."

"I'm not looking for work right now, thanks," Horn said.

Bonsigniore appeared to lose interest. "Fair enough," he said with a shrug, then turned to Mad Crow. "Joe, you got it?"

"Yessiree," Mad Crow replied. He pulled a fat envelope from his jacket and laid it on the table.

Still staring at Horn, Bonsigniore said, "You excuse us now, okay? Joe and me . . ."

"Sure," Horn said. He got up and moved to a

table about twenty feet away. When a waiter came over, he ordered coffee. Then he sat facing Bonsigniore, trying to study him without being obvious.

So what have I learned? he asked himself. *Not much I can use. He likes pastrami and Betty Grable and George Raft. He doesn't like people eating around him. He likes to take little girls away to the mountains with his friends. The man who found the girls—his procurer—is dead. Maybe that's the job he's thinking of offering me.*

And now, most important of all, I know for sure he's one of the three men in the photos. His two big, fancy rings nail it down. The beefy man with the rings: That's Vincent Bonsigniore.

As for him, he knows a lot about me, except for the most important thing: That I know he molests little girls. And that he had my friend killed.

And now, what can I do about it?

A shadow fell over the table, and Horn looked up to see Gabriel Falco sitting down across from him.

"Well," Falco said. "It's the tough guy from the alley." His face wore an almost imperceptible grin, as if he'd just heard a joke that only he could appreciate.

Horn put his coffee cup down carefully. "How's it going?" he asked.

Falco shrugged. He waved over a waiter and said, "Coffee and a piece of pie. Apple if you got it." His voice had the metallic sound of the New York streets.

Horn took his first good look at him. Falco was average height and weight, with a thin Clark Gable mustache, but he gave off hints of speed and strength. Above the corded neck was a face of angles, including a strong jaw and cheekbones that would not have been out of place in Mad Crow's family tree. The brows, like Bonsigniore's, were heavy and dark, and the surprisingly pale eyes reminded Horn of those of a predator bird—wide and absolutely without depth. He seemed to carry no extra weight on his frame. It was as if something had consumed the excess flesh, burned it off to lighten the man for the things he needed to do.

Remembering the darkness of the alley and the ache in his kidney, Horn felt something stir and begin to grow in him, and he knew it was fear. The same thing that had taken over and immobilized him in the mountains of Italy. The thing that gets to you if you think too much, open the door to it. The man sitting across from him had killed someone in prison and could have killed him that night behind the Dixie Belle, might have killed him if the struggle had gone a little differently. And one more thing: This could be the man who ended Scotty's life. *Sure, I'm afraid of him*, Horn thought. *But . . . I don't have to let him know it.*

"Waiting for your boss to finish up?" Horn asked.

Falco was working on his slice of pie. It was apple and looked good, but he attacked it the way a fire would consume a dry stick you threw into it. Although he didn't look up at Horn's question,

276

Horn knew the man was reflecting on it, wondering how much Horn knew about even simple things like who he worked for. Horn half-regretted the question, told himself he shouldn't appear to know too much. *Maybe you should let him be the smart one*, he thought. *You're the dumb-ass out-of-work cowboy, he's the city slicker.* But in the next breath, he told himself: *I'll never find out anything that way.*

Falco seemed amused by the question. "Sure. Waiting for the boss," he said. "He barks, I jump."

"But you stay busy with other jobs too, don't you?" Horn asked.

"That's right." Falco finished the pie, pushed the plate aside, and sat there with the half-smile on his face. "You know a few things about me?"

"Sure. Got real interested in you after you and your friend ganged up on me the other night. I asked around. Not long after that, I was watching you hanging from an airplane out at the Medallion Ranch. What's the matter, Vinnie not paying you enough?"

Falco didn't seem offended. "Vinnie pays me good, but he only needs me for things every now and then. Rest of the time . . . well, if you're the best stunt man in the business, you're going to work steady."

Horn gave a low whistle. "And modest, too."

"I leave that to other people," Falco said. "You, for instance. What I hear, you got lots to be modest about. One day you're a hotshot movie star, with guys like me doing your stunts so you won't get

277

your hair mussed. Next day you're a caretaker for some rundown piece of property, cutting weeds."

"I do all right," Horn said. Strangely, the sarcasm stung him. Maybe because it was true. *Stop defending yourself. Go after him.*

"I've got more going on than just weed-pulling," he went. "Lately, I've been busy looking for my daughter. She's not exactly my daughter, but I think of her that way. I promised her folks I'd find her, and I mean to."

"Good for you," Falco said. "You do that."

"For a while, I thought she was with a man named Anthony Del Vitti—you know, that friend of yours, the one who liked to use a knife—"

"He wasn't very good with a knife," Falco broke in. "I'm a lot better. Maybe you'll get a chance to see some day."

"Maybe. But then somebody killed Del Vitti, and it turned out she wasn't with him. So I'm still looking." He knew he was saying too much. He'd promised Mad Crow not to say anything that might get him in trouble with his partner. But, sitting across from this man whose very looks had the power to chill him, he knew he couldn't just sit silently. He had to talk, to probe, to see what Falco was made of, to see what he knew. Horn felt as if he'd been riding in a field and a gate had swung open onto a new piece of land, unexplored and a little dangerous, but full of possibility. He wondered what would happen if he rode through.

Falco helped him decide. "It's like Tony told you:

278

Be careful where you look," the man said, elbows on the arms of his chair, fingers templed. Horn could see old scar tissue on the back of one hand. "You should've listened to old Tony. Now he won't be giving out any more advice. Somebody put a bullet through his eye, messed up his nice bathrobe."

For a few seconds, Falco's words, and the arrogance behind them, shocked Horn into silence. A new and disturbing thought crowded its way into his head. Could he have killed Del Vitti?

"You know a lot about it, don't you?" Horn asked him.

"Just what I read in the papers," Falco said. "I try to keep up on all the crime news." Horn realized that Falco was regarding the cut near his eyebrow. It was healing but still noticeable. "So, you learned to stay out of fights?" the other man asked casually.

Smug son of a bitch, Horn thought, aware that he and Falco were behaving like two boys in a schoolyard contest, the kind that starts with words and ends in shoves and blows. *Push him right back.* "You bet," he said with exaggerated casualness. "I like peace and quiet. And my daddy taught me never to go up against two guys at once. You'll lose every time, he'd tell me. But then he'd say you don't have to be ashamed of that, 'cause anybody who'd gang up on another man is basically low and yellow. Yes, sir, that's what he'd tell me. What do you think?"

"I think the next time I see you, you won't walk

out of the alley." The smile stayed in place. Horn couldn't hear any bluster in Falco's words. Just promise.

"Oh, my goodness," Horn said, wanting to see how far this would go. "Guess I'll have to stay out of alleys now. But tell me something: Since you lost your partner, the pretty boy with the little knife, who you going to get to help you out?"

Falco lolled back in his chair. "Do you a favor," he said. "I'll be alone this time."

"Great. Do I need to look over my shoulder, or do you come at a man from the front?"

"Why don't you ask your friend?"

"Huh?"

"Your friend. You know, the guy who went out the window."

A blood-red film descended over Horn's eyes. He didn't feel himself kick back the chair, didn't feel himself lurch around the table. Vaguely, he heard shouting. When his eyes could focus again, he was standing over Falco, his right hand knotted in the tablecloth, stomach muscles clenching until they hurt, ready to lunge for the man's throat. But Mad Crow's face was inches from his own, and Horn felt the Indian gripping him hard by the shoulders. He took a breath, ready to push his friend aside. But at that instant he saw Falco sweep aside his jacket with his left hand and rest his right lightly on the polished butt of a handgun nestled in some kind of holster under his left arm. Horn stopped himself, breathing heavily.

Although Falco's eyes were narrowed, his expression hadn't changed perceptibly. "Come on," he said quietly. "Here or someplace else. I don't care. If it's here, I put one in both of you and walk out through the kitchen. Nobody saw me, 'cause everybody in this place gets amnesia. That what you want?" His fingertips tapped the gun butt. "Right here, cowboy? Right here in the O.K. Corral?"

Horn took a breath. He heard a voice and looked around. Bonsigniore's three men were on their feet, hands in their jackets, as the waiters quickly exited. The old woman in black remained bent over her food, paying no more attention to them than she would to the voices of the actors in a radio drama heard faintly from the next room.

Mad Crow held him wordlessly, face twisted with the effort. Bonsigniore himself spoke again to his men: "I said sit down, all right?" He gestured imperiously, the overhead light glinting off the stones on his little finger. Then he turned to Falco: "Gabe, get out of here."

Horn relaxed a little, and Mad Crow, watching him carefully, stepped aside. Falco stood and arranged his jacket. He and Horn stood within a foot of each other. Horn could smell the other man's breath. He thought of two animals approaching each other in the wild, sniffing to determine which one would turn tail.

Falco leaned forward. "You're a funny guy," he said, almost in a whisper. "Difference between you and me, I just handle business, but you take everything personal. If you turn into a job for me, I'll take care of you. If not . . ." He spread his hands wide, palms up, brushing Horn's coat. "We leave each other alone. Don't make yourself my business." He turned and left.

Horn saw that his hand, still clenched around the tablecloth, was shaking. *Too late for that, Gabe,* he thought.

CHAPTER 18

Out on the street, ten minutes later, Mad Crow raged at him.

"What was that all about? You said you wouldn't get in the way. Then you start mixing it up with that guy—"

"That was Falco."

"I thought it was. You went crazy, you know that? Vinnie said I got to keep you out of his sight. He's mad. John Ray, I can't afford to get on his bad side, I told you that."

"He was pushing me. He said he killed Scotty."

"What?"

"Well, he just about said it. He came close enough to satisfy me. The son of a bitch did it. He thinks I can't do anything about it. Maybe he's right."

The Indian leaned up against his Cadillac, looking grim. "He could have killed you right there," he said. "Both of us, maybe."

"You should have stayed out of the way."

"And let you take him on? Oh, sure. You would've chewed him up, just like you did little Junior. Only difference was, this guy carries a gun."

Horn glared at him. "You saying I should be afraid of him?"

"I'm saying you didn't show good sense in there. Sometimes you get all crazy, other people got to look out for you."

"You should have—"

"Stayed out of the way, I know. You really think I should have turned loose of you, let you at him?"

Horn glared some more, then let out a deep breath. "No," he said finally. "I guess I ought to thank you."

"There'll be another time."

"You know something?" Horn said. "I killed a few men in the war, one or two up close. I still think about it, have bad dreams. I looked in Falco's eyes just now, and I knew he could kill me dead and go eat a good meal and get laid and sleep like a baby. And it's people like *that* scare me."

"That's not Sierra Lane talking," the Indian muttered.

"I know."

He found Maggie with one of her ranch hands in the tack room off the stables, repairing a worn latigo on a saddle. "Where's Clea?" he asked.

Maggie looked up briefly, then resumed work. "Went for a walk. Addie showed up, and the two of them went off awhile ago. Looked like they had a lot of catching up to do."

"Where?"

"Now, don't worry. They took the north road,

where it parallels the fence for a couple of miles. I told them to turn around when they get to the bend in the road. They'll be back soon." She looked up at him again. "Relax, John Ray."

"I'm relaxed. When did Addie get here?"

"Couple of hours ago. She hitched a ride with some delivery man, and he acted like it was a privilege to bring her all the way out here."

"That's Addie. She'll never be without a ride. Or anything else she needs. It's good of you to put up with all of us campers here, Maggie."

"I don't mind. Addie even brought an overnight bag, so I guess she plans to stay awhile."

He told her what he knew about Addie, including the time the two girls had run off together, and he finished by telling her about the night down on Central Avenue.

"I'd never have guessed they were the same age," Maggie said.

"Addie's a year or two older."

"More like five, I'd have said. No matter how old she is, though, she knows a few things. Including men. You should have seen the looks she got from Miguel and Tomás. And she could tell."

"A heartbreaker."

She nodded, smiling, still focused on the cinch strap. "Why did you call her? I thought you didn't want—"

"Didn't want word to get around about Clea being here. I still don't. But I haven't been able to get through to her, get her to open up to me about why she ran away. I won't take her home until I know. She and Addie were always close, and something tells me Addie can help. She said she'll try."

"Hope you're right."

"How's the mare?"

"She's ready. Told me so."

He went outside and sat in one of the worn chairs on the patch of grass in front of Maggie's converted bunkhouse. Before long, he heard girls' voices and turned to see Clea and Addie coming down the road. He went to meet them.

"Hi," Addie called out.

"Hi, girls." Clea wore Maggie's dungarees and cotton shirt, while Addie wore well-pressed slacks and a pastel blouse. Both were sweating in the midafternoon heat.

Clea seemed even more than usually subdued. "I think I'll go wash up," she said, heading for the cottage. When she was out of earshot, he asked Addie: "Anything?"

She shook her head. "I tried," she said. "I asked her over and over. She just shakes her head. You can tell there's something bothering her. She's changed a lot. But whatever it is . . ."

"Well, I hope you'll keep trying. Will you stay with us for a while? You girls can share the bed, I'll be on the couch, and Maggie's been sleeping in the stable lately."

"Sure," she said readily. "I'll call Mama and let her know. She'll yell at me, but I'm used to that. And now I better go wash up too."

"Do me a favor," he called after her. "Tell Maggie I'll be back for dinner."

He pulled up in front of the Fairbrass house in the Hancock Park neighborhood, on a quiet street shaded by sweet gum and coral trees. The houses were solid and patrician, done in the city's usual mix of architectural styles. It was the middle of the afternoon, warm verging on hot. After some hesitation, he had decided not to call first. He wanted to avoid letting Paul Fairbrass know he was coming. Fairbrass would insist on being there, and Horn wanted Iris to himself. Much the way he had butted heads with Falco, he wanted to confront Iris abruptly with his questions. The answers could determine whether it was time for Clea to come out of hiding and go home.

The house was an impressive two stories, white, in what some people would call French chateau style. He rang the bell several times and got no answer. After a minute, he went along a walkway that led to the back, and there he found Iris in the garden. She was on her knees, working the dirt with a trowel, and she wore a loose-fitting blouse, pants, and a wide-brimmed hat against the sun. Not far away, where the garden bordered a spacious backyard, a middle-aged Oriental man stood on a ladder, pruning the limbs of a pepper tree.

"You always did like digging in the dirt," he called out. "Digging and planting things. Remember our fruit trees?"

She sat back on her heels, raised the brim of the hat, and looked at him. There was no welcome in the look, only resignation.

He walked over. "You don't look glad to see me."

She shrugged. "If you had good news, you would have called right away," she said. "Also, since Paul asked you to deal with him, you probably know I wouldn't have invited you over just for a visit. So why are you here?"

"I talked to Clea."

"What?" She put down the trowel, got up distractedly. "When? Is she all right?"

"She sounds all right," he said. *Start lying, but make it good.* "She must have heard I was looking for her, and she telephoned. Wouldn't tell me where she was. She just said she doesn't want to come home."

"I don't understand." Iris pulled off her hat and brushed a strand of hair out of her eyes, then looked at her hand, realizing she'd left a streak of dirt across her face.

"I don't either. I was hoping you could help me."

She looked at him suspiciously, and he knew the conversation was going to be difficult.

"If we could go inside where it's cooler, maybe I could explain," he said.

She hesitated a moment, then motioned him toward the back door. They entered the kitchen, where she indicated they could sit at a breakfast table. The kitchen was large and sunny, with bright yellow walls and shiny appliances, including a built-in dishwasher. He imagined Clea sitting at the table, eating her favorite breakfast of toast, cereal, and bananas. Two doors led to the rest of the house, but they were closed, and he could see no farther. *Mrs. Bullard sat me down in her parlor, not her kitchen*, he felt like saying. *And her house is even nicer than yours.*

She went to the freezer, extracted an ice tray, and began to crack the cubes loose. A minute later, she placed a tall glass of ice water in front of him.

"You remembered I like lots of ice," he said, taking a long drink. A telephone rang somewhere farther back in the house. She excused herself and went to answer it.

He sat there for a few minutes and, when she didn't return, he went to look for her. He found her in the living room, talking on the telephone while standing at a table beside one of the front windows. He eavesdropped on her conversation as he browsed around the room, but the talk seemed to be about something she had bought at a store and wanted to return, so he stopped listening. His real reason for following her, he admitted to himself, was curiosity about her house, about the new life she and Clea had entered into with this man Fairbrass. The living room was elegant and well-furnished, if a little too feminine for his taste. As Iris stood with her back to him, he studied her in the context of the room, the comfortable furniture, the family photos on the table next to her. He had always thought of her in their old world, but he could see that this was her world now. *She looks right at home.*

When she hung up, he pointed to a framed photo of Clea on the table. "Your husband gave me a copy of that, to help me look for her," he said. "I think it's the best picture of her I've ever seen."

"Paul took that," she said. "We all like it."

"Scotty told me he was at the party where you and Paul met."

"Oh, that's right. I remember Scotty was there. It was a big party, at Mr. and Mrs. Bullard's place. I was there, of course, because I was one of the old company girls. When the invitation came, you had just . . . you know, had just gone. I wasn't handling it very well, you being in prison, and I guess I was grateful for the chance to get out, see people, so I went."

Her expression told him she hoped to avoid talking about the divorce. He hadn't the heart for it either. They went back to the kitchen, and Iris waited for him to resume.

"Clea said she doesn't want to come home," he said. "It's pretty clear to me nothing's going to happen until I find out why."

"Will you talk to her again?" Iris asked. "I mean, do you think she'll call you again?" She reached over to the counter beside her and picked up a pack of Viceroys, extracted one, and lit it. Her motions were measured and precise and seemed designed to give her time to gather her thoughts.

"I think she might. I have the feeling we can clear all this up in a few days. But I'm not going to do anything more to find her until I know . . ." He paused, searching for the words.

"Know what?"

"Know if she has anything to be afraid of here."

She inhaled deeply and blew the smoke off to the side, then lowered the cigarette to a square ceramic ashtray in front of her, where she shaped the ash carefully, even though it was still short. Her expression had not changed.

"I'm not sure I know what you mean."

"Look, Iris, I think we're running out of time. Don't ask me how I know. I've got to find out what's wrong. You need to be honest with me about your girl. If you're not, I don't know what will happen."

"If I don't tell you what you want to know, I may not get her back. Is that what you're saying?"

"No. You might still find her. Your husband might. The police might. But I think your chances are better with me, because she trusts me. And I'm starting to feel stubborn, because I think there are things you haven't told me. She's afraid of something." *Go on, tell her.* "I think she's afraid of Paul."

Her eyes went wide, and her mouth gaped. Then, improbably, she laughed. "Afraid of Paul?" She laughed again, louder this time, and the laugh turned into a coughing fit. She reached for his glass and took a drink.

"Oh, John Ray, you're so wrong," she said finally. "Paul's an angel to her. He loves her as if she were his own. I really think he would die for her."

"I'm glad you think it's funny."

"No, I'm sorry. It's just that you're so wrong. Whatever problems Clea had here, whatever made her run away, it had to do with me, not Paul."

"Prove it."

"What?"

"Convince me."

She stared at him, her look almost hostile. Then she got up and went to a cabinet, where she found a bottle of scotch. She poured herself three fingers in a small glass and sat down facing him, both hands wrapped protectively around the glass. She didn't offer him a drink.

She said nothing, just stared, and he could almost hear her thinking. *Got to keep her talking*, he thought. *Or she might decide to throw me out.* "You know, you really haven't changed all that much," he said to her. "Just little things. One is, you're drinking better stuff now. Must be nice to have a husband who can afford—"

"Don't be sarcastic, John Ray. If I married Paul, it was because I loved him, and I knew he loved me and Clea. It *is* nice to be able to afford things, and I won't apologize for enjoying them. And no, I don't usually drink in the middle of the day," she said, looking down at her glass. "You're making me nervous, that's all. I don't drink nearly as much as before. I decided I never want to get into that kind of behavior again. I have a husband and a daughter who expect me to be . . ."

"Upright."

"I said don't be sarcastic. What do you know? I've changed more than you can even guess. I look back at the kind of person I used to be—angry about things, going on binges, fighting with you, neglecting her—and I just want to forget that woman."

"You're too hard on yourself."

She said nothing, just looked into her glass. Somewhere in the house, he could hear the ticking of a large clock. A minute went by, then two. He pulled something out of his pocket and slid it across the table toward her. It was a snapshot, face down. She didn't pick it up, but the grim set of her face told him she knew what it was.

"It's her, isn't it?" he asked. "You don't have to look at it again. Just tell me you know it's her."

Her face twisted, became helplessly ugly as she fought the emotion. Then it took her over and she began to cry silently. Her eyes glistened and overflowed as she looked down at the photo she couldn't pick up. He handed her his handkerchief and let her cry as he talked.

"I've learned a lot of things," he began, even as he admitted to himself that all his ideas fell short of absolute certainty. "About Wendell, and how he used to take Clea up to the Bullards' lodge in the mountains, where old man Bullard and some others would get together. It was always one young girl

293

or another, some as young as Clea in this picture. I don't know why Wendell did it. Maybe it was because he was just a nobody behind a hotel desk, and he wanted old man Bullard to owe him something. Maybe he liked rubbing elbows with men who were more successful than he was. Whatever it was he wanted, he was willing to use his little girl as the admission fee—"

"Don't," she said in a tiny voice. She reached out and laid a hand over the photo, patting it gently, almost caressing it, as a mother would soothe a frightened child. "Don't."

"And I learned that along with Scotty's father and your husband, there were a couple of others. One was an old gangster named Vincent Bonsigniore. The other, I'm pretty sure, was someone named Calvin St. George, who runs a bookstore in Hollywood and who was the one who took the pictures up at the lodge."

He pocketed the picture without turning it over. "If you knew it was her, why did you lie to me when I showed it to you after Scotty's funeral?"

"Why didn't I admit to you I knew that someone had been abusing my daughter years earlier? How could I? You don't know how much I blamed myself for what happened. But that doesn't mean I'm ready to confess everything to the world. I never wanted you to know. And I don't want Paul to know. You have to promise me—"

"I've got no reason to tell him."

"Promise me."

"I promise. Now you need to tell me some things. First of all, it *was* Wendell, wasn't it?"

"You just said—"

"I need to hear you say it. Was it Wendell?"

"Yes." Her face was grim.

"Did you know about it while it was going on?"

"No. Not really. But let me just tell you; it's easier that way." She picked up her glass, put it back down, took a deep breath, and began.

"I heard Clea crying one night and went to her. Wendell was always a sound sleeper. She told me she'd had a nightmare. I comforted her for a while, and then she began telling me a story about a trip with her father one day while I was at work. It sounded like a little girl's fantasy, but there were some details that bothered me. A few days later, I found some photos in one of his drawers—I admit I was snooping. They were awful, with little girls. They were probably the same pictures Scotty gave you. And I found one of Clea, the same one you showed me.

"I went a little crazy. I confronted him that night. He admitted everything. He . . . he came apart. Right in front of me. It was like watching someone dissolve down into nothing. He told me he'd always had this weakness for young girls, and that he knew other men who had the same fascination, and that they . . ."

"I know," he said.

"He said he'd sinned and was ready to accept his punishment. Actually used those words, even though he'd never struck me as any more religious than the next person. But he had some kind of strange loyalty to those other men and wouldn't name them."

"So you never had any idea about Arthur Bullard?"

"No, of course not," she said, and the hate twisted her face. "How could I have kept working for his company? How could I, years later, have gone to a party at his house? Wendell obviously didn't tell me where they took the girls either. If I'd known it was the lodge, I would never have agreed for the three of us to join Scotty up there for that weekend."

"All right," Horn said. "So you divorced Wendell."

She nodded. "I put Clea in the car the next morning, and we drove to Reno. I rented a room and stayed there just long enough to divorce him, and then we came back."

"What about him? Did you tell the police?"

"No," she said. "To this day, I don't know if I did the right thing. It wasn't because I had any love left for him—that was gone, every ounce. It was just that he was so . . . destroyed. He cried that night. He swore he'd never touch another girl. He begged me to let him go someplace and try to start a new life."

"So you did. I'm not sure it was the right decision either. There were other little girls, you know, past and future."

"Wendell said when he told the others what had

296

happened, they would break up and scatter. I wanted to believe him. I hoped it was true."

"It wasn't," he said.

"I know that now. Every day I know it. I feel as guilty as he was."

"No, you're not," he said. "Important thing is to get Clea home and to make sure these men—what's left of them—get put away. I've got an idea about how to get some information to the police about them. That should do it. Now, about Clea . . . I need to know what went on before she left. Paul tells me you were fighting. What about?"

"I don't know," she said vaguely. "Little things. Everything. She just seemed very angry."

"Any chance she could remember anything at all about those times at the lodge?"

"You're thinking *that* was it? I don't see how she could remember. She was so young. And besides, more than ten years had gone by. Why would it suddenly come up?"

"That's what I'm wondering. When did the fighting start?"

"I think it was just a few days before she ran away." She paused to reflect. "Do you want to know what scares me the most? The idea that somehow she blames me for what happened all those years ago. I know it sounds fantastic, because so much time had gone by, and we were happy in so many ways. But it's the only explanation I can come up with. That she somehow remembered it and blamed me for it."

"Did anything unusual happen around the time she left?"

"I don't think so. She was out of school for the summer and at home most of the time. Sometimes friends would come over, or she'd go visit them. And one day all of us went to . . ." She stopped, took a breath. "Oh, God. We went to the funeral. All of us."

"What do you mean? She wasn't at Scotty's funeral."

"No," Iris said slowly. "Arthur Bullard's."

"Clea went to his funeral?"

"Yes. I thought it was a little strange. She asked to go. I think it was just curiosity. She'd never been to a funeral, but we thought it would be all right, so we took her. She seemed strange on the way home, almost as if something had happened at the funeral. And then those awful fights began, and one morning I went in to awaken her, and her bed hadn't been slept in."

He felt confused. "The funeral. I don't get it. I mean, if she knew that old man Bullard had been one of the men at the lodge, I could understand his death setting her off. But they all wore masks . . . hoods. And she was so little."

"I know," Iris said. "At the time, I just thought that it was a mistake to take her to the funeral, that maybe it was just too morbid for her. Now I wonder if it was something else."

"I think we'll find out now," he said. "Clea's going to tell us. We just have to ask the question right, that's all. She'll be back home, and everything will be all right. And then I'll only have one thing left—doing something about Scotty."

He got up. "Thanks for being honest with me. Maybe it's best if you don't tell Paul I was here. I'll just go out the back way."

She followed him out the door and through the garden to the path that led to the front of the house. She looked tense, as if something remained unsettled. At the path, he turned, listening to the *snip, snip* of the gardener's shears up in the pepper tree.

"A long time ago," he said, "we were talking about other people's houses, and you said you envied anyone who had their own Japanese gardener. Well . . . congratulations."

She said nothing. He noticed again the mark her dirty hand had left on her forehead and reached toward her, intending to wipe it away. But she flinched, and he stopped.

"What is it?" she asked.

"Sorry. You've got a little dirt on your face."

She rubbed at it halfheartedly, but a trace of the mark remained, like a small shadow passing over her.

"There's one thing I didn't tell you," she said, taking a breath and letting it out. "He's alive."

"Who?"

"Wendell. I told you he died in San Francisco. It was a lie."

CHAPTER 19

Horn was on the road at first light, when the westernmost ridge of the San Gabriel Mountains lay to the north like giant sleeping cattle, still almost indistinguishable from the night sky. The Ford did not take well to extreme heat, so he wanted to cover some miles before the sun was far up. An old Army canteen full of water lay on the seat next to him, along with a paper bag holding a sandwich he'd hastily put together in Maggie's kitchen. He had reluctantly awakened Maggie before leaving, just to tell her he'd be gone most of the day.

He drove east about ten miles until he hooked up with the two-lane road that wound up through the San Fernando Pass and beyond. After an hour, the road had climbed a thousand feet or so, and not long after he'd switched off his head-lights, he felt the first rays of sun warming the back of his neck through the rear window. Far below to his right, he could make out the dark slash of the Los Angeles Aqueduct. People said it was the aqueduct's water that made the desert bloom hereabouts, that turned the dry San

Fernando Valley into a place of orchards and homes.

That was true. But, like most L.A. stories, it had its dark side. While lobbying for a plan to divert water from the slopes of the Eastern Sierra and carry it hundreds of miles down to L.A., certain big operators in business and government had secretly bought up huge swaths of valley land, planning to cash in when the desert turned from brown to green. The young Arthur Bullard, Scotty told him once, was at the time building up his own real estate business. He watched those men and learned from them—and, before long, was one of them.

Another hour, another thousand feet, and a dark, imposing range of mountains rose up ahead and to his right. He passed cars and trucks heading down into L.A., some of them loaded with produce from up the coast. He stopped at a small diner, one of the few signs of civilization on the road, to have a cup of coffee and ask directions. The waitress had never heard of his destination, but the owner, after some reflection, was able to help. "Funny," he said. "That place has been up there long as I can remember, and you're the first person ever asked me how to get there."

He drove on, thinking about what Iris had told him. Wendell Brand had begged her to help him disappear, and believing in his sincerity, his shame and repentance, she had agreed to make up a story for him. She was the only one who knew where he had gone, she said. He had chosen a place where he thought no one would look for him, and Horn had to agree it was an inspired choice. His place of refuge struck Horn as a gigantic, mirthless joke.

He found the turnoff about two miles past the diner—no sign, just a dirt road off to the right that began to climb almost immediately and soon was deep in sage and chaparral. The road was barely more than a single lane, full of turns and badly graded. He drove slowly. The road rose steeply now, the Ford beginning to labor with the altitude. He pulled over to rest the engine for a while and ate his sandwich. It was Spam, something he'd had more than enough of during the war, but he was hungry.

After another half-hour of driving, Horn estimated he was close to a mile up. The chaparral gave way to pines. Still no road markers, no signs of people or structures. Just when Horn began to wonder if he had taken the wrong path, the road leveled off, and he saw a stone gate up ahead.

He drove through and saw spread out before him a collection of wood-and-stucco buildings clustered around a spacious grassy area. In the middle was a round stone well, with bucket and pulley. The buildings' architecture was simple but strong and suggested pictures he'd seen of some of the old California missions. Rising from the largest building was a modest bell tower. Here and there he saw men wearing hooded robes of white cotton, each one working at some kind of task.

He got out and, after asking directions of one of the robed men, found his way to a work site behind a nearby building, where several men were putting up the timbered frame of what looked like a shed or storeroom. The man supervising the work was big, with hood thrown back on his shoulders to reveal a large, curly head and vivid red beard.

"Are you the abbot?" Horn asked him.

The man nodded. "Brother Timothy."

"I'd like to see Wendell Brand. Brother Wendell."

The abbot regarded him without expression, his large, work-hardened hands clasped in front, their backs covered with wiry, pale-red hair. "We allow visitors only for special events, or on emergencies," he said quietly. "We're a working order. We try to focus on what we have to do and leave the world outside."

"This is a kind of emergency," Horn said earnestly. "I'm his brother . . . uh, his brother-in-law Wesley, and I have an important message from his ex-wife."

"You've never visited before."

"I know. You could say we're not close."

After staring at him for another moment, the abbot nodded. He spoke briefly to one of the other monks, who then walked off. "He'll go find Brother Wendell," the abbot said. "I'll show you where you can wait for him." He led Horn to the main building, which apparently held the chapel and bell tower. They entered through a side door and were in a kind of meeting room with a simple round wooden table, six chairs, and a crucifix on the wall.

"He'll join you here," the abbot said, indicating for Horn to seat himself. "But only if he wants to see you."

Brother Timothy seemed in no hurry to leave. He stood regarding Horn with mild curiosity. "You look like a working man," he said.

"I've done my share."

"When Brother Wendell came to us several years ago, he had what you might call a white-collar background; he wasn't used to hard work. But he's different now. Here, we all learn the satisfaction of labor in the right cause."

Horn nodded, only partly listening. He glanced out the window. "When I imagine a monastery, it's in a place like this," he said. "Somewhere on a mountaintop or 'way off in the desert."

"Yes," Brother Timothy said. "We're not near anything here. Just God and the sky. And maybe something else."

"What's that?"

"If you go in that direction," the abbot said, pointing off to the northeast, "eventually you drop off the mountain and enter the great desert. Just where mountain and desert meet is the San Andreas Fault. You know what that is?"

"Sure," Horn said. "From the big quake."

The abbot nodded. "Years ago, we had a monk here named Brother Mark. He was old and a little

. . . you know, sometimes he would say things that we couldn't quite understand. But he believed that the fault in the earth led straight down to Hell." The abbot smiled. "Most of us would just listen politely. And Brother Mark would go on to say that God put us here on the mountain for a reason, to watch over the fault and make sure that nothing evil ever came up and walked the earth. And you know something? Even though his stories sounded fanciful, to this day some of the brothers debate whether they might be true."

"How does Wendell vote?"

"I think Brother Wendell is among those who have a healthy respect for the power of Satan." The abbot looked out the window again. "Here he comes. I'll leave you now." He stuck out his hand. "It was good to meet you, Wesley."

Horn sat for a moment, hands clasped on the table, wondering at his nervousness. His hatred for Clea's father threatened to take him over, turn him into the raging thing that could easily have beaten Bernie Rome Junior to death. What would he say to him? He clenched his fists briefly, relaxed them, forced himself to breathe deeply.

The door opened, and Wendell Brand entered. He was not a large man, and he looked almost lost in the billowy robe. Unlike the abbot, he wore his hood fitted loosely over his head. Once, he might have been called almost delicate, but Horn could see that the life here had hardened him, browned his face and chipped his nails. He looked at Horn curiously, his face relaxed. Except for the eyes, which always seemed in motion, and which were framed by extra lines suggesting wariness, or pain.

"You wanted to see me?"

"That's right."

"I don't have a brother-in-law."

"But you do have an ex-wife, don't you?" Horn gestured toward one of the chairs, and after a brief hesitation, the other man sat. "Do you know who I am?"

Brand shook his head.

"I'm John Ray Horn."

"Oh. Of course." Brand's tone was simply polite. "You're the movie actor."

"Not anymore."

"Iris told me about you. She writes every now and then, and sometimes she sends money—not for me, but for the order. I've asked her to pray for us, and I believe she does so. Iris is a very good woman."

Horn looked around the small room and then out the window, where the mountain sun burned strongly but where a cooling breeze riffled the branches of an evergreen on the far side of the clearing. He felt contempt for his own politeness, his failure to deal simply and directly with the little man across the table. He wanted to feel Wendell Brand's neck between his fingers.

He took a deep breath and heard the words begin to tumble out as if spoken by a stranger. "I'm here about Clea," he said. "I'm here about the hunting lodge, the men you took her there to be with, the pictures you took of her, the things . . . the things you did . . ." He stopped, the rest of his words stuck in his throat.

Wendell Brand had shrunk back in his chair, crossing his arms over his chest, the thin hands receding into the large sleeves until they disappeared. But his expression did not change. His mouth worked for a few seconds, and then he said, "I knew someone would come. Someday."

"It's me. I've come."

"Iris told you."

Horn nodded.

"She said she wouldn't tell anyone. I forgive her." Brand looked down at the scarred surface of the table. "I've never forgiven myself. But God has. That's why I'm here. I've come to the place where I can ask God's forgiveness and know it's there."

"That's nice," Horn said. "But right now it's me you should be worried about, not God."

Brand shook his head. "I'm not accountable to you," he said quietly.

"Do the rest of the brothers know?"

"No. Just the priest who comes to hear our confessions. This is between me—"

"And God. I know." Horn allowed himself a small smile. "Religion really comes in handy sometimes, doesn't it? I come from a religious family, had a man of God for a father, and my Daddy could deliver a sermon that had the ladies crying and rolling their eyes, then come home and beat me to a pulp for sassing him. Then ask God to forgive *me*." He felt himself slipping away from the matter at hand. "How do you feel about ruining your daughter's life?"

"God will look after her," Brand said. "Her mother will look after her. So will her new father. With God's help, he'll be a much better father than I was—"

"Stop talking about God," Horn cut in. "I'm getting tired of it. I want some information from you. I want to know about the men at the lodge, how they operated, what happened there. I especially want to know the one name I don't have."

Brand shook his head. "The others have to answer for themselves," he said. "I won't condemn them."

Horn got up slowly, Brand's eyes following him warily. *In another minute*, he thought, *I'll be shaking like a leaf. Or I'll kill him.* "You sick little piss-ant," he said, looking down at him. "You'll tell me. You'll tell me every single thing I want to know."

"No," Brand said, staring back at Horn, looking almost brave in his oversize robe. "Each man has custody of his own soul."

"Oh, yes," Horn went on. "Because if you don't, I'll wreck the nice little life you've built up here, all snug and secure, going around in your hood so you can hide your face whenever you're feeling guilty about something. You're still covering your face, Wendell, just like in the pictures of you and your friends—have you noticed?

"I'll start by going out there and ringing that bell, ringing it until every godforsaken monk, or brother, or whatever you call each other gathers around. And then I'll tell them just what you did to your own daughter and all those other little girls. And what I don't know, I'll make up. And then I'll find me a cop who just loves to nail the men who hurt children, and I'll show him the pictures—that's right, I've got them—and then I'll tell him where to find you. And he'll come up here and drag you down this mountain, back into the world you tried to run away from. And we'll make Iris testify, you can count on that. And somewhere along the line, between the arrest and the trial, I'm sure the cops will tell you in great detail just what cons like to do to child molesters."

He stopped, out of breath. After a moment, he sat back down. Brand's eyes, still on him, had gone wide. His face seemed to have taken on the color of his robe, like a chameleon's skin. Neither one spoke for a long time. Then Brand cleared his throat, got up from his chair, and walked to the window, where he stood with his back to Horn.

"This is very hard," he said finally. "Would you mind asking me questions?"

"Not at all. Glad to make it easier for you. How many in the group?"

"Four."

"Names?"

"I only knew one. That was Mr. Bullard. He's dead now, isn't he?"

"That's right."

"Iris told me. In a way, that makes it easier to talk about all this, since he was always the leader, the organizer. Anyway, I worked for him at the hotel. We didn't use names at the lodge, so the others were just faces to me."

"So your faces weren't covered all the time?"

"Just during picture-taking."

"How did you join?"

"Mr. Bullard asked me. I was surprised, once I met the others, because they were all well-to-do, and I was just a clerk. I think the only reason he was interested in me . . ." His voice trailed off.

"Clea was the reason, wasn't she?"

Brand nodded, his back still to Horn. "She was such a beautiful little girl. Iris and I had brought her to some sort of company party, and Mr. Bullard . . . well, he noticed her."

"How did he find out you . . . uh, you liked little girls?" Horn tasted sourness in his throat. *Careful*, he thought.

"I don't know, except that he was a brilliant man, and he had the ability to focus on people's weaknesses, use them for either business or personal reasons. It may have been something I said. Somehow he just knew."

"Did he offer you money to bring her to the lodge?"

Brand was silent so long that Horn thought he hadn't heard the question. But he had. "Yes, God help me."

310

"And how many times did you take her there?"

"I don't remember exactly. Four or five times."

"Who brought the other girls?"

"Club. It was his job to bring the girls."

"Who?"

"Club. That was the name Mr. Bullard gave him. I told you we didn't use names at the lodge, but he gave each of us a nickname. He was Spade. I was Heart. The other man was Diamond."

"That's very cute," Horn said. "Just like four poker buddies. I suppose you were Heart because you were the sensitive one." When he got no answer, he went on. "Now. Tell me what happened up there."

"All right." Brand braced both hands against the window sill, as if his legs had suddenly weakened. "It was either just picture-taking, or sex with the girls while pictures were taken."

"Was Clea—?"

"No! The youngest girls were just for pictures. Actually, they were more for the benefit of myself and Diamond. We preferred the youngest, and basically all we wanted to do was look. I never touched Clea in a bad way, either there or at home. The other two, Mr. Bullard and Club, wanted sex, but their girls were older, up to fifteen or so. Sometimes Club would bring two girls, one older and one younger, so we all—"

"So no one would feel left out. Nothing worse than standing around while somebody else has a good time."

311

"Go ahead," Brand said. "Ridicule me. Nothing you call me can be as bad as the names I call myself."

"Oh, I'm just getting started. Where did Club find the girls?"

"He didn't talk about it much. But after a while, I understood that he—or, actually, someone who worked for him—would go looking in poor neighborhoods, and they would pay off the mothers or fathers, and no one would complain."

Go ask Alphonse Doucette about that, Horn thought. He stared at Brand, chewing his lip. "The sex," he said finally. "Even the older girls, they must have—"

"They were drugged," Brand said quickly, shifting his eyes over Horn's shoulder, about where the crucifix would be. "Club always gave them something. In a drink, as soon as they arrived. He said some of them would barely remember what happened."

"But the littlest girls wouldn't need drugs, would they?"

"No. Most of them thought it was just some kind of game with a camera."

"Is that what it was to Clea? A game?"

"Yes." It was barely a whisper. "I asked her to help me keep it a secret from her mother, and she agreed, because that was part of the game."

Enough, Horn thought. *Enough about her. Talk about something else.*

"Describe Club to me."

"Well, he was big. Not tall, but stocky, fleshy.

And he had heavy features and heavy eyebrows. He always wore two big rings, one on each—"

"All right," Horn said. "I know him. What about Diamond?"

"He was the photographer. He took all the pictures, and he was very good at it."

"Could he have been a professional photographer?"

"I suppose so, but I always got the impression it was more of a hobby for him."

"Could he have been a book dealer?"

"I really have no idea," Brand said. "Mr. Bullard said we weren't to talk about personal things, and we didn't. I do remember that he probably came from a longer distance than the rest of us, because he was often late. Oh . . . and that he smoked an odd kind of cigarette, one that smelled different than the ones I was used to. He offered me one once, but I didn't like it."

"What did he look like?"

"Nice-looking, well-built. He was about my age. I was almost thirty then, and he was probably in his early thirties. The other two were much older. Because his interests and mine were . . . you know, similar, I probably spent more time talking with him. He seemed to know Mr. Bullard better than the rest of us. I think he was probably single, because Mr. Bullard would sometimes tease him, saying, 'Don't worry, I'll find a nice girl for you.'"

"After Iris found the pictures . . . what did Bullard say when you decided to leave?"

"He knew he had nothing to fear from me. I

was just an ordinary man who happened to have a pretty little daughter. He asked me to give him the photos I'd been keeping, to make sure no one else ever saw them. And he reminded me never to talk about any of this. Except for what I told the priest, I kept the promise. Until today."

Horn stood up. "You were right to tell me. Sometimes keeping a secret is harder than telling it." *I need to get out of this room and get some air*, he thought. *I can't keep my hands off him much longer*. He started for the door.

"I told you more than I ever told the priest," he heard Brand mutter. "I told you everything except . . ."

"Except what?" Horn stopped at the door, turned.

"Except about that last time, that last night. The night it all changed for me. It wasn't Iris who made me leave the group, you see. She just happened to find the pictures. I was ready to leave."

Horn stood staring down at the back of the hood. He could barely hear the voice.

"We had taken pictures of Clea and another girl," the man said softly. The words came out in a rush now, unstoppable, almost like a confession. "There was supposed to be an older girl there that night, but instead another small one was delivered. A little Mexican girl, about ten, I think. So we took pictures of both of them, and afterward Diamond and I went out into the main room for a smoke, and Mr. Bullard was in the kitchen fixing a drink, when . . . when I heard Clea scream. We all ran toward the bedroom. Club was in there with both of them, on the bed . . .” Brand began coughing, as if the words wouldn’t come up into the air. “He was—”

Horn grabbed him from behind, lifted him from the chair, spun him around, and pinned him against the wall, his fists knotted in the folds of the robe. The other man’s hands fluttered in front of him, his eyes on the floor.

“Did he?” Horn demanded, shaking him. “Did he?”

“Not Clea,” Brand said, the word almost lost in the cloth. “He was raping the other girl. She was unconscious; I think he may have hit her. We pulled him off. He was crazy, cursing us. But Mr. Bullard got him under control. He began lecturing him, in that quiet voice, about our rules.”

“Rules?”

“About how only the girls thirteen and older were there for sex,” Brand went on in a reasonable tone. “About how we couldn’t risk injuring the younger girls. Injuring them . . . or worse. And that without rules, we were no better than anybody else.”

“No better than . . .” Horn repeated the words in a monotone, releasing Brand from his grip, allowing him to sag down against the wall. He turned, looking almost blindly for the door.

“All the time, Clea was screaming,” Brand said softly, “but not like the kind of screams you usually

315

hear." His eyes came up, and there was no focus in them. The voice sounded far away. "It was almost like a baby crying."

"She *was* a baby," Horn said. He opened the door and walked outside, breathing deeply in the thin air. He looked around for a few seconds as if lost. Then he strode to the bell tower and went inside, where he found the thick, knotted bell pull. He reached up and grabbed a knot, heaved downward. The rope descended slowly, and at first nothing happened, but then the bell high above clanged once. He pulled again, putting all his weight on it, letting the rope carry him up, then drop him as the bell clanged again, the sound echoing in the tower. He worked the rope for a full minute until the tones of the bell sounded steadily over the grounds of the monastery. When he stopped, out of breath, he turned to see dozens of monks standing in a loose semicircle outside the building, regarding him. The abbot was there, his face troubled.

"Brother Wendell has a confession to make," Horn yelled to them. He saw Brand leaning in the doorway, about to emerge from the room, his face white. Horn went to his car, got in, and started the engine. "You may have to encourage him, but he knows confession is good for his soul. It's something about his daughter."

He drove too fast down the mountain road, the Ford's well-worn tires occasionally skidding in the dirt and gravel. *Sierra Lane would probably have*

316

handled that a little differently. It was afternoon, and shadows were gathering in the tall pines. The woods looked like a perfect place for children to play. When they were boys, he and Lamar would have loved a setting like this for their games, he thought as he wrestled with the wheel. They would cast themselves as frontiersmen, explorers, Indian scouts, whooping and hollering among the tree trunks and boulders.

But then again, he thought, these were deep woods, with steep drop-offs. Before long it would be dark and increasingly treacherous, and little children could get lost in there.

CHAPTER 20

Horn sat out in front of Maggie's place, a glass of her bourbon in his hand, listening idly to the sounds from the kitchen, Maggie and the two girls bantering. Even Clea sounded happy.

Up there on the mountain, high above the fault in the earth, he had briefly entered a place that his father would have known from the old texts, a place where evil and human life intersect. It frightened and saddened him, so he could only wonder at its effect on Clea. How much of it could she remember today? He heard her laugh at one of Maggie's jokes, and the laugh sounded like it came from someone who had emerged from a dark place, looked around, and decided to be part of things again, part of cooking and laughing and all the rest. *Maybe*, he thought—and it felt like a prayer—*maybe she's out of there for good.*

He thought about the mysterious Diamond and wondered why he felt it was so important to uncover the man's identity. Hadn't he already answered most of the important questions? Bonsigniore had had Scotty killed to keep him quiet. He still wanted the photos and would eventually figure out who had them. Still left unanswered was the precise nature of Clea's relationship with Bonsigniore's henchman, Del Vitti, but that would surely be cleared up in time.

Horn's priorities were clear: Keep Clea safe, and find a way to make Bonsigniore pay for Scotty's death. Horn didn't know if Diamond could help bring this about, or even if the man was still alive. But he was the last missing piece in a puzzle that Horn had first confronted that night with Scotty in his father's office. Horn had to find him.

A good-looking, well-dressed man who would have been around thirty back then. With his contacts, Arthur Bullard doubtless had known countless men like that. One of the photos in Bullard's office had shown him with his hunting club, a couple of dozen men standing in a grove of trees with their weapons. Easily half the men in the picture could have fit that description. Even Paul Fairbrass, Iris's respectable new husband, fit it—and he could have crossed paths, social or professional, with Bullard. But Horn quickly rejected the idea. It would be too fantastic to imagine that Iris could have unknowingly married two men capable of molesting her daughter. *Hell*, thought Horn, *Wendell could even have been describing Scotty, if you think about it.*

He paused. What about Scotty? Did that make any sense? Of course not. After all, he had shown Horn the photos, had condemned his own father for them. If Scotty had been part of it all, why would he be the one to reveal it? And how could Helen Bullard have known about her husband's secret life and not known about her son's?

And yet . . . Scotty's words came back to him: *I wanted him to be proud of me.* Horn had no trouble understanding how a man could hate his father and at the same time hunger for his approval. How much did Scotty want that, and what would he have done to obtain it? Recalling the photo Scotty's mother had presented to him during his visit, Horn grudgingly admitted to himself that his old friend had been reasonably proficient with a camera.

It was because of Scotty that Horn had gone to Geiger's bookstore. Was it because Scotty had suspected he might find something there, or had he known it for sure? The night that Scotty faced him over his father's desktop and its array of photos, was he condemning only Arthur Bullard, or himself as well? Was that night the beginning of a confession, an elaborate game in which Scotty hoped John Ray would guess the truth? And wouldn't this secret knowledge, this shared experience between father and son, have given Vincent Bonsigniore an even greater reason for sending an assassin after the son of Arthur Bullard—to retrieve the photos and silence the man who was betraying him?

No. Horn pushed the thought back down into his unconscious, ashamed of giving it a place in his mind. *Not Scotty.* The idea was too farfetched. He knew him too well. No, he would still put his money on Calvin St. George, the man who dealt in dirty pictures, who displayed a photo of a small girl like a trophy in his shop, the man who lied when he told Horn he didn't recognize a picture from Bullard's collection. *You're my favorite*, Horn said to St. George silently. *And we're going to talk again.*

Another concern pressed in on him. He knew it was time for Clea to go home. His talk with Iris had finally convinced him that Clea faced no obvious threat from either of her parents, and he had run out of excuses for keeping her. Still, he hesitated. She seemed to be enjoying herself here, emerging from the fright of seeing Anthony Del Vitti dead, relaxing for the first time in quite a while. He knew she wanted to stay. For his part, the longer he stayed with her, the better his chances became of getting her to open up about why she had left home. Finally, he admitted that it was good simply to have her around, helping him learn to be a father again, even if only for a few days.

But how much longer could he keep her before her parents learned where she was?

He heard Clea's voice. "Hey, your corn bread looks ready," she said. "Aren't you hungry?"

As he went inside, Maggie opened the oven and took out the corn bread he had made. She had put together a pot of chili, and they sat down to dinner. As they ate, Addie entertained the others with stories of looking for work as a model at some of the big department stores.

"I was in the restaurant at Bullocks Wilshire at noon the other day when Marlene Dietrich came in," Addie said. "Her chauffeur was carrying her hatboxes and all the things she'd bought. She was wearing a man's suit and a man's shirt, and high heels," she went on breathlessly. "She walked to her table. The whole place just stopped."

"Marlene Dietrich," Maggie said, a faraway look on her face. "She's so glamorous. Those cheekbones."

"She ain't got nothing you ain't got, old girl," Horn told her, digging into his chili. She punched his arm lightly.

Addie did a wicked impression of a certain department store executive informing her casually that there were occasional demands for lingerie models. If she could stop by the store that evening, he'd gone on, they could determine if she was suitable for the job.

"And did you go?" Clea asked.

"Sure I went," Addie said. "Turned out there wasn't exactly the job he described, but you might say I got my foot in the door of the company. Or another part of me."

There was a small, awkward silence, and Maggie shot him a wry look that said, *Listen to her, will you?* As Horn looked at the other three faces around the table, he was struck by the differences. Clea was still a girl—a little awkward but coming out of it, her beauty not quite ready to blossom, her

322

open gaze shrouded by her secrets. Maggie's once-vibrant looks were still visible but had receded into something more calm and internal, more identified with the whole woman than just the face. Addie's beauty was like a bouquet of fresh-cut flowers, its aroma on the wind. But as with Clea, there was something subtly sad about her too, as if one were watching a speeded-up film of the life of a flower. *She burns almost too hot,* Horn thought.

Later that night, as he slept, he encountered Addie in a dream. It seemed natural to see her there, and natural to find that he wanted her. She stood on the dirt road where he'd seen her before, except now she wore that white two-piece swimsuit she'd worn in his car, with the matching hair band. She glistened all over, as if she'd just stepped out of the surf, and the look she gave him said enough. Guilt rose in him, and he began looking for words to tell her that they shouldn't be there, that she was Clea's friend. But immediately he felt foolish over the guilt. *It's only a dream,* he told himself. *You can do anything in a dream.*

He felt a hand at his shoulder and knew that she had come to him, had left Clea in bed to come out and find him on the couch, and he rolled over and opened his eyes. But it was Miguel the ranch hand.

"*Señora* say you come out, please."

It was just past midnight. He followed Miguel out to the stables and there, in the mare's enclosure, was a shiny new colt. It stood wobbling on stilt legs, its oversized head bobbing as it looked around, taking in this new world. The mare, wrung out, sat up weakly, leaned over, and licked her newborn, giving it long, slow, swipes with her gigantic tongue.

Maggie leaned on the rail, looking as exhausted as the mare. "Hey," she said. "Old cowboy like you, I knew you wouldn't mind being woke up for this."

"I wouldn't have missed it," he said, patting her elbow. "Everybody all right?"

"Fine and dandy, except for Mom and me. But we'll catch up. I'm going to start right now," she said, indicating the bedroll she'd laid down on a pile of smoothed-out hay in an empty stall next door. She went over and lay on it. "Just going to rest awhile," she said drowsily. "The boys will be around. You can go back to bed anytime."

He rested his arms and chin on the rail for a while, talking in a low voice to the mare and foal. It was something he did around horses, something most horse people did without embarrassment. He told Bonnie she had done a good job, and he told the colt he was welcome in this world and to be careful with the standing and walking because all that took practice.

After a few minutes he went over and lay down next to Maggie on the blanket. It was a little cool in the stable, so he pulled over an Indian blanket and spread it over them. He gently lifted Maggie's head and placed it on his arm, and she rolled toward him and rested her arm on his chest. She smelled of soap and hay.

"The sire's a champion quarter horse, and the mare's got good blood too," she said, her voice slowed by sleepiness. "I think I might breed this one."

"That'd be nice. What name you going to give him?"

"Thought I might call him Sierra. If you don't mind."

"That'd be real nice."

"You still talk to horses."

"Heard me, huh? Well, I bet you do too."

"John Ray, I'm so sorry about Raincloud." They lay looking up into the rafters, almost whispering in the dark. "I was off someplace when it happened—rodeo in Tucson, I think it was. By the time I got back, you were in jail. I was never sure if I heard the way it really happened. Would you tell me?"

"I don't mind," he said, and began to tell her.

He'd never told the story from beginning to end, but it came naturally because it had been in his head for years, just waiting to be told. It started with Bernard Rome Junior and how his daddy sent him off to one of those private schools in the East, where Junior learned about polo and how to ride English-style. And then he came back and started apprenticing under Bernie Senior, learning how to run a studio, but always trying to impress people with how cultivated he was. One day this rich girl from New York was visiting, and Junior was squiring her around the studio, wearing his polo outfit. She said she'd just love to see him ride, maybe do a little jumping, and he couldn't say no. The horses he usually rode were in his father's stable out in Malibu. But he looked around the back lot, checked out the studio horses, and decided Raincloud was his mount.

So he had his English saddle fetched from his car and had the horse made ready for him. Raincloud had never worn this kind of saddle and was skittish about carrying Junior, who was twitchy at the reins and who reeked of expensive cologne. The stable hands were nervous, but Horn was at home between pictures, and no one had the gumption to say no to Junior.

He rode out to some fenced-in acreage behind the studio and began taking Raincloud over some low fences. Horse and rider did fine for a while, the young lady clapping at each jump. Then Junior decided to tackle a higher fence. He spurred Raincloud to a gallop, and they raced toward it. The horse had the grit for it, but Junior balked at the last second. He hauled back on the reins, they broadsided the fence, and Raincloud's right foreleg snapped between two of the rails.

Horn paused in the telling. All that, he told Maggie, was what he heard from others. He didn't get involved until someone called him at home, and he smoked up the roads to the studio. He found Raincloud lying out by the fence, surrounded by studio people. The vet was there, and told him there was no hope, the break was too bad. Do you want me to do it? the man asked him. No, Horn said. I'll do it.

He went to see Doolin, the studio armorer, a small and stooped man who was rumored to have fought the Black and Tans in the streets of Dublin decades earlier. Doolin tended to the great assortment of weaponry, some real and some bogus, used by the studio in its action movies, set from the streets of New York to the American west to the Khyber Pass. Horn asked for his .45-caliber Army Colt replica, 1873 model, and Doolin pulled it from a shelf and handed it over to him in its holster. You have bullets for this, don't you? Horn asked.

You want blanks, right?

No. I want lead bullets.

Doolin reached to the back of another shelf and handed him a box of .45 shells adorned with a sticker that read CAUTION: LIVE AMMU-NITION. NOT FOR USE ON SET.

I know you've got a bottle here somewhere, Horn said. I want that too. I'll pay you back. Doolin hesitated, then was gone for a moment and returned with a half-full bottle of Old Crow.

Horn swigged what was left, loaded the cylinder's six chambers, went back out to the field, and told everyone to leave. He pulled out his pocketknife, sliced through the latigo, and wrestled the ridiculous saddle off the horse, then he gently slid off the bridle. He sat for long minutes, cross-legged, with Raincloud's great head cradled in his lap. The animal's eyes were full of pain and fear as Horn talked to him. Others watched from a distance, but no one could hear the words.

Finally, he stroked the horse's muzzle one last time, cocked the weapon, placed the gun barrel dead center between the eyes, closed his own eyes, and pulled the trigger.

Then he went looking for Junior.

He found him in the commissary with the New York girl, sitting at a table with Bernie Senior and Bing Crosby, who was under contract over the hill at Paramount but who was an old golfing buddy of the studio chief. The four were having a late afternoon cup of tea. "Excuse me," Horn said, hauling Junior out of his chair. "We've got some business about a horse."

Although on the short side, Junior was solidly built and athletic. He took one swing at Horn, and that was it. Horn slapped him twice across the face, then dragged him out the door of the commissary and flung him down the flight of steps onto the pavement. As Junior tried to crawl awkwardly off the pavement onto the grass, Horn descended the stairs and began to work on him. People gathered around, yelling, but no one stopped him because he was wearing the gun. He didn't know how long he worked, but at one point he became aware that his knuckles were starting to ache, Junior's screams were hurting his ears, and the grass was speckled with red. Finally, Mad Crow pulled him off— someone had had the good sense to call him. And not long afterward, the police arrived.

"I guess you know the rest," he said. "Felony assault, they called it. When Bing Crosby showed up for the prosecution and started signing autographs outside the courthouse, I sort of knew how it would go. And when Mr. Rome told me he was going to make sure I never worked for any studio, well . . ."

Her hand patted his chest. "You should put it away," she said. "I hope some day you can do that." She was silent for a long time after that, and he thought she might be asleep. But then she yawned mightily. "You were a son of a bitch, John Ray," she said in a barely audible voice. "Leaving like that." He knew what she meant; the leaving had nothing to do with prison.

"I know."

"Too late to do anything about it now."

"I know. Go to sleep, Maggie."

She said one last thing—he thought it sounded like *I would have waited for you*, but the words could have come from inside his own head—then turned away from him.

He lay there but couldn't sleep. After a while, when her breathing became regular, he worked his arm free and, after a quick look into the maternity stall, left the stables. He walked across the dirt road to the pasture, clambered up onto the fence, and sat there with his heels hooked over the second rail. The pasture smelled of trampled grass and horse dung. He rolled a handmade and lit it, enjoying the first puff as always, the slow pull of the smoke into his lungs. He looked up at the night sky. It was the time of the new moon, and here in the country the dark was almost total. He looked around and located the moon high up, just about midpoint in its loop through the dark. Its image was barely there, just a crescent swipe of pale light, the color of bone, against the darkness. It was Clea's moon, her favorite. He hadn't seen it for a long time.

Inside, he made his way to the bedroom to check on the girls. Approaching the bed quietly, he saw that Clea was alone in it. A rustling sound told him she was awake.

"It's me, honey."

"Oh. Hi."

He sat on the edge of the bed. "I've got some news for you. The mare had her baby."

"Really? That's wonderful." She stirred, half-sat up. "Is it a boy or a girl?"

"It's a boy. They're both doing fine. He's up on his legs already. You should see him, he's all gangly."

"I want to see him."

"You can see him tomorrow. Where's Addie?"

"She went outside. I think she's in the hammock."

"Well, it's probably cooler out there," he said. More rustling. "I . . . I told her about Tommy."

"What do you mean?"

"I thought when you called her, you told her about him. That he was dead. But she didn't know. I told her, and she . . . she got very . . ."

"Why would she care? She told me she hated his guts."

"She loved Tommy."

What the hell? He sat on the edge of the bed, waiting for more. After a while, she began to talk, her voice sleepy but controlled. "When we first met Tommy, he dated both of us. I liked him a lot, even though I was a little scared of him too, because he was so much older. But Addie was crazy about him. She chased after him, and they saw a lot of each other. She's so pretty, I never really understood why he seemed to like me better. He just did. And when I left home, I went straight to him, and he took me in. And he never saw her after that."

"Maybe she was too old for him," he said, the sarcasm heavy in his voice.

"What? Why would you say that?"

"Never mind, honey. So you told her Tommy was dead. Did you tell her how he died?"

"Yeah." She drew a ragged breath and sounded on the edge of tears. "I think . . . she thinks you killed him."

"Didn't you tell her—?"

"I did. But she said you hate Tommy because Tommy beat you up one night, and she was there. You didn't kill him, did you?"

"Honey, I already told you I didn't. You can believe that." He leaned forward and straightened out the top sheet, the way he had done when she was small. Sometimes dreams would disturb her, and he would come in and find the bedding all in a knot.

As he fussed over the sheet, he tried to think. If Addie Webb had been in love with this piece of trash Del Vitti, then her night out with Horn had most likely been an act. The Dixie Belle was a setup, and Del Vitti and Falco were waiting for him. Might have killed him, at least sliced him up good and proper. He had a new respect for Addie's intelligence and cunning. He hoped that he would eventually find a way to convince her of the truth about Del Vitti's death.

Sitting back up, he thought about turning on a light but decided against it. "I'll talk to her tomorrow," he said.

"Do you think she'll be all right?"

"Oh, she'll be just fine. Like I keep telling you, Addie can take care of herself. Listen, can I ask you a few questions about Tommy?"

"I guess." She yawned.

"How did you meet him?"

"I just ran into him. At the malt shop across the street from the high school. He was really nice and polite, and you should have seen the way the other girls looked at him. You know, it's funny."

"What?"

"Well, I got the feeling that it wasn't just an accident. I mean, that maybe he had wanted to meet me, you know?"

"Uh-huh. Do you know what kind of work he did?"

"He told me he worked for a man named Vincent, and Vincent was very rich and liked pretty girls, and one of Tommy's jobs was to find girls to go out with Vincent."

"Did you think there was anything wrong with that?"

"No. Not if they wanted to date him. Tommy said Vincent would take them out to nice places like the Brown Derby."

Well, not exactly. "Did you ever meet Vincent?"

"No." Another yawn.

"Ever know any of the girls?"

"Oh, no. Tommy said they all came from other parts of town." She was quiet for a long time. Then: "Addie helped him."

"What do you mean?"

"Helped him find girls. And once I got the idea that she went to see Vincent."

Dear God. So that's what little Adele was up to.

As if sensing his surprise, she went on: "I know Addie better than anybody. She acts crazy, but she's really sweet. The only thing is, the place she comes from . . . she told me once that her father— he's gone now—used to come to her room at night, starting when she was . . ." She stopped.

"You don't have to tell me any more, honey. So Addie does some wild things."

"She likes to be sexy. She wants men to like her."

"I've seen that."

"She's my best friend."

"Good." He reached over and rearranged her pillow. "You want to go back to sleep?"

"Maybe in a little bit. Can you stay for a while?"

"Sure I can." Her words warmed him. He couldn't recall when she had last asked for his company. He was sure it had been years. Probably the night he had left for Cold Creek and she had screamed and cried behind her locked bedroom door. He adjusted a pillow behind his back. "You just close your eyes. I'll be right here."

He began talking to her quietly, the way he had done years earlier. When she was little, he would make up bedtime stories about silver ponies and magic carousels and little girls who discover herds of wild horses up in the mountains and lead them down to the sweet-grass valleys before the snow begins blowing. Sometimes the stories were about a little girl named Clea, sometimes about others. She didn't seem to mind either way, as long as he told them.

So, this night, he talked to her. But this time the stories weren't made up. There was too much he needed to say. He told her about how he had missed her every day since that night he had left. About how he missed having her for a daughter, but he knew that her new father was a good man and that she had a good home to go back to when she was ready.

If there was anything she ever wanted to talk to him about, he said, he would listen—even if it was something that happened years ago and she could barely remember it. He would listen, because some things shouldn't be kept to yourself. Sometimes what you needed most in the world was just somebody to listen.

He paused, wondering if she had dropped off to sleep. "Your moon's up tonight," he said in a quiet voice. "I saw it out there awhile ago and thought about you. It's brand new, so thin it's almost not there. Remember what you said, a long time ago? It's special because it's like a new baby, just born. 'Last night,' you said, 'the sky was all black, and now we have this new, funny-shaped moon, just hung up there to start brightening things. It'll grow, even faster than me,' you said, 'and pretty soon it'll be fat and yellow and we can read storybooks from the light it gives off.'"

He thought he heard a sound from her, but when he looked over at her rounded shoulder in the dark, there was nothing.

"You probably didn't notice this big ugly belt buckle of mine," he went on softly. "I meant to show it to you. It's something I made in the . . . something I made while I was away. I took this hunk of steel and faced it with silver plate. And then I got some copper wire and inlaid a design on the silver. I'm not much of an artist, but if you look close, you'll see a couple of horses, one big, one little, with riders on them. And way up in the right-hand corner, with the last piece of wire, I made a little squiggle. That's a crescent moon. And the two riders . . . well, I guess that's supposed to be me and you, headed off to—"

Another sound, more distinct this time. He turned toward her. Her shoulder was shuddering, and he could hear strangled sobs, as if she was trying to choke off the sounds with her hand. He grabbed her and drew her to him, and she flung an arm across him, gripping his arm as if it were a life preserver.

"Oh, baby. Let it out, honey. Let it out."

The sobs came full-throated then, wailing and full of pain, as if they were years' worth of pent-up cries. He patted her shoulder, not knowing what else to do, just telling her it was going to be all right now, whatever it was, it was going to be all right. He would make it all right, he said, even as he asked himself how he possibly could.

"I saw him," she cried.

"Who?"

"The man with the rings."

"The man with the . . . When?"

"At the funeral. For Scotty's father. I saw him there. And I remembered his face, and the rings on his hands. And his hands had black hair on them. And how one of his hands grabbed me and held me, while he was doing things to that other little girl. I wanted to leave so bad, but he wouldn't let me. He said I should watch. It was a long time ago, but when I saw his face, and the rings, I remembered."

He gripped her tightly. "I know about it. You're never going to see him again. And someday you'll be able to forget all of it. Do you hear me?"

"No," she said, her voice thickened with tears. "I didn't think about it for a long time. But now I can't stop. When I saw him, he saw me too. And the way he looked at me . . . I just keep seeing his face, over and over."

"Is that when you ran away? After you saw him?"

He felt her head nod against his shoulder, felt the wetness there.

"But why didn't you just tell your mother? She could have helped you. Your new father—"

"I couldn't have talked to him about that," she said.

"Your mother, then."

"She's the reason it happened," Clea said, her breath heaving again. "She let it happen to me."

"Honey, she didn't know."

But there was no reasoning with her. She lay there crying, and all he could do was hold her. Finally, when her sobs finally subsided to breathless gasps, and he could feel his chest drenched from her tears, she turned her face up to him. "You came after me, didn't you?" she asked.

"You bet I did, little girl," he said, gripping her hard. "You bet I did."

In a few minutes she was asleep. *His name was*

Vincent, he said to her silently. *You don't ever need to know that.*

It didn't take him long to find his old footlocker. It was in a corner of Maggie's tack room, under a worn saddle blanket. There was no lock. Opening it, he saw Sierra Lane's old cavalry boots and hat, the brim pinned up jauntily on one side. Close by were the familiar gun belt and holster, done in plain leather. Underneath, neatly folded, were the pants and the blue shirt with its array of buttons. He pulled out a wide sheet of tightly rolled-up paper and unrolled it.

Okay, Indian, maybe I lied a little. Maybe I did keep one of my posters.

It was the one-sheet for *Wyoming Thunder*, and it showed Sierra Lane astride Raincloud, galloping full-tilt toward the viewer against the background of a stormy sky. The cowboy gripped the reins in his left hand while his right swept his hat high and wide. Dust billowed under Raincloud's hooves, and horse and rider seemed one, almost like a centaur, swept up and lost in the joy of running.

He replaced the poster and, at the bottom of the trunk, found what he was looking for, a heavy bundle wrapped in oilcloth. He unwrapped the cloth and held the Colt in his hand, feeling the grip, testing the balance. One more thing, and soon he had fished it out too: A small, heavy box bearing a label that said CAUTION: LIVE AMMUNITION. NOT FOR USE ON SET.

CHAPTER 21

"I don't need you on this," Horn said as Mad Crow guided the Cadillac eastward on Hollywood Boulevard, the top down, the midmorning sun warm on the dashboard.

"White man make joke," Mad Crow said. "You have no idea what you need, my friend. You need me to watch over you, like an overweight guardian angel. To keep a rein on you. Mostly, you need me to make sure you don't come uncorked again, the way you did that time with Junior. In short, you need me to keep you out of Cold Creek. Reach us a couple of RCs from the back, will you?"

Horn shrugged, not in the mood to argue. He half-turned, dug two bottles out of the cooler on the backseat, shook off the ice, and pried off the tops with an opener from the glove compartment.

"Thanks," Mad Crow said, taking a long swig. "You ever wonder why they never asked us to sink our big feet into the cement over there?" He pointed to Grauman's Chinese Theatre, passing on the left, where a few tourists were idling over the stars' footprints out front.

"Next to Ronald Colman and Greer Garson?"

Horn said. "Somewhere between Gable and Lombard? Gosh, I don't know. Must have been some kind of oversight. I keep thinking the phone'll ring some day, and it'll be Sid Grauman saying, "Mr. Horn, my most sincere apologies for neglecting you. I just saw *Wyoming Thunder*, and it's a masterpiece. I want to immortalize you today. And don't forget to bring your sidekick, what's his name.""

"An oversight," Mad Crow said, hitting the brakes as a bell rang and the STOP arm flew up on the traffic signal up ahead. They heard a yell and saw a young man on the sidewalk waving at them enthusiastically.

"Fan of yours?" Horn inquired.

"Could be; I don't know," the Indian said, saluting him back with the RC bottle. "Most likely he's just waving at the car. I get a lot of that." He looked sideways at Horn. "I know, you think I'm crazy to enjoy all the attention. I don't care. I like it. You be all morose and private if you want to. Me, I'm going to put the top down, drive in the sunshine, and wave at all the nice people."

The GO signal flew up, and he stepped on the gas. "Now what's this thing you didn't want to talk about on the phone?"

"She opened up to me last night," Horn replied. "Clea. It's starting to make sense. When Iris and her new husband took her to Arthur Bullard's funeral, she saw Bonsigniore there. And she remembered him from the lodge. He had tried to rape her. She was little more than a baby—"

"Oh, man." Mad Crow gripped the wheel and shook his head, his face twisted into something ugly.

"And it came back to her at the funeral. Not only that, *he* saw *her*. He must know that she remembers. All this time, I thought the lodge was something 'way back in the past for her, just a bad time she could grow out of. I didn't know she was in any danger today. But it's all connected. She ran away because she blamed her mother for letting her father do all that to her. But most of all, because she had seen that man's face again after all these years."

"You think he's after her?"

"I know he is. If he'd have Scotty killed to cover up what he did, why not Clea? I think he would have sent someone to get her soon after the funeral if she hadn't run. I also think it was a kind of miracle she wound up with Del Vitti, because he was one of the few people who could protect her."

"But he was Vinnie's boy," Mad Crow said. "I don't get it."

"I don't either, altogether. But Clea told me she met Del Vitti around the high school and that it didn't seem accidental. Long before she spotted him at the funeral, I think Bonsigniore was trying to keep tabs on Clea. He could have sent Del Vitti to casually check up on her, get to know her, try to see if she was any kind of risk. It would have been insurance for him. Most of the girls who went up to the lodge were from poor families,

341

families that could be paid off. Clea was different. Her new father had money. Bonsigniore couldn't afford to take the chance that she might be a threat to him someday. So he sent Del Vitti to keep an eye on her."

"Okay, but that doesn't explain—"

"What happened at Del Vitti's house. I know. I think he fell for her, that's what happened."

"You're kidding."

"No. Clea told me he was a perfect gentleman, never laid a hand on her. I think he was in love with her. After the funeral, Bonsigniore must have made it clear that he wanted her killed—may even have ordered Del Vitti to do it. But just at that moment, she showed up at his front door, asking him to take her in. And he did. He decided to be her protector. Bonsigniore figured it out and sent Falco over to kill them both. But just before he was killed, Del Vitti managed to hide her, and save her."

Horn stretched his arms overhead to work out the stiffness from his lack of sleep. "He was a snake," he said. "But I owe him for that."

"What's that under your shirt?"

"The old Colt. I dug it out of my footlocker last night. This is serious from now on, Indian. We aren't talking any more about getting a girl back to her parents. Somebody wants her dead. She's safe at Maggie's for now, but every day that goes by, they're closer to finding her."

"What do you have in mind?"

"First off, getting the police in on this. With my record, they won't listen to me—"

"Afraid I wouldn't do much better," Mad Crow cut in, "considering my line of work."

"But I know someone they'd listen to. Helen Bullard."

"The widow?"

He nodded. "She's a tough old bird—ruthless, even, just like her husband. She carries a lot of weight in this town. She told me there's nothing she wants more than to nail whoever killed Scotty. I'm going to tell her all I know and let her use the information any way she wants. If she doesn't want to do it, I'll talk to Paul Fairbrass. He's a solid citizen too. But I don't think he knows as much about hating as Mrs. Arthur Bullard."

"Good luck with that," Mad Crow said, sounding dubious. Without looking, he tossed the empty bottle over his shoulder. It bounced off the back-seat and landed on the floor. "What else?"

"Now that I know the kind of danger Clea's in, I want to get her out of town. If she went home, she wouldn't be safe. Iris and her husband can always have me arrested later, if that's what they want to do. Right now, I want to make sure she's a long way from Bonsigniore and his people. Any thoughts about that?"

Mad Crow hesitated. "Maybe. I got a good friend in San Bernardino. I staked him to a truck and horse trailer a long time ago, and he owes me. I could call him, see if he'd put her up for a while."

"Good. I'll go with her. You can stay in touch with me, let me know if the problem clears up at this end. If not . . ."

"I know what you're thinking," Mad Crow said, looking grim. "Somebody is going to have to go after him. And Falco. And anybody else who gets in the way. Are you up for that, amigo?"

"No." Horn allowed himself to smile at the idiocy of it. "It's a lot easier to play a hero than to be one."

"Sometimes you find out things about yourself you didn't know were there."

"I know," Horn said. "I found out a few things in Italy, none of them very pretty. Anyway . . . there's one other thing. It's about you."

"Yeah." Mad Crow, eyes straight ahead, drummed his fingers on the steering wheel. "About me and my friend Vinnie."

"That's right. You and your partner."

"He left his calling card with me the other night."

"What does that mean?"

"After that day we met up at the Alexandria, he told me you were trouble, I should fire you. He said someday he might have to deal with you, and if I was in the way, he'd deal with me too, and it wouldn't be good for me or my business. I told him I respected his sage counsel and I'd think about it."

Horn listened silently.

"Other night, after we closed, somebody filled up a Budweiser bottle with gasoline, stuck a rag in the top, lit it, and busted it against my back door. Not a lot of damage, it just singed things a little bit. But I got the message."

Horn made a face. "Look, Indian, I didn't know things were headed this way. I try never to get up against a man's business. But that's where we are. He wants Clea dead. You can't be on both sides in this."

Mad Crow made a U-turn and docked the Cadillac at the curb near their destination. He turned and gave Horn a slack-jawed grin. "So fuck him," he said. "The fat guinea, him and his fat little fingers with the fancy rings."

"You mean it?"

"Sure. The little girl comes first. Let's take care of this business, okay? Starting right here." He gestured toward the storefront a dozen yards away.

"Okay." Horn started to get out.

"Wait a minute. Can I have that, please?" Mad Crow held out his hand. After a few seconds, Horn pulled the Colt from under his belt, and Mad Crow put it under the seat. "You won't need it. I forgot the most important reason you need me around: to keep you from shooting up the saloon and scaring all the dancing girls."

"Fine with me," Horn said. "We're here just to talk."

"That's right. You be the good-natured, slow-witted cowboy. If the need arises, I'll be your slightly unpredictable companion."

The little bell tinkled as they entered Geiger's

bookshop. The only person inside was a business-suited customer sitting in one of the soft leather easy chairs, a large book balanced on his knees. He looked up furtively.

A heavy curtain parted behind the counter, and Calvin St. George came out. His eyes quickly took in Horn and Mad Crow, and although his expression did not change, he seemed to sense that his store was about to be disturbed. He gave no sign that he recognized Horn. "May I help you?" he asked in a flat tone.

"Sure," Horn said. "Remember that talk we had? Well, I've thought of a lot more questions I need to ask."

"Ahh . . ." St. George rested his fingertips lightly on the glass atop the counter, his eyes darting between the two visitors and the customer in the chair. "I don't, ah . . ."

Mad Crow quickly worked out his own role. He walked around behind the customer, bent over, and stared at the open book in the man's lap.

"Whoa, Nellie," he said loudly. "John Ray, come here and look. This gal's on some kind of a *trapeze*. How the hell can she do that? No, wait a minute, it's more like a—"

The man slammed the book shut, grabbed his hat, and left, causing the little bell to ring furiously. Following him to the door, Mad Crow flipped over the CLOSED sign and drew the door's shade down to cover the glass.

St. George quickly retrieved the book and

deposited it under the glass-topped counter. "That was very rude," he said to Horn. His voice was steady, but his fingertips tapped nervously on the glass.

"I suppose," Horn replied. "But you don't want an audience for this, do you?"

"If you make trouble here, I'll call the police."

"No, you won't." Horn took a seat in the chair vacated by the customer. "It'll just cause you grief. Looks to me like a lot of your business is illegal. So if you have us tossed out of here, somebody in Vice will get a call about you. They'll close you down, and you'll go to jail. Who's got more to lose?"

When St. George didn't answer, Horn reached over and patted the seat of the chair next to him. "Come on over here and talk to me, Calvin."

St. George stood still. His attention was on Mad Crow, who was moving around the room, occasionally taking a book from a shelf and leafing through it. "What about?" he asked.

"Men who like to look at pictures of underage girls," Horn said flatly. "Just like the picture I showed you last time I was here. You recognized it, even though you said you didn't. I want to know why you lied to me and what you know about these men."

St. George looked directly at Horn. "You probably think I'm afraid of you. I'm not. I've dealt with threats before."

"Is that so? And how do you deal with them, Calvin?"

"Get out," St. George said, raising his voice slightly.

Horn was about to reply, but just then he heard Mad Crow whistle softly through his teeth. "John Ray, this is just bee-*yoo*-tiful. I bet this book is worth a lot of money." He held it up for St. George to see. "Isn't it?"

"Please be careful with that," St. George said, sounding almost bored. "That's a *Decameron*, printed in Italy in 1813. It's in fine condition. The engravings alone—"

"This one," Mad Crow said, opening the book to a full-page illustration. "This is an engraving, right? This is pretty enough to put on my wall. Can I have it?"

St. George sighed. "The book will cost you—"

"No, just this page." Mad Crow gripped the top corner and began to pull. The sound of tearing paper was surprisingly loud.

"No!" St. George was across the room in an instant. As he grabbed at the book, he ran into Mad Crow's open hand, which closed on his throat and maneuvered him back against the bookshelves.

"Go sit in the chair and talk to my friend, Calvin," the Indian said conversationally. "I'll just keep looking at your collection here, see if anything strikes my fancy." He spread his fingers, and St. George sagged, clutching at his throat. After a brief hesitation, he made his way to the chair and sat.

Mad Crow carefully realigned the page, which

had about an inch torn from its binding, and replaced the *Decameron* on the shelf, then resumed his browsing.

"No time to be polite," Horn said to St. George. "I've got some ideas about you. I think you're the man who took that picture I showed you, along with a lot of others. All underage girls, all of them molested, some worse than others. You're one of the molesters. They're good-quality pictures, and you're a good photographer." He pointed to the framed photos of the young woman and the girl. "And," he said, looking around the store, "you also deal in roughly the same kind of material."

A look of disbelief grew on St. George's face.

"You fit the general description, and you're even the right age for the man I'm looking for," Horn went on. "What kind of cigarettes do you smoke?"

The other man swallowed. "Chesterfield."

"Ever smoke anything else?"

"No."

"I think you're lying. You ever hear of Arthur Bullard?"

"Of course I have. He died the other day. And you mentioned him when you came in."

"Good memory, Calvin. How about Vincent Bonsigniore?"

"I don't know," St. George said sullenly. "I don't think so."

"Wendell Brand?"

"No." St. George shook his head. "What does this—"

"Don't interrupt. Let me just tell you the whole theory, to save time. I think you're the fourth man, Calvin. You and the other three took all those girls up to the mountains for your awful games, and you were the photographer."

"No." St. George's face had begun to resemble Wendell Brand's at the moment Horn threatened him. It appeared to be infected with dread and fear.

"There's one other thing you need to know," Horn said. "One of the girls was my daughter."

St. George looked as if he wanted to sink inside the overstuffed cushions and disappear. His eyes darted around the room. Somewhere among the books, Mad Crow was whistling tunelessly.

"Listen," St. George said. "You are terribly, terribly mistaken about this. Yes, I did recognize the picture—"

"How?"

"Mister Bullard brought it in one day, along with some others. That's right, I knew him. He was one of my best customers. We had an arrangement. Whenever I received anything especially fine, I would call him and he would come look at it, to see if he wanted to add it to his collection. One day he pulled those photos out of his pocket and showed them to me. It was very casual. He just laughed and said, 'Of course, I know you could never handle anything like this, but I thought these might interest you.' That was all. I didn't ask him where he got them, and he never mentioned them again. And—" He took a breath, as if willing himself to calm down. "And I never saw any of those pictures after that until the day you came in here. Naturally, I lied to you. You could have been a policeman, for all I knew, and those pictures are dangerous."

Horn cracked his knuckles, thinking. The man sounded convincing, but Horn needed a target for his hate, and he wasn't ready to abandon his ideas about St. George. "I don't believe you," he said, putting as much threat as he could into the words. "You were lying to me then, and you're lying now. Which is worse, Calvin—being caught with a few dirty pictures or putting a hood over your face and raping a little girl?"

Something passed over St. George's face. He got up and went behind the counter. "I'd like to make a call," he said. "Do you mind? I think it will help answer some of your questions." When Horn nodded in assent, he picked up a telephone and dialed a number, and Horn thought he could hear a ring somewhere in the distance.

"Wally?" St. George said into the receiver. "It's me. Would you come down, please? There's someone I want you to meet." A pause. "I know, but it's important. Don't worry about getting dressed, just come down. Now."

A minute passed. Horn heard a door close, and then the sound of someone descending a narrow circular staircase he had barely noticed in the rear of the store. A young man appeared, wearing short pants, sandals, and a brightly striped pullover and wiping his hands on a dish towel.

"Wally, this is Mr. Horn," St. George said to him from the leather chair, pointedly ignoring Mad Crow, who appeared lost in his browsing. "He's looking for some information, so I'd like you to answer some questions for him. First, what were you doing upstairs?"

The young man was tall and blond and well-built. He was probably about twenty, and he had the casually handsome but unformed look that Horn had noticed in Vincent Bonsigniore's nephew at the lunch table. He looked uneasily back and forth between Horn and St. George.

"I was, uh, doing the breakfast dishes," the young man said.

"And why was that?"

Wally laughed nervously. "You know, Cal. I always do them."

"And what were you going to do next?"

Wally stopped drying his hands and, unsure what to do with them, clasped them in front, wrapped in the damp towel. "Fix lunch, naturally."

"That's good," St. George said encouragingly. "Wally, how long have we lived in the apartment upstairs?"

"Well, you've lived there ever since you took over the store," Wally said, smiling at Horn as he warmed to the conversation. "I've lived there since we met a couple of years ago."

"Wally, Mr. Horn noticed the pictures I took of

the young woman and the little girl. Would you tell him who they are and why I took them?"

"That's Clara, your niece, and her daughter." Wally shot Horn a conspiratorial look. "You said you took them because your brother's a cheapskate who pestered you until you agreed to do it for free."

"That's right," St. George said. "Now, Wally, please tell Mr. Horn whom I prefer to use as a model. And be honest."

"Me," Wally said proudly. He turned to Horn. "You should see the apartment. I'm all over the place. He says I'm his muse, and that I—"

"That's fine, Wally. You can go back upstairs. Please call me when lunch is ready."

The young man left. "I wouldn't have told you any of that," he said in a voice grown calm, "except that in your hunger for certitude and revenge, you had fixed on a fantastic image of me. And only the truth would shake you out of it." He steepled his hands in front of him, brow knitted, like a schoolmaster forced to deal with a particularly difficult student. "I don't molest little girls, Mr. Horn. I don't even begin to fit the description of those men you've told me about. Now that you've met Wally, I think that should be clear to you."

Horn turned to Mad Crow, and both nodded at each other. "All right," Horn said.

St. George drew himself up. "Now please take charge of your crude friend and get out of my store."

CHAPTER 22

As Mad Crow gunned the Cadillac up through the pass toward the Valley and Maggie's place, Horn retrieved the Colt from under the seat. He muttered under his breath.

"Hard to see a good theory blown all to smithereens, ain't it?" the Indian said.

"I wanted him to be the fourth man," Horn said. "He still could be, except . . ."

"Except it's a lot less likely. He just doesn't fit. Can't see him getting all worked up over any member of the female sex, no matter what age. Guess that leaves you without anybody to look at, doesn't it?"

"I guess it does." *Except for Scotty*, a small voice said inside his head. His silent answer came quickly: *I don't want to think about that.* Horn took off his hat, ran his hand through his hair, and laid his head back on the seat, letting the sun warm him. "Listen, I appreciate you coming along today. You were right. This was one of those times when I could have done something I'd regret."

"Don't mention it. You're the excitement in my life these days. Gasoline bombs in the night, a killer on the loose . . ."

354

"I don't want you to get so close to all this that you—"

"Get burned? That's the excitement, my friend. You know, I told you I was sorry for not saying anything the night Del Vitti brought the girl over to my place. That's still true. I suppose I'm trying to be helpful in order to make up for that. But there's another reason."

His head still tilted back, Horn turned to look at Mad Crow through slitted eyes.

"Back when I met you, I'd just finished being the third Indian from the left in some Hopalong Cassidy epic. I had one line: *Drums talk, tell us you lie*. I still don't know why you put in a good word with Bernie Rome, but—"

"Told you why," Horn said, sounding bored. "I thought you and I would make a good team. Turns out I was right."

"Anyway, after you did, I found myself working regular and eating good and feeling a hell of a lot better about things. I was able to bring family out here, the whole package. I turned a corner when I started working with you. I don't know if I ever said a proper thank-you—"

Horn put his hat back on to shade his eyes. "Just wake me up when we're there, okay?"

"Clea!"

Mad Crow was yelling for her before his Cadillac had rolled to a stop in front of Maggie's cottage. "Where are you?"

She came out the door, followed by Maggie. "Uncle Joe," she said, sounding pleased.

"She's one of the few who can get away with calling him Joe," Horn said to Maggie as he got out.

Mad Crow boosted himself up heavily onto the back of his pinto-hide seat, swung his legs over and, ignoring the door, dropped to the ground. He strode over and stood close to the girl, hands on hips.

"Well?" he demanded.

She shook her head, feigning ignorance. It was an old game.

"Well?" he asked, louder this time.

"Hello, Joe, what do you know?" she yelled, a broad smile creasing her face.

"That's right," he boomed. "And I say . . . 'Hey, little girl, lemme give you a *twirl!*'" With the last word, he grabbed her around the waist, lifted her high, and spun her around three times. She screamed, delighted.

"Damn, you're big," he said, setting her down, pretending to gasp. "What happened to that little bitty thing I used to swing around in the yard? Last time I'll be able to do that."

"It's good to see you, Uncle Joe," Clea said.

"Double for me, girl," Mad Crow responded, flashing a smile at Maggie. "Hey, wait a minute. Almost forgot." He strode over to the Cadillac, retrieved something from the backseat next to the cooler, and brought it over to Clea. It was a gift-wrapped parcel. "Heard you had a birthday just the other day."

She kissed him on the cheek, said, "Thank you," and hurried inside to unwrap it.

Horn shook his head. "What's the matter?" Maggie asked.

"I don't know. Look at her today, all happy to see Joseph and get a present. Last night she seemed just broken to pieces."

"I know," Maggie said. "Amazing, isn't it? I think it just has something to do with being seventeen." She turned to Mad Crow. "Can you stay for a while?"

"Sure. My place doesn't open up for a few hours. Let's have a great big lunch."

"You two do that, but I have to go somewhere," Horn said. "Pasadena. I have to see a rich lady about something."

"Mrs. Bullard?" Maggie was interested. "She was in the society page the other day. She lives in one of those mansions. You know, I wouldn't mind coming along. Get away from this place for a while."

"Admit it, girl. You want to see how the idle rich live."

"I do not." She seemed defensive.

Horn immediately regretted what he'd said. "Well, hell, come along. You've been cooped up here for days, what with me and Clea and the mare. Indian, can you watch Clea and Addie 'til we get back in an hour or so?"

"Addie's gone," Maggie broke in. "She took off early this morning without saying goodbye."

"Damn," Horn muttered. "Wish I knew what she was up to. I'm afraid she's going to be trouble."

"I'll be happy to mind Clea," Mad Crow said to them. "Take the Caddy, you two. Ride in style for a change." He tossed Horn the keys.

"You're sure Mrs. Bullard wouldn't mind an uninvited visitor?" Maggie asked Horn.

"Depends on the visitor. Way I see it, anybody who's hobnobbed with the Duke of Windsor ought to be able to swagger into any place in Pasadena and start ordering the help around without batting an eye."

He went inside to make a quick call, then came out. "She's out shopping but'll be back before long. Let's go."

He turned to Mad Crow and said quietly, "You won't need it, but if you do, her husband Davey's deer rifle is on the wall of the living room."

"Go," Mad Crow said. Then he hollered toward the house. "Clea! I want to see the new colt!"

When Horn guided the convertible into the Bullard driveway, he saw Helen Bullard by the front door, watching as her maid unloaded several shopping bags from the trunk of her car. She came over to greet him.

"Hello, John Ray," she said. "Nice to see you."

"Mrs. Bullard," he said. "This is my friend Margaret O'Dare."

Helen Bullard smiled at her. "How do you do? Won't you both come in?"

"We can only stay a little while," he said. "I have some information for you."

A few minutes later, Maggie was settled into a lounge chair on the back patio with a glass of iced tea, enjoying the view of the arroyo. Horn sat in the living room with their hostess, who had changed from her shopping clothes into a silk lounging robe and high-heeled slippers.

"I have to go away for a while, and I'll be out of touch," he told her. "But before I go, I have something for you. You wanted to know when I had found out anything about Scotty's death and who was behind it."

She nodded, waiting. Her hostess face had disappeared, and in its place was something hard and focused.

"His name is Vincent Bonsigniore," he said. "You may have read about him in the paper. He's a gangster, basically. He runs a lot of businesses here in L.A. for his bosses in New York, some legal, some illegal."

"I know the name," she said. "He's been here in my house, at a party we gave once. Arthur said they had business connections, but this man was not a typical business associate. I didn't like him." She wound the fringe of her sash around one thin finger. "And the young woman he brought with him struck me as cheap."

"Bonsigniore was part of a group of men who

spent time with underage girls. Your husband was one of the group."

She blinked at that, and her nostrils flared slightly. "Go on."

She knew some of it but maybe not all of it, Horn thought. *Whatever this does to her, she's not going to let it show.* "Scotty found a collection of pictures among your husband's papers. Bonsigniore wanted them back, and he had Scotty killed for them."

"You're sure."

"I'm sure." He handed her a manila envelope with a small note clipped to the outside. "This is his name and address here at the top," he said, pointing to the note. "Do you know anyone in the police department?"

"I sit on a board that oversees investments in some of the poor neighborhoods. We sometimes consult with the police. I had lunch not long ago with one of the deputy chiefs."

He nodded. "I don't know how much you or the police can do with this information, but it's yours now. You need to know that this man is one of the most powerful gangsters in this city. He kills people whenever they get in his way; I know of at least one more besides Scotty. To be that powerful, you need friends in the police department, so he probably has a few. Whoever you approach about this, just be careful."

She compressed her lips in a thin line, briefly carving dark valleys under her cheekbones. "I think what you're saying is that no matter what I do, he may get away with this."

"Mrs. Bullard, people get away with things all the time."

She lifted the manila envelope. "Are these the pictures?"

"Yes, ma'am. I guess they belong to you now."

She glanced at the note again. "This other name and phone number underneath—who is that?"

"I wrote that down just as an afterthought," he said. "This man has nothing to do with Scotty. But you may want to talk to him."

"Why?"

"He's someone who wants Bonsigniore as badly as you do."

She looked out the big window over the expanse of lawn. "I'm not sure that's possible," she said.

He and Maggie stopped for lunch on Colorado Boulevard in Pasadena, then drove back to the San Fernando Valley. A few miles short of her place, they passed a billboard advertising a new housing development—two-bedroom bungalows, attached garage, special terms for veterans—and saw bulldozers leveling acres of land. The development was called Vista del Sol, the billboard proclaimed. A little farther on was the developer's office, a stucco creation done up to resemble a miniature Alhambra, painted in garish orange and blue and festooned with penants. It sat in the middle of nothing.

"There goes another orange grove," said Maggie. "One of my neighbors who's been breeding horses out here since the thirties has just sold out to a developer. Said he couldn't turn down the money. They told him there was room for almost a hundred homes out where he and his family have been living."

"What'll happen to him?"

"He's going to move up the coast, where land is cheaper," she said. "I'm afraid the bulldozers'll come after me someday too."

"Don't sell. Hell with 'em."

"It's not that simple, John Ray. The Valley isn't the place you remember, where you and Iris used to live. It's more crowded, it's noisier, the air's not as clean. Too many cars, too many people. Davey and I've talked about it. We may not last much longer either."

"Sorry to hear that. You're good folks. Listen, Maggie. I just want to say thanks."

"For what?"

"You know. For everything. For taking us in. I don't know what I would have done with Clea—"

"Don't mention it. You're good folks too, both of you. Stay as long as you like."

"We're leaving tomorrow," he said. "It's time."

"Well, I'll be sorry to—" She stopped, leaned forward in her seat. "Who's that?"

He had turned off the road onto Maggie's driveway, and the buildings lay about a hundred yards ahead. As the car drew nearer, they saw

Miguel and Tomás leaning over a third figure seated on the ground, propped against the outer wall of the cottage. It was Mad Crow.

Horn hit the brakes in front of the little group, jumped out, and ran over. Mad Crow sat with shoulders slumped, head down. Flecks of blood darkened the shoulder of his embroidered shirt, and Horn saw a glistening patch of dark red above his right ear.

"Find Clea!" he yelled at Maggie. He knelt down in front of Mad Crow as his friend muttered something. "What?"

"She's gone," the Indian said.

Horn felt a wave of dizziness, almost nausea. He reached out, gripped both of Mad Crow's shoulders hard. "Was it—"

"No," Mad Crow said, looking up for the first time, his face streaked with pain and shame. "It was her father. Fairbrass."

Maggie brought a pan of water and a towel and began dabbing at the bloody spot. Mad Crow winced, cursing. "God, I'm sorry," he said.

"What happened?" Horn asked.

"We were in the stables for a while, and then we had something to eat." His words were slurred, as if he were drunk. "Afterward, I lay down on the couch, figured I'd close my eyes for just a minute. When I woke up, this guy was sitting there with a gun on his knee, not pointing it, just holding it."

"Fairbrass?"

"No. Some guy."

"Did he have a bandage on his face?"

"He had a scar there, where some stitches had been."

"Sykes." Horn was working hard to keep the anger out of his voice—anger at his old friend for letting this happen.

"Then Fairbrass came out of the bedroom with his arm around Clea. He told me who he was, said he was taking her someplace safe. They walked out to the car. He told her she should thank Addie for telling him where she was."

"*Damn*. That little . . ." Horn tried to collect himself. "What did Clea do? Did she fight him?"

"No," Mad Crow said wonderingly. "She looked a little dazed, but she went with him. He was talking to her all the time, telling her she was going to be okay and everything. The guy sounded like he really cared for her."

"I don't give a shit about that," Horn said. "How did you get hurt?"

"Well, we were out by the car. I asked Clea if she wanted to go with him. She looked at me for a long time and finally nodded her head. But just then she remembered the present I got for her and said she wanted it. She tried to go back inside, but Fairbrass had ahold of her tight, and she started to cry, and I went for him. Wasn't going to do anything serious, just get him to turn loose of her so she could go get her present. But the other guy stepped up behind me and laid his handgun upside my head. Next thing I remember, I was sitting by the wall with the two boys shaking me."

He braced himself against the wall and tried to get on his feet, but immediately fell back down to one knee. "Damn. I'm seeing everything double." He resumed a sitting position, head drooping between his knees. "I'm sorry, John Ray. I let you down."

Horn patted his shoulder but could think of no words of comfort. *You sure did, old buddy*, he said silently.

Maggie took him aside. "He took a good crack on the head, may have a concussion," she said quietly. "We need to get him to a doctor." She hesitated. "The nearest hospital is miles away, but I know a vet close by. He's better with animals, but he does people just fine."

"All right, point me to him," he said. "I'll drive him there in his car, and you can have one of the boys follow me in mine. I won't be coming back here." He looked around almost wildly, as if for guidance.

"What are you going to do?" She moved around into his line of vision and took hold of the front of his shirt. "You opened up your old trunk last night and got some things, didn't you? Talk to me."

"What am I going to do? You tell me." The anger spilled out, and it choked his voice. "I could try kidnaping Clea from her father—if I could find them—but somehow I don't think that would work.

All I know is, somebody wants to kill her, and she was probably safer here than anywhere else. Her father means well, but he doesn't have any idea about how much danger she's in or how to protect her. I can try to find him and talk some sense into him, but I've been lying to him for days, and he's got no reason to trust me."

His shoulders sagged. "Sierra Lane would know what to do. I don't."

Aided by Miguel and Tomás, he maneuvered Mad Crow into the front seat of the Caddy, then started the engine. Maggie gave Mad Crow an awkward hug, then looked searchingly at Horn. "You just be careful," she said.

"I'm sorry I brought you all this, Maggie."

He rang the doorbell, but its tones sounded too decorous for his purposes, so he banged on the door with his fist.

"Who is it?" He could hear the alarm in her voice.

"It's me, Iris. Let me in."

"John Ray? What—"

"I need to talk to your husband."

"He's not here."

"Where is he?"

"I don't know. What's the matter?"

He felt like a fool, standing there talking to her through the door. "Goddammit, Iris, let me in."

"Stop it. You're frightening me."

He leaned against the door, head down, trying

to think straight. He needed to convey the danger that Clea was facing, but do so without sending Iris into hysteria or causing her to call the police on him. He forced himself to sound calm.

"Listen. I won't do anything, I promise. Just want to talk to you for a minute. All right?"

The door opened, and he stepped inside. She looked distraught. Her hair needed brushing, and she gave off the scent of nerves, like stale clothing.

"Paul came after Clea," he said quickly. "She was staying with me at a place out in the Valley."

"I know," she said. "He told me just before he left."

"I lied to you when I said I hadn't found her. But I was only trying to protect her. Look, there's no soft way to say this. Somebody wants to hurt her. The same person who killed Scotty. I don't think your husband realizes—"

"He does," she said quietly.

"What?"

"He knows someone's looking for her, that she's in danger. He told me he's known for some time, was sick knowing about it, but kept it from me because he didn't want me to worry. As soon as he found out where she was, he decided to take her someplace safe."

"Where?"

"He wouldn't tell me. Said it was better if I didn't know. He plans to call as soon as they're settled in."

"I don't like this," he muttered, looking around

the room, too nervous to sit down. "Why doesn't he just go to the police? I had reasons for keeping them out of it. But he's a solid citizen, they'll believe whatever he tells them. Why is he trying to handle this on his own?" He turned to her. "If he calls you, call me. I'll be at my place. Even if he says it's not a good idea, call me. I need to talk to him."

She shook her head. "I can't promise, John Ray," she said. "I trust his judgment."

"Do you? His man Sykes hit Joseph with a gun, cracked his head open. How's that for judgment?"

"I'm sorry. Truly I am. I hope Joseph's all right. But I know Paul loves Clea, and he'll protect her. And when all this is over, we'll all be a family again."

His gaze fell on the framed portrait of Clea, the one that made her look almost glamorous. *That's not her anymore*, he thought. *Right now, she's just a scared kid again.*

"Let's pray it turns out that way, Iris."

As he paused in the doorway, she regarded him almost fondly. "You look terrible," she said.

"Well, you're a knockout, as always."

She brushed the hair out of her face. "Sure I am. I used to think I could handle anything. Now, I imagine her getting hurt, and it makes me sick."

"Oh, I think you're going to get through this," he said. "I was telling Joseph the other day that marriage number three is going to be the charm for you. I'm sorry it didn't work out for us, but I do want you and Clea to be happy. So maybe it was a good thing you met Paul. If I remember right, Scotty told me he introduced the two of you at that party. If that's the way it happened, then my old buddy had good instincts."

"Well, it didn't happen exactly that way," she said. "It was a party, and I think Scotty was there. But it was his father who introduced me to Paul." A tiny smile, barely there. "Isn't that funny? Arthur Bullard is responsible for some awful things in my life, but I guess I should be grateful to him for that one thing."

It was late afternoon when he reached his place in the canyon. The first thing he checked was the mailbox, but all he found was a note from Harry Flye exhorting him to spend some time repairing the crumbling rock-and-concrete wall that ran across the front of the property. He cursed his landlord loudly enough to hear a small echo from the far side of the canyon.

Rummaging through his larder, he rustled together enough food for a passable supper, which he ate out on the porch. One thought occurred to him. He dug up the number of Fairbrass's office at the Long Beach plant and placed the call through the long-distance operator. Finding him there would be almost too easy, he reflected, and although it was after business hours, it was worth a try. He listened to the phone ring several times before he replaced the receiver.

He felt useless, helpless. He had found Clea and lost her, just at the moment when he had become aware of the peril she faced. He had run down Scotty's killers, only to acknowledge that he was powerless to impose justice on them. The Colt sat on a table by the couch, mocking him. It was thought of as a hero's gun, but it had spent its life firing blanks. Except, he reminded himself, to end the life of a good animal that deserved better.

Self-pity demanded a few drinks, so he pulled out a glass and a bottle of Evan Williams and began working on it. When the level was down three inches, it was dark outside, so he turned out the light, lay down on the sofa, and closed his eyes. A small thought, tiny as a worm, began gnawing around the edge of his consciousness. But before he could identify the thought, he slipped into sleep. . . .

He awoke to a scream. He knew it was her, and he gathered the breath to shout out her name before he realized it was the shrill ring of the phone. His hand unsteady with tension and alcohol, he picked it up.

"Is this Horn?"

"Yeah."

"Dewey Sykes. We met out at your place."

"I know who you are," Horn said, sitting up on the couch. He looked at his watch; it was past two-thirty. "You coldcocked my friend from behind. He owes you, and so do I."

"If you say so," said Sykes, sounding unconcerned. "But we've got more important things to talk about."

"Where's Clea?"

"She's here with her father."

"Where's that?"

"Listen, just let me talk. We've had some trouble. We went down to Mr. Fairbrass's plant in Long Beach, thought we'd go in one of the side gates and hide her there. But somebody either was waiting or followed us. They fired some shots. We took off, and I think we lost them."

Horn shook his head to try to clear out the bourbon. "Is she all right?"

"She's fine. Shaken up, but fine. The shots took out two of our side windows in the back. Lot of glass and noise, but nobody—"

"Why are you talking to me?"

"What do you mean?"

"Why isn't Fairbrass on the phone?"

"He's, uh . . ." Sykes lowered his voice. "He's shaken up bad. Nobody's ever taken a shot at him before, and he's not handling it very well. I thought I'd better step in. This is the kind of thing I get paid for, anyway. Listen, before all this happened, Clea told us the Indian mentioned that you might take her out of town. Is that right?"

"He has a friend in San Bernardino."

"Sounds good to me. I don't like the situation here, so San Berdoo would work just fine."

"Do you know who you're up against, Sykes?"

"Mr. Fairbrass told me someone wants to hurt the girl. That's all I need to know."

"It's Vincent Bonsigniore. The name mean anything to you?"

"Holy Mary," Sykes breathed.

"That's right. I don't know if your boss knows that or not, but you need to know it. You're the one out in front."

"Thanks for telling me."

"I've got to get hold of Mad Crow," Horn said. "When I do, I'll meet you—"

"No, we're coming over to your place," Sykes said.

"Absolutely not. This canyon's a dead end. If they're following you—"

"They're not. Anyway, we're already there. I'm calling from the pay phone outside the garage, about ten minutes from you."

Damn. "Get here as fast as you can," Horn said and hung up.

CHAPTER 23

"Indian?"

"Oh, Jesus, I just got to sleep. My head feels like—"

"I'm sorry. Listen, I've got a problem. Clea's coming here."

"What? Where are you?" Horn heard Mad Crow knock over something as he sat up. "Damn. What time is it?"

"It's a little before three. I'm home. Sykes just called. Somebody took a shot at their car, and they're headed this way. They want to get her someplace safe, like we planned, and it looks like San Bernardino is on again."

"Fools," Mad Crow said, his voice still full of sleep. "Is she all right?"

"I think so. I need one last favor from you. I'd rather not ask it, but I don't know how many of Bonsigniore's men are out there looking for her."

"You want some protection," Mad Crow said with resignation. "Somebody to ride shotgun."

"Something like that. Are you in shape for it?"

"I reckon I'll do it for the little lady," the Indian sighed in a poor imitation of Sierra Lane's drawl.

"Tell this guy Sykes I'm going to clean his clock for him when all this is over." He paused. "I'm almost an hour away from you. Can you wait?"

"We have to. Just hurry." He saw headlights out the front window. "They're here. I've got to go."

He went down and unlocked the gate. The Packard pulled up with Sykes at the wheel and his two passengers in the rear. Both side windows in the back had been shattered, leaving only a few jagged icicles of glass. Horn waved Sykes through and told him to pull around behind the cabin so the car wouldn't be visible from the road. Soon, all three had joined him on the porch.

Clea had her arm around Paul Fairbrass's waist as they came wordlessly up the steps. He looked stricken and out of breath. Horn took them inside and had them sit on his couch, the only comfortable seat. He motioned Sykes back out to the porch.

"Tell me exactly what happened."

"Pretty much like I said," Sykes began, the light from inside illuminating the fresh scar and the pinprick marks left by the stitches on his left cheek. "I think they were waiting for us at the plant, although I can't imagine how or why."

"I think I can," Horn said. "Addie Webb. She told your boss where to find Clea, and I'm guessing she also told Bonsigniore that Clea was with the two of you."

Sykes narrowed his eyes. "She's a kid. That doesn't make sense."

374

"She's a young woman, she's been cozy with Bonsigniore, and she's a little cracked," Horn shot back. "She thinks I killed her boyfriend—the same one who cut you, by the way—so she got back at me by having Clea taken away. She's jealous of Clea for stealing that boyfriend, and now she's trying to get revenge on her. The way Addie sees things, they don't have to make sense."

"Well," Sykes said, "she could have made things a lot simpler—"

"I know. By calling Bonsigniore in right away. All I can guess is that she didn't want his boys tearing around the O Bar D, maybe hurting Maggie or her ranch hands."

"Or maybe you?"

"I don't know anything about that. Look, she's put her friend Clea in the worst kind of danger, and she scares the hell out of me," said Horn. "What happened at the plant?"

"Somebody fired three shots at us just as we were going into a side entrance," Sykes continued. "You saw how close they came. I got a glimpse of a car with two or three men. I stepped on it, got us inside, and the guard closed the gate. Then we left by another gate—it's a big plant—and headed this way. I was careful coming here, and I don't think anybody followed us."

"What happened to Fairbrass?"

"Don't know, but it's pretty clear he's never had anybody fire a gun in his direction before," Sykes said wryly. "On the road, he had trouble breathing.

It might have been his heart. He seems better now, but he's still shaky. Anyway, we came here. He wasn't crazy about the idea, but I get paid to take care of him, and it seemed to me I'd better make some decisions. So here we are."

"How's Clea doing?"

"Not bad," Sykes said, and Horn thought he could hear respect in his tone. "Soon as Mr. Fairbrass started having trouble, she stepped right up, started taking care of him. I think she's got what it takes."

"Good," said Horn. "Here's what's next: I'll take you to a safe place in San Bernardino, but we need some help. I've got a friend coming over to drive with us—the same one you laid out with your little gun barrel today."

Sykes chuckled. "He's not going to be very happy to see me. I don't always fight fair."

"We'll worry about that later. He'll be here inside an hour, and we'll go."

"All right," Sykes said, and descended the steps. "I'll go down to the road and watch, just to make sure nobody surprises us."

Inside, Horn found Clea sitting on the couch. "He's in the bathroom," she said. "His face felt hot, and I thought he should splash some cold water on it."

"Are you all right? You look pretty chipper for somebody who's been through all this excitement in one day."

"I suppose," she said slowly, looking down. "I was

really afraid when somebody shot at our car, and there was glass everywhere, even in my lap. Then Mr. Sykes was driving us really fast, and that was scary too." She leaned forward, hands clasped, her body drawn inward protectively. "And sitting in the car, I was thinking how much time I've spent in the last few days being afraid. There was the funeral, when I saw the man and he saw me. Then there was Tommy and what happened at his house." She raised her head to look at him. "I'm really tired of being afraid. It's the worst thing I can imagine, being afraid all the time. Don't you think so?"

"I sure do."

"Well, I told myself I'm going to stop it."

"Just like that?"

"Yes. Bad things can happen—maybe even *will* happen—but I'm not going to waste my time worrying about them." In the partial light from the table lamp, he saw some of Iris's features in her face.

"Well, I'm with you, girl. Hope you don't mind if I take some lessons from you."

"You? You're not afraid of anything."

He started to answer that, then thought better of it. "Honey, how do you feel about being with him? Tell me the truth."

"You mean Paul?" Horn was happy she didn't say "Daddy." "I think I'm all right now. I know he loves me. All the way down to Long Beach, he told me how worried my mother has been. I suppose I shouldn't blame her for anything bad that happened to me when I was little. But I needed somebody to blame. Does that make sense?"

"Perfect sense. You know Iris divorced me, and I'm not happy about that. But I won't let anybody tell me she doesn't love you. When we get all this straightened out, you belong back with her."

She nodded soberly, and he noticed for the first time how tired she looked.

"Did you tell Paul about seeing the man at the funeral?"

"I tried to, in the car. But he didn't seem to want to hear about it."

The worm was stirring in his mind again. He had the feeling that when it finished nibbling away all the excess underbrush that clogged his memory, something important would stand revealed.

As he tried to form another question, Fairbrass came out of the small bathroom. His face was damp and pale. "That's better," he said, smiling ruefully at her. "I'm sorry I was such a handful."

"Don't be silly," Clea said.

"We'll be leaving in less than an hour, soon as Joseph Mad Crow shows up," Horn told them. "Clea, I'd take it as a personal favor if you'd use the time to lie down and rest. Paul and I can talk outside."

They stepped onto the porch, and Horn closed the door. "Are you all right?" he asked.

"I suppose," Fairbrass said. "I don't respond well to stress, and you might say today exceeded my quota. I wasn't in the war. I envy anyone like you who could stand up to combat."

They sat on the steps. "Don't envy what you don't know about."

"Now that I've complimented you, I want you to know I think it was despicable of you to hide Clea from us."

"I had my reasons," Horn said. "They had to do with protecting her. Nothing else. And while I had her, she was safe. That's more than you could say down in Long Beach. So don't lecture me."

Fairbrass sighed. "Anyway, soon we'll be someplace where we can draw a breath."

"Why didn't you call the police in on this?"

Fairbrass looked surprised. "They've been looking for her for weeks."

"No, I mean the shooting."

The other man shrugged. "I don't know. It all happened so fast." He pulled a cigarette from a flat box and offered one to Horn, who shook his head. When Fairbrass struck a flame with his lighter and touched it to tobacco, an aromatic scent drifted over the porch and out into the trees.

"Do you have any idea who shot at you?" Horn asked.

"I hope she can't hear us," Fairbrass said. "This talk might trouble her."

"Don't worry. The door's closed."

"All right. Well, I just assumed it had something to do with this Tommy character. We know he's dangerous. Now it looks like he has dangerous friends. I wish I'd known enough to keep her away from him at the very beginning."

"You don't have to worry about Tommy. He's dead."

"Really? How do you know?"

"I saw his body."

"Well . . . I'm glad to hear it. But I thought he was still a menace to her, and that's why I wanted to get her away."

"I suppose that makes sense," Horn said. "I've been thinking about a lot of things lately, trying to make sense of all of them. You're going to think some of them are really unimportant. Like where you used to live."

"What do you mean?"

"Before you met Iris and married her. Where did you live?"

"Long Beach. My father wanted me near the plant. After he died, I stayed in the same house until Iris and I decided to buy the place in Hancock Park. Why on earth does that matter?"

"I'm not sure it does. By the way, you remember that photo of Clea you gave me? I didn't realize that you took it until Iris told me. It's very nicely done, almost professional."

"Thank you," Fairbrass said curtly. "It's just a hobby."

"Do you have a darkroom?"

"Yes, I have a darkroom. In the garage. Again, what does this have to do with anything?"

"You know, I think I will try one of those cigarettes of yours, if you don't mind."

"Of course." Fairbrass opened the flat cardboard

box, and Horn took one out. "They're Turkish," Fairbrass said, lighting it for him. "An expensive habit, I suppose, but my father used to smoke them, and I got to like them too. There's a cigar store on Wilshire that stocks them."

"They're different," Horn said, exhaling. "I'm not sure everyone would enjoy them. Why, just the other day I met a man who told me he didn't like the smell of them."

"Who was that?"

"Maybe I'll tell you his name later." Horn stood up and stretched and remained there, looking down on Fairbrass. "You asked what these questions of mine have to do with anything. Well, I've been looking for a man who fit a description. A man who was a good photographer. Who smoked an unusual cigarette. Who would have had to travel a long distance to get up to a hunting lodge in the San Gabriels, maybe all the way from Long Beach."

Fairbrass sat motionless, his cigarette a tiny glow in the dark, not even looking up.

"When you started fitting that description, I wouldn't believe it, because it was too crazy," Horn went on. "The idea that Iris would be married twice to scum who abused her little girl. It would never happen like that. The odds were too long. Unless . . . unless someone set it up that way."

His chest felt tight, and he strode to the end of the porch, then back. The worm had cleared away most of the leaves and branches now, and Horn could make out the shape of something. He sat down heavily in the rocker and regarded Fairbrass's back. Across the canyon, a nightbird called.

Finally Fairbrass spoke. "It was Arthur Bullard's sick sense of humor," he said in a voice so faint that Horn had to strain to hear him. "When he introduced us at that party, I thought he was just being a good host. Then I fell in love with Iris and couldn't believe how lucky I was. I loved her daughter too—I didn't recognize her, of course, because by then she was much older. Iris and I married. And then that awful day came when she described her first husband to me. Although she wasn't specific, she hinted at the reason their marriage ended, and as she talked about him, I realized I had known him. And . . . and Clea."

She told this bastard Fairbrass more about Wendell Brand than she ever told me when we were married, Horn thought resentfully. *Maybe because she knew I wouldn't have handled it very well.*

"You called him Heart, didn't you?"

Fairbrass half-turned, but in the weak light from the front windows his profile was almost invisible. "Oh, Lord, you know it all, don't you? After what Iris told me, I should have given you credit for being smarter. Yes, that was the name we called him. I didn't learn his real name until the moment Iris began talking about him. The only person we knew by his real name was Bullard; he didn't want the rest of us to know anything about the others."

"So Iris told you about Wendell Brand," Horn prompted him.

"And I realized just how manipulative Arthur Bullard could be, holding the strings and making people dance like puppets. Seeing me marry Iris, become a father to Clea, must have seemed like the ultimate joke to him. I almost could have killed him for trying to play God with me. Except for the fact that his terrible joke also brought me so much happiness. So maybe the final joke was on him."

Just what Iris said, Horn thought, but he didn't want to give Fairbrass the satisfaction of hearing the words spoken.

"That was when I told Bullard I'd had enough of his games and his string-pulling," Fairbrass went on. "Heart—Wendell Brand—had dropped out long before then. When I left the group, there were just those two."

"Spade and Club," Horn mused. "You didn't know who Vincent Bonsigniore was at the time?"

Fairbrass shook his head. "I found out later. One day I saw his picture in the paper along with a story, and I understood how dangerous he could be. And then there was that day at Bullard's funeral, when Clea and I both saw him at the same instant. She took my hand and squeezed it so hard . . . he looked at both of us, and I could see it all in his face. He knew she had recognized him, and I knew she was in danger."

"Why didn't you protect her?"

"I tried," he almost shouted. "I went to the man, begged him to leave us alone, told him she was no threat. He just sat there, playing with those enormous rings. He told me one of his men had been keeping an eye on Clea, and soon he would have to decide what to do about her. Such arrogance! As if he had the power of life and death, and the rest of us had no appeal. I tried to think of something else to do, but then Clea disappeared, and I suppose I panicked."

"You came to me."

"Yes."

"And told me just what you thought I needed to know."

"What I told you was mostly true—that I thought she was with this man who was calling himself Tommy. For a long time, I even thought that was his real name. What I didn't tell you was that I suspected he worked for Bonsigniore."

"Did you tell Sykes that? The guy who got his face cut up while he was trying to do a job for you?"

"No," Fairbrass said, his voice sounding tired again. "I could have been more honest with him. I was trying to keep things secret. A lot of things."

"Just for the record, Tommy—Anthony Del Vitti—was trying to protect Clea when Bonsigniore had him killed. Did you know that?"

"No, I didn't," Fairbrass said. "If that's what happened, I'm deeply grateful to him. I couldn't love her more if she were my own."

Horn laughed out loud. There was no mirth in the sound; it could have been a hangman's laugh. "You self-righteous piece of—"

"Please lower your voice," Fairbrass said urgently. "I don't want her to hear."

"This is the little girl you molested, over and over," Horn said, trying to choke back the rage.

"We never touched her."

"I know, I know. You just took her picture. You left it to Bonsigniore to rape some poor little girl with Clea watching."

"We . . . we tried to stop him." Horn could hear the surprise in Fairbrass's voice. "Did she tell you about that?"

Horn chose not to answer. "She'll always have nightmares about it."

"Yes," the other man said, almost in a whisper. "I wish I could change that."

"And what about the other girl? I suppose Bullard threw in a little extra money for her parents. And what about all the others? Do you wish you could change what happened to them too? Or are you just concerned about your daughter?"

When Fairbrass didn't answer, Horn pressed ahead. "And I suppose you never laid a hand on her, all the time she was living under your roof."

"As God is my witness," Fairbrass said. "I don't expect you to understand, but . . . look, I have certain urges. Wendell Brand shared them. In my case, it's purely visual, connected with my photography. I just enjoy the sight of . . . you know.

Whatever else went on in that place, that was the work of the other two."

His words came out slowly and deliberately, but now there was something inevitable about them, as if they had finally found their long-awaited audience.

"You have to understand," he said. "The girls . . . the girls must be very young. By the time Iris and I married, Clea had grown out of that age, and my interest in her—my love for her—was strictly a father's. It still is."

"How much of this does Iris know?"

"Nothing. Absolutely nothing. If she ever found out, it would kill her. You know that."

Horn sat silent, almost ignoring the other man for a while. Of the many people injured in this story of weakness and exploitation, Iris's situation was one of the saddest and most unlikely. Each of her marriages, it seemed, only took her deeper into misery. What was there about Iris that attracted men like Horn, full of rage and shame, and men like Brand and Fairbrass, possessed of some of nature's darkest impulses? She wasn't to be blamed for any of this. Instead, he pitied her for whatever chemistry she possessed that brought such men to her and cast such a shadow on her life. *She's had enough unhappiness*, he reflected. *I'm sorry some of it came from me.*

Iris would have to find out about Fairbrass, of course. Would the disclosure, as he said, kill her?

A long time had gone by, and he realized Fairbrass was speaking to him. "What?"

"I said, what are you going to do?"

When all this is over, I think I'll probably kill you. The words were on his lips, ready to be spoken, when he heard a faint sound down by the road. A moment later, Sykes's shape emerged, his shoes crunching on the gravel of the driveway. "Get inside," Sykes said in a low voice.

He and Fairbrass moved into the cabin, where Clea was lying on the couch. Sykes mounted the steps and paused in the doorway. "I heard a car engine for a few seconds, but it stopped. No lights, either. It's too early for—"

A dark red flower bloomed around the back of Sykes's head, and tiny petals spattered the doorframe just as Horn heard a distant sound that sounded like the splitting of a branch. Sykes's face took on a quizzical look an instant before he pitched forward. The sound of his head and chest meeting the floor was startlingly loud in the small room.

CHAPTER 24

The next few seconds flashed through Horn's mind like short, jerky scenes in a badly edited movie:

Sykes lying inert, the back of his head glistening red, a shard of curiously unbloodied skull, with hair attached, perched on his shoulder. Clea's strangled gasp, followed an instant later by a shout from Fairbrass, full of surprise and despair. Another cracking sound, almost simultaneous with the soft thud of a bullet imbedding itself in the couch near Clea's shoulder. Her face pale with fear. The weight of the Colt as Horn grabbed it from the side table, then his backhanded blow that sent the table lamp to the floor, the bulb shattering, the room now in darkness.

Sharpshooter with a rifle, he thought. "Don't anybody move." He dropped to the floor, grabbed Sykes's sleeve, and dragged the heavy form into the room, then scuttled around the body and slammed the front door. "Let's all get behind the couch." He joined them there, where they huddled amid the sounds of their own heavy breathing.

"Oh, God. Dewey." Fairbrass's voice was a tightly

strung wire. "They killed him. What do we do?"

"Give me a minute."

Think. Sykes said two or three men. At least one has a rifle and is a good shot. They're probably down by the road now, coming up. Before long they could post themselves around the cabin to guarantee no one leaves, then decide what to do. They can take their time, since no one lives close enough to interfere. Gunshots after dark out here on the wild end of the canyon could be someone going after raccoon or 'possum. Sykes put it well: I don't like the situation here. *We have to get out.*

He moved around the couch and swept his hand over the floor, searching for the box of shells. He found only the telephone receiver and realized the phone had crashed to the floor along with the lamp. When he lifted it to his ear, it was silent. He moved to the door, where he listened intently for a few seconds. Kneeling, he felt underneath Sykes's body until he located the man's gun in a holster on his right hip. It felt like a short-barreled .38, a plainclothes cop's gun. Fumbling with the unfamiliar weapon, he managed to break open the cylinder and confirm that the gun was loaded. Back behind the couch, he pressed it into Fairbrass's hand. "Take this," he said.

"I've never fired a pistol. Just a .22 rifle, when I—"

"I don't care. You point it, and you pull the trigger. Use both hands if it helps. Aim just a little low. Don't jerk, but use some force when you pull. Simple as that."

"You can do it," Clea said.

"All right."

"Now we're going out the back," Horn told them, "before they have a chance to get around us. Follow me, and try to stay low." He hoped they couldn't hear the tension in his voice.

Hands outstretched in the dark, they made their way to the rear of the cabin, where a single dirty window faced the back slope. Horn wrenched it open, stuffed the Colt in his belt, climbed through, and dropped to the soft ground, then helped the others, Clea first.

The bulk of the Packard blocked their way. Reaching through the window, Horn felt for the keys and found none; they were doubtless in Sykes's pocket. Remembering that he had left the gate unlocked, he briefly considered piling everyone in the car, hot-wiring the engine, ducking low, and hoping to get past their pursuers and down to the canyon road. But he hadn't enough time or the proper tools. So he led the other two around the car to the path that wound its way up the hill. "Single file," he said in a low voice. "No talking."

The first five minutes were rough going, since there was almost no light in the trees. Horn knew the path, but occasionally the other two would stray off it and have to claw their way out of branches that swiped at their faces. Halfway up, he stopped to listen. At first there was nothing; then, far behind, he heard a voice calling out, somewhere near the cabin. The voice was answered by another. However many there were, he thought, they would eventually figure the cabin was empty and begin moving up the slope. He led the other two on.

Minutes later, they came out on the plateau and were walking along the weedy ground where he had wielded his scythe just a few days before. They could make out the pale, indistinct shapes of what remained of Ricardo Aguilar's estate—the great house, outbuildings, pool, and tennis court.

Mad Crow could do little for them, Horn concluded. He hoped that when his friend arrived, he would assess the situation and have the good sense to stay out of it and call in the police. Their only hope, he reasoned, was to keep climbing and make it quickly to the north-south path that traveled the crest of the canyon's west wall, then follow it south toward the ocean. After a half-mile they would come to other houses, some with telephones, and could make their own attempt to call for help.

He led them around the ruins of the big house to where the ground began to slope slightly downward, and there they found the path and turned left. Soon the trees closed in again. Behind him, Horn heard Fairbrass breathing heavily. "We're doing fine," Clea whispered to him, but her own tone sounded anxious.

Suddenly Horn heard something. "*Shhh*," he

said. A few seconds went by, and there it was again—up ahead, a voice calling out. It sounded less than a hundred yards away. The answer was not long in coming. It sounded more faint and came from behind and to their left. Finally, another voice answered from even farther away; Horn could not place the direction.

They were outflanked. One of the men had made it quickly up through the darkened underbrush south of the path in order to cut off a possible escape. There were three of them, and they had spread out, going about their task in a smart and methodical way.

"We have to go back," Horn said quietly.

"Oh, no," Fairbrass said hopelessly.

"Come on." Moving even more quickly, they headed back toward the estate. The three pursuers were closing in on them. Horn could think of nothing except taking cover. Maybe the darkness would shield them until help arrived, he hoped. But he knew better. The three men out there in the dark would find them.

As they walked across what had once been Aguilar's sprawling front lawn, he quickly fixed on a plan. "This way," he said. "Be very careful." They climbed over the broken, hip-high wall that marked the front of the main house, then threaded their way among a jumble of old concrete, jagged tile, and charred beams that were all that was left of the mansion. From his daytime explorations, Horn knew the approximate shape and layout of the place. They were now in the living room, which contained the ruins of a stone fireplace. The smell of ashes told him that bums and other casual visitors still built fires there. To the left would have been the hallway that led to the dining room and kitchen. Halfway along the remnants of the hall, feeling his way, he stopped them. "Here."

The door had burned away from the masonry frame, leaving a black and gaping hole only partly blocked by charred wood and other debris. Horn cleared away the largest pieces of stone and wood, then stepped tentatively down into the hole and gestured for them to follow. They descended a dozen stone steps to the bottom, then stood there, breathing cooler air.

It was Aguilar's stone-walled wine cellar, and it had survived the worst of the fire. Others had discovered it too, of course, and the wine was long gone, some of it carted off, other bottles smashed by vandals. The place had an overpowering sour smell. It was pitch-dark down there, but Horn had once looked around it by flashlight and knew the dimensions of the room.

"Careful of broken glass," he said. As they felt their way like blind people, he led them to one of the far corners and had them huddle under a crazily tilted set of shelves. "Stay here and be quiet, and you'll be fine," he told them with more confidence than he felt. "I'm going up there to keep a lookout."

"Do you know who they are?" Fairbrass asked hoarsely.

"Well, they're obviously sent by your friend Vinnie," Horn said. "But do I know their names? I'm pretty sure I know one of them. I guess I expected to run into him again someday."

He reached out for Clea and encountered Fairbrass's hand, which was reaching for his, as if asking for reassurance. Awkwardly, he squeezed the other man's hand, then found Clea in the dark. He cupped her cheek for a few seconds, feeling its warmth, then heard her say, "Be careful," and left them.

Outside, he peered around, trying to recall the layout of the ruins, looking for a place to take cover. He remembered something and moved off in a northwesterly direction for a few dozen yards until he came to it. One of Aguilar's guest houses had once stood here. Now all that remained were parts of the outer wall's foundation. The nearest corner formed a waist-high V. The apex faced the big house, and one of the two arms, each roughly six feet long, afforded him cover from the man who would be approaching up the trail from the south. This would have to do. He settled in behind the wall and tried to make himself comfortable.

It was still predawn, and the young moon, now nearing the horizon, was too slender to give off much light, but the sky held a layer of haze that reflected the far-off lights of the city, casting the faintest illumination onto the ground. Pale objects, particularly the crumbled marble and granite remnants strewn about, seemed to glow. The pieces that stood upright or leaned against each other looked to Horn like tombstones in a neglected cemetery.

He glanced down at his arm, noted that his white shirtsleeve gave off the same glow as the stone, and cursed himself for not considering it earlier. He stripped off his shirt and undershirt, and rolled them into a tight bundle. Carefully, he laid the Colt on its side atop the wall, barrel facing outward, and tried to think of anything except dying.

The gun that won the West, he mused, looking down at the Colt. *I just hope this one can handle a single job here at the Villa Aguilar. They say Wyatt Earp used one of these at the O.K. Corral. Did he have any trouble holding it steady?*

He listened, straining to hear anything from the path. He heard nothing but the crickets and an occasional voice in his head.

What are you doing, John Ray?

What the hell do you care? You're dead. But since you ask, I'm listening for some guy who wants to kill me as dead as you are.

I think he's on his way. Others, too.

I know that. I'm kind of busy right now, Scotty.

Just trying to be helpful. You know, this sounds like the big shootout in the last reel, where you always—

Goddammit.

Sorry. Anything I can do?

Horn felt the sensation begin to grow, just as it had during that fierce Italian winter among the rocks and ice. As before, it started in the pit of his stomach, where it fluttered like a flight of demented butterflies, and spread to his arms and legs, where it turned muscle into jelly. His right hand began to shake ever so slightly.

Someone is coming to kill me. He sat on the ground and leaned forward, hugging his knees, trying to squeeze the feeling until it died. But he knew it had dug in and would only grow, would speed up his breathing and heartbeat and bring palsy to his limbs. The fear had returned, like an old enemy he had tried to forget but who had never forgotten him.

Scotty?

Yeah.

Were you afraid when you died?

Was I ever. But that's not a fair question. It's hard to be brave when you find yourself suddenly flying out a window, you know what I mean? Let's talk about you instead, cowboy. If anybody knows a few things about being strong, silent, and heroic, it should be you.

Doesn't count. That was just acting.

You were in the war. You even killed a few Krauts.

Doesn't count either, and I've already told you why. At your funeral, remember?

All right, look at it this way: If you can't handle these guys, you're going to be as dead as me.

Now you're making it even worse.

How about Clea?

What do you mean?

If you can't stand up and do what you have to do, what do you think happens to her?

396

Horn's eyes scanned the tree line as he thought about Scotty's words. Or were they Scotty's? Funny, he could hear Clea's voice too: *I'm tired of being afraid. I'm going to stop it.* He saw her under their Christmas tree the year he became her father. He saw her astride Raincloud that first time, and the carousel horse. He saw her reaching for the ring, her face screwed tight in little-girl concentration.

He saw her dead.

He shifted position in the dirt, kneeling forward, leaning on the broken stone. Something eased inside him, something warmed the muscles that had felt so chilled, something steadied the hands that rested now on the wall.

He would not see her dead.

The fear was not gone, but it had receded into a tight little lump. It huddled down there, somewhere in his stomach, waiting for the day when it could return. In some wonderment, he flexed the fingers of his hands. They felt not palsied but strong.

Horn realized that the shapes out there had taken on a few more degress of definition. The irregular pillars of jumbled concrete were more distinct, and as he turned his gaze to his left, the sky looked faintly pale over the silhouette of the big house and, farther off, the eastern rim of the canyon. It was first light.

As his eyes swept back across the plateau, he saw a movement where the path broke the tree line about a hundred yards away. It was the man.

He carried a pistol, not a rifle, and slowly entered the clearing at a crouch. His white shirt was pale in the dim light.

They may be slick and dangerous, Horn thought with satisfaction, *but they're city boys, and they've never chased after anybody in the woods at night.*

Don't forget: A single-action has to be cocked before it'll fire. It takes extra time, but that's the price you pay for having an authentic gun in your movie. Wouldn't mind having my old M-1 with me right now.

He slowly pulled back the hammer on the Colt until it clicked, then sighted down the long barrel and waited. The man had left the path for the high grass and was not approaching directly but angling slightly off to the right. His route would eventually take him into the ruins of another guest house, where Horn would lose sight of him. Before that happened, Horn reckoned, the man would approach within twenty or thirty yards of him. Not close enough to guarantee results with a hand-gun, but he would have to take the shot.

He waited. The man approached the ruins, head swiveling back and forth, moving more easily now. Instead of the cautious gait of a hunter, he walked with a near-swagger, arms swinging loosely. To Horn, there was something familiar about him, but he had no time to think about it. At the last moment, just before the figure was obscured, Horn pulled the trigger.

Amid the quiet, the gunshot was explosive. The Colt bucked in his hand, more than it did when loaded with blanks, and he berated himself for not allowing for that. As the figure dived to the ground, Horn knew he had missed. The answering shot was quick. Horn saw the muzzle flash from near the ground just before he shut his eyes and ducked behind the wall.

A few seconds went by, and Horn peered over the jagged top of the wall, re-cocking the gun. Nothing at first, then he spied a pale smudge in the grass where the man had gone down. He drew a bead on it, but before he could fire, the man sprang up and dashed for the nearest pile of rubble, where he took cover. More seconds elapsed, then suddenly a shot from the rubble, and Horn heard the slug plow into the front of the wall. *He knows where I am.*

Breathing heavily behind the wall, Horn wondered how he could draw the man out. He carefully peered over the top, searching out the pile of ruins, but saw no movement. *Don't want to waste shots, but I need to make him move.* He aimed at the largest mass of ruins and fired, watching the slug kick up chips and hearing it ricochet away with a keening sound. But nothing moved.

Suddenly another shot, this one from a spot twenty yards to the right, and Horn ducked again. *Sonofabitch. He moves each time he shoots. Maybe that's how I'll get him.*

He felt along the ground until he found a foot-long stick. He poked its end into his wadded-up shirt and undershirt, then used his left hand to move it slowly above the top of the wall. It only took a few seconds before another shot boomed out. It missed, and this time Horn forced himself to keep his head high, eyes sweeping the area. There was the man, loping from a chunk of rock toward the ruined guesthouse he had been approaching when Horn took his first shot. Horn squeezed off a quick shot, knew he had missed; then, trying to lead the running figure, he pulled the trigger again.

He heard a cry.

The man was down. "Goddamn!" Horn heard him yell across the distance in a high-pitched voice. "He shot me!"

Horn stood up. He saw the man writhing in the grass. He knew him now: Dominic, Bonsigniore's nephew, the one with the smart mouth who wasn't allowed to sit with the big boys but was nonetheless sent out to kill.

"Oh, shit!" the young man groaned. "Gabe! I'm shot!"

That's right, Gabe, he thought. *Come and get your boy. Come over here and let me—*

Just before he heard the crack of the rifle, he felt the slug whiz past his ear close enough to rip the air. He ducked behind the wall instinctively even as he realized with dread that the shot had come from behind. He swiveled around on his knees just in time to see the silhouette of the rifleman against the lightening sky where he stood atop a pile of rubble only twenty yards away, taking aim. The second shot plowed into the dirt between Horn's knees. Reflexively, almost panicky, he raised the Colt, but he had forgotten to cock the single-action weapon and lost a split second doing so before he could fire back, and he barely had time to aim. He pressed himself back against the V of concrete, trapping himself, knowing there was no place to go.

The third shot blasted a hole in the wall only inches from his face, stinging his cheek and filling the air with the smell of grit and dust. Horn fired again, knowing his shot was wild but desperately trying to throw off the other man's aim. Then, clearly, as if he and the gunman stood in the same room, Horn heard the man lever the next shell into the chamber. Aiming more carefully this time, Horn pulled the trigger but heard the hammer fall on an expended cartridge. No more bullets. As if in slow motion, he saw the other man raise the gun, imagined he could look all the way down the dark barrel to the shiny lead projectile just before it—

He shut his eyes tight, feeling frail and foolish but knowing that no man wants to see the bullet that kills him. He waited. A second passed, then two.

When he opened his eyes, something had changed. The silhouette on the skyline had become two, both in violent motion. Then they sank out of sight, and Horn heard a hoarse, brutal exhalation that was cut off as soon as it began. After that, nothing.

He stood up again, ashamed at the weakness in his legs. But he had no time to reflect on what had happened, because of the scream. It came faintly from behind him, and the voice was Clea's.

CHAPTER 25

The scream was followed quickly by gun-shots—one, two, several more, wild firing. Horn clambered over the V and through the debris that led to the house, then over the low outer wall into what had been the area between living room and hallway. At that point he could see the door to the wine cellar. There was an unsteady light within, and the indistinct form of a man framed in the doorway.

As Horn drew near, he saw that the man was holding a flashlight and shining the beam down into the cellar. A figure moved into the beam. It was Paul Fairbrass. He held Sykes's gun in his hand, aimed at the man in the doorway, and Horn could hear the dry clicks as the trigger was pulled, over and over. Then Fairbrass's face twisted and he howled in what sounded like rage. He flung the empty gun at the figure and then threw himself on the man, swinging his fists.

A single muffled shot, and Fairbrass fell back, his face bloody. Another scream from within. Now the man in the doorway began to descend the steps, playing the beam of light around until it fell on what he sought. He moved in that direction.

Stumbling and almost falling on loose rock, Horn reached the threshold and flung himself down the steps and onto the dark figure. The man began to turn, but Horn caught him on the side, driving him full-force into a row of shelves. The two of them spun off the shelf, broke apart, and landed heavily on the stone floor. Horn heard a clattering sound as something fell.

He leaped up. The only light came from the flashlight, which lay on the floor and cast its beam uselessly against the base of a wall. The other man was a shadow in the corner. Did he have his gun? Horn waited for the blast, the impact of the bullet.

"That you, cowboy?" the other man asked softly, the New York accent even more pronounced. "I told you not to get in the way." He reached out onto a nearby shelf, his hand fumbling there for a second, then he came forward. *He's lost his gun*, Horn thought.

"You first, then her," Falco said evenly. "It's all the same to—"

Horn crouched and drove into him, plowing his shoulder into the man's chest and driving him back against the wall, forcing the breath out of him. Seeing an advantage, Horn cocked his fist, aiming it at his opponent's head. But he saw Falco's right hand come around in a looping curve, something glinting in the dim light, and Horn's neck exploded in fiery pain. He cried out.

"Like it?" Falco muttered, pressing the broken bottle deeper, grinding it into flesh and muscle. The pain was worse than anything Horn could remember—worse than the bullet in his shoulder. He felt Falco wrench the bottle out of the wound and saw the bottle now poised in front, ready for the throat. Horn bellowed in desperation, grabbed the other man's wrist with his left hand and gripped Falco's throat with his right. The other man made a fist with his free hand and drove it into Horn's ribs, then again.

The two wrestled upright for a moment, and then Falco hooked a leg behind Horn's knee and forced him backward to the floor. They rolled there, gasping, Horn's hands locked on wrist and throat, Falco pummeling him on the face now.

"Clea," Horn managed to gasp. "Run." He heard movement toward the stairs.

Falco kneed him in the groin, and Horn felt a shock of nausea. A memory of an old bar fight in San Antonio surfaced, and he sank his teeth into Falco's ear, tasting blood. Falco jerked his head away with a groan, but his left hand worked tirelessly, slamming the side of Horn's head over and over. Horn began to feel faint. He widened his eyes, but everything looked gray. His hands ached. He bore down on the other man's throat with what felt like his last bit of strength but felt only corded muscle under his fingers.

Another blow to the head, and he knew he was going to pass out. *Don't let go of him.* Then another.

His ears were ringing like the bell at the mountaintop monastery. He opened his eyes one last time to spit in Falco's face and was almost blinded. The face was awash in light, shining like the full moon, panting mouth agape, eyes wide in surprise. Falco turned his head and blinked, trying to make out who was behind the flashlight. At that moment the barrel of his own gun extended slowly into the light, almost gently, until it came to rest on Falco's temple. He felt it and tried to jerk away, but Horn's fingers held him fast.

The deafening blast took away most of one cheek. Falco stiffened, then relaxed as shock set in. The second shot was more accurate, taking him dead center in the side of the head.

Horn kicked him away and lay there, gasping. The flashlight dropped to the floor and went out. He reached out until he met Clea's hand and drew her to him.

She was crying softly. "I thought you were going to die," she said.

Me too, he thought, but instead said to her, "Now, how could that happen if I've got you around to take care of me?"

Outside, a voice he recognized called his name. "We're in here," he said. "We're coming out."

His foot brushed against a leg near the bottom of the stairs. He knelt down and pressed two fingers against Fairbrass's throat, moving them twice in search of a pulse. Nothing.

As he stood, Clea touched his arm. "Is he—"

"Better not stop," he said quickly. "Hold on to me, honey. This way."

Mad Crow stood in the gray light, his expression apprehensive. He was dressed in hunting khakis, as if for some kind of recreational weekend, and his head was bandaged with gauze where Sykes had hit him. A shotgun rested loosely in the crook of his right arm.

Horn stumbled as he mounted the stone steps into the light, and Clea steadied him, just as she had assisted Paul Fairbrass up the steps of the cabin. "You're getting pretty good at helping older men up the stairs," he told her.

Mad Crow raised his eyebrows in a question.

"Falco's in there," Horn told him.

"I shot him, Uncle Joe," Clea said in a tone she might have used to relate something that happened to her at school.

"You hush," Horn told her. "We don't need to talk about that."

Mad Crow approached. "Godalmighty, but you're bleeding like a stuck pig. What happened?"

"He came at me with a broken bottle. How does it look?"

"An unholy mess, that's how," Mad Crow said, grasping Horn's shoulder to turn him slightly. "But I bet it's skin and a little muscle and nothing vital. We need to wrap it quick, though."

"My shirt's over there."

A couple of minutes later, Mad Crow had improvised a bandage from Horn's undershirt, securing it over the wound with the sleeves of the shirt tied tightly under his right arm. "Get you to a doctor," he muttered as he knotted the sleeves.

"Pretty soon," Horn said. "What happened out here?"

"It was Billy did it," Mad Crow said.

"Who?"

"Billy Looks Ahead. You tangled with him at my bar, remember? He was staying at my place after he got behind in his rent and his landlady threw him out. He heard me start up the car. When I told him where I was going, he just invited himself along."

"I thought he specialized in Japs."

"He's not particular. Anyway, we found Sykes, figured you had taken off in this direction, so we followed. Heard shots. Billy was able to get behind the guy with the rifle. How many were there?"

"Three total," Horn said. "We've got a wounded man somewhere over there." As he pointed in that direction, he saw Billy Looks Ahead rising from the tall grass. He was bare-chested, and his face, chest, and arms had been darkened with what looked like dirt and soot. His long hair was held in place with a head scarf. He carried no gun, but as Horn watched, he wiped the blade of a Marine Corps knife with a fistful of grass.

"He's not wounded anymore, John Ray," the Indian said quietly.

Looks Ahead scabbarded his knife and walked a few yards over to where grass gave way to the path. He sat down cross-legged in the dirt facing them, and from that distance it appeared that he had closed his eyes.

"That was Bonsigniore's nephew," Horn said.

Mad Crow cursed under his breath. "Well, he was sent out on a man's job, wasn't he?"

"I owe Billy," Horn said. "I want to tell him so."

"Not now," Mad Crow said. "He needs some time. Just leave him alone for a while." He turned to Clea. "How are you doing, darlin'?"

"Just fine, Uncle Joe," she said brightly—a little too brightly, Horn thought. "I'm tired, that's all."

Horn put his arms around her and hugged her, then motioned Mad Crow to move off a few paces with him. "Her father's in there, too," he said in a low voice. "Falco killed him. I want to get her out of here as soon as we can. She's going to need her mother."

"All right. What do we do with all this lowlife trash?"

Horn thought for a moment. "You'll find a pick and shovel in the toolshed behind the cabin. Gather up all their weapons and ID, watches, rings, and stuff, and bury them in the woods. Our friend Bonsigniore will never know what happened to them. He'll guess, but he won't know." He paused. "There's a car down there somewhere."

"We saw it. I'll leave it parked right in front of Vinnie's goddam house."

"Don't get carried away. Just leave it someplace far from here, all right? I'm sorry to put all this on you, Indian."

"Don't worry about it. I'm just wondering—"

"Sykes and Fairbrass? They can't just disappear. Here's my idea: Put them in their car and leave it parked down in Long Beach somewhere. When they're found, the police will ask who had it in for Paul. Iris will tell them somebody was after Clea and Paul was trying to protect her, and she also knows Bonsigniore was one of the group at the hunting lodge. It won't take the police long to make the connection. He'll have some heat on him."

"I hope it's enough heat to keep him away from the little girl," Mad Crow said.

"He lost three men tonight," Horn said. "One of them was a relative. This won't make him quit, but it'll make him stop and think, at least for a while."

"What if it doesn't? What if it just makes him mad?"

I'm tired of being afraid, said a girl's voice in his mind. "Then somebody'll have to go after him."

"Now, that sounds more like Sierra Lane," the Indian said. "Go on, get out of here."

Horn went to Clea. "You want to go home?"

She nodded, a half-smile on her face, and he wondered what was going through her mind.

They started down the trail that led to the cabin. When the trees closed in, she stopped, reaching out for him. "My legs are so rubbery," she said. "Just like the baby horse. Isn't that funny? I don't know if I can—"

He picked her up and began to carry her. She wrapped her arms around his neck, as she had countless times when she was small. He felt her yawn.

"Paul protected me," she said.

"I know he did, honey."

"I think he knew he was going to die, and so did I. He shot the gun over and over, and then it didn't work anymore, and he just walked over to the door—"

"*Shhh*. I know," he said. "Why don't you rest?"

She yawned again, audibly this time. "I'm so sleepy." Her head settled onto his shoulder.

He stumbled on a root but caught himself. He was exhausted but, oddly, he felt strong—ready to carry her as long as he had to, until the sun was high.

CHAPTER 26

The Santa Monica beach ran off in both directions in a long, sandy curve. It was a near-perfect Sunday, and the beach was dotted with families who were sunning and swimming and playing, the children calling to each other like magpies. Mad Crow spotted Horn and walked unsteadily over the mounded sand until he reached him. "This spot taken?"

Horn, stretched out on his back, looked up from under the brim of his hat. He had taken off his shirt, and the two-week-old wound on his neck was starkly visible next to the white strap of his undershirt, healing but still angry-looking, with patches of iodine rimming the scabs.

"Pull up a stretch of sand and set yourself down, stranger," he said.

Mad Crow sat heavily and placed a large paper bag between them. "Where are the girls? Are we going for hamburgers, or what?"

"They've gone for a walk down the beach," Horn replied. "Take your shirt off. Get some sun."

"Silly-ass white man's habit," Mad Crow said. "I'm brown enough already."

Out over the ocean, midway between the apex of the sky and the horizon, a skywriter's plane dived and circled as it slowly inscribed a message in a long plume of smoke.

"Oh so good," Mad Crow said, squinting to read it. "Something like that."

Horn watched the plane paint another letter. "O-So Grape," he said. "He's advertising O-So Grape soda."

"Can't stand the stuff." Mad Crow reached into the bag and plucked out a still-cool Blue Ribbon and an opener. "You want one of these?"

"Sure. Why do you think we invited you?" As Horn opened it with a hiss, he focused on something far down the beach, waved an arm broadly, and said, "They're coming back."

"So how's she doing?"

Horn took a pull from the beer and rested the bottle on his chest. "Not real well," he said. "What do you expect? She just turned seventeen, and she's been through more than most people see in a lifetime. Iris is trying to make things normal for her, seeing friends and all that, and she starts school in a couple of weeks. But I don't know." He exhaled loudly, a long sigh. "There are doctors —I knew some in the Army—who work on people like her, people who are bothered by things they remember."

"How did you know them?" Mad Crow asked casually.

"Maybe I'll tell you some time. Anyway, I'm

going to try to find one here and get Iris to have Clea talk to him."

"Good luck. I don't need to ask you if you're ever going to tell them about Paul Fairbrass."

"No, sir, you don't," Horn replied, his eyes on the skywriter again. "When he died, he was trying to protect her. That's all they need to know. Especially Iris. She had two losers, me and Wendell. If she wants to think Paul was a good man, I suppose it's all right with me." He let a handful of sand sift through his fingers. "One time, I could have killed him myself. Now, I don't know. I guess I'd rather remember the way he ended up."

"I talked to Iris for a few minutes last night when she called to get the four of us together," Mad Crow said. "I was amazed. She loses a husband and almost loses her little girl, and you can hear all that in her voice. But you can hear something else—"

"I know." Horn shook his head wonderingly. "Iris is . . . just Iris. Inside, where it counts, she's plenty strong. Even after all this, she'll go on and raise her girl and . . . survive."

"Any chance for the two of you to—?"

"No," Horn said. "Too much happened. But I told her I'll be around for Clea anytime she needs me."

"Well, I guess I will too," Mad Crow said. From a trouser pocket he extracted a folded-up news-paper article. "You said you were going to tell me about this."

Horn studied the clipping, dated two days earlier. The headline read MOB BOSS MYSTERIOUSLY SLAIN; GANG RIVALS SUSPECTED.

"I said I knew something about it," he said, handing it back. "I never said I was going to tell you."

"Dammit, John Ray—"

"Sorry, Indian. I made a promise."

Mad Crow looked disgusted. "That sounds like some kind of cowboy-honor crap."

"Maybe it is. Just don't ask me. What matters is you've lost a business partner. I guess you'll be needing another one." He tilted his head back. The skywriter had departed, and the tribute to O-So Grape was growing wispy in the offshore wind.

Mad Crow was studying him. "What's the matter?"

"Oh, just thinking about something I said to a lady the other day about how people get away with things. It's even more true now. I remember Arthur Bullard, who abused children and who died respected. And Wendell Brand, who damaged his own daughter and other girls and who ran away to hide behind God. Where's the punishment for men like that? Even Addie Webb, who turned against her friend and probably sent killers after her. Think she feels guilty? She'll buy a new dress and go out dancing. Who's going to call down any justice on her?"

Mad Crow forced a smile and nudged his friend in the ribs. "It's real life, John Ray. Not a movie. Sierra Lane would wrap it all up and clap the

415

varmints in the hoosegow and ride away, but you can't do that."

"Sierra Lane wouldn't be dumb enough to get stuck with a broken bottle in a fight," Horn said.

"Wasn't going to say that." Mad Crow looked up. "But I don't care what anybody says. People still need heroes. Even make-believe ones. Hell, especially make-believe." He grinned broadly. "Know what you need? To get back to work."

"I've been thinking about that," Horn said. "I guess I'm ready. I could use the money. In fact, I could use a little in advance against the next job, if you don't mind. You know, groceries and stuff."

"Sounds good to me," Mad Crow said enthusiastically. "Look, here they come." He stood and waved.

Iris and Clea, wearing swimsuits and floppy hats, waved back. Horn thought he could make out a faint smile on Clea's face, but her hat brim cast a heavy shadow, and he couldn't be sure.

He had learned about Vincent Bonsigniore the day before, sitting at a lunch counter down on Central Avenue, working on a plate of pork ribs and greens with Alphonse Doucette seated beside him.

"Could be you drive a long way for nothing," Doucette said.

"I don't think so," Horn said. "I bet you've got a story to tell me."

"Why should I tell you anything?"

"Because I hooked you up with her."

"With who?"

"You know who I mean. If it wasn't for me, Vincent Bonsigniore would still be sitting up there in his house, planning ways to kill some people and hurt others. And you'd still be hating him for what he did to your sister's girl. I don't want to get you in any trouble, so I won't tell anybody. But I hated him too—maybe more than you did—and I just want to know."

Doucette wiped his mouth, got the counterman's attention, and pointed to a slice of pie under the round glass cover. When it arrived, he dug into it and began to speak around his food.

"I'll just tell you a f'rinstance kind of story," he said, his voice musical and soft. "Mighta happened this way, mighta not. Let's suppose a rich lady calls up Mister Bonsigniore and tells him she got something for him, something she know he wants. Some pictures. Says she know they important to him, and she 'fraid he might come after her. Says she'll give 'em to him if he leave her alone, call everything square. Naturally, he very interested.

"Let's say she drive in her nice car over to his house, 'way up there off Mulholland. He expecting her, and he meet her in the driveway and take her inside. They already know each other a little bit. She very well dressed, got a lot of style. Inside, they talk, he offer her a drink, everything proper. He a dangerous man, everybody know that, but this lady important herself, and she act like she not 'fraid of him, and he respect that.

"So she give him the pictures and leave in her nice car. And Mr. B, he sit up for a while with his drink, then he go to bed." The Creole stopped to chew.

"And?"

"And let's suppose they was somebody else in the lady's nice car when she park it off to the side, around from the front where nobody keep an eye on it. And this person sneak out of the car while she inside and find a way inside the house, where he hide in a cleaning closet. Like I say, Mr. B, he a dangerous man, but he don't feel anybody really dangerous to him, 'cause he only got two men in the house, and they playing cards in the dining room.

"And let's say this person wait a long time there in that closet smellin' like furniture polish, 'til everybody asleep, and then he slip a nylon stocking over his head and make his way up those stairs. He hear snoring, and he go in this bedroom, but he find this old lady asleep there, and he leave without bothering her. Next door turn out to be Mr. B's room. And there he pull something out of his shoe, and he fix him real good. And just after Mr. B feel his throat cut, but before he die, he hear somebody whisper a name, a little girl's name. And so he go to Hell remembering that name."

Amen, Horn felt himself saying, almost as his father might have said it.

"But just then the light come on, and there somebody in bed with him. She sit up, all white, looking at all the blood. And she want to scream, but he do this—" Doucette put a finger to his lips in a hushing motion. "—and she be quiet. Just froze there."

Horn never knew what made him ask. "What did she look like?"

"Young," Doucette said. "You not surprised, huh? But she not a child, not this one. Beautiful young lady, dark hair. Funny thing: She look almost familiar to him, you know?"

Yes, he thought. *I know.*

"But that's just a story." Doucette wiped his face one more time, laid money on the counter, and got up to leave.

"My treat," he said. "Now we even."

The woman who answered his knock on the door wore the same soiled apron. Her resigned expression shifted into recognition when she saw his face. "My husband's not home," she said.

"Yes, ma'am, I know. I just saw him leave," Horn said.

This did not reassure her. He pressed on quickly.

"Mrs. Taro, your husband doesn't owe money; I'm not here for that. I know I didn't behave very well the last time, but this is different. I just need a minute with you, and I'll be gone." He tried to smile reassuringly.

She reluctantly opened the door wider, and he stepped into the living room, where he stood awkwardly.

"The man I work for wants you to know he made a little mistake in his bookkeeping," Horn told her. "Seems I collected too much from your husband."

"Too much?" She seemed to be having trouble with the idea.

"Yes, ma'am. He wanted me to return this to you." He handed her some folded bills.

She held them without counting them, looking dumbly at him. "Well, thank you very much," she said finally.

"One other thing," he said. "Man I work for says there's one condition. He wants to make sure this money doesn't go for gambling. Said I should ask you to promise to spend it on yourself and the boy. Clothes and food and things like that."

She nodded slowly. Wisps of gray-tinged brown had escaped the pins holding her hair in a bun on the back of her neck. She reminded Horn of a photo he had once seen, a shot of a farm wife during the Depression, her face a map of toil.

"Naturally, I don't want to go behind your husband's back. But you think you can promise me that?"

"Well, I guess I can," she said softly.

"That's good. I saw your boy for a minute the last time I was here. Is he around?"

"Uh-huh." Her expression brightened. "He's out by the side of the house, swapping comic books with a friend of his." She led him to a side window of the shabby living room. Looking

420

out, he saw the boy sitting with another boy about his age on a sidewalk that led to the back of the house. His lame leg was tucked protectively under him. Between the two boys stood several stacks of comic books, and they appeared to be bargaining heatedly.

"What's his name?" Horn asked.

"Orville," she said. "After his grandfather."

"Is that his friend Lee?"

"How'd you know?"

"Oh, he mentioned him. He said Lee likes Sunset Carson, for some strange reason."

"I wouldn't know about that," she said vaguely.

"I just remembered something," he said. "I'll be right back." He went out to his car and returned with a roll of heavy paper about two feet long. "I'd like to leave this for Orville, if it's all right with you."

"You want to see him?" She started for the window.

"No, that's all right. Maybe you could just give this to him."

She unrolled the stiff paper partway down. It was the poster for *Wyoming Thunder*. "He told me he likes the movies," Horn said.

"He sure does," she said. "But he doesn't have anything like this. You're very nice to—" She looked at the image more closely. "Oh, my goodness. Is this you?"

"I guess I ought to go." He opened the door.

"It's you, ain't it?"

Funny, he thought. *The boy wanted to know the same thing.*

He paused in the doorway. "Yes, ma'am, it's me," he said finally. "And I'd appreciate it if you'd tell him that."